PRAISE FOR THE NOVELS
OF HEATHER CULLMAN

Bewitched

"Readers will be *Bewitched* by Heather Cullman's tender late-Regency romance. . . . Delightful."
—BookBrowser

A Perfect Scoundrel

"A delightful, lighthearted Regency romp from a talented writer. Enjoy!"
—Kat Martin

For All Eternity

"A skilled romance writer. . . . Intriguing setting and highly sensual love scenes."
—*Romantic Times*

"Moves like a whirlwind . . . humor in just the right places . . . wonderful characters."
—*Rendezvous*

continued . . .

D1022845

HEATHER
CULLMAN

 SCANDAL

A SIGNET BOOK

SIGNET
Published by New American Library, a division of
Penguin Putnam Inc., 375 Hudson Street,
New York, New York 10014, U.S.A.
Penguin Books Ltd, 80 Strand,
London WC2R 0RL, England
Penguin Books Australia Ltd, 250 Camberwell Road,
Camberwell, Victoria 3124, Australia
Penguin Books Canada Ltd, 10 Alcorn Avenue,
Toronto, Ontario, Canada M4V 3B2
Penguin Books (N.Z.) Ltd, 182–190 Wairau Road,
Auckland 10, New Zealand

Penguin Books Ltd, Registered Offices:
Harmondsworth, Middlesex, England

First published by Signet, an imprint of New American Library,
a division of Penguin Putnam Inc.

First Printing, January 2003
10 9 8 7 6 5 4 3 2 1

 REGISTERED TRADEMARK—MARCA REGISTRADA

Printed in the United States of America

PUBLISHER'S NOTE
This is a work of fiction. Names, characters, places, and incidents either
are the product of the author's imagination or are used fictitiously, and
any resemblance to actual persons, living or dead, business establishments,
events, or locales is entirely coincidental.

For Jennifer Brimer and David Reines
My cherished friends

CHAPTER 1

North Riding, Yorkshire, England, 1798

"Dead?" Gideon Harwood echoed, his mind reeling in shock. Of all the things he'd expected to learn here, that Lady Silvia Barham had died most certainly did not rank among them.

The swag-bellied majordomo nodded his wigged head in affirmation, his gimlet eyes growing round as he glanced over Gideon's shoulder to the gravel drive beyond. Gideon didn't have to follow the servant's gaze to know the source of his consternation. It was Jagtar, his *sirdar,* as the station of personal attendant was referred to in India, and even Gideon had to admit that the tall Sikh with his wiry black beard, his scarred, teakwood-hued face, and starkly contrasting white turban could be a very menacing sight indeed to those unaccustomed to it. The fact that he wore a lethal-looking *kirpan,* as the symbolic Sikh dagger was called, tucked into his blue silk waist sash did nothing to diminish the impression of barbarity.

To the majordomo's credit, he gaped only for the briefest of moments before returning his attention to the man before him. Nodding again, this time rather stiffly, he confirmed, "Dead, yes. Her ladyship expired unexpectedly five days ago."

The word unexpected seemed rather an understatement for the abrupt and startling untimeliness of her ladyship's demise, Gideon thought, the news dealing him a devastating blow. Indeed, Stiles, one of several Bow Street Runners he had hired to find his younger brother, Caleb, had spoken to Lady Silva on what had apparently been the day of her death and had carried back an invitation from her to call at his leisure. According to the runner, she claimed to have information about Caleb, the contents of which were too delicate to entrust to anyone but Gideon himself.

Gideon, of course, had been elated by the news. After two months of searching, an excruciating time filled with endless dark moments punctuated by all-too-brief glimmers of hope, they had at last discovered a piece to the puzzle of his brother's baffling disappearance. Galvanized by this new hope, he'd naturally come posthaste. But he had arrived too late. Again. He was always too late, it seemed. As a result, he had once again failed those he loved when they needed him most.

A paralyzing weariness swept over Gideon at the thought of his failures and the tragedy they had spawned, leaving him feeling drained, used up. Lady Silvia was dead, and without her help he might never find Caleb. Unless . . .

His eyes narrowed with sudden speculation. If his memory served him correctly, and at the age of twenty-nine he had no reason to believe that it had grown faulty, Lady Silvia and Lord Gilbert had been inordinately fond of each other. That being the case, it was possible that she had confided in her husband about Caleb. Praying that his reasoning would prove sound, Gideon refocused his attention on the majordomo.

"I truly am sorry, sir," the man was saying in a funereal tone. "Perhaps I can be of assistance?"

Gideon nodded. "Indeed you may. You can announce me to his lordship."

The majordomo couldn't have looked more affronted had he requested that he dig up Lady Silva and present him with her corpse. For several moments his mouth flapped open and closed in wordless indignation; then he boomed, "Must I remind you, sir, that his lordship is in deep mourning?"

"I am well aware of that fact, I assure you," Gideon smoothly countered. "And while I truly do regret disturbing him at a time like this, it is imperative that I speak with him on a matter of some urgency. So please do be good enough to inform him that Mr. Gideon Harwood is calling."

"Harwood?" The man's smooth forehead puckered into jagged creases. After repeating the utterance at least a dozen times, his brow cleared and he ejected, "Harwood, yes. But of course." He smiled and bobbed his head. "Now I remember. Her ladyship informed me that you were to call—why, it must have been on the very day she died, God rest her soul. She said that you were to be received without delay. I believe she said your family had once resided in our village." His demeanor was decidedly less frigid than it had been mere seconds earlier.

Gideon smiled, relieved to be finally getting somewhere with the man. "That is correct—?" He cast the servant a querying look.

"Leighton, sir," the majordomo supplied with a bow.

Gideon acknowledged the introduction with a cordial nod. "To answer your question, Leighton, my father was Joseph Harwood, curate of Fellthwaite parish for nineteen years. He is buried in the churchyard. I, myself, was born and lived my first seventeen years in the old rectory." If Leighton was anything at all like the Fellthwaite residents he remembered, his pedigree as one of their own was certain to gain him favor, and perhaps an audience with his lordship. Wishing to cement the veracity of his claim, he added, "As I recall, a gentleman named Pryor used to occupy your position. I do hope nothing untoward has befallen him?" There was nothing like naming names to establish one's legitimacy.

It appeared that he was accurate in his reasoning, for Leighton's smile broadened. "Pryor is my cousin, sir. I assumed his position when he retired a year ago last month." His tone was positively warm now. "If you will pardon me for prying, sir, might I inquire as to the nature of your business with his lordship?"

Hoping to gain the man's sympathy, Gideon explained about his brother's disappearance and her ladyship's cryptic message.

The majordomo remained silent for several moments after he finished his account, his expression thoughtful. Then he cleared his throat twice and said, "I am sorry, Mr. Harwood. As much as I regret doing so, I must inform you that his lordship is not receiving at this time. He gave strict orders to that effect."

Never one to give up on matters of importance without a fight, Gideon opened his mouth to argue, to plead, if necessary, when the man leaned forward. Glancing nervously around him, Leighton whispered, "I do believe that his lordship is at the churchyard, visiting Lady Silvia's grave." With a conspiratorial wink, he straightened back up again, adding in a low voice, "Of course, you did not hear it from me."

Gideon smiled. "Never. You are the soul of discretion, Leighton." Nodding his thanks, he made his way down the steps to where Jagtar stood crooning in his native tongue to the horses, which had grown restless during the exchange at the door.

The Sikh straightened at his approach, his demeanor, as always, deferential but never subservient. *"Sahib?"*

Gideon shook his head. "I am afraid that I shan't be speaking with her ladyship now, or ever. She died five days ago."

Jagtar, who had been aiding Gideon in his quest to find his brother and thus understood the importance of his interview with Lady Silvia, looked genuinely grieved by the news. "Ah. Such unhappy tidings. Many regrets," he murmured, his soft accent and melodious cadence lending a pleasing singsong quality to his voice. Bowing his head in proper deference to the deceased, he added, "What must we do now, *Sahib?*"

"Her ladyship may have confided whatever she knew about Caleb to her husband, so I must speak with him. He is presently at the churchyard." He pointed to the opposite end of the village, where a single tower jutted up from behind a stand of ancient yew trees. Unlike many hamlets in England, where the lords of the manor had built their houses a distance from the town, thus segregating themselves from the villagers, Fellthwaite Hall stood in the village itself, towering majestically above the humble yet charming cottages that huddled around it. "I do not know how long he will remain there, so I—"

Ooof!—Gideon's horse, Abhaya, snorted and tossed his head, a bit of fractiousness that caused Sarad, Jagtar's gray gelding, to dance a nervous jig.

Shweet! Shweet! Tat! Tat! Tat! Jagtar's constant companion, Kesin, a *sharmindi-billi,* or slow loris, as the queer, owl-eyed primates were called in the English-speaking world, poked his wooly cream-and-brown head from the pouch tied to Jagtar's saddle, emitting a sharp, scolding twitter in protest to having his nap disturbed.

Jagtar chuckled. "A thousand pardons, little one," he said, extending his arm to his indignant friend. The beast grasped the proffered limb with its almost-human-looking hands and sinuously climbed to his master's shoulder, where it perched and expelled a series of chirps and whistles. The Sikh laughed and turned back to Gideon. As if translating the animal's complaints, he said, "The little beggar is hungry, *Sahib,* as are the horses. Where may I get food for them, please?"

Gideon considered the question, then pointed to the pale Yorkshire brick inn visible just down the road. "There. At the Three Lamb Inn." Mr. Galloway kept the best stable in the county, just as his wife distinguished herself as an innkeeper with both the bounty of her table and the cleanliness of her beds. At least that had been the case when he'd lived here. Since the Galloway family had adhered to those standards for the six generations they had owned the inn, Gideon felt safe in assuming that matters hadn't changed much over the past twelve years.

Handing Jagtar several coins, he said, "Tend to the horses, and then kindly arrange for dinner and rooms for the night. I daresay that the horses can use a rest after the hard manner in which we rode them. I shall meet you at the inn in an hour." Because of the poor road conditions in this part of the country, coupled with his desire for speed, Gideon had chosen to ride rather than take the elegant coach he had purchased to transport his sisters to his newly acquired estate in Lancashire. He had been in the process of settling the girls in the house there when he had received Stiles's message.

Jagtar accepted the coins with a nod. *"Bahut acha"*— very good.

"Oh, and Jagtar?"

"Sahib?"

"You will find fruit for Kesin at the shop two doors down from the inn on the opposite side of the road." Damn if he hadn't developed a fondness for the comical little creature himself.

Jagtar brought his palms together beneath his chin and inclined his head in the Indian gesture for respect. *"Dhany-avad"*—thank you. With that he set off, scolding the naughty Kesin, who now tugged at his turban. Smiling at the droll pair, Gideon started toward the churchyard.

Now walking down Mucky Lane, an aptly named road given its miry condition when it rained, Gideon observed the village he had left what felt like a lifetime ago. It was exactly as he remembered, seemingly untouched by the hand of time.

Which is something that most certainly cannot be said for me, he thought, grimacing at his reflection in the bakeshop window. The nine grueling years he'd spent in India, first serving in and later commanding the armies of the rajas and Rajput chieftains, had left their mark upon his face, stripping away the soft vestiges of youth that still graced the faces of many men his age. His was the face of a life lived hard: a lean, predatory visage made up of razor-sharp planes and deeply etched lines, the skin stained dark from the sun.

Of course, he'd been paid handsomely for his bartered youth. In fact, his banker had confided that the fortune he'd accumulated in India made him one of the wealthiest men in England. And hadn't that been his goal all along? Hadn't everything he'd done, every battle he'd fought, every wound he'd suffered, every moment he'd endured beneath the brutal Indian sun, his flesh scorched and his body screaming with bone-crushing weariness, all been borne out of a lust for wealth?

Turning from the window, Gideon admitted that it was true, just as it was true that that lust had, in the end, caused him to fail the very people he had sought to help by gaining riches. Those people were, of course, his beloved family. And while they in no way blamed him for the chain of misfortune that had fractured their lives, he blamed himself. After all, if he had not been so vain in his desire to be their hero, to rescue them with dazzling wealth, he would have returned to England in time to save them from their suffering. And they had suffered. All of them.

Terribly.

A knife turned in Gideon's heart, as it always did when he contemplated his sins. If only he had been satisfied with a smaller fortune, a less grandiose dream. If only—

For several moments Gideon waged a battle within himself, fighting the savage emotions that welled up inside him at the thought of what his "if onlys" had cost his family. Taming it into the now-familiar hollow ache, he forced his attention back to the panorama that was Fellthwaite Village.

White limestone cottages, many graying with age, mingled with redbrick shops and multihued gardens, lending the tiny town a gay, dappled appearance. On his right was the rough stone farrier's stable, where he and Caleb had passed many a boyhood hour watching in awe as Mr. Witty, the jolly, barrel-chested blacksmith, worked magic on bits of iron. To the left was the cobbler and clogger shop, supplier of the endless parade of heavy, wood-soled clogs that he and his siblings had outgrown, lost, or ruined on a monthly basis. And over there, behind the wall so fragrantly dressed in honeysuckle, jasmine, and sweetbriar, stood the tiny ivy-draped cottage of Mrs. Porrit, a blind widow who nonetheless baked the best ratafia biscuits in the village.

On he continued, past the crumbling medieval village hall and the Jacobean grammar school. Though he recognized several of the villagers he met, none appeared to recognize him, so he simply returned their polite nods and continued on, unable to spare the time to renew their acquaintance.

After passing four more shops, a row of low, cozy-looking cottages, and a pair of elderly women out tending their garden, he reached the village green. The churchyard lay at the end of the path that cut through the far side of the green. As he crossed the broad, tree-shaded expanse of grass, the scene of so many memorable village celebrations, he spied a quartet of little girls engrossed in a game that had once delighted his sister Bethany.

Using bits of stone to build sheep folds and fir cones as sheep, the smaller ones, of course, serving as lambs, the girls pretended to be sheep farmers, an occupation that provided the livelihood for the majority of the nearby cottagers. At the moment they clipped their sheep, their index and middle fingers acting as shears as they moved in a scissoring motion around the fir cones, their voices raised in a chorus of bleats punctuated by giggles. Charmed, Gideon paused a few seconds to watch, remembering Bethany as she had looked the last time he'd seen her play the game.

She must have been about nine at the time, and had looked so enchanting with her dark hair tumbling around her dirt-smudged face and her sapphire-blue eyes dancing with mischief, as they had always done in those days. He and his siblings had been inordinately spirited children, or so their mother had once lamented. However, unlike he and Caleb, who could be quite wicked in their naughtiness and often landed in the suds because of it, Bethany's mischief had been innocently sweet and endearing in its light-hearted silliness. Bethany was still sweet and endearing, and still enjoyed an occasional spree of tomfoolery, though, sadly, she would never again be innocent—a heartbreak, the blame for which he placed squarely on his own shoulders. The fact that his youngest sister, eleven year-old Bliss, had never enjoyed the true innocence of childhood at all, well, he laid that fault at his door as well.

So many memories, so many reminders of what should have been, but would never be.

With a sigh, Gideon resumed his trek. Now coming to

the path that led to the churchyard, the Road Home, some called it, referring, of course, to the heaven they hoped to attain when they were laid to rest in the sacred ground ahead, he noted that like the village, the pleasant white-poplar-lined walkway remained exactly as he remembered it . . . as did the flowers edging it.

With some reluctance he studied the prismatic skeins of snowdrops, primroses, and forget-me-nots that wove around the silvery tree trunks, his throat growing tight as he envisioned his beautiful mother kneeling among them. It had been she who had planted the flowers, she who had cultivated the knots of rosemary, the symbol of remembrance that formed the border of the cheerful garden. How like her in her love for the parishioners to make gay a place that held such sadness. How very typical of her compassionate nature to try to bring comfort to those so needful of its peace. Then again, she had been everything that was good and fine, a true inspiration to all who knew her.

Desolate agony ripped through Gideon at the vivid memory of his mother. How he had loved her and wished to make her proud. Yet, in his zeal to do so he had failed her most of all. Choking on his sorrow, he more marched than walked the remaining distance to the churchyard and slipped through the timber lynch gate.

Like the rest of Fellthwaite, the thirteenth-century church appeared unchanged by time. The same, unfortunately, could not be said for the churchyard itself.

Unlike when his father was curate and his mother had so lovingly tended the property, the grounds surrounding the church were choked with weeds. Only the yew trees lining the stone perimeter wall had somehow escaped the neglect ravaging the rest of the lawn.

As Gideon walked along he recalled the conversation he'd once had with his father about the yews. According to his sire, they were well over a thousand years old, an ancient reminder of earlier, more pagan times when the long vanquished Brigante warriors had stained their faces blue with woad and worshiped before the monolith that still stood in the south corner of the yard. He had also explained that yews were the pagan symbol of death, adding how they were believed to absorb the putrid miasma that many thought emanated from the graves at sunset. In short, the trees were planted to protect the village from the vile contamination of death.

Smiling faintly at the absurdity of the superstition, Gideon spotted Lord Gilbert Barham, kneeling before a mound of raw earth in a posture that proclaimed profound grief. Not wishing to intrude upon what was clearly a private moment, Gideon discreetly proceeded to where his father was buried.

Unlike his mother, who had died in his absence, he'd had the chance to bid his father a final farewell. Thus, as he stood before his father's grave, upon which someone had planted cowslip and pansies, he felt none of the anguish that assailed him every time he thought of his mother. True, he'd failed his father as much as the others, having broken the deathbed vow he'd made to safeguard the family. But it was he who was haunted by his betrayal of trust, not his father. And for that he was eternally grateful.

After whispering a prayer for his father's soul, he pressed his hand against the sun-warmed slate tombstone and silently pledged to right the wrongs caused by his broken promise. Resolving to honor the new vow at any cost, he turned from the grave to survey the four tiny ones beside it. There beneath a burgeoning cover of primroses lay his siblings, babies who had either been stillborn or had failed to live past their first year. He remembered the occupants of those sad graves well, even though he had been young when they had made their brief appearances on earth. Kneeling down, he read the names inscribed on each small headstone.

The first was a girl named Cherish, a plump, bonny baby who had come a year after Caleb, only to die of measles eight months later. Then there were Benjamin, Ethan, and Jeremy, in that order, all of whom had been born two or three years apart in the nine-year interval between Bethany and Bliss. Benjamin and Ethan were born tragically still, while Jeremy had lived a mere week.

Offering a prayer for each of the babies' innocent souls, he stood up and glanced toward his lordship.

Lord Gilbert now stood as well and prepared to take his leave. Judging it best to make the encounter appear accidental, Gideon timed his departure so that he would meet his prey at the lynch gate.

Arriving there just as his lordship prepared to pass through, Gideon exclaimed in a surprised voice, "My word! If it isn't Lord Gilbert Barham." Though his lordship's appearance had altered a great deal over the years, time having thickened his bull-like build into portliness and coarsened his once-fine features, Gideon easily identified him by his distinctive copper hair.

His lordship whipped around in a swirl of black mourning coat, wariness creeping across his pale face as his amber-eyed gaze swept Gideon's length. His features tightening, as if displeased by what he saw, he snapped, "Do I know you, sirrah?"

"Indeed you do, though I fear that it has been a great while since we last met, and that I have changed much in the interim," Gideon replied, unfazed by his lordship's uncharacteristic asperity. It was grief, of course, the strain of which often robbed the bereaved of their manners. Sketching a brief bow, he continued, "I am Gideon Harwood, eldest son of Joseph Harwood, your former curate. Perhaps you remember my family?" He prayed that his lordship not only remembered them, but would also recall either seeing Caleb recently, or hearing news of him.

His lordship continued to stare at him, his stance tense and his thicket of eyebrows drawn together in an expression of—what? Annoyance? Puzzlement? When he finally deigned to respond, his voice was hoarse and edged with a curious note of uncertainty. "Harwood, you say?"

Gideon smiled politely and nodded. "Yes."

The lines between his lordship's eyebrows deepened for a moment; then his brow cleared and he nodded back. "Harwood. Yes. Of course." He nodded again, as if validating the recollection. "Fine man, your father. Been dead—what? Ten years is it?"

"Twelve."

Another nod from his lordship. "Twelve, yes." His gaze again traveled Gideon's length, this time slowly, arresting when it touched his boots. Contemplating them as if they were objects of rare curiosity, he murmured, "Well, well. Gideon Harwood. So what brings you to Fellthwaite after all these years?"

Gideon glanced down at his boots as well, wondering if he had inadvertently stepped in something nasty. But no. Aside from a veneer of road dust from his journey, they appeared respectable enough. Not quite certain what to make of his lordship's unwarranted attention to his footwear, he replied, "I came to speak with you and Lady Silvia on a matter of considerable importance. Indeed, I was on my way to call just now. How very serendipitous that we should meet like this."

Lord Gilbert looked up then, his mouth tightening into a crescent of pain. "Her ladyship is dead," he rasped, his bluntness exposing a grief too raw for delicacy. "It was an accident—a fall on the garden steps."

Though his expression of shock was feigned, Gideon's sorrow was real, for he had genuinely liked and respected Lady Silvia. Hoping that his voice reflected the sincerity of his regret, he said, "Please accept my deepest sympathies for your loss, my lord. Her ladyship was a fine woman, one of the finest I have ever had the privilege to know. You may be certain that I shall always remember her kindness to my family and hold her memory dear."

His lordship smiled faintly at his words. "As I recall, she harbored a particular fondness for you and that limb of Satan you called your brother. What was his name?"

"Caleb," Gideon supplied, his hope sinking at the question. Surely his lordship would remember Caleb's name if he'd had recent news of him? Then again, grief did queer things to the mind, including making one forgetful.

"Ah, yes. Caleb. Her ladyship used to find his antics most diverting. Indeed, she often said that if she were to have a son, she would wish him to be exactly like Caleb." Lord Gilbert sighed. "My poor, darling Silvia. Such a pity that she never had children of her own. It was the sorrow of her life, and mine." He seemed to lose himself in memory for a moment, a sweet one, judging from the tender smile tugging at his lips. Then he regained his sense of time and place, his smile fading as he said, "I believe that you have business with me?"

Gideon inclined his head. "Indeed I do." Clinging to his last, admittedly tenuous threads of hope, he explained his quest.

His lordship listened carefully, now and again nodding when Gideon made a salient point. When, at last, he fell silent, having told what pitiful little he knew of his brother's disappearance, Lord Gilbert shook his head. "I am sorry, truly I am. But her ladyship never confided whatever it was she knew of your brother."

Though his response came as no real surprise, the words dealt Gideon a crushing blow. Feeling sick and bruised with defeat, he said in as light a tone as he could muster, "Well then, that is the end of it, I suppose, so I shan't detain you any longer. Please accept my apologies for intruding upon you during your time of mourning." Remembering to bow, he added, "It has been a pleasure to renew your acquaintance, my lord. I hope that we will meet again under happier circumstances." His farewell thus tendered, he turned to leave.

"You appear to have done exceedingly well for yourself, Harwood."

Gideon froze, taken aback by the unexpected nature of the remark. "Pardon, my lord?" he said, pivoting around to gaze at the other man in question.

"You look quite prosperous." Lord Gilbert advanced toward him, gesturing at Gideon's clothing with a sweep of his hand. "Indeed, if I do not miss my guess, your Hessians were made by Finster's in Pall Mall."

Wondering what had prompted the conversation and where it was leading, he glanced down at his admittedly costly Finster boots, saying, "I have been very fortunate, yes." When he looked back up again, he saw that his lordship was watching him with a queer, almost calculating expression. It was an expression that vanished in the next instant when he saw Gideon looking at him.

Now smiling with jovial charm, an abrupt shift in demeanor that Gideon could only attribute to the capricious idiosyncrasy of grief, his lordship said, "With all of your newfound wealth, you must spend a great deal of time in London. Most men in your position do, you know. Many even seek entrée into the *ton.*"

Aware of the contempt with which the *ton* viewed commoners like him who had made their fortunes in India, Gideon emitted a short, snorting laugh. "I have no more interest in society than they have in me. The same holds true for London and her more opulent pleasures. I go to town only when business dictates that I must and stay for as brief a time as possible."

"Indeed," his lordship intoned, seeming to carefully consider Gideon's words. "Hmmm. I must say that you are going about matters in a sensible fashion. The *ton* can be rather, er, cool to outsiders, especially those of common birth. It is why I never took Lady Silvia to town when I was forced to go there on business. Being of common birth and a modest nature, she would have found the experience most disagreeable. As her husband, it was naturally my duty to shield her from all unpleasantness."

"Most commendable of you, my lord," Gideon replied, again wondering at the direction of the conversation.

Apparently there was none, for in the next instant his lordship clapped him on the back and boomed, "Well, it was good to see you again, my boy. Do give my regards to your sister Bethany, and best of luck in finding your brother."

Gideon nodded. "I will, and thank you." As he watched Lord Gilbert Barham pass through the gate, he grimly reflected that it was going to require much more than mere luck to find Caleb. At this point, it was going to take a bloody miracle.

CHAPTER 2

London

"*D!* I see a *D*. Do you see it, Caro?"

"Yes, I do believe you are correct, Amy," replied the exceedingly elegant and well-connected Lady Caroline Riddell. "What do you think, Mina?"

Mina, as Lady Wilhelmina Edicott, daughter of the immensely wealthy Earl of Cranham was fondly referred to by her friends and family, couldn't have looked more thrilled by her friends' conclusion. "Yes! Yes! It is most definitely a *D*," she cried, her pale blue eyes shining and her normally pasty cheeks awash with color as she peered at the plate before her. "Surely you agree, Helene?" She transferred her gaze to the sable-haired girl at her right, her euphoric expression tainted by anxiety.

All eyes shifted from the dear but decidedly frumpish Mina to the dazzling Lady Helene Dunville. Beautiful Helene was not only the daughter of the politically powerful Duke of Hunsderry, she was the acknowledged toast of the Season, an influential position that made the younger set defer to her out of a sense of awe.

Now puckering her famous ivory brow—famous in that it had been praised in at least eight sonnets that Season— Helene considered the letter in question. "I think that it rather resembles an *O*." She nodded once. "Yes. There is simply no doubt about it, it is an *O.*" Slanting Mina a sly, sidelong glance, she finished with, *"O,* as in Offchurch."

The game they played was an old one, born of an ancient superstition that claimed that a maiden could divine the identity of her future husband by placing a snail on a pewter plate. According to the belief, the snail would track upon the plate the first initial of the last name of the man the maid would someday wed. Because marriage was the desired outcome of any Season, the pastime was a favorite among the girls of the *ton,* who would spend hours at gatherings performing the ritual and then guessing at the identity of the man for whom the resulting initials stood.

This particular gathering was an intimate breakfast party given by Helene, the purpose of which was to gossip about the ball they had all attended the night before. Their speculation about several of the gentlemen in attendance had led them to consult with garden snails that had been hastily procured by the Duke of Hunsderry's elegantly liveried footmen.

Hence, they now sat at a small, round mahogany table in what Helene grandly called the Print Room, a name that referred to the selection of hunting prints displayed on the Pompeian red walls.

Mina, who had begged to go first, looked crushed at the mention of Lord Offchurch, a viscount whose lack of looks, conversation, and grooming made him the object of much ridicule among the ladies. Her previously blissful expression now much as it might be if the Naples biscuits she adored suddenly ceased to exist, she admitted, "I-I suppose that it could be an *O.*"

"Well, I say that it is a *D,*" Caro declared, giving Mina's arm an affectionate squeeze. "What do you say, Julia?"

Lady Julia Barham, who was currently suffering through her third Season, and had thus played the tiresome game more times than she cared to remember, heaved an inward sigh and dutifully leaned forward to study the plate.

"*O* or *D*?" Caro prodded.

Helene sniffed. "Really, Caro. I do not understand why you insist on bothering Julia. Can you not see how very bored she is by our company?"

Julia smiled at Caro, who was quickly becoming her

bosom bow. "It isn't the company I find tedious, just the game," she explained. And it was true. Though famous Helene did try her patience, she could never accuse the girl of being boring. As for Amy, Caro, and Mina, well, Amy's sauciness could be diverting, Caro was clever, and Mina was simply a dear.

"Mmm, yes. But of course you would be bored, dear," Helene said. "You must have played the game dozens of times by now. After all, this is—what?—your fifth Season?" She regarded Julia with an air of horrified fascination.

"It is her third, and you know it," snapped Caro.

The famed forehead furrowed. "Did I? Hmmm." Helene assumed a pose of pensive contemplation, a pretty, if calculated, posture that had prompted more than one gentleman that Season to wax poetically upon the picture she made. At length, she nodded. "Yes, yes. I do believe that you are correct, Caro. How very silly of me to forget. Now that you have prompted my memory, I also seem to recall that she was not an utter failure her first Season. You had— was it two proposals your first Season, Julia, dear?"

"It was six her first Season," Caro answered for her friend. "And as if that were not quite enough for any girl, she received four more in her second Season, and two so far this year."

Helene's eyebrows rose in mock surprise. "An even dozen? No wonder our game holds no charm for you, Julia. After turning down twelve proposals, you must be quite out of prospects."

Having spent much of the current Season fielding similar observations, Julia simply shrugged. "That has yet to be seen. Whatever the case, I shall not wed without love, and I did not love any of the men who proposed." That much was true, on both counts, though it constituted only a small part of the reason for her refusal to wed.

"Love?" Helene's eyebrows raised a fraction higher. "Bah! A clever girl seeks a coach-and-six and an income that will keep her in style. If you have any sense at all, you will forget about love and take what is offered, or you might find yourself a permanent resident of the shelf you presently occupy."

"I would scarcely call Julia on the shelf." This was from Lady Amy Manners, the pretty, golden-haired daughter of the estimable Marquess of Shepley. "Furthermore, I must say that I envy her parents' tolerance in the matter. She is beyond fortunate that they are allowing her to wait for her perfect match."

Tolerance was hardly the word Julia would have assigned to describe her parents' feelings toward her refusal to wed. Dismay, frustration, and anger all fitted with a more precise accuracy. Indeed, not a day passed that her father, the socially prominent Marquess of Stanwell, did not lecture her on her duty to make a brilliant match. Her mother, who prided herself on being London's premier hostess, was just as relentless in her nagging and never missed an opportunity to harp on the shame of having a daughter in her third Season.

Though Julia would have liked to believe that their vexation stemmed from concern for her future, she knew better. Her parents cared only about their position in the *ton*. Because they believed that her failure to wed was beginning to dull their social brilliance, her father had recently decreed that he would choose a husband for her, if she failed to select one for herself by the end of the Season. Having endured several excruciatingly interminable evenings in the company of one or another of her father's candidates, she could only shudder at the prospect. But what was she to do?

Before she could contemplate her dilemma, Mina prodded, "So, Julia? Is it an *O* or a *D*?"

"Oh, do stop being such a goose, Mina," Helene snapped. "It is obviously the letter *O*." Her prose-provoking lips curled into a malicious smile. "*O,* as in Offchurch, your most promising suitor."

For a moment Julia was tempted to tell Helene exactly what she thought of her spiteful baiting, to brutally inform her of the real reason their set suffered her disagreeable presence: because their parents insisted that they do so to further their own friendships with Helene's highly esteemed parents. Reminding herself in the next instant that to do so would serve only to provoke yet more censure from her parents, she resisted the urge and instead said, "It is a *D*, as in Denney." She smiled at Mina. Though the girl had never voiced her feelings for Lord Denney, an angelically beautiful viscount with a bookish bent, Julia had seen how awkward she became in his presence and guessed that she harbored a crush on him.

"Lord Denney?" Mina's doughy cheeks blushed a becoming shade of pink, thus confirming Julia's suspicion. "But his lordship has never betrayed so much as a passing interest in me."

"That is because you have never given him any encouragement, dear," Julia returned, giving the plump girl by her side a fond hug. Poor Mina. Every time Lord Denney strayed within a yard of her, she became hopelessly tonguetied. Resolved to promote her friend to the best of her ability, she added, "If you like, I shall have Mama seat his lordship between the two of us at the picnic she is having at the end of the month. That way, I can help you converse with him, should you need me to do so."

"You would do that?" Mina exclaimed in a breathless voice.

Julia nodded. "Of course I would. Are we not friends?"

"Oh, yes. Yes! Forever." It was Mina's turn to hug Julia.

Smiling, Julia hugged her back. No doubt her parents would interpret her request as an interest in Lord Denney for herself, which, of course, would result in him being thrown in her path at every turn. Oh, well. If she was clever, and she prided herself on being so, she could arrange to have Mina by her side at such times and thus encourage a match between the pair. Once his lordship saw past Mina's lumpish exterior, and she was certain that he would, given his scholarly nature, he was bound to be as taken with her as she was with him. Satisfied that something good might possibly come out of this otherwise wasted morning, she turned her attention back to her companions, intent on tendering an excuse and taking her leave.

Before she could utter the words, Helene said, "Now that you have settled matters so very neatly for Mina, per-

haps you would like to try your luck, Julia." Her delicate
eyebrows lifted in genteel challenge. "Unless, of course,
you fear that the snail will fail to make a letter?"

Failure to make a letter naturally indicated spinsterhood.
And while it was true that Julia had no wish to wed at the
moment, she hoped to do so someday—after her younger
sisters were grown and free of their aunt Aurelia's tyranny.

"So?" Helene goaded, snapping her fingers at the nearby
footmen, indicating that one was to remove the used snail,
while the other brought a selection of fresh ones.

Not about to give Helene satisfaction by begging off,
Julia took the silver tongs a footman offered and plucked
a snail from the dozen or so on the presented salver. As
she waited for it to do its magical duty, her mind again
strayed to her aunt. The story of Aurelia and the folly that
had led to her presence in their lives was one that Julia
and her sisters had heard at least a hundred times, a dreary,
cautionary tale that was repeated often in hopes that they
would learn from their aunt's mistakes.

Once the toast of the *ton*, Aurelia, who Julia's father
never failed to stress had been an exceedingly stubborn and
headstrong chit, had eloped with a man her parents had
forbade her to wed. Her parents had been justified in their
prohibition, for the man had turned out be a complete
scoundrel. He had been shot during their tenth year of
marriage, while bedding another man's wife, thus leaving
Aurelia a penniless widow. With nowhere else to turn, she
had thrown herself on the mercy of her family.

Because Aurelia's parents had died in the interim, it had
fallen to Julia's father, the new Marquess of Stanwell, to
decide his wayward sister's fate. In the end he had consented to take her in on one condition: that she serve as
an example to his daughters to illustrate the wretchedness
that came from defying one's parents. In order to do this
effectively, she was reduced to the station of servant and
charged with the duty of overseeing the girls' upbringing.

From the very beginning it had been clear that Aurelia
loathed her position. Indeed, she made no bones about the
fact that she despised children and often let her bitterness
guide her in her dealings with Julia and her sisters. That

was not to say that she beat her charges without reason, or that she hit them unduly hard when she deemed a switching necessary. Truth be told, she seldom raised her hand. Nor did she subject them to any other sort of maltreatment that would be readily apparent to the casual observer. No, her method was worse, far more insidious and damaging to their young lives: She deprived them of all love and joy, making their lives as grim as she had made her own.

At least she had done so until Julia had become old enough to defy her. Now a woman grown, it was within Julia's power to shield her sisters from their aunt's malice, and she did so with a fortitude that had made Aurelia back down from every confrontation they had had thus far. And she was determined to continue doing so until she could either convince her parents to rid them of Aurelia, or her sisters were grown. Exactly how she was going to evade her father's edict that she wed this Season, well—

"*K?* Or is that an *H,* do you suppose?" murmured Mina, interrupting Julia's rumination.

Caroline leaned over to examine the snail's handiwork, her forehead creasing beneath her face-framing tumble of chocolate-brown curls. After tipping her head this way and that, she pronounced, "It is an *H.* The outer lines are far too straight to be a *K.* Do you not agree, Julia?"

Julia, too, studied the plate before her. Though the lines were distorted, as they always were during snail experiments, it did look rather like an *H.* Nodding, she said, "I do believe that you are correct, Caro."

"An *H,* you say? Hmmm," Helene said, stroking her lyrically immortalized jaw in a contemplative manner. "I seem to remember you turning up an *H* when we played this game at Mary Montworth's picnic last week."

There was a pause of silence as everyone considered, and then Caro nodded. "Helene is correct. Do you not remember the awful time we had thinking of gentlemen whose names begin with an *H*?"

Julia did remember and it made her shudder to do so. Heaven help her if the game was as prophetic as it was alleged to be, and she ended up saddled with one of the three men in the *ton* whose names began with an *H.*

"Yes, now I remember as well," said Amy. "If I recall correctly, we settled on Clive Hartshorn, Earl of Wolton. He is younger than Augustus Hungate, Earl of Trendall, and ever so much richer than Viscount Huxham."

Lord Wolton—he of the mincing walk and affected lisp. Julia cringed at the mere thought of him. If he was the best that fate had to offer, she would take spinsterhood any day of the week.

"Lord Wolton? Perhaps," Helene mused, still stroking her jaw. "Or seeing as that it is Julia, who is set on a love match, it could be a commoner, someone we have never before considered."

The very notion of one of their illustrious number wedding a lowly commoner stunned the other women into silence. Caroline was the first to recover. "What a hateful thing to say, Helene!" she exclaimed, her cheeks flushing a dusky rose in her indignation. "Our Julia would never be brought to such a low pass."

Amy giggled, a sure sign that she was about to say something saucy. "Given the choice between a handsome and wealthy commoner, or Lord Wolton, I would take the commoner without a second thought. Especially if the commoner was someone like Mr. Gideon Harwood." Another giggle. "There is an idea. *H* as in Harwood."

Ever since the mysterious Mr. Harwood had deposited his enormous fortune in one of several banks owned by Amy's family, he had become a figure of much speculation among the *ton*—especially since he had shown no interest in entering their elite society. Not that they wished him to join them or that they would accept him should he try. It was just that they were used to the nabobs, as they referred to commoners who had made their fortunes in India, trying to gain eminence by infiltrating their ranks, and they were thus mystified that Mr. Harwood showed no inclination to follow suit. Truth be told, several *ton* members had actually voiced outrage at his behavior, interpreting his actions not as the wisdom to know his place, but as a snub of their society.

Mina frowned at the mention of the notorious Mr. Harwood. "A man like that would never do, Amy. We know nothing at all of his background and nobody seems quite certain as to how he came about his fortune. Indeed, it is rumored that he did not make it in India at all, as he claims, but as a pirate. In view of the fact that no one in polite Indian society has ever heard his name, at least according to Lady Waddell, and she is lately returned from Calcutta, it makes perfect sense to suspect that he acquired his wealth in a less-than-honorable fashion."

"Perhaps," Caro intoned. "Then again, India is an exceedingly large country. If his wealth were founded in diamond mines, as others say, he most probably spent his years out in the wilds and thus had no contact with English society."

Yet another giggle from Amy. "Whatever the case, you must admit that he cuts a most dashing figure."

"Does he?" This was from Mina, the only one among them who had never seen the object of their speculation. Her expression forlorn, as if she felt left out because of that fact, she begged, "Please. Do tell me what he is like."

"He is dark," Helene supplied with a disdainful sniff, "like a farm laborer. So dark, in fact, that I shall not be at all surprised if he turns out to be the half-Indian bastard of an unsavory English adventurer."

"He told Papa that he is from Yorkshire, which makes him as English as you or I," retorted Amy, visibly stung by Helene's criticism of her father's richest depositor. "And if Papa believes it to be true, then I do too. Besides, he is not so very dark as all that. His eyes are quite light—gray, I believe, and his hair is more brown than black."

Helene shrugged. "If you say so, dear." She couldn't have sounded more condescending.

Amy opened her mouth, no doubt to press her point, but Caro cut her off. "Whatever Mr. Harwood's nationality, we must all agree that he is exceedingly tall." Frowning first at Helene and then at Amy to remind them of their manners, she added, "If I do not miss my guess, he stands well over six feet tall."

"He is also well formed. You can be certain that he re-

quires no padding in his shoulders or calves, and his waist-
line is quite trim," tossed in Amy, shooting Helene a
mutinous look.

Another shrug from Helene. "You shall get no argument
from me on that count."

Nor would they get one from Julia. Gideon Harwood
did indeed possess an excellent figure, a fact that she had
discovered for herself when she'd barreled into him at the
Temple of the Muses, Mr. Lackington's fashionable bookshop in Finsbury Square.

Her cheeks burned at the mere remembrance of the mortifying incident. Though Mr. Harwood had done the gentlemanly thing and claimed all responsibility for their collision,
they both knew that the fault was entirely hers. To be sure,
she had been so elated at having finally found the third
volume of *Account of Voyages Undertaken by the order of
His Present Majesty for Making Discoveries in the Southern
Hemisphere,* Mr. John Hawkworth's final entry in the thrilling chronicles of Captain Cook's travel adventures, that she
had rushed headlong into the poor man, oblivious to everything but her eagerness to purchase her prize. No doubt
she would have fallen onto her derriere from the impact
had he not pulled her into his arms to steady her.

The burning in her cheeks intensified as she involuntarily
relived the moment. Though he had held her only the briefest of seconds and in a most impersonal manner, she
couldn't help but be aware of the body beneath his clothing. He felt so hard and powerful, so aggressively male—a
far different creature from the pale, soft beings that squired
her about the dance floor at every ball. To Julia's shame,
she could still feel the solid warmth of his body and the
sweet but oddly unsettling shock of excitement that had
raced through her as she pressed against him.

"And how do you find Mr. Harwood, Julia, dear?" inquired Helene. "Given your . . . mmm . . . accident at
Lackington's, you have had a much more—shall we say
intimate?—view of him than the rest of us." By the arch-
ness of her voice, it was clear that she already knew the
answer to her question.

Julia cursed her lapse of judgment in relating the incident

to her circle. Blast! Wasn't it just her luck that Helene would somehow discern her unorthodox attraction to the man? Praying that the other women had not detected it as well, she cautiously replied, "He is tall and rather dark, yes. And his manner is civil enough." She shrugged one shoulder in a way that she hoped would convey nonchalance. "I cannot say that he made much of an impression."

"Indeed?" Helene murmured, her raised eyebrows challenging the lie.

Fortunately for Julia, Mina was blind to the subtle byplay between her and Helene and unwittingly came to her rescue by demanding to know, "But is he handsome?"

"Well? Is he, Julia?" purred Helene.

Is he? Julia thought. Odd, but she had never stopped to consider whether Mr. Harwood was handsome. He was intriguing, yes. Attractive? Undeniably so. But handsome? After mulling the question for several moments, she shook her head. "No. I do not think that I could call him handsome. He is far too"—she made a helpless hand gesture as she grappled for a term to describe her impression of him. Unable to find one that fit, she settled on—"bold. He is too bold looking to be handsome."

"Bold?" Mina looked genuinely perplexed. "Whatever do you mean by bold?"

"Yes. Please do explain yourself, dearest Julia," said Helene. Unlike Mina, Helene appeared to know precisely what Julia meant.

"It is just that he is so . . ." So what? The word virile instantly came to mind. Not about to share that particular observation, especially not with Helene, she changed the flow of her thoughts and weakly explained, "It is just that his features are a bit . . . um . . . unrefined for my tastes."

"He may not be pretty, but I would hardly call his looks unrefined," contradicted Amy, who had actually been introduced to the man. "I would say that they are"—like Julia, she, too, had to pause to search for a word to describe the hard-to-define Mr. Harwood. Unlike Julia, however, she did not flinch from stating her honest opinion—"manly," she finally concluded with a nod. "Yes, the word 'manly' fits Mr. Harwood to perfection. Unlike many men in the *ton*, his looks leave no doubt whatsoever as to which sex he belongs."

Always the innocent, Mina frowned and said, "I have never had any trouble distinguishing between the men and the women. Which gentlemen do you find confusing?"

"I did not mean to say that I find the question of their sex confusing, rather that they appear to have some confusion about it themselves," Amy replied, grinning at her own naughtiness. When Mina continued to look uncomprehending, she sighed and explained, "Fops, dear. I was referring to fops like Lords Shipdam, Fiskerton, and Wolton, none of whom I find the least bit appealing." Heaven help them, she giggled again. "Unlike Julia, I happen to find manly men like Mr. Harwood far more attractive than fribbles like Lord Wolton."

"Oh, I did not say that I find Mr. Harwood unattractive," Julia blurted out before she could stop the words.

"No!" ejected Helene in mock surprise.

"Yes," Julia admitted, miserably aware that Helene would never let her live down her unwitting confession.

Mina's frown deepened in her consternation. "And Lord Wolton? Do you find him attractive as well?"

Again Julia's response just slipped out. "Good heavens, no!" The horror in her voice was unmistakable.

Helene chuckled. "Ah. Well, then perhaps it shall be *H* for Harwood after all."

Julia merely smiled. *H* for Harwood? Never. She would never choose such a man for herself, no matter how attractive she might find him, and her parents would most certainly never match her to a commoner. Not even to one as wealthy as Gideon Harwood.

CHAPTER 3

It could be *H* for Hartshorn after all, Julia reflected miserably as she strolled along the spectacularly lit Grand Walk of Vauxhall Gardens with Clive Hartshorn, Earl of Wolton. To her dismay, his foppish lordship was the latest selection in what had become her parents' endless parade of matrimonial prospects, an offering they seemed especially keen on her accepting. So keen, in fact, that they had lured her here tonight under the pretext of attending a concert by Mr. Donovan O'Keefe, an Irish tenor who was the current musical darling of the *ton,* well aware that she would have balked had she known that the outing was yet another of their matchmaking ploys. The perpetrators of the detestable plot presently followed close at her heels, now and again interjecting comments that were clearly contrived to further Lord Wolton's admiration of her.

Not that his lordship requires any prompting in that direction, Julia thought, slowing her already snail-like pace to accommodate her escort's mincing stride. Judging from the nature of what he no doubt considered his seductively whispered puffery, and the annoying but meaningful way he kept groping her elbow, it was apparent that he held her in the highest regard—heaven help her! If her parents were truly as set on having the popinjay for a son-in-law as they appeared to be, she might very well find herself being addressed as Lady Wolton by the end of summer.

More than a little alarmed by the prospect, Julia pasted

a smile on her face and nodded as they passed several acquaintances. As dictated by fashion, her party now promenaded the main Vauxhall walkways, as one always did upon their arrival at the Gardens, where they could see and be seen by everyone who was anyone in London society. And it appeared that everyone of the first description was there tonight, milling about in a glittering sea of evening dress that stretched as far as the eye could see. The crush was due, of course, to the popularity of Mr. O'Keefe, a triumph on his part, to be sure.

Steeling herself for what was certain to be a tedious evening, despite the promise of fine music, Julia dutifully murmured, "Fascinating," to whatever conclusion Lord Wolton had just drawn from his comparison of the city's snuff shops, then turned her attention to the visual feast that was Vauxhall Gardens, seeking respite in its splendor.

It was like something out of a fairy tale, a veritable miracle of sparkling waterfalls, fantasy grottos, lush lawns, and Gothic pavilions, all dotted with classical statues and illuminated by an infinite number of twinkling rainbow-hued globe lamps. Indeed, everywhere one looked was a spectacle to dazzle the eye. There were covered colonnades and secluded mazes of alleys in which one could take a leisurely stroll, and clearings sprinkled with temples and alcoves that begged a person to tarry. There was even a smuggler's cave, complete with a glittering treasure. And a row of charming booths that sold quaint fairings. Oh, and one must not forget the musical bushes, beneath which underground orchestras played fairy music. And then there were porticoes adorned with pillars and paintings, Chinese lanterns, and light cascades, and—

Snap! Snap! Lord Wolton snapped his fingers before her face, imperiously commanding her attention. "Lady Julia?" *Snap! Snap! Snap!* "I wealize that you, as a woman, have vewy limited mental facilities, but please do twy to follow my line of weasoning."

She? Possessed of limited mental facilities? Julia could only stare at him, rendered speechless by her outrage. How dare he, who could not so much as pronounce the letter *R*, presume to question her intellect? Why—why—! She was about to deliver a tart retort, when she felt a sharp jab in her lower back. It was a poke from her mother's fan, of course, a familiar warning from her parents, who were well aware of her unfortunate propensity to air her views when provoked. Too incensed to let his lordship's insult pass unchallenged, Julia shot her mother a mutinous glower.

Another jab, this one more urgent.

Again Julia glanced over her shoulder, mutely conveying her defiance.

By the threat on her parents' faces, it was clear that they would never let her hear the end of the matter if she said or did anything to discourage Lord Wolton's suit.

For several seconds Julia continued to wrestle with her governing impulse, weighing the satisfaction of unburdening her affront against the endless lectures she would endure from doing so. At last judging the price of satisfaction too steep, she swallowed her withering riposte and forced what she hoped was a contrite expression on her face. "A thousand pardons, my lord," she said, willing herself to smile in her most beguiling manner. "I must confess to being quite diverted by the sights. The Gardens look exceptionally stunning this evening. Do you not agree?"

Her apology had the calculated effect, for his lordship's pursed lips promptly curved into a most forgiving smirk. "Indeed they do look lovely, Julia, as do you," he drawled, his grasp tightening on her arm as he stumbled on the gravel paving for what must have been the tenth time that evening. It was his high-heeled shoes, of course, the lofty height of which made navigating the rough grade of the Vauxhall paths a very dangerous undertaking indeed. Though such heels had gone out of fashion for men years earlier, fops cursed by a lack of height occasionally still wore them.

Now steady, thanks to his liberal use of Julia's arm as a handrail, his lordship added, "Did I tell you how vewy wadiant you are tonight? How youh eyes scintillate with the luminawy nitid of twin stahs, and how the incandescence of youh lucifewous smile eclipses the sun with its bwilliance?"

He had not, but Lords Sothcott, Drewell, and Clapper had all presented that exact word bouquet to her at a ball

given the night before. That meant she had either become
exceedingly radiant of late, or that the line was the compliment du jour among the men of the *ton*. Guessing it to be
the latter, she smiled with a delight she did not feel and
tendered the same response she had given the other men.
"I thank you for your charming speech, my lord, though I
fear that it is unwarranted." A well-bred girl naturally displayed modesty when faced with effusive praise.

"Nonsense, my dear," boomed her father, more dragging
than escorting her doll-like mother in his rush to walk at
their side. "His lordship speaks the truth. You look most
radiant this evening. Why, you quite outshine every woman
here tonight, except, of course, your dear mother." He patted the white-gloved hand clinging to his arm and smiled
down at his wife, who simpered prettily in return. Now
directing his attention to Lord Wolton, he added, "As you
have no doubt heard, Wolton, our dearest Julia is considered to be an Incomparable by the *ton.*"

Julia cringed at her father's blatant exaggeration. While
it was true that she was much admired by the *ton,* their
regard came more from her well-bred manner and position
as the Marquess of Stanwell's daughter than from any extraordinary physical beauty on her part. Oh, that was not
to say that her looks were wanting. Truth be told, she was
rather pleased by what she saw when she gazed in the mirror. For though she could not lay claim to having the
brightest eyes, or the prettiest face, or the finest figure in
London—those honors belonged to famous Helene and
rightfully so—her looks were an agreeable blend of the
physical attributes the *ton* currently held in favor. Add her
rich dowry and Barham blood, which was said to be royal,
and she never lacked for suitors.

"I must say that you two look quite the thing together,"
contributed her mother, her nod mirrored by both her
bouncing golden curls and the extravagant black plumes in
her silver crepe turban. "Only see for yourself." She in-
dicted a looking-glass alcove to their right.

Never one to pass up an opportunity to preen, Lord Wolton promptly followed her directive, wheeling toward the

alcove with an eagerness that made him come perilously close to losing his balance. Now viewing his reflection with open admiration, he murmured, "We do make a devilish fine couple. Do you not agwee, Julia, deah?"

Julia obediently nodded, though as often was the case while in company, her actions in no way resembled her actual thoughts. Odd was the word that came to mind as she watched his lordship's pink-gloved hands adjust the frills at his throat and then smooth the lines of his awful coat. And it truly was awful. Indeed, whatever could have possessed him to have it made up in cloth in such a vile shade of prune?

Gripped by horrified fascination, the kind one usually reserved for the sight of diseased beggars, Julia contemplated the hideous but fashionable garment in question.

Apparently his tailor was not all that he should be, for the liberal padding in the chest and shoulders was easily detectable. Repressing her urge to make a face in distaste, she shifted her scrutiny to his waistcoat. Unlike Lord Wolton's coat, it met with her full approval. Made of gold tissue upon which was worked an ostentatious floral design of silver-gilt beads and green-and-pink foil spangles, his lordship's waistcoat was nothing short of a masterpiece. Of course, it was far more suited to a court visit than a concert at Vauxhall—as was the profusion of lace frills dripping from his wrists and neck. And while she was on the subject of his neck—

Julia paused to consider his stiffly starched neckcloth, which extended over his chin in an obvious attempt to hide its weakness, then glanced at the cheeks above it. Goodness! Was that rouge she spied? Surely no one flushed such perfect crimson circles? Deciding that he had indeed been dipping into the rouge box, she moved on to what she judged as his rather nice green eyes, in spite of his tendency to squint, her gaze finally coming to rest on his flaxen hair. Someone, most probably his valet, had brushed it forward from his crown to frame his narrow face in an artistically stacked arrangement of tight curls.

She was just wondering how many curling papers it had

taken to achieve the elaborate coiffure, when his lordship noticed her studying him. Vainly mistaking her curiosity for admiration of his person, he smiled smugly.

Julia saw her parents, who stood behind them and were thus reflected in the mirror as well, exchange a look of supreme satisfaction. "Yes. Fine," her mother echoed in a dulcet voice. "Then again, our Julia is always in looks. Why, just last week her hair was compared to gold reflecting the fire of sunset." Briefly touching one of the golden-red ringlets draped over Julia's shoulder, she continued, "Lord Busby compared her eyes to candlelit amber in his latest poem. Oh, and Sir Ludlow said that her teeth—"

"We all look particularly fine this evening," interrupted Julia, who was rather beginning to feel like a horse on the auction block. Not about to be sold to Lord Wolton for any price, she changed the subject by saying, "I heard you mention earlier that you purchased a new gig, Lord Wolton. Do tell us all about it as we walk to the orchestra rotunda." If his lordship were like every other man in the *ton,* he would seize the opportunity to brag about his new acquisition.

True to form, his lordship wasted no time in sharing the particulars of his new highflier, as the fashionable high-wheeled phaetons were called, describing every detail in depth, all the way down to the exact sheen of the varnish used on the undercarriage. He had just launched into a tedious description of the horses he had purchased to pull it, when she heard a feminine voice more bellow than call, "Julia? Julia Barham! Do wait!"

Amy. Of course. No one else in her acquaintance had the audacity to hail her in such a bold manner. Following the sound of the voice, she turned, smiling at Amy as her friend raced to where she stood. By the expression on Amy's face, it was clear that she was bursting with news. Following close on her heels in a blur of drab brown skirts was Amy's beleaguered abigail, Miss Philpot.

"Oh, Julia!" Amy cried, showering gravel hither and thro as she came to a skidding stop. "You will never guess who Papa brought with us this evening." She was practically dancing in her excitement.

"Lady Amy! You will address Lord and Lady Stanwell this very instant," Miss Philpot chided between huffing breaths. With her spare figure, brisk manner, and careworn face that looked frozen with infinite disapproval, Miss Philpot was the exact sort of dragon one thought of when they heard the word "abigail."

Amy had the good grace to look chastened as she dropped a pretty curtsy and murmured an appropriate greeting. That formality completed, she again looked at Julia. "As I was saying—"

"And Lord Wolton," Miss Philpot prompted in a severe tone. "Really, Lady Amy, I simply do not know where your manners have flown tonight to ignore a gentleman in such a fashion."

Judging from the way Amy wrinkled her nose at the command, it was not so much a lack of manners but a hearty dislike of his lordship that made her ignore him. Nonetheless, she did as directed, after which she widened her eyes at her abigail in exasperated query. Miss Philpot nodded primly. "Very well, Lady Amy. You may speak with Lady Julia. But please do remember that you are a lady and refrain from making a spectacle of yourself."

Always one who knew the side on which her bread was buttered, Amy inclined her head in agreement and then turned her attention back to the party before her. Now the very picture of demure maidenhood, she sweetly implored, "If you please, Lord and Lady Stanwell"—she smiled and nodded at Julia's parents—"Lord Wolton"—a nod in his direction, but no smile—"might Julia be permitted to walk with me for a moment? I have ever so much to tell her, and I do not wish to bore you with my silly chatter. I promise that we shall stay close at hand." Though her supplication was innocent enough, Julia could see from the gleam in her eyes that she was up to her usual mischief.

A quick, urgent glance passed between Julia's parents, as if each were demanding that the other think of an excuse to keep Julia trapped in Lord Wolton's company. Before either could speak, his lordship answered for them. "I was about to explain the pahticulahs of handling the weins. In view of the fact that Julia is unlikely to undewstand such complexity, I see no weason why she should not walk with heh little fwiend." He fluttered his hand in a patronizing gesture of dismissal.

Without waiting for his blessing to be echoed by Julia's parents, Amy grasped her friend's arm and unceremoniously hauled her away. Giggling, she mimicked, "Since Julia is unlikely to undewstand such complexity, I see no weason why she should not walk with heh little fwiend." Another giggle. "The stiff-rumped fribble, or I suppose that I should say stiff-wumped fwibble." A snort. "Does he not make your foot itch to kick him?"

"Hush, Amy. He might hear you," Julia cautioned, casting an uneasy glance back to where his lordship now pantomimed his driving technique to her parents. Miss Philpot walked several paces behind her and Amy, eyeing a nearby cluster of foxed rakes with an expression daunting enough to stop them cold as they surged forward to accost the young ladies in her charge.

Amy shrugged one lilac-satin-clad shoulder, unconcerned by the notion of offending Lord Wolton. Now looping her arm through Julia's, she said, "You know as well as I that his lordship is far too involved in dazzling himself with his own brilliance to take note of anything that we feeble-minded females might say. That fact aside, can you truly claim to have never suffered from the urge to kick him, especially when he flaps on about the inferiority of the feminine mind?"

"Well, no," Julia admitted with a sheepish grin.

Amy nodded her satisfaction. "I must confess to being relieved. For a moment, I feared that it might be *H* for Hartshorn after all. Speaking of the letter *H*"—she hugged Julia's arm in hers, her face animated with renewed excitement—"you shall never in a thousand years guess who Papa brought with us this evening."

"I am sure I cannot," Julia replied. And it was true. Any number of people, men, in particular, could have elicited such ebullience from Amy.

"Guess," her friend demanded, giving the arm she held an insistent tug.

Julia made a helpless gesture with her free hand. "Umm.

Let me think. Is it Mr. Crawford? I believe you said that your father commissioned him to renovate his bank on Threadneedle Street." As everyone in their set knew, Amy thought Mr. Joshua Crawford, one of London's leading architects, to be beyond dashing. And since Mr. Crawford was the youngest son of Seymour Crawford, a viscount of no small means, he was of high enough society to be publicly hosted by Amy's hierarchy-conscious father.

"No. No! I said *H,*" Amy exclaimed in an exasperated voice. "Think, Julia, think!"

Julia did exactly that, her mind running over the short list of men in the *ton* whose surnames began with an *H.* Finding none with the attributes to put Amy in such a pucker, she sighed and shook her head. "I give up. Who is it?"

Amy hugged her arm so hard that Julia feared she would have a bruise from it on the morrow. "It is *H,* as in Harwood!"

"What!" Julia came to an abrupt halt, stunned that Amy's widowed father would not only play host to a man of such questionable reputation, but would also allow his young daughter to act as hostess. Certain that she had misheard, she clarified, "Are you saying that your father is here in the company of Mr. Gideon Harwood—*the* Gideon Harwood?"

Amy's head bobbed up and down in a dizzying motion. "Yes. Yes! Papa invited him to join us tonight and oh! He is ever so wonderful. Come, you must let me have Papa introduce him to you."

Meet Gideon Harwood? Julia's heart seemed to freeze in her chest. It was unthinkable—impossible! After the mortifying way in which she had run him down at Mr. Lackington's bookshop—heavens! What he must think of her! Besides, what use could she possibly have for such an acquaintance? Since he would never be a part of her set, the introduction would serve only as an inconvenience, saddling her with the obligation to acknowledge and perhaps even converse with him should they accidentally meet in the future. And what could she possibly have to say to such a worldly man that would not make her sound like an utter

ninny? Worse yet, what would the *ton* have to say should
they spy her speaking to him? Considering the nature of
the speculation about him, she could only imagine how
tongues would wag.

Yet how could she *not* meet the man who fascinated her
so? And she had to admit that she was fascinated to no end
by him—by his mystery, by his physicality, by the beguiling
masculinity of his presence. He was so unlike anyone she
had ever met before, foreign and exotic, a world apart from
herself and her dull, sheltered existence. Indeed, she could
not remember a time in her admittedly untried life when
she had been so attracted to a man.

And there lay the crux of her resistance to meeting him:
She was frightened of the intensity of her attraction to him.
Not, of course, that he posed any real danger to her heart.
Being of such disparate stations, nothing could ever come
from her attraction, not even if she wished it, which she
most assuredly did not. No, it all came down to the fact
that she disliked the feelings he aroused in her. They bewildered and unnerved her, making her feel helpless and out
of control. And she hated feeling helpless.

"Come." Amy gave Julia's abused arm another tug. "I
promised to meet them at the orchestra rotunda."

"Well . . ." Julia vacillated, grappling for a reason, any
excuse at all, to avoid meeting the unsettling man. Desperate now, she glanced back at her parents, hoping to see
them signaling for her return to their fold. Better to suffer
Lord Wolton's tedium than the sensations she feared would
overcome her in Mr. Harwood's presence. To her dismay,
her parents seemed caught up in his lordship's performance
and paid her no mind at all.

As she looked away again, Miss Philpot approached.
"Lady Julia?"

Julia smiled at the woman, praying she carried news that
would provide for her escape. "Miss Philpot?"

"Your parents bade me to inform you that you may walk
to the orchestra rotunda with Lady Amy. They will meet
you there."

"Oh, perfect!" Amy squealed. "Come. I simply cannot
wait for you to meet him."

Feeling as if the air had been knocked from her, Julia allowed herself to be pulled into the opulently garbed current of humanity that now streamed toward the beckoning organ music that wafted through the light-festooned trees.

Down the Grand Walk they were swept, past the curved arcade of gaily lit supper boxes, in which visitors could enjoy the Garden's legendary fare, and through the Piazza, an imposing domed structure that boasted a spectacular chandelier with seventy-two lamps. Glancing back as they passed out of the Piazza and into the Grove, where the orchestra rotunda was erected, Julia noted that Miss Philpot remained close at their heels. Her parents and Lord Wolton, however, were nowhere to be seen, swallowed up in the surging swell of plumed headdresses and flower coronets.

Only half listening as Amy chattered on about the gown she was to wear at an upcoming ball, Julia stepped into the Grove. Formed by a quadrangle of colonnades and illuminated by fifteen hundred globe lamps that sparkled among the foliage like fallen stars, the Grove was a dreamlike vision that made one long to pinch oneself to confirm that one was indeed awake. In the center of the chimerical vista, set like the solitary jewel in a fairy queen's crown, was the lavish orchestra rotunda.

As Julia and Amy joined the throng gathered before the rotunda, Amy frowned and said, "I was to meet Papa and Mr. Harwood to the left of the stage, but I do not—oh, there they are."

Julia looked in the direction of Amy's nod, her heart jumping to her throat as she spied the men, who stood slightly apart from the crowd, engaged in an animated conversation. Though Amy's father was by no means a small man, he seemed almost dwarfed by Gideon Harwood's remarkable height, as did the other men present. Then again, there wasn't a man in London who would not fade into insignificance next to Mr. Harwood's imposing figure, Julia decided, smitten anew with awe. Still far enough away to observe him without him noticing her doing so, she allowed her gaze to roam over his splendor, noting every detail of his appearance.

He wore an exquisitely tailored black coat that was cut away in the front to reveal a waistcoat of silver silk embroidered with an intricate striped pattern of black and red scrolls. Layered beneath the waistcoat was an under waistcoat of gleaming scarlet satin, its high-rolled collar creating a bright frame of color that drew the eye to his neckcloth.

Unlike Lord Wolton and many of the other men in attendance tonight, Mr. Harwood had forgone frills, choosing instead a plain neckcloth, which he wore tied in a perfect knot beneath his strong chin. The contrast of the stark white linen against his sun-bronzed skin was dramatic, to say the least. Unable to make out the rest of his face for the shadows, Julia dropped her gaze, shocked to find herself perusing his unmentionable regions.

Though she normally tried not to notice such places, she could not tear her gaze away from his snug pearl-gray breeches, and the fascinating way they clung to his muscular hips and thighs . . . and other places. As Amy had commented the morning of the snail experiment, there was no doubt whatsoever as to which sex he belonged. The indelicate thought had just crossed her mind when she heard the author of the observation giggle. Suddenly aware that she gawked, Julia flushed and looked away.

"He truly is a glorious sight, is he not?" her friend inquired slyly.

"Yes," Julia somehow managed to squeak past her choking mortification. After all, it would have done no good to deny her admiration. Amy had caught her gaping. Wondering if anyone else had noticed her indiscretion, she glanced around. No one appeared to be paying her the least bit of mind, including Miss Philpot, who was indulging in her favorite pastime of glowering disapproval at everyone in her sight. Relieved, Julia again turned her attention, albeit more discreetly, to Mr. Harwood.

She was now a scant three yards away, a distance that closed rapidly as Amy quickened their pace. As she struggled to compose herself for the upcoming introduction, rehearsing the words she would utter in her mind, Lord Shepley looked up and noticed their approach. A handsome man, from whom Amy had inherited her stunning

legacy of thick golden hair and clear green eyes, his lordship smiled in welcome as the women approached.

"Why, it is Lady Julia," he exclaimed with genuine pleasure. "Always a delight to see you, my dear."

Julia sketched what she hoped was a pretty curtsy. "Lord
Shepley," she murmured, stealing a glance at Mr. Harwood
through her lashes as she dipped, trying to read his face.
Did he recognize her from the bookshop? Did he even
remember her? It was impossible to tell from his blandly
cordial expression. While one part of her hoped that he did
remember her, that he had found her every bit as unforget-
table as she had him, another part hoped that he had forgotten her and her clumsiness, thus giving her the
opportunity to form a fresh impression. Her curtsy now
completed, she rose, looking expectantly at Lord Shepley,
waiting for him to tender an introduction.

His lordship did not disappoint her. "Lady Julia Barham,
may I present Mr. Gideon Harwood, lately of India?"

Thus given permission to look directly at the man by his
side, Julia smiled and did exactly that. As Lord Shepley
continued the introduction, explaining, "Lady Julia is the
daughter of the Marquess and Marchioness of Stanwell,
both dear friends of mine," Julia reacquainted herself with
his face.

It was exactly as she remembered, lean and tan with
steel-gray eyes that revealed nothing yet seemed to speak
volumes to those who knew how to read what was in their
cool depths, which, regretfully, she did not. True, he was
not precisely what she would call handsome, at least not in
the currently accepted sense of the word. Yet there was
something about the boldness of his sharp-planed cheeks
and the strength of his high-bridged nose that quickened
her pulse in a way that the *ton*'s almost effeminate ideal of
manly beauty did not. His was the face of a real man, a
stalwart one who lived life hard and savored it to its fullest.

As she now gazed at his firm mouth, noting its pleasing
shape, he said, "A pleasure, Lady Julia," in a timbre that
sent a thrill down her spine. He then sketched what she
had to admit was an exceedingly polished bow, treating her
to an excellent view of his hair. It was beautiful hair, thick

and fashionably cut in a long crop that fell naturally, she suspected, given its inherent wave, in the stylish tousle so many men labored hard to achieve. She especially liked the color, the way the sable darkness was streaked with gleaming chestnut and russet highlights.

Tearing her gaze away as he straightened back up again, so as not to appear overly bold, Julia inclined her head in acceptance of the introduction, dismayed to find that her carefully rehearsed speech had quite flown her mind. As she looked up again, struggling to recapture it, she saw that he was no longer looking at her, but at a point beyond her. As she watched, his eyes widened briefly and then narrowed, as if in query or wariness. Mystified as to what had prompted the peculiar response, she stepped aside, turning slightly as she moved to follow his gaze.

It was her father. The blood had drained from his face, and he stood stiff and still, his eyes taking on an oddly hunted look as he stared back at Mr. Harwood. Not quite certain what to make of the curious byplay, she glanced several times from one man to the other, neither of whom moved so much as a muscle the entire time.

"Ahem!" Lord Shepley cleared his throat as he too looked from man to man, marking their perplexing tension. "Er—I say, Harwood, are you and Lord Stanwell acquainted?"

The intensity of Mr. Harwood's gaze seemed to increase as it bore into her father. "Are we, Lord Stanwell?" he inquired, his voice textured with a wealth of meaning.

Though her father blanched a shade whiter at his words, his voice was steady and demeanor confident as he replied, "If we are, sir, I fear that you have me at a disadvantage."

Mr. Harwood smiled then, a thin, wintry smile that did nothing to soften his harsh expression. "My apologies, my lord. It seems that I have mistaken you for someone I once knew, a man by the name of Barham, the lord of my childhood village. I must say that you bear a remarkable resemblance to him."

Her father turned positively ashen.

"A Barham relative, perhaps?" Julia's mother chimed in, seemingly oblivious to the bristling between the men.

Opening her carved ivory fan to cool herself from the gathering heat of the crowd, she added, "Barham men have a tendency to bear a striking resemblance to one another. You have said so yourself on several occasions, Bertie."

"The man could be a relative, yes—a distant one," her father murmured, his gaze still locked with Mr. Harwood's.

Inquisitive by nature, especially when it came to other people's affairs, her mother said, "Hmm, yes. Now let me think. He could be referring to the Berkshire line of Barhams. There are three of them, I believe, and one has a rather fine village near Lambourne." Smiling brightly at the object of her prying, she inquired, "Do you, by chance, hail from Berkshire, Mr. Harwood?"

Her father raised his eyebrows slightly at her question, a gesture that was answered by a tilt of the head by Mr. Harwood. "Do you?" her father finally echoed, giving a faint nod that had nothing whatsoever to do with the question and everything to do with his silent communication with the man before him.

Mr. Harwood slowly shook his head. "No. I am from Yorkshire, my lady, the North Riding region."

Her mother frowned at his response. "I cannot recall any Barham relatives in North Riding. Can you, Bertie?" Her gaze was on her husband now.

His remained on Mr. Harwood. "There is one, yes, but a very distant one—a cousin four times removed, I believe, who has an estate in that region." His eyes narrowed almost imperceptibly as he spoke, and he again nodded, a gesture so minute that it would have gone unobserved had Julia not been watching him so closely. "However, as we have never met, I cannot attest to the resemblance between myself and the man."

"Could he, perhaps, be the lord of your village, Mr. Harwood?" her mother inquired.

Mr. Harwood shrugged one shoulder. "Perhaps."

"Then perhaps—"

Whatever her mother wished to say was cut off by, "Lowd and Lady Stanwell? Lady Julia?"

All gazes turned to where Lord Wolton tottered toward them, waving his patterned silk handkerchief to command

their attention. Julia could not help noticing that he favored
his left ankle, no doubt having twisted it without her arm
to brace him against the hazards of his high-heel shoes.
Now recapturing Julia's arm with a proprietary air, he inclined his head in greeting to Lord Shepley.

Lord Shepley nodded back. "Lord Wolton." That formality complete, he introduced his lordship to Mr. Harwood.

As he always did when he did not quite approve of someone or something, which was most of the time, Lord Wolton lifted the quizzing glass that dangled by a gold chain
from his coat and raked the other man with his gaze in an
insultingly thorough manner. Judging from the way his nostrils twitched and the contemptuous curl of his lips, he most
probably would have cut Mr. Harwood had the introduction been tendered by a man of lesser station than Lord
Shepley. As it was, he offered only the slightest of nods.
Rather than bow, which was the appropriate response from
a commoner being acknowledged by a peer, Mr. Harwood
returned Wolton's nod in equal measure, an affront that
made Lord Wolton stiffen with outrage.

Turning his back on Mr. Harwood in a deliberate snub,
Wolton said, "Lowd Stanwell. Lady Stanwell. My deawest
Julia." He gave Julia's elbow a meaningful squeeze as he
uttered the word "deawest." "I have managed to secuwe
chaihs foh the pewfowmance. I have taken the libewty of
having the footmen set them thehe." He used his free hand
to indicate to where a pair of footmen stood guard over
four chairs set beneath a bower of lights opposite from
where they stood. "Do come now. I have owdewed we-
fweshment to be bwought."

As he uttered the words, the crowd around them broke
into wild applause. Julia glanced up to see Mr. O'Keefe
taking the stage. "Come," Lord Wolton repeated, urging
her to the chairs. Seeing no other choice, she allowed herself to be led away, but not before she nodded to Mr. Harwood in cordial farewell.

Mr. Harwood, however, did not acknowledge her courtesy. He did not even see it. He was again engaged in a
staring match with her father.

CHAPTER 4

Scratch! Scratch! Scratch!

Gideon looked up from the contract he was reviewing to see his majordomo, Simon Rowles, standing at the open door of his cozy, book-lined study, softly scratching at one of the gilded door panels in a bid to gain his attention. "Rowles?" he responded, arching one eyebrow in query.

The servant's hand paused midscratch. Unlike the cadaverous beings of decrepit stateliness that helmed the neighboring town houses on fashionable Grosvenor Square, Rowles was not only relatively young for a majordomo, having recently reached the distinguished age of thirty, he was a swarthy, roguish-looking fellow with a cocky grin and a wry, satirical wit. At the moment he appeared uncharacteristically sober. "The Marquess of Stanwell, sir. He is demanding to see you on a matter that he purports to be of some urgency."

Gideon glanced at the longcase clock to the left of the door. Its ornate brass dial read seven forty-five. Though his lordship's call came as no surprise, the earliness of the hour he had chosen to make it did. Then again, he doubted if the man had slept a single wink the previous night. Guilty minds seldom rested. Smiling darkly at his philosophical thought, he nodded. "Very well, Rowles. I will receive him in here."

Rowles bowed and then departed to do as he was instructed.

Gideon resumed studying the papers before him. Well, at least he went through the motions of doing so. Though his eyes were on the words, his mind was on the upcoming encounter with Lord Stanwell, wondering what the man would do or say. For the life of him, he could not even begin to imagine what could be said to defend or justify a case of bigamy. And Lord Stanwell was clearly guilty of that particular crime. How could he not be? He had been married to Lady Silvia for twenty-seven years at the time of her death, an interval during which he had fathered the chit who had been introduced as his daughter the night before. And there was no doubt whatsoever as to the girl's parentage. Not with those eyes and that hair.

He also suspected that Lady Silvia had been his lordship's first and therefore legal wife, given the fact that his lordship had been little more than a youth when he had wed her. As for the legality of the marriage itself, well, since his father had performed the nuptials and had recorded the entry in the village church registry, he had every faith in its legitimacy. He was trying to remember the specifics of that entry when Rowles announced his lordship.

Gideon waited several moments before looking up, a ploy calculated to illustrate his mastery of the situation and thus establish his control of the meeting. When his lordship had cooled his heels for what he deemed a proper interval to suit his purpose, he pushed the papers aside and acknowledged him with a cool nod. "Stanwell."

Lord Stanwell inclined his precisely curled and queued head in return. To his credit he appeared perfectly at ease, revealing none of the trepidation he no doubt felt inside. "Harwood. Good of you to receive me at this ungodly hour."

"Hmmm, yes. Now that you mention the fact, it is rather early for a call," Gideon replied, languorously stretching his spine as he leaned back from his imposing Chippendale desk. Now lounging in a deceptively relaxed pose, he rested his chin atop his steepled hands, fixing his visitor with a steady gaze as he inquired, "To what do I owe the honor, my lord?" He already knew the answer, of course, but he could not resist toying with the man.

His lordship smiled, a taut, strained expression that betrayed a crack in his composure. "I have a proposition. One that I am certain you will find quite interesting."

Gideon's eyebrows raised a fraction at his response. "Indeed?"

Lord Stanwell nodded.

"Pray tell."

"Since my business involves a matter of some delicacy, may I suggest that we discuss it in private?" He cast a meaningful look at Rowles, who hovered on the threshold, no doubt hoping to collect gossip about their illustrious caller to carry to the servants' hall.

It was all Gideon could do to hide his grin at the thought of how his housekeeper, the devout Methodist Mrs. Courter, would look should she catch wind of the true purpose of Stanwell's visit. Willing himself to frown instead, he glanced at the majordomo and quizzed, "Is there something you wish, Rowles?"

Always the model of decorum when circumstances dictated, Rowles sketched an elegant bow. "I was wondering if your guest would be requiring refreshment. Breakfast perhaps?"

Gideon had to bite his tongue to repress his chuckle at the servant's impudence. So much for decorum. Then again, he'd hired the man more for the amusement he provided than for his skills as a majordomo. Shooting the servant a look meant to quell any further indulgence in witticisms, he returned his attention to his caller. "Lord Stanwell?" he politely inquired.

His lordship shook his head, his amber gaze darting this way and that to avoid Gideon's now-probing stare. Another chink in his armor of calm. "No, no. Nothing. I—" His skittish gaze arrested abruptly on the crystal decanters ranging the sideboard to his right. "Well—*ahem!*— perhaps I could do with a brandy. Mmm, yes. A brandy would be very nice, indeed." Chink number three.

"A . . . brandy?" Rowles echoed in a choked voice.

Again, Gideon suppressed a grin. His lordship had just provided Rowles with a particularly tasty morsel of tittle-tattle. By the time the servants finished chewing over Lord

Stanwell's early-morning request for spirits, they would no doubt have him cast in the role of an inveterate tosspot who relieved himself in drawing-room corners and puked at the dining table. Hard-pressed to maintain his impassive facade in the face of that diverting thought, he nodded at the servant and said, "You heard his lordship, Rowles. A brandy. Or would you care to serve yourself, Stanwell?" Again he deferred to his lordship. Such a perfect host, he.

His lordship's dithering gaze skittered back to the decanters. "I will serve myself, thank you."

Gideon nodded again. "Very well, then. You may leave us, Rowles. And please close the door behind you."

Now alone, Gideon waited until Lord Stanwell had poured himself a ration of his finest brandy and loitered awkwardly at the sideboard before again addressing him. "Do sit, Stanwell," he said, indicating one of the two Chinese elbow chairs flanking his desk. "Or should I, perhaps, address you as Lord Gilbert? After all, that is the name by which I know you."

"And rightly so, for it was indeed my name when I acquired Fellthwaite Village," his lordship replied, crossing the room in several long strides. Now settling his stocky frame into the designated chair, he explained, "I came into the world as Lord Gilbert Barham, third son of the Marquess of Stanwell. As a third son with two exceedingly healthy and sober older brothers, I had no expectations whatsoever of gaining the family titles, and thus expected to spend my life simply as Lord Gilbert. Truth be told, I was happy as such."

He sighed then and closed his eyes. "You see, my father was a harsh, cruel man, a tyrant whose standards for his heir were impossible, to say the least, and I was relieved to escape his tyranny. Though it shames me to confess the fact, I was terrified of him—so terrified that I was reduced to a craven coward whenever he so much as looked in my direction. It is because of my cowardice that I find myself in my current pickle." Sighing again, he opened his eyes, his expression haunted and his gaze imploring as it locked with Gideon's. "If you will permit me to explain my situation, I believe that you will not judge me so very harshly."

Though Gideon doubted if that last would prove true, he had to admit that he was more than a little intrigued. Not about to give his lordship the advantage by revealing his interest, he schooled his face into a mask of bored indifference, a look he had perfected for the purpose of bargaining with the notoriously miserly Rajput chieftains. "As you wish, my lord."

His lordship nodded and took a long—and no doubt fortifying—swallow from his glass. His voice now raw from the burn of the strong liquor, he began. "Let me preface by saying that I truly loved Silvia. She was my first love, my heart's blood, and I would have been content to live out my days by her side in Fellthwaite."

"Then why did you not do so?" Gideon felt compelled to ask out of loyalty for the woman who had shown him and his family great kindness.

"As I said, I was terrified of my father, and even my love for Silvia was not enough to give me the strength to defy him." His lordship now stared at his glass, his thumb restlessly tracing the smooth rim. After several rotations, he shook his head. "I have so much to explain, I scarcely know where or how to begin."

"Perhaps you should start by telling how you came into the title," Gideon said. It seemed as good a starting place as any.

"It was the influenza. Perhaps you remember the outbreak that occurred twenty-two—no, it was twenty-three years—ago?"

Gideon nodded. He did. He had been six at the time and had barely survived his own battle with the disease.

Lord Stanwell nodded back and took another drink. "My father was in the midst of arranging a match between my oldest brother, Averil, and Lady Cordelia Fitch, the Duke of Kilminster's daughter, when the influenza took the prospective groom. Kilminster was, and still is, a man of enormous power, both socially and economically, and a match joining our families was a coup my father was loath to surrender, even in the face of my brother's death." He quaffed the remainder of his brandy in one long swallow, clearing his throat to soothe the sear of the liquor before resuming his explanation. Now staring into the empty tumbler, he continued. "Because my second brother also fell victim to the disease, I was now the heir and the duty fell to me to wed the girl."

"And did the girl have nothing to say about the change in husbands?" Gideon inquired, appalled that a parent would so callously pawn his child.

His lordship shrugged one shoulder. "She had no more choice in the matter than I did."

"There is always a choice," Gideon reminded him harshly.

"Not for a coward." Lord Stanwell looked up then, his eyes pleading for understanding. "You did not know my father, Harwood. I simply could not tell him about my marriage to Silvia. Had he even suspected that I was wed to a commoner, and to a lowly miller's daughter, no less, well, I do not even wish to speculate upon what he might have done. Besides, once I actually had the title in sight, I found that I rather wanted it. I—"

"Wait." Gideon held up his hand to halt the other man's speech, unable to believe what he was hearing. "Exactly how was it that your father did not know of your marriage to Silvia? I cannot imagine how you could have hidden such an important matter from your family."

"As a mere third son, my father wasted neither time nor thought on me. Indeed, he most probably would never have acknowledged my existence at all had my mother not insisted that he do so. After she died"—another shrug—"we spoke only when we met by chance. As long as I remained clear of scandal he was free to ignore me and I was at liberty to live my life as I pleased. Because of his disregard, he was ignorant of the fact that I owned Fellthwaite. You see, the estate was forfeited in lieu of a large debt owed to me at the gaming table and thus never numbered among the Barham properties. I still keep it separate for reasons I need not explain."

The very thought of carrying on such a deception for so many years boggled Gideon's mind beyond all comprehension. So much so, that he could not keep a note of incredulity from creeping into his voice as he asked, "How in the world did you manage to keep your wives ignorant of each other's existence?"

"It was far more simple than you might imagine, for Silvia had no interest in London, and Cordelia is interested in nothing else." He held up his empty glass, seeking permission to refill it. At Gideon's nod, he rose and made his way back to the sideboard. As he replenished his drink, he explained, "Silvia never questioned me when I attributed my frequent absences from Fellthwaite to business. She was a simple woman, who was content to live a quiet life in the country. As for Cordelia"—there was a clink of glass against glass as he replaced the stopper in the decanter— "I sometimes wondered if she even noticed my absences. Like many couples in the *ton,* we lead separate lives. That is not to say that we do not care for each other. Were I not so fond of her and our children, I would not be here."

Though Gideon suspected that the visit had been prompted more from a sense of self-preservation than from any great love for his family, he let his lordship's pretense of devotion pass unchallenged. He did so not out of understanding or sympathy for the man's plight, but because he did not see it as his duty to bring him to justice. Indeed, considering the weight of his problems with his own family, doing so was the furthest thought from his mind. However, since his lordship was here and clearly feared what he might do with his damning knowledge, he might as well make him pay a small measure by letting him squirm like a worm on a fisherman's hook. With that punitive purpose in mind, he chuckled darkly and replied, "You mentioned a proposition earlier, one, I suppose, with which you intend to buy my silence?"

His lordship nodded as he resumed his seat. "Yes. As I said, I am very fond of my family."

"I shall judge how fond by the magnitude of your offer," Gideon countered. "Do proceed."

His lordship drank deeply of his brandy, then said, "I know that you are an exceedingly wealthy man, Harwood. If the accounts of your fortune are true, then your wealth matches, or even exceeds, my own. In view of that fact, I realize that it would be foolish to attempt to buy your silence with money."

"How very astute," Gideon interjected dryly. "So?"

"So—" His lordship indulged in another tipple. "So, I am prepared to offer you something that you cannot, with all your wealth, buy. Something every man in your position covets but has no chance of gaining on his own."

"Which is?" Gideon was genuinely intrigued and took no pains to hide the fact.

"The *ton.* I am offering entrée into London's highest circles."

Gideon emitted a derisive snort. "You will have to do better than that if you expect me to remain silent. Please believe me when I say that I have no interest or use for the *ton.*"

"Do you not?" Lord Stanwell raised his wiry bronze eyebrows, his expression smugly challenging. "Think, man, think! Just imagine what such an opportunity could mean to your family, especially your sister."

"Sisters," Gideon said, willing himself to ignore the other man's directive and the temptation it presented.

"Sisters," Stanwell echoed with another significant lift of his brows. "All the more reason to consider my offer. With my patronage, your sisters will move in the highest circles, gain powerful friends, and make fine marriages. If I recall correctly, the women of your family are blessed with uncommon beauty. Such extraordinary looks paired with your wealth and my sponsorship should allow them to marry into the aristocracy. In short, they shall enjoy every advantage afforded those of noble rank, as will their children and all future generations. As for your brother, you are far more likely to find him with all doors open and every resource at your disposal."

Of course his lordship was right. His family would benefit immensely from such an opportunity. Yet how could he, in good conscience, allow himself to profit from Lord Stanwell's sins? And that is exactly what he would be doing if he accepted the man's bribe. Then again, where was the real harm in doing so? Lady Silvia was dead and thus beyond being hurt by her husband's deception. As for Lady Stanwell, she was now his sole wife, though not his legal one since in the eyes of the law they were never truly wed. Gideon contemplated the troubling detail for several beats, seeking a way to right the wrong in his mind.

Hmmm. Perhaps his acceptance of the bribe might not be so egregious if his lordship agreed to legally wed her ladyship. Indeed, in forcing his lordship to do so, he would actually be remedying the injustice done to the woman. Yes, and—

No. No! Gideon gritted his teeth, his conscience springing forth to battle his temptation. It would be worse than wrong to accept such a bargain. It would be disgraceful—immoral. No. He would not entertain such an offer. He could not. Not if he wished to retain even a shred of honor and self-respect.

In spite of his noble intentions, his resolve remained dangerously shaken as he growled, "Exactly how do you intend to work such a miracle, Stanwell? I doubt the *ton* will accept me on your say-so."

His lordship shrugged, visibly unfazed by the prospect of what most men would view as an onerous task. "I am prepared to offer you my greatest prize, my treasure, to ensure your acceptance."

"Which is?" Heaven help him, he had to ask.

"Why, my daughter Julia, of course."

"What!" Gideon more roared than uttered the word in his shock. That the man would sacrifice his daughter to save his own skin—good God! Was there no end to his villainy?

Lord Stanwell smiled, clearly mistaking his outrage for startled surprise. "Yes, I am prepared to give you my dearest Julia's hand in marriage." He couldn't have looked smugger or surer of himself. "I promise you, Harwood, you cannot lose with my daughter by your side. Not only is she a respected member of the *haut ton,* she is greatly admired for her charm and beauty. As such, she is naturally much sought after for a bride. To date she has had a dozen offers from noblemen of the first description, all of whom she refused. Her suitors were, of course, crushed by her rejection. Now if you were to win her, especially with my blessing"—he spread his hands to illustrate the magnitude with which the feat would be viewed—"why, the *ton* will most certainly clasp you to its bosom."

"Yes, and you can rest secure in the knowledge that I shall never reveal your foul secret at the cost of branding my wife a bastard and myself as big a villain as you for entering into such an arrangement," Gideon bit out.

"That too," Stanwell confessed with a galling air of nonchalance. "Nonetheless, it will be you who will be coming out on the winning end of our bargain."

"Provided that your daughter will accept an offer from me. And what makes you so certain that she will do so?" Not that he would ever consider such a marriage. Of course not. Not only would it be dishonorable to do so, he simply was not attracted to the girl, who in his opinion was insipid in both looks and manner.

Now visibly certain of victory, his lordship replied, "She will wed you because I shall command her to do so. She is a malleable chit." Before Gideon could respond, he added, "I can promise you that Julia is everything you could wish in a bride. Not only is her breeding impeccable, she has been thoroughly schooled in the wifely arts. Thus she is prepared to manage your household, supervise your servants, and regulate your family. Why, just imagine how your sisters will benefit from her example." He nodded, his smile coaxing. "Think, Harwood. Just think! Under her tutelage they will learn how to go about in society and show themselves at their best advantage. I guarantee that they will blossom into perfect ladies under Julia's direction."

Gideon did think. He thought about the letter he had received from Bethany the day before expressing her despair over Bliss's ungovernable nature and her own inability to curb it. Poor, sweet Bethany. She was hardly in a state fit to deal with their young sister's wildness. Then again, it seemed as if no one was. That the three seasoned governesses he had thus far employed to tame the child had failed to last in their positions more than a fortnight spoke volumes of the trouble he had on his hands. Could

Lady Julia Barham, perhaps, be the solution to his problem?

The moment the thought entered his mind, Gideon tried to dismiss it. Yet it refused to leave. After all that his sisters had suffered from his neglect, he owed them the best life he could give them. And the best in life went beyond the obvious material effects, all of which he had already given them. The best meant comfort, happiness, and peace. That being the case, would it really be so very wrong to wed Lady Julia Barham if doing so meant buying Bethany the peace she would gain from knowing that Bliss was in guiding hands? As for the incorrigible Bliss, she could not help but to be improved by Lady Julia's refined ways, and such improvement would most certainly add to her happiness. And they would all benefit from the comfort to be derived from him having a properly trained wife to set right the shambles he presently called his estate. The more he weighed the advantages of the union against the eternal damnation he would no doubt suffer for entering into the bargain, the further his resolve slipped.

"Well?" Lord Stanwell pressed. "Have we an agreement?"

Gideon shook his head. He had to be sure. "Not so fast. What guarantee do I have that your daughter will take my sisters and household in hand, and do so with the proficiency you claim her to possess? Do not forgot that I have met the girl, and she strikes me as overly young to have much experience in such matters."

"She is twenty, hardly a child by anyone's measure. However, to answer your question, her experience with children comes from her dealings with her younger siblings, to whom, I feel compelled to point out, she is selflessly devoted. She spends much of her day in their nursery granting them guidance and counsel. Everyone who sees her with them comments upon her natural fondness and talent for managing children. She is firm, but kind. As for her experience in household matters, I can say only that she has done admirably on those occasions when she has been called forth to manage our home in her mother's absence."

"That is hardly what I call a guarantee," Gideon countered, though he had to admit she sounded ideal. What did it matter that he found her physically less than alluring?

Lord Stanwell nodded. "Very well, then. If she fails to perform in her domestic duties as promised, you have my word that I shall rectify the situation by personally seeing to it that you have the best housekeeper, abigail, and governess to be had in all of England. The best servants naturally reserve their services for the aristocracy."

"Naturally," Gideon murmured dryly.

"So you see? You cannot lose."

"Perhaps not on that score," he said, his eyes narrowing as he was struck by a new and exceedingly important consideration. "However, you seem to have forgotten one small detail in all of this. Bethany and Caleb both lived in Fellthwaite, and often saw you in the village. No doubt they will recognize you and guess at your secret."

"Not if you tell them that I am a relative of the master of Fellthwaite Village. If you do so straightaway, marveling at the rare coincidence that has made the daughter of a distant cousin of Lord Gilbert catch your eye, they will believe you easily enough. Indeed, why would they not? Besides, as my wife mentioned at Vauxhall, Barham men all bear a striking resemblance to one another. I might also add that four of us are currently named Gilbert, after one of our more illustrious ancestors. Those details coupled with the fact that I have changed much over the years—" He broke off with a sweep of his hand. "So you see? You truly cannot lose."

"So it would seem," Gideon said, considering his words. Lord Stanwell was correct in that he had changed a great deal since Bethany and Caleb had last seen him. So much so that he, himself, most probably would not have recognized him had he passed him on a London Street, displaced from the familiar setting of Fellthwaite. His lordship was also accurate in that they would believe him to be a mere relative of the village's master if he, their brother, told them that it was so.

"Then you accept?"

Gideon held up his hand. "On three conditions." Good

God! Was he really considering entering into the sordid bargain? The answer was yes. He would enter into a bargain with the devil himself if in doing so it would benefit his family.

"The conditions?" his lordship quizzed.

"Number one." He held up one finger. "You must remarry Lady Stanwell, make her your legal wife."

Lord Stanwell chuckled and drained the remaining contents of his glass. "Already done. I have convinced her ladyship that I wish to marry her all over again to demonstrate to the *ton* how much I adore her. Being a female, she naturally finds the notion impossibly romantic." Another chuckle, this one accompanied by a head shake. "With the plans she is making to celebrate the occasion, it is certain to be the event of the Season. As my future son-in-law, you will, of course, be invited."

"Of course," Gideon muttered, not relishing the notion. "Your second condition?"

"Number two." He flashed two fingers. "Our marriage must look like a love match to the world. Only then will my family gain genuine acceptance into the *ton*. This means that I must court your daughter, and she must pretend to become infatuated with me. At least when we are in public." He only hoped that he was up to the charade. It was going to take an extraordinary talent for acting to convincingly feign interest in the tedious milk-and-water miss.

His lordship's lips curved into a most reassuring smile. "As I said, Julia will do as I say, and I shall instruct her to dote upon you as if you are the answer to her maiden's prayer. Who knows? Perhaps she will find you so. You are not without certain manly charms, or so my wife informed me last night." He chuckled and shook his head. "Females."

Gideon smiled back tautly. "For my part, I promise to show your daughter every kindness and consideration due to her as my wife." Not that he truly thought Lord Stanwell cared how he treated the girl. Nonetheless, he had every intention of honoring his vow, and he genuinely hoped that the chit would find a measure of happiness within their union.

"Your third condition?" his lordship asked, impatiently waving aside Gideon's honorable pledge. Ah, fatherly love.

"Number three." Three fingers. "Your daughter must agree to be unfailingly kind to my sisters. She must understand that they are my first consideration, and that my sole purpose for entering into this marriage is for the advantages it will bring them."

"Of course. Of course." Lord Stanwell bobbed his head several times to the affirmative. "She shall be the soul of benevolence."

Gideon gazed at the other man for several moments, coming to terms with what he was about to do. Then he sighed and nodded. "Very well."

"Then we have a bargain?" His lordship could not have looked more triumphant.

"If all my conditions are met, yes." Heaven help him. He had just sold his soul to the devil.

CHAPTER 5

"It is barbaric, and I shall not allow it," Julia exclaimed in shocked accents as she gazed at her sister Jemima, who stood at the end of the long schoolroom table reciting a particularly laborious selection from Shakespeare's sonnets. To her horror, the eight-year-old child was strapped in a "spider," as the torturous iron collar and backboard combination was commonly referred, a painful, posture-perfecting device that Julia herself had been forced to endure every day of her young life between the ages of six and twelve.

The perpetrator of the outrage, her aunt Aurelia, who presently lorded over the cheerless schoolroom from a comfortable leather wing chair at the head of the table, rose at the sound of her voice. A tall, aristocratically beautiful woman with rich auburn hair and the striking amber Barham eyes, Aurelia could not have looked more elegant or icily remote than she did at the moment, standing ramrod straight in her simple yet fashionable gown of brown and cream linen. Now poised for what had become her daily confrontation with her eldest niece, she snapped, "The board is necessary, Julia. The child stoops." Her frigid gaze shifted to Jemima, her razor-edged voice sharpening with accusation as she added, "Had the willful chit not ignored my repeated admonishments to stand straight, I would not have been required to resort to such measures. As it is"—a dismissive shrug—"she shall grow accustomed

to the device by and by, and in time will hardly be aware
that she is wearing it."

"One never grows accustomed to such misery," Julia retorted heatedly, kneeling on the bare wooden floor to wrap
a protective arm around her sister, board and all. "I
never did."

Another shrug from Aurelia. "That is because you were
overindulged as an infant. Everyone knows that too much
coddling in infancy spoils one's constitution. Jemima, on
the other hand, has been under my guidance since birth,
so she suffers no such weakness. In view of that fact, she
should bear up against the rigors of the backboard without
the untoward discomfort you claim to have endured."

"No, she will not. She shall never be forced to bear up
to the backboard, or to any other form of unnecessary discomfort. Not while I have a breath in my body," Julia said,
her fingers shaking with fury as she began to unlatch the
complicated series of heavy leather straps and steel buckles
lashing the brutal contraption to her sister. As she un-
clasped the iron collar, soothingly stroking the reddened
skin beneath it, Jemima ducked her face away from her
aunt to shoot Julia a quick look of gratitude. With her pale
golden curls and robin's-egg-blue eyes, little Jemima was
the only Barham daughter who favored their fair mother.
Overwhelmed by tenderness at the sight of tears streaking
the child's pale cheeks, Julia planted a kiss behind her ear,
hugging her close as she promised, "It will be all right, love.
I will speak with father about the matter. I am certain—"

"It is your father who ordered the board," Aurelia interrupted, her sharp voice lashing through the room like the
crack of a whip. "It seems that Lady Mabley saw Jemima
at her daughter's picnic last week and commented upon
her poor carriage to several of the ladies in your mother's
circle. Your mother was, understandably, distressed when
the observation reached her ears and took to her bed with
a megrim. When your father learned what had happened,
he bid me to remedy the girl's defect. And as we all know,
I am your father's most humble servant." Bitterness spilled
over into her voice as she uttered that last.

Julia smiled and winked at her dejected sister, seeking

to reassure her. "All the more reason for me to speak with him," she countered evenly, at last liberating the girl from her prison of iron, leather, and wood. Taking her now-free sister's hand in hers, she stood, saying, "Come, Jemima. You may accompany me downstairs and take air in the garden while I consult with father. I daresay that you have not set foot outside the nursery all day. You must come as well, Maria."

She held her other hand out to her twelve-year-old sister, Maria, who sat at the table pretending not to notice the scene unfolding before her as she studiously deciphered whatever tedious, and no doubt pedantically moralizing, French parable their aunt had assigned her to translate. Judging from the soft hiccups coming from the girl, a sure sign of distress in Maria, the translation had been assigned as a punishment. Knowing Aurelia as well as Julia unfortunately did, the subject of the piece would most probably be revealed to be a searing condemnation of whatever infraction the woman had determined Maria to be guilty of.

When Maria hesitated in accepting Julia's invitation, her gaze darting nervously between her sister and her aunt, Julia prompted, "Come, dear. I am sure that Aurelia will agree that you could both benefit from some exercise." That was a lie, of course. Aurelia would never have willingly acknowledged their youthful need for sunshine and exercise, not knowing, as she did, how much her charges enjoyed their frolics in the garden. Indeed, had the woman been given her way, she would most probably have imprisoned the girls in their barren attic nursery, robbing them of the pleasures and company to be found in the outside world.

Maria's skittish gaze arrested on Julia for a moment, her brown eyes full of longing and her small white teeth tugging furiously at her bottom lip. Then she hiccuped and looked at her aunt. "My lady?" Though the utterance was a simple one, soft and devoid of inflection, it spoke eloquently of the tragic extent to which Aurelia had crushed the child's spirit.

Wanting nothing more than to strangle Aurelia for so thoroughly cowing her beloved sister, Julia too looked at Aurelia and echoed, "My lady?" Unlike Maria, her voice was laden with meaning, promising a battle should the woman not deliver the desired response. Truth be told, she almost hoped that her aunt would deny the request, thus giving her leave to vent a measure of the blistering rage that smoldered within her.

Apparently her aunt was in no mood for conflict today, for she nodded once in curt dismissal. "Very well. You are both excused. However, I shall expect you back at your lessons promptly at half-past three."

Maria practically bolted up in her eagerness to escape, only to remember herself in the next instant. Hiccuping several times in quick succession, she dropped a deep curtsy, her delicately sculptured face flushing a fiery red as she murmured, "Thank you, my lady. You are most"—*hiccup!*—"kind."

Jemima abruptly dropped Julia's hand and followed suit, her sister's example reminding her of her own manners.

Aurelia frowned. "Do keep your back straight when you curtsy, Maria. You look like a puppet with a broken string. As for you, Jemima"—her disapproving gaze pounced on the younger girl—"how many times must I tell you not to rock when you dip?"

"I thought that your curtsies were lovely. Perfect, in fact," Julia contradicted, the sight of Jemima's crestfallen face making her hands itch anew to strangle their wretched aunt.

Poor, darling Jemima. All she wanted in life was a measure of kindness and an occasional word of praise, not so very much to ask. It was the same with Maria. Unfortunately, since their parents seldom spared them more than a passing glance, and they were allowed little fraternization with the servants who adored them, they were left with no choice but to look to Aurelia for affection and approval. But, of course, Aurelia never gave it. She never gave anything that was good, or kind, or could be mistaken for affection to her charges. Thus, it fell to Julia to provide it. And, heaven help her, she gave as best she could, working so very hard to fill their yearning need. At times she even felt as though she were succeeding. But at other times— heartbreaking moments like this—she despaired, questioning whether her love alone was enough to fill the void in her sisters' souls. They were awfully big voids, after all, ones that should have been filled by constant love and nurturing from their parents, grandparents, and every single person who touched their young lives.

Jemima met Julia's gaze then, smiling faintly at her praise, an expression that never quite reached her wide blue eyes. Such old eyes for one so young, Julia thought, her heart wrenching at the sight. Sad eyes, full of disillusionment and weary defeat. Maria's eyes were much the same—as were her own. For beyond their name, beyond their blood, the strongest bond the three sisters shared was their legacy of lonely longing for affection.

"Come, loves," she murmured, squeezing the words past the sorrow swelling in her throat. Holding out her hands again, she injected a cheery note into her strangling voice and added, "I saw Mr. Mullock this morning, and do you know what he said?"

Jemima shook her head, while Maria skirted the schoolroom table, her gaze nervously flitting to Aurelia as she went.

"He informed me that the goldfinch eggs he showed you in the topiary obelisk last week have hatched. He said that he would be glad to hold each of you up to see the babies if you wish him to do so." Bless Mr. Mullock, the jolly head gardener, and his unfailing kindness to her sisters.

Maria, who adored animals and no doubt would have adopted a menagerie of strays had Aurelia allowed the girls to keep pets, brightened visibly at the news. "Did they all hatch? Oh, and are the babies all quite well?" she exclaimed, grasping Julia's left hand while Jemima latched onto her right one.

Julia smiled, pleased to have brought a sparkle to her sister's eyes. "I do not know, Maria. I was hoping that you would take note and report your findings to me. However, judging from the vigorous chirps coming from the shrubbery, my guess is that the nest is full and the birds are all in fine feather. It—"

"Jemima. Maria," Aurelia's voice cut in.

Julia stiffened at her aunt's harsh tone, her simmering

anger roiling to a full boil as she felt Maria wince and Jemima tremble.

"My lady?" her sisters chorused in dutiful unison, the flush of anticipatory pleasure draining from their cheeks as they half turned to acknowledge their scowling aunt.

"Do have a care for your gowns. I will not have you returning to the schoolroom as filthy as beggars." It was a warning, of course. A malicious one meant to lessen the children's pleasure in viewing the birds.

Giving the small hands that still clutched hers a quick squeeze of reassurance, Julia tossed over her shoulder, "If they soil them, we shall have them washed. We had five laundry maids in our employ at last count, so you can rest assured that you shall not be required to clean them yourself." With that, she pulled her sisters from the room, closing the door behind them with a resounding slam.

No one spoke as they trooped down the narrow stairs, the only sounds marking their passage being that of Maria's hiccups and the scuff of their soft-soled shoes against the rough wooden steps. As with most noble households, the nursery and schoolroom were located on the upper floors to save the Barham parents from being disturbed by their children's racket. Not that Aurelia permitted the girls to engage in madcap play, nor was their infant brother, Bertie, allowed untoward crying by his bevy of nurses. No. It was just that with children, there was always the possibility of an eruption of disagreeable noise.

It wasn't until they had descended to the third floor of their sumptuous Upper Brook Street mansion, and were halfway down the elegantly appointed corridor that Maria broke their silence. "I do believe that you are the"—*hiccup!*—"bravest person I know, Julia. Indeed, no one else has the courage to talk back to Aunt Aurelia in such a bold manner. How I wish that I—"*hiccup!*—"were so very brave"—*hiccup! hiccup!*—"perhaps then, she would not have dared to tear up the play I was writing."

Julia halted midstep, taken aback by her sister's report on their aunt's latest outrage. "She did what?"

"She tore up Maria's play," Jemima piped in, her childish

voice shrill with indignation. "And it was a very good play. I was to act the part of the pirate princess."

Maria nodded. "Aunt Aurelia said that plays are the worst sort of rubbish, and that in writing one I am no better than the lowest Grub Street hack. She also said that"—*hiccup!*—"engaging in amateur"—*hiccup!*—"theatricals promotes an unladylike boldness of action and a displeasing elevation of the voice." *Hiccup hiccup!* "As punishment for my vulgarity, she is making me translate a story about the downfall of an heiress with a fondness for the stage."

Of course she is, Julia thought angrily, hard-pressed to keep herself from marching back up to the schoolroom and taking Aurelia to task for her latest act of cruelty. Knowing better than to do so, aware that the vindictive woman would punish Maria should she learn that the girl had reported her spiteful action, she replied, "Aunt Aurelia is wrong. Amateur theatricals are a harmless enough pastime. Why, I cannot think of a single girl in the *ton* who has not written or performed in at least one." She nodded to reinforce her point. "However, since Aurelia is set against theatricals and will not suffer you writing your play in the nursery, you must write it during our time together. If you like, we can perform your finished work in the garden with Mr. Mullock and his assistants as an audience." Aurelia knew better than to intrude upon Julia's time with her sisters, so there would be little danger of the woman learning of their forbidden enterprise.

The light flew back into Maria's eyes. "Can we really do that?"

"We can, and we will," Julia promised, pressing a kiss to the top of the girl's head. Like golden-haired Jemima, Maria, with her unruly mane of copper curls and thickly lashed brown eyes, showed promise of growing into a great beauty. Now dropping their hands to hug their slight forms to her sides, she added, "By the by, I think that you are both exceedingly brave—every bit as brave as you think me to be. And I am beyond proud of you."

Maria drew back slightly to stare up her, frowning her incredulity. "Brave? Me?"

"Yes, you. You are both brave, because no matter how badly Aunt Aurelia treats you, you always have the courage to remain kind and loving to those around you. To love takes great courage, and the strength of your love is the true measure of your bravery."

"Is that why Aunt Aurelia hates me so, then? Because she is not brave?" Jemima inquired with a gravity that should have been beyond her tender years.

"No! Oh, no, darling," Julia exclaimed, wanting to weep at the hurt behind her sister's words. "Aurelia does not hate you. No one could ever hate someone as dear as you." She fell to her knees and grasped Jemima's shoulders, forcing her to meet her gaze so she could be certain that the child understood her words. "Aurelia is a sad, bitter woman whose heart was badly broken years ago. The break never quite mended, you see, so she finds it difficult to love anyone. The way she is, the way she acts, has nothing to do with you—either of you!" She released one of Jemima's shoulders to convulsively grasp Maria's hand. "No matter what she says or does, you must never think that you deserve her unkindness. You have done nothing to earn it. Nothing! And if she cannot see how very wonderful you both are, well, then, to hell with her!"

"Julia!" Jemima and Maria chorused in shock at their sister's use of profanity.

"I mean it," Julia said with a firm nod. "To the devil with Aunt Aurelia. She does not deserve the honor of loving you. Moreover, you do not need her love. You have plenty of other people who love you, worthy ones."

"We do?" Maria could not have looked more dubious, an expression mirrored by Jemima's face.

Another nod from Julia. "Of course you do. Mother and father love you enormously, as does Grandfather Kilminster." When her sisters continued to look doubtful, she added, "There is Mr. Mullock. Does he not always take time to show you the wonders of nature every time you venture into the garden?" At their nods, she nodded back. "And Cook, why, did you know that the only reason she bakes jumbles is because she knows how much you like them?" Jumbles were delicate, lemon-flavored biscuits that were cut in the shape of bowknots and sprinkled with sugar. "Oh, and how about Mary-Margaret, the nursery chambermaid? Does she not always have a story, or a jest, or a song to cheer your day when she sees you?"

"They do seem to be fond of us," Maria admitted slowly. By now, her hiccups had all but vanished.

"As does Mr. Brice," Jemima chimed in. Mr. Brice was the weathered old coachman who just happened to have a soft spot in his heart for children. "Remember the cunning sugar-paste birds he gave us after church on Sunday when Aunt Aurelia was not looking?"

"See?" Julia smiled and nodded yet again. "That proves my point exactly. You do not need Aunt Aurelia's love, not when everyone else in the house loves you so."

"I suppose not," Maria conceded, smiling back.

Jemima, too, smiled. "No."

"But of all the people who love you, can you guess who loves you most of all?" Julia playfully quizzed.

Her sisters exchanged a grin, easily catching the spirit of the game. "Who?" they demanded to know, though, of course, they already knew.

"Why me, of course, sillies!" With that, she lunged forward and grabbed them both in a fierce hug.

"And that is best of all," Maria declared, hugging Julia back. When Jemima followed suit, practically hurling herself at Julia in her eagerness to join in on the fun, Julia collapsed back under their weight, laughing beneath their hugging assault. As they wrestled about on the thick Savonnerie carpet runner, their laughter ringing around them like the joyous tidings of a Christmas bell, Julia rolled against something hard, something that felt suspiciously like a pair of feet. Large ones.

"Ahem!" The owner of the feet cleared his throat.

Praying that it wasn't their father, Julia poked her head around Jemima's shoulder to match the face with the feet. It was Cuthbert, the majordomo. She smiled her relief. Beneath his patina of venerable crustiness, Cuthbert harbored the heart of a prankster. He was displaying that penchant now as he grinned at her and her sisters, visibly amused by their boisterous antics.

"Cuthbert," she acknowledged with as much dignity as she could muster in her admittedly undignified position.

"My ladies." Always the epitome of courtesy, he bowed as formally as if she and her sisters were princesses seated on their thrones. "Your father bade me to convey his desire to speak with you, Lady Julia. He awaits you in the library."

"Excellent. I wish to speak with him as well," she replied, grimacing as she extracted a tendril of her hair that had somehow become trapped in her mouth. "I was on my way downstairs to find him when I was waylaid by this pair of monkeys." She nodded at her sisters, who lay collapsed atop her, giggling with the giddy silliness of youth. Grinning at the rare sight of their glee, she added, "Could I, perhaps, prevail upon your kindness by begging your assistance in removing them?"

He grinned back, his age-mottled skin crumpling into a multitude of cross-hatching creases. "But of course, my lady. Monkey removal just happens to be a particular specialty of mine." Holding out a hand to each of the younger girls, he said, "If you please, monkeys?" When they took his proffered hands, their giggling renewed by his tomfoolery, he hauled them to their feet, saying, "Up we go, then."

Now free, Julia sat up, mortified to discover that the skirt of her yellow-and-blue print day dress had somehow become twisted and was now rucked up well past her knees. Her cheeks burning, she tugged it back down again, stealing an anxious glance at Cuthbert to see if he had witnessed her shocking display. To her relief he wasn't looking at her, but at Jemima, who was animatedly describing a monkey she had seen in Hyde Park dressed up like Napoleon Bonaparte. Thus assured of her modesty, she turned her attention to her hair, one side of which had come loose and now dangled across her cheek.

As she felt for the pins that should have been anchoring it, Cuthbert turned back to her and offered her his hand. "If you will permit me, my lady?" Gratefully, she accepted his aid in rising. When she was on her feet, he indicated her hair. "If I might be so bold?" At her nod, he extracted several U-shaped hairpins that had come loose, and handed them to her.

"Oh, dear. I must look a fright," she murmured, again feeling her hair, this time to assess the damage to her coiffure.

"You could never look a fright, my lady," Cuthbert gallantly responded, "though you might do with a bit of tidying before going to your father. Perhaps you will allow me the privilege of attending to the monkeys while you see to the matter?"

Julia smiled and nodded, perfectly at ease with the notion of placing her sisters in the warmhearted man's care. "If you please, Cuthbert, my sisters wish to go to the garden. Mr. Mullock has promised to show them a nest of newly-hatched goldfinches."

Cuthbert nodded back, then directed his attention to her sisters. "Ah, yes. I know the very nest. However, before going to the garden, might I suggest that we visit the kitchen and request a crust of bread for the mother? No doubt she can use some refreshment, as could you ladies after your romp. If my nose does not deceive me, I smelled the aroma of baking wigs when I passed the kitchen not more than a half hour ago." Wigs, flat, yeasty buns flavored with nutmeg, ginger, and cloves, ranked among her sisters' favorite treats. Thus, it took no further enticement to persuade them to accompany him.

As they walked away, chattering childish nonsense to the indulgent majordomo, Julia called out, "Maria? Jemima?"

When they looked back, she pointed to the Cuthbert's back and mouthed, "He loves you, too."

They grinned, a sight that kindled her heart, then resumed their trek to the kitchen.

Julia rushed to her chamber to tidy herself. A quarter of an hour later she was knocking at her father's library door, armed with complaints against Aurelia and arguments against the use of backboards. Though she did not really expect him to heed the former, her numerous complaints against her aunt having thus far fallen on deaf ears, she fervently prayed that he would at least listen to her case against the latter.

"Yes?" his voice called out in response to her knock.

"It is I, Julia. Cuthbert said that you wish to see me."

Several moments later the door swung open, opened by—*her father?* Julia frowned, taken aback that her imperious father would stoop to extend such a humble courtesy, especially to her. After all, he seldom troubled himself with anyone else's comfort or feelings, unless, of course, he had something to gain in doing so. Highly irregular! More irregular yet, he was smiling that false, fawning smile he employed when wooing the *ton.* Now looping his arm around her waist in an unprecedented gesture of fatherly affection, he drew her into the library, booming, "Come in! Come in, my dear. I must say that you look exceptionally lovely today, a veritable picture of youthful radiance. The sight of you has quite brightened my day."

His flattering speech instantly put Julia on her guard. She, who he regularly referred to as a thorn in his flesh, brightening his day? Again, it was beyond irregular. Her frown deepening, she murmured, "Is something amiss, Father?" It had to be for him to be behaving so queerly.

"Amiss?" He chuckled as if she had just authored a particularly droll witticism. "Of course not. Whatever makes you ask such a thing?"

"It is just that you seem so . . . so"—she shook her head, trying to think of an appropriate word to describe her impression of his conduct. When she could think of none, at least none that would not bring him offense, she settled for— "happy. You seem inordinately happy this afternoon."

"And why should I not be happy, pray tell?" he inquired, practically beaming at her as he led her across the impressive green and ivory library. Decorated in the grand rococo style, three of the four walls were covered by mahogany bookcases that ranged from the polished oak floor to the magnificent plasterwork ceiling, their every shelf filled with leather-bound books, marble busts, and other tastefully decorative gewgaws. The fourth wall boasted a splendid marble fireplace and chimneypiece, flanked on both sides by several floor-length Venetian windows that overlooked the terraced formal garden.

Again at a loss for a response, Julia weakly replied, "I

merely meant that it is rather early in the day for you to be so cheerful." Truth be told, it was early for him to be up and about, much less in good humor. Indeed, her parents seldom rose before noon and almost never emerged from their respective chambers before three, having usually not returned home from their social rounds before dawn.

"Ah. But this is a special day. One that shall no doubt hold a place of honor in your memory forever." He stopped before one of the pair of tapestry-upholstered sofas that overlooked the garden. "Do sit, my dear, while I impart my good news."

Her wariness now metamorphosing into suspicion, the dreadful, sinking kind one felt when they sensed that they were not going to like what they were about to hear, Julia did as directed. When she was seated and her father had settled himself by her side, she prompted, "Well?"

He contorted his lips in what was no doubt intended to be a grin, displaying both rows of his slightly yellowed teeth. "Congratulations, my dear. You are to be wed."

Her heart dropped to the pit of her stomach with a sickening thud. "W-what?"

His smile seemed to waver; then it broadened and he repeated, "You are to be married. Is it not wonderful news?"

Julia merely stared at him for several beats, too stunned to do anything more. Then she somehow managed to gasp, "No—no! It cannot be true."

"I assure you that it is. You will be wed before the end of the Season."

"But how—what—I mean, why—" She broke off, gesturing helplessly as she fought to master the panic tangling her thoughts.

He chuckled, a light sound edged with darkness. "Should you not be asking 'who'?"

Who? The word took a moment to penetrate her frantically scrambling mind. When finally it did, it triggered an alarming image. Lord Wolton! It could be no one else. Unable to speak for the horror of the thought, she shook her head over and over again, her gaze mutely imploring him to tell her that it was not so.

"It is Gideon Harwood."

Julia felt her jaw drop, even more surprised by the name of the groom than by the news of her impending marriage. Gideon Harwood? Of all the men in London—

"Why?" she blurted out.

Her father frowned, his patience growing visibly thin. "Why what? Why did he offer? Or why did I accept him?"

"Why on both counts," she replied, grasping to make sense of what she was hearing.

He shrugged. "He offered because he wishes you for a wife. Why else? That a man should desire to wed you should come as no great surprise, not after the number of offers you have received."

"The men who made those other offers did so after courting me for a respectable period of time to make certain that we suited. Mr. Harwood met me for the first time last night," she pointed out. In instances like this, their encounter at the bookstore most definitely did not count as a meeting. "Considering the briefness of our acquaintance, he cannot claim to know me, not even the slightest bit. Why would any man wish to marry a woman he does not know?"

Another shrug from her father. "You should know the answer to that question readily enough. You look in the mirror every morning, do you not?"

Julia emitted an unladylike snort of disbelief. "Mr. Harwood hardly seems the sort of man to wed a woman solely for her looks. By the same token, I am not the kind of woman to marry a man who would select a bride based on such cabbage-headed reasoning."

Her father's mouth took on an ugly twist. "Willing or no, you shall wed him, Julia. Make no mistake about it."

Oh, they would see about that! Now changing her tactics, hoping to strike at her vain father's inflated sense of social conceit, she inquired, "Of all the men who have sought me for a bride, why are you forcing me to wed Gideon Harwood? Not only is he a commoner, but both his past and his character have been repeatedly called into question by the *ton*. In view of that fact, whatever will your noble circle say when they hear that you have matched me to such a person?"

"They shall not say a word. They shan't dare," he ground out from between his teeth. "Do not underestimate my influence in the *ton,* daughter, or my ability to make any match I choose acceptable to them."

"But why would you do such a thing?" she countered, unable to imagine why her father would go to such lengths on behalf of a mere commoner. It was not as if he had anything to gain from the match. She shook her head in bewilderment. "Judging from your discourse with Mr. Harwood last night, you cannot expect me to believe that you harbor a fondness for him. Indeed, had anyone asked me last night what you thought of him, I would have said with certainty that you despised him."

"Then you would have been wrong." He more spat than uttered the words. "Damn it, Julia! Why must you always be so blasted stubborn on the subject of marriage?"

"You know why," she flung back. "I have told you over and over again."

He grunted. "Your childish prejudice against Aurelia hardly qualifies as a credible reason."

Childish prejudice! Why—"Perhaps if you spared Maria and Jemima more than a passing glance, you would see how very wretched they are," she exclaimed. "The poor darlings are terrified of Aurelia, and she wickedly preys upon their fears."

"They are girls, and girls are unhappy creatures by nature," her father parried harshly. "That point aside, it is right that they fear Aurelia. How else is she to make them obey her?"

"Through love and kindness," Julia thrust back. "True obedience comes from a desire to please. Jemima and Maria obey Aurelia only to spare themselves the pain of her displeasure."

Her father shrugged, contemptuously dismissing her argument. "What do the methods matter as long as the results are satisfactory? And I am exceedingly satisfied with their progress." When she opened her mouth to argue, he cut her off with a chopping hand motion. "Aurelia will remain in charge of the girls, and that is my final word on the matter."

"Then I shall not marry Gideon Harwood, and that is *my* final word on *that* matter," she hurled back.

"You shall, damn it!"

"I shall not. You can drag me to the altar, but you cannot force me to speak the words!"

For several long moments they engaged in silent battle, Julia sitting stiff and bristling as she defiantly returned her father's cold, furious gaze. When, at last, her father spoke, his voice was taut and urgent. "If you truly love your sisters as much as you claim, you will do as I say."

Julia frowned, caught off guard by his change in strategy. "No. If I truly love them, I will stay at home where I can shield them from Aurelia's spite."

"You will not have a home to stay in if you do not wed Gideon Harwood. None of us will."

Again, he caught her off guard. "Pardon?"

"I am sorry, Julia. I had hoped to spare you the true reason for this marriage. Unfortunately, you have left me with no choice but to tell you." He sighed and shook his head, his expression regretful. "The truth is that you must wed Mr. Harwood in order to pay your mother's gambling debt to him."

"Mother gambles?" Julia choked out. It was the first she had heard of her mother's vice, and vice seldom passed the sharp-eyed notice of the *ton* without provoking scandalized comment.

Her father nodded. "Your mother has an inordinate fondness for the card table. However, until now her debts have been manageable enough, so I saw no reason to worry myself over the matter. Then again, she has never before gambled with Gideon Harwood. Though I shall never be able to prove it, my guess is that he cheats. The bastard is simply too damn lucky not to be guilty of hocus-pocus. Unfortunately, he is also cunning and—"

Julia waved her hand to halt his rant. "Are you saying that mother offered marriage to me as a wager?"

"No, of course not. Your mother would never do anything so very vulgar."

Had Julia not been so overwhelmed by everything else her father was saying, she would have been wounded by his claim that her mother had refrained from the wager not out of love for her, but out of a desire to avoid vulgarity. Now wanting nothing but to make sense of what she was hearing, she shook her head and said, "I do not understand any of this."

"To put it bluntly, your mother lost a great deal of money to Mr. Harwood. Everything we own, and more, to be exact."

Julia gasped her dismay. "Oh, no!"

He nodded, his expression grim. "Oh, yes. When I called on Harwood this morning, begging on your mother's behalf that he forgive the debt, he handed me a most shocking proposition: He said that he will pardon the debt if you consent to be his wife. If you refuse, he will call in the debt. If he does, everything we own will be auctioned, and within a fortnight we will be living in the streets. My guess is that he planned all this, that the idea planted itself in his mind when he met you at Vauxhall."

"But how? When?" Julia shook her head. "I mean, how was it that Mr. Harwood had the opportunity to wager with mother? He does not belong to the *ton,* and I cannot imagine mother gambling outside her circle."

"It happened at the Bittlestons' rout last night, after our visit to the Garden. If you will recall, you begged off attending by pleading a headache."

Julia nodded. It was true. After several hours in Lord Wolton's company, she had not had to pretend to have a headache.

Her father nodded back. "From what I can ascertain, Harwood persuaded Shepley to allow him to attend the affair with him. Once there, it was simple enough for the scoundrel to lure your mother into playing with him. Within two hours of doing so, he had achieved his vile purpose."

"But why is he so very set on having me?" Julia asked. It was too impossible to believe. "By all accounts, Mr. Harwood is wealthy enough to buy a dozen brides, should he desire to do so. To be sure, there are peers who would gladly exchange their daughters for the fortune he would bring their families."

"True, but he could never buy a bride like you, not one who can gain him certain entrée into the *ton.*"

Julia gasped her comprehension.

Her father inclined his head, confirming her conclusion. "Make no mistake, Julia, Harwood is a man with high aspirations, and he is ruthless enough to sacrifice anyone or anything that gets in the way of his ambitions. Thus, I have no choice but to allow him to wed you. Surely you see that it is the only way out of this tangle?"

Unfortunately she did see, just as she saw that the marriage was the only way to save her sisters and brother from being forced to live in the streets. Oh, blast the detestable Mr. Harwood! How dare he use her in such a manner? And blast her mother. Her mother was a woman grown and should have known better than to gamble so deeply. As for her father, well, double blast him. He should have done more to rein in her mother's gambling and thus he shared her guilt. Her siblings, on the other hand—

Julia's insides knotted into a sickening coil as she pictured her sweet sisters and their cherubic brother dressed in rags and shivering in the cruel London streets. Poor darlings. They were utterly blameless in all this and should not be made to suffer for their parents' weakness. Damn it! They would not suffer. She would not allow them to do so.

Feeling as if someone had just pulled the world out from under her, Julia sighed her surrender. "I must marry him, I suppose. And that is that."

Her father had the good grace to look ashamed. "Er—I am afraid that that is not exactly that. There is a bit more to the matter."

"More?" Julia echoed faintly.

"The bastard put several conditions on the bargain."

Though she hated to ask, Julia knew that she had no choice but to do so. "What conditions?"

"One is that you must pretend to fall in love with him.

He wishes the world to believe that your marriage is a love match."

"Impossible!" Julia spat. And it was. How could she possibly pretend to love someone she so thoroughly loathed?

Her father scowled at her response. "Unless you wish to see your siblings living in the streets, you will do your best."

Of course he was right. Now feeling the beginnings of a headache lurking in her temples, she murmured, "I will try."

He nodded, visibly satisfied by her obeisance. "He also wishes you to take his household in hand after you are wed."

"Fine." It was a simple enough request.

"The third and last condition is that you must never reveal any of this to anyone. That includes your mother." When she opened her mouth to ask why, he silenced her with a wave of his hand. "Harwood does not want your mother to know of his blackmail, so as to be free to court her patronage in the *ton*. No doubt she will give it readily enough if she believes that he graciously forgave her debt. She is also likely to view your marriage to him with favor out of a sense of gratitude. In short, you must never let her so much as suspect that you know about her debt."

"Yes, yes," Julia miserably agreed.

"Good." Her father smiled and nodded. "Mr. Harwood will call on you tomorrow afternoon to outline his plans to court you. No doubt he will also have ideas on how you should conduct yourself in order to convince the *ton* of your mutual infatuation. I expect you to be at your most charming."

"Of course." What did it really matter what she agreed to at this point? Her life was over.

CHAPTER 6

There were some fashion foibles that certain women should shun. The rage for wearing white was one that Lady Julia Barham should avoid at all costs, Gideon decided, pasting a cordial smile on his lips as he bowed to the object of his less-than-favorable observation. Indeed with her pale ivory complexion and regrettable reddish gold hair, he could not imagine any color that could be less flattering. As he straightened back up from his bow, his gaze again filling with the sorry sight of her, he could not help wondering at her unfortunate choice of attire.

Hmmm. Could it be that she was cursed with poor eyesight? That would certainly explain her failure to see how her virginal white gown with its missish puffed sleeves and prim, lace-trimmed ruff made her look like a whey-faced dowd. It was also possible, he supposed, that she actually liked the hideous frock and believed that it complemented her insipid looks. After all, one could not always account for the tastes of others.

Her ladyship inclined her head in regal acknowledgment of his bow. "Mr. Harwood," she uttered in a clipped, precise voice.

Gideon tightened his smile to keep it from faltering. Good God. What ever had possessed him to make him think that he could marry this bloodless paragon of overbred maidenhood? Not only was she utterly lacking in

looks—not that looks were his first priority when judging
a woman's merits, mind you—but there was absolutely
nothing in her manner to suggest that she might at least be
good company. To be sure, judging from her icy demeanor
and the disdainful pursing of her pale lips, he doubted if
she were the least bit familiar with genial words like tolerance, humor, and amiability.

For several moments he seriously reconsidered his bargain with Lord Stanwell, wondering if, perhaps, he had
been a jot hasty in agreeing to this match. Then he reminded himself of his reasons for doing so, the privileges
that the union would bring to his family and the incalcula-
ble debt he owed them, and he grimly resigned himself to
his wretched fate. Perhaps matters might not be so dismal
if—

"Mr. Harwood?" The words sliced through his thoughts,
ringing with rebuke.

Gideon heaved an inward sigh and reluctantly forced
himself to refocus on the woman before him. By the frown
creasing her brow, it was clear that she had said something
that required a response from him. Unable to imagine what
that response should be, yet wishing to set a tone of civility
for their interview, he urged his fixed smile a fraction
broader and improvised. "A thousand pardons, my lady. I
fear that I was momentarily diverted by"—he glanced over
her shoulder in search of an appropriate object to which
he could ascribe his lapse in attentiveness—"your celestial
globe," he smoothly inserted, choosing the first likely object
to fall beneath his gaze. "It is a particularly fine example,
the finest I have seen in London."

"It is French," she replied shortly. "My great-grandfather
purchased it in Paris half a century ago. I believe that it
dates from the seventeenth century."

"Indeed," he murmured for a lack of anything more con-
versational to say.

She nodded, a gesture so stiff that he wondered if she
had slept wrong the night before and thus had a sore neck.
"Mr. Harwood, do excuse me if what I am about to say
seems overly abrupt or rude, but we both know the reason

for this meeting and it has nothing whatsoever to do with globes or other such chitchat. If you do not mind, I would prefer to address the matter at hand, and be done with it.''

Gideon narrowed his eyes, taken aback by her candor. He had expected her to play games, to dance around their business and cloak the issues in a veneer of inane banter. But it appeared that he had been wrong, that there might actually be pluck and a measure of intellect beneath the haughty Lady Julia's milk-and-water appearance. His interest piqued, he replied, "As you wish."

"Excellent. Shall we sit?" She stepped back, gesturing to one of the spacious room's seating groups, consisting of a facing pair of sofas. With their formal serpentine backs and sparsely padded celadon-and-white damask upholstery, the dainty gilded-wood sofas could not have looked more exquisite or torturously uncomfortable. Then again the Gold and White Drawing Room, as the majordomo had referred to the aptly named space, appeared to have been decorated more to dazzle the beholder than to provide comfort for its occupants.

Everything in the coldly elegant chamber was calculated in its perfection, from the pristine white walls and coved ceiling, both of which were lavishly decorated with gilded plasterwork, to the five ornately wrought gold chandeliers and matching wall sconces, all laden with expensive white beeswax candles. As one would expect from a family of such an ancient and noble lineage, the walls were hung with an assortment of dynastic portraits that, judging from the subjects' clothing, dated everywhere from Henry VIII down to the current period.

When they reached the sofas, Lady Julia signaled that he was to occupy the one on her right, politely if coolly inquiring, "May I offer you refreshment, Mr. Harwood?"

"No. Thank you." Truth be known, he had no intention of staying any longer than was absolutely necessary. He had decided as much on his ride here today, determining that he would outline what was to be done in the simplest and most businesslike of terms, and then take his leave. No fuss. No muss. Since, by her own admission, Lady Julia was eager to do the same, he saw no need to waste precious time on trifling niceties. Thus he waited until she had seated herself on the opposite sofa, then sat himself, commencing without preamble, "Shall we proceed, then?"

"Yes. Of course." Another of her stiff-necked little nods. "We do have a great deal to discuss. However, before we begin, I feel as if I must explain our lack of chaperonage. No doubt you are wondering at the absence of an abigail?"

Gideon nodded, though truth be told, he had been wondering nothing of the sort. Then again, there was nothing about her ladyship's person that he found the least bit enticing, so he was in no danger of being overwhelmed by the sort of ruttishness that would require dampening glares from a dried-up matron.

At his nod, she replied, "Considering the shocking nature of our business, my father decided that our discussion would best be conducted in private. To be sure, were the unsavory details of this matter to become known, our family would, quite naturally, be ruined. But then, you already know that or you would not be here."

Shocking business? Unsavory details? Ruined? Gideon shot her a quick glance, caught off guard by her words. One would think by her speech that her father had confessed the nature of his sins to her. Curious to find out if what he suspected was indeed true, he said, "Perhaps you should tell me exactly what your father told you, so that I will know where to begin our interview."

She flushed at his words, giving proof that there was blood rather than ice water flowing through her veins, her amber eyes darting away from his steady gaze to stare at a place somewhere in the proximity of her feet. Her voice quavering with barely contained—what?—anger? chagrin? indignation?—she declared, "If you possess so much as a fiber of human compassion, sir, you will not humiliate me by forcing me to speak of my parent's shameful weakness. I can assure you that no one could have been more appalled or dismayed than I when I learned of it. This entire matter is unspeakably monstrous. A disgrace." She looked up then, and he saw the emotion in her face that he had been unable to read in her voice. It was resentment, pure and simple.

That it was directed entirely at him came as no great surprise. Why, he could only imagine what a blow it must be to her aristocratic pride to be forced to wed a lowly commoner—a far worse one, no doubt, than learning of her father's bigamy. And he was now quite certain that the craven Lord Stanwell had indeed confessed his crime to his daughter. What else was he to make of her bitter little dialogue? Yes, and now that he had considered the matter more thoroughly, he would probably be safe in attributing a measure of her antipathy toward him to the fact that he had dared to challenge the code of justice popularly held by nobles: that their crimes should go unmarked and un-punished simply because they were of the peerage and thus above the law. That a mere commoner would have the unmitigated gall to confront her high-and-mighty father with his wrongdoing must rankle her to no end.

Rankled himself by the thought of such conceit, he more snapped than said, "Since you appear to understand where matters stand in that regard, we will proceed to planning our courtship. Me being from an inferior station"—a little salt for the wound to her arrogance—"I am, of course, un-familiar with the courtship rituals favored by the *ton*. Per-haps you would care to enlighten me?" Not that he required any such instruction from her, having engaged a particularly experienced valet who could direct him in such matters, should he find himself in need of help. No. It was just that he wished to rub the salt in by forcing her to actually think about what lay ahead of her.

She shrugged, a gesture as imperious as it was dismissive. "The conventional course of courtship begins with a formal introduction. I should think that even you would know that."

"Ah. But this is hardly what could be termed as a con-ventional courtship, Lady Julia, is it?" he countered, rub-bing the salt yet deeper.

To her credit, she merely nodded, her expression void of the turmoil that had to be roiling beneath her coldly proud facade. "While that is true, Mr. Harwood, we must proceed as if it were conventional, at least we must if you wish it to be believable to the *ton*. And gaining acceptance into the *ton* is your sole reason for entering into this marriage, is it not?" The scorn in her voice was unmistakable.

"Perhaps not the sole reason, but certainly one of the more compelling ones," he unabashedly admitted. At least she hadn't deluded herself into thinking that he desired her person.

"Well then, in that instance it would be advisable to follow the tenets of courtship put forth by the *ton*. And the first on the list demands a formal introduction. It is usual for the gentleman to ask a credible third party to introduce him to the girl who has struck his fancy."

"That hardly seems necessary since we have already been introduced."

"Yes, but not publicly. As I understand matters, you wish our marriage to appear to be a love match. Correct?" She peered down her nose long enough to grace him with a querying look.

He nodded.

"Then you must appear to be smitten by the sight of me and beg for an introduction. And it must be done in the presence of the entire *ton*, though"—she sniffed, a singularly contemptuous and unpleasant sound—"exactly how you shall manage such a feat, I do not know. As you, yourself, pointed out, you are of a significantly lower station, so you are unlikely to be invited to any affair that will allow you to do so."

Not just a lower station, but a *significantly* lower station. It seemed that Lady Julia wasn't above tossing a little salt herself. Unfortunately for her, he was not wounded by her reference to his inferior social standing, so her salt did not render the desired sting. Grinning now, to illustrate that failure, he drawled, "Do not worry your head on my account, my dear. Lord Shepley has taken care of that detail."

She blinked and frowned, drawing back slightly, as if in incredulous disbelief. "He has?"

"Yes. He has invited me to the ball he is holding in honor of his daughter two nights hence."

"Oh? And exactly what sort of blackmail did you use to obtain the invitation?" The instant the words left her mouth, she bit her lip, flushing a rather interesting shade of beet red as she rushed to explain. "Er—it is just that Lord Shepley generally invites only members of the *haute ton* to his affairs, especially those honoring Amy. Do forgive me. I did not mean to suggest that you would actually blackmail him into an invitation."

Like hell she didn't. Then again, could he really blame her for jumping to such a conclusion after the bargain he had struck with her father? Unable to fault her on that score, he nodded his acceptance of her apology. "I can assure you that I came by the invitation honestly. If you must know, it was the size of my deposit in his lordship's bank that prompted it. Apparently my wealth has done much to elevate my station in his eyes." He paused to chuckle. "That, and the fact that his daughter begged him to invite me. Lady Amy seems to be of the opinion that my presence will add luster to the occasion."

Another of her disdainful sniffs. "I am sure that she does."

"Meaning?" He regarded her with raised eyebrows.

The challenging question hung in the air between them for several seconds; then she seized it and flung back, "I simply meant that Lady Amy is prone to silly schoolgirl crushes. Never fear, though. They seldom last past a fortnight. Amy is rather fickle in her affections, but"—she frowned and shook her head—"Amy and her affections are neither here nor there, are they?"

"No. So do let us return to the business at hand."

She nodded, her frown deepening. "Then I suppose it is settled. We will be formally introduced at Lord Shepley's ball on Thursday evening. We should most probably discuss how to go about it so as to ensure that matters proceed smoothly."

He shrugged. "No need. Your father has already devised a plan."

"What?" If the furrows in her forehead got any deeper, they would crease her skull. "Whatever do you mean?"

"Exactly what I said. Your father has already devised a plan for our introduction. I am surprised that he did not outline it to you."

She stared at him for several moments, her eyes slowly

narrowing. Her mouth thinning with displeasure, she demanded, "Exactly what is your game, Mr. Harwood? I thought you said that you did not know how to go about our courtship."

He shrugged again, deliberately ignoring her pique. "No game. I did and I do not."

She out-and-out snorted at his response. "You must have at least an inkling to have so cozily arranged matters with my father."

"We have arranged an introduction, nothing more. Your father said that I was to consult you for further details." That much was true. Like Lady Julia, Lord Stanwell seemed to think that anyone below the station of viscount was utterly lacking in breeding.

"In that instance, you should have had the courtesy to tell me of my father's plan, so as to save me from wasting time on matters that have already been arranged."

"I just did."

"You should have mentioned it when I first broached the subject of an introduction." The accusation was punctuated by a singularly scornful sniff.

Yet another shrug. "Do forgive me. I was operating under the false assumption that you knew of the plan." Of course he had been doing no such thing. He had allowed her to ramble on simply because he wished to see what she would say.

By her expression, it was apparent that she did not believe his explanation. Nonetheless, she accepted it, saying, "In the future, please do be kind enough not to make any more such assumptions."

"Fine."

"Well then?"

"Well then, what?" he inquired obtusely, though he knew perfectly well what she was asking. It was just that he did not care for the dictatorial manner in which she was asking it.

"Well then, do tell me of my father's plan for our introduction." By her tone, it was an order, not a request.

Gideon graced her with an abbreviated bow. "But of course. Your wish is my command, dear lady."

His insolence earned him a withering look.

Questioning anew the wisdom of the bargain he had made, Gideon explained, "I am to await your father's signal, which he will give when he is in what he deems as appropriate company to serve as witnesses, and then approach him begging for an introduction. He will, naturally, agree, saying that you had spied me with Lord Shepley at Vauxhall and have been unable to speak of anything else since. In short, he shall instigate the rumor that you were smitten with me at first sight."

"If you are a gentleman, you will pretend to be equally enamored with me. A gentleman would say that he has been languishing with love for me and fears that he shall perish if he does not make my acquaintance," she pointed out with yet another of her sniffs.

"If one must engage in pretentious banter in order to earn the title of gentleman, then I fear that I must refrain from trying."

"A thousand pardons, Mr. Harwood. I should have guessed that such a feat would be beyond your capabilities."

"Apology accepted, my lady. You may consider yourself pardoned," he returned, refusing to be pricked by her barb.

Still another sniff. "You are too kind, sir."

He pulled his handkerchief from his pocket. "Not at all." Then he extended the neatly folded square of blue silk. "Here."

She viewed his offering with visible confusion. "Excuse me?"

"It is obvious from your repeated sniffing that your nose requires blowing."

The nose in question promptly rose several inches into the air. "I can assure you that my nose is quite clear, Mr. Harwood. I also feel obligated to point out that a gentleman would never be so vulgar as to notice such a condition in a lady."

"But we have already established that being a gentleman is beyond my capabilities, have we not?" he reminded her, returning the rejected handkerchief to its resting place.

"Yes. And your actions just now have served simply to confirm my opinion."

Gideon chuckled, which judging by her face was not the response she desired. "I am glad to hear that we have managed to settle at least that much."

"Yes, and I wish to settle the remainder of our business before the day grows much older," she retorted waspishly.

"Ah, yes. Our business. Now where were we?" He knew exactly where they had left off, but he was having far too much fun baiting her to stop now.

"Our introduction at Lord Shepley's ball." Her exasperation was unmistakable.

He made a show of thinking, then nodded. "Yes. Now I remember. After we are introduced, we are to dance, during which we must look appropriately bewitched by each other. That done, I shall return to your father and his friends and ask permission to court you."

"I see that you do not intend to waste any time," she observed dryly.

He shrugged. "What is the point in doing so, when the outcome will be the same?"

"Nonetheless, I do hope that you intend to allow a decent period of courtship before having our engagement announced."

"A month, no longer. We will be married two weeks later."

"What!" She blanched a shade whiter, if such a thing was possible, and a hunted look crept into her eyes. It was the first honest emotion she had displayed since beginning their interview.

Gideon nodded, pleased to have fractured her shell of aristocratic ice. "I have several rather pressing family matters to attend to in Lancashire, so I cannot spare any more time than that. That means that you must work especially hard on your performance. If you chatter constantly about me to your friends and acquaintances, they should be convinced enough of your infatuation that the announcement of our marriage shan't come as any great surprise to them."

"B-but six weeks?" She shook her head over and over

again. "Impossible! Why, it will be whispered that you compromised me and that we have to be wed lest there be a seven-month baby."

"Compromise? Hmmm. Now there is an intriguing notion." He made a show of furrowing his brow, pretending to be seriously considering the idea as an option. Keeping his voice to a murmur, as if musing out loud, he said, "Let me see now. If I were to compromise you Thursday night, we could be wed in, oh, a fortnight at the most. Then we could dispense with this nonsense." He nodded, as if warming to the idea. "Yes. And if we exert an effort to make your seduction appear exceedingly passionate in nature, why no one will think to question our love."

She could not have looked more appalled. "Surely you jest?"

For several moments he was tempted to say no, to take her down yet another peg. Then his innate sense of gallantry overrode his annoyance at her arrogance, and he nodded. "Yes, though I must admit that the idea does have its merits."

She made a derisive noise, one that made him instantly regret his clemency. "It most certainly does not have merit. I, for one, would never participate in such a display. No respectable woman would willingly allow herself to become the object of scandal."

"Yes. And anyone can see that you are, above all else, a paragon of respectability." He flung the words like the insult they were meant to be. Hot color flooded her cheeks, and her spine straightened with a brutality that made him wonder that it did not snap. Once, twice, thrice she opened her mouth, as if trying to expel her indignation. Before she could open it a fourth time and perhaps succeed in her vexed purpose, he said, "Since we do not wish your reputation to be tainted by the slightest breath of scandal, I shall charge you, who are such a flower of propriety, with the duty of deciding how we will progress from our introduction."

Though she looked as if she would rather tell him to go to the devil, and in truth he expected her to do so, she surprised him by evenly replying, "You must call on me the morning after the ball. If you wish to appear especially mitten, you will bring me a nosegay. After you have called several times, you must include a sweet, such as a basket of strawberries or a beribboned box of bonbons. Later on you may bring me a fan or a book of poetry." She smiled with an infuriating air of superiority. "In spite of what you might think, Mr. Harwood, I have a bevy of suitors and they are likely to be present when you call. If they are to judge your intentions toward me as true and honorable, you must impress them with your romantic fervor. Please believe me when I say that their report to the *ton* will have much to do with whether or not you gain your desired acceptance into their ranks."

Gideon snorted at the notion of her suitors. "If your admirers are all as witless as that popinjay Lord Wolton, they should be simple enough to convince."

"If you say so, Mr. Harwood," she returned in a patronizing voice.

"I do," he snapped, nearing the end of his patience. "What else is to be done?"

"We must be seen in public together as often as possible. I assume that you are not cow-handed with the reins?"

"I can handle a gig, if that is what you mean."

"Fine. Then you may take me driving in Hyde Park at the fashionable hour. May I assume that you know when that is?" By the smugness of her expression, it was clear that she assumed no such thing.

"Of course I do," he lied, not about to give her the satisfaction of admitting his ignorance. No doubt his valet, Gilchrist, could enlighten him as to the specifics. "What else?"

She thought for a moment and then replied, "You may squire me to the theater, but only in the company of my parents. They have boxes at King's Theater and Covent Garden. Considering the circumstances, I am sure that my father will be amendable to including you in our party whenever we attend. You would also do well to ask my father to include you in some of his more manly pastimes. After all, it is important to appearances that my parents seem to accept you. If they welcome you, there is a good chance that other *ton* members will follow suit."

Though the last thing in the world he wished to do was spend time with her father, Gideon saw that there was no help for it, so he nodded. "Fine. Is there anything else?"

"Well"—her gaze darted to her feet—"In order for our charade to be truly successful we must, er—" She bit her lip, her cheeks again staining a beet red.

"Must what?" he prompted impatiently, growing bored with the tedious subject.

"We must . . . mmm . . . act like lovers."

So much for boredom. "Oh?"

She nodded, her gaze still glued to her feet.

"And how do you propose we do that?" He really wanted to know.

She made a helpless little hand gesture. "We must do things like—like sit together and whisper, as if sharing endearments. And you must compliment me at every turn. It would also help if you clung to my every word, as if fascinated. And—and well"—she shot him a rather desperate look—"you take my meaning, do you not?"

He pretended to think on what she had just told him, ticking off, "Let me see, now. Whispered endearments. Compliments. Clinging to every word." He paused to frown. "Are lingering glances across the room in order?"

"I suppose so. Yes."

"And holding hands?"

"Um . . . after an appropriate interval of time, yes."

"Which is?"

"Considering the shortness of our engagement, I suppose that it will be permissible to do so"—she shook her head and looked up at him—"oh, I guess it will have to be the week before we announce our engagement."

Again he pretended to contemplate the matter, and then inquired, "How about kissing?" He simply could not resist asking.

Her gaze flew back to her feet. "Kissing?" she squeaked.

"Yes. It is when two people, usually ones who bear a measure of affection for each other, express their feelings by caressing one another with their lips."

"I know what a kiss is," she snapped, casting him a venomous look.

"Seeing as how you are so very respectable, I could not be sure."

If looks could kill . . . "You may kiss me when our engagement is announced. However, I would appreciate it if you would refrain from doing so again until the moment you must kiss me in order to seal our marriage vows."

He would most definitely have no problem honoring that request. "Fine. Is there anything else I should know?"

She seemed to consider, then sighed and shook her head. "I am sure there is more, but at the moment I cannot imagine what it is. As you can probably understand, this is all rather trying for me, and I am not properly able to think."

"I can assure you that I do indeed understand." And he did. After all, this was hardly a carnival of chuckles for him either.

For several moments thereafter they remained silent, each lost in their own thoughts. Gideon was about to take his leave, having concluded that their interview had come to an end, when Lady Julia murmured, "Is there anything you wish to add to all of this, Mr. Harwood?"

Was there? There was. Well, at least something he felt obligated to say out of a sense of decency. For in spite of what the supercilious Lady Julia might think or say about him, he was a gentleman. Nodding, he quietly replied, "Only my promise that I will make the best of this situation. I sincerely hope that you will do the same."

Her lips tightened and she drew herself up straight, as if she were a martyr mounted on her high horse. "What choice do I have?" she inquired tersely, her eyes flashing with self-righteous reproach. "Please know, sir, that I shall do whatever I must to save my family from shame and ruin, regardless of the cost to myself. It is my duty to do so."

"How very honorable," he sneered, infuriated by her saintly outrage. If she were anything like her father, and he was beginning to suspect that she was, judging from her demeanor, then the only thing she was truly interested in saving was her precious position in society.

She reverted back to sniffing her disparagement. "Considering the circumstances, Mr. Harwood, I must wonder if you even know the meaning of the word 'honor.'"

He had to admit that she had every right to question his honor. After all, if he were truly honorable, he would never have consented to her father's bargain. Then again, if honor were so blasted important to her, she would have refused to participate in this charade and damn the consequences. Not that there would have been any. At least not from him. Truth be told, had she refused to sanction her father's plan and had told them all to go to the devil, he would have kept silent forever out of admiration for her ethics.

Heaving an inward sigh, he glanced at the woman across from him. She sat rigidly erect, as if someone had shoved a rod down her spine, stabbing him with her hostile gaze.

If only she had had the character to say no. If only he'd had the strength to deny the temptation of the bargain. If only. But, of course, as with all of his "if onlys," it was too late to mend matters now.

CHAPTER 7

Julia had been at Amy's ball for well over an hour, and Gideon Harwood had yet to appear.

Not that she cared.

Not a jot.

Indeed, nothing could have pleased her more than if the blackguard took himself back to whatever God-forsaken hellhole he had crawled from, and never returned.

But, of course, that was a lie. She did care. She had no choice but to do so.

Julia smiled cordially as she curtsied to Lord Farndell, a genial but exceedingly gawky young earl, thus concluding the final figure of the cotillion they danced. If Mr. Harwood did not come tonight, she could be almost certain that he had decided to call off the bargain he had made with her father. Then they would be ruined. And it would all be her fault. As her dance partner escorted her back to her aunt Aurelia, who was often called upon during the Season to serve as her chaperon, Julia cursed her ungovernable temper.

She had behaved abominably toward Mr. Harwood when he had called two days earlier, like a shrew—the worst sort of termagant—baiting and pricking him at every turn. Heaven help her, she had been unable to stop herself from doing so, in spite of her good intentions. And she had indeed planned to be on her best behavior when she had entered the room that afternoon, promising herself that she

would take the utmost pains to be all that was amiable
and pleasing.

She had also vowed that she would not do or say anything that might prompt him to rethink the bargain and
thus endanger her siblings. But then, well, what could she
possibly say in her own defense? He had been so arrogant,
so blasted smug and sure of himself, as if what he did was
somehow just and righteous, that she had been unable to
contain her outrage. The way he had spoken to her—why,
one would have thought that he was of the nobility and
she a mere commoner from the lack of deference he had
shown her. He was insufferable, that is what he was. Yes,
he was an insufferable, blackmailing scoundrel, the worst
sort of villain.

Oh please, God. Let him come tonight and beg her father's permission to court her. She had just proposed a
bargain to the powers that be, promising to bridle her
tongue and temper her pride with humility in exchange for
a second chance with Gideon Harwood, when Lord Farndell interrupted her negotiations.

"A pleasure, as always, my dearest Lady Julia," he
gushed, gazing at her as if she were the sun around which
his world revolved. "Indeed, I cannot think of a greater
pleasure or privilege in life than dancing with you." Now
coming to a stop before her aunt, who sat in one of the
chairs lining the ballroom walls, looking regal yet appropriately unassuming in her dark blue sarcenet gown, he captured both of Julia's hands in his and hugged them to his
heart, impetuously murmuring, "May I be so bold as to say
that you dance as lightly as a rose petal on a soft spring
breeze? That the beauty of your smile warms my heart,
and that the music of your laughter lifts my soul on wings
of euphoric gladness?"

Julia nodded her acceptance of his rhapsodic gallantry.
Excessive flattery, it seemed, had become all the rage
among the gentlemen of late, for she had yet to have a
dance partner that evening who had not waxed poetic over
her charms. "You may, my lord, and thank you," she said,
favoring him with a gracious smile.

His homely freckled face split into an answering grin,

revealing a broken front tooth and several crooked lower ones. "You would be granting me the greatest of honors if you would permit me to call on you tomorrow."

"It is I who shall be honored if you do," she said, which was not only the correct response, but also the expected one. Besides, she genuinely liked Lord Farndell. Indeed, for all that he was behaving like a lovesick dolt this evening, she knew that he had no more desire to court her than she had for him to do so. They were friends, jolly ones, but nothing more. No doubt his current display of fawning buffoonery could in some way be attributed to his recent tiff with the high-spirited Lady Lucetta Burney, whom he loved and fully intended to marry.

Now lifting her hands to his lips, his lordship made a show of extravagantly kissing first her left and then her right one, between which he murmured in a sighing voice, "I shall count the seconds until that moment arrives, my dearest Lady Julia." Concluding his honeyed speech with a look of wry deviltry, which she answered with a conspiratorial smile, he bowed and departed. Julia arranged herself in a graceful pose in the vacant chair beside Aurelia, unfurling her fan to fend off what was rapidly becoming the torturous heat. That the ball was a triumph was apparent from the crush of people crowding the room, all of whom hailed from London's highest circles.

They also ranked among the city's most perfumed circles, Julia decided, her head beginning to throb as she was assaulted by a sickeningly sweet mélange of lavender, frangipani, musk, and attar of roses. Add the smell of burning beeswax emanating from the two hundred and fifty candles that blazed in the ten cut-glass chandeliers overhead, and the faint yet pervasive aroma of the food laid out on two long tables in the adjoining room, and it was almost more than she could bear. No. Not almost, she amended, giving her fan a particularly violent wave in a desperate attempt to clear the air. It was more than she could bear.

Just when Julia was certain that she would either suffocate or be sick if she remained in the oppressive room a second longer, Caroline appeared before her. As always, she was dressed in the height of fashion, in an ivory silk gown overlaid with a gold net half robe, both delicately trimmed with gleaming gold quilling. "Lady Aurelia. Lady Julia," she said, inclining her Grecian-coiffed head first to the older woman and then to her friend. "If you please, Lady Aurelia, may Julia withdraw to the retiring room with me? I find myself rather overcome by the heat, and would be exceedingly grateful for her company."

Julia, too, looked at her aunt. "Please? I must confess to feeling overcome as well." The appeal was a formality, of course, one voiced strictly for the sake of appearances. After all, it would never do to let on that there was discord within the family.

Aurelia swept Julia with a critical eye, her skillfully rouged lips pursing, as if she did not at all approve of what she saw. "Very well." She nodded once, brusquely. "You are looking overly flushed, Julia. Perhaps it would be for the best if you retire from view until your color subsides. High color is most unbecoming to delicate complexions such as yours."

"Yes. I am sure it is," Julia returned with unruffled irony, well aware that just about everything in respects to her person was unbecoming in her aunt's eyes. Unlike her younger sisters, however, she refused to take Aurelia's criticism to heart, so she remained impervious to the woman's constant onslaught of slings and arrows. Now rising, she added, "Should my mother have a need for me, please direct her to the retiring room." Not that she actually expected her mother to grace her with her attention. Were her mother the least bit inclined to pay her mind, she would not have requested Aurelia's services as chaperon this evening. Granting her aunt the courtesy of a parting nod, Julia looped her arm through Caroline's, and together they skirted the edge of the dance floor, their progress slow as they wended their way through the assemblage.

As they squeezed around a trio of ancient peers, all of who wore old-fashioned powdered wigs and gestured broadly as they engaged in a loud political debate, Julia said, "I cannot thank you enough for rescuing me, Caro. I truly was feeling overcome by the heat."

"And I must thank you," Caroline countered with a

smile. "Had you not consented to accompany me to the
retiring room, I would have been forced to return to my
mother and she would have insisted that I dance with Lord
Sorley. I saw him approaching as I took my leave. Merci-
fully, I escaped before Mother took note of his presence."

Lord Sorley was an odious, rat-faced earl whose plump
pockets more than made up for his lack of looks and social
graces in the eyes of the *ton*'s matchmaking mothers. To
Caroline's infinite horror, he had recently abandoned his
pursuit of famous Helene, having no doubt suffered one
too many rebuffs from the haughty beauty, and had now
redirected his attention to her.

Julia made a face at the mention of the detestable man.
"I would hardly term what Lord Sorley does on the dance
floor as dancing. He quite ruined my slippers for all the
treading he did on my feet the last time I was pressed into
partnering him."

"Nor would I, though to listen to him boast of his popularity as a dance partner one would think that he was quite
the master of London's ballrooms."

Julia sniffed at his lordship's unwarranted conceit. "Well,
judging from the way he barks at the servants, he is scarcely
a master of patience, so he will no doubt have gone off
after less-challenging prey by the time you return from the
retiring room."

The women fell silent as they squeezed sideways through
a narrow fissure between a knot of whispering matrons and
a convergence of drunken young rakes. When they reached
the end of the human channel, Julia resumed their conversation by inquiring, "By the bye, have you seen Mina this
evening? When I attended the reception at Ackermann's
Repository with her and her parents on Monday last, we
encountered Lord Denney, who prettily begged us each to
save a dance for him at tonight's ball. And you know what
a crush Mina has on Lord Denney. Since she wishes to
look her best, she made me promise to seek her out and
give my opinion of her new gown."

Caro sighed, her face taking on an expression that suggested the greatest of tragedies. "The poor dear has the
most dreadful spot at the end of her nose and does not

wish Lord Denney to see her in such a state, so she has
been hiding in alcoves all evening. The last time I saw her,
Amy was offering to filch the Venetian paste she claims
her aunt Cecily always carries in her reticule, promising to
apply it so that it will perfectly cover the spot. My guess is
that Mina accepted the offer, and that they have now retired to a private place to apply it. After all, it would never
do to be caught using, much less possessing, cosmetics."

"Yes," Julia murmured, her heart going out to Mina. As
if the poor dear didn't have enough problems with her
looks, her complexion had a distressing tendency to erupt
into spots.

By now they had reached the four sets of double ballroom doors. As they stepped out onto the third-floor gallery and strolled toward the opposite end where the ladies'
retiring room was located, Caro changed the subject by
saying, "I hear tell that Lord Wolton sprained his ankle
yesterday afternoon while viewing horses at Tattersall's,
which, I suppose, would explain why he is not sniffing about
you this evening. Lord Wickham said that Wolton's grief
must be blamed in the entirety on his shoes." She shook
her head, as if marveling at such folly. "One would think
that the popinjay would have the good sense to leave off
his high-heeled shoes while at Tattersall's. Wearing them
there seems rather pointless since there are no ladies present to be impressed by his enhanced stature. Do you not
agree?"

Julia laughed. "Yes. Then again, perhaps it was not vanity, but a simple wish to be tall enough to examine the
horses' teeth that prompted him to wear them."

Caro slapped her hand over her mouth, stifling her laughter at her friend's scathing riposte. "Oh, Julia. You truly
are wicked," she gasped when she had regained enough
control to speak. "I do not know anyone else who—" She
broke off abruptly, her brown eyes widening as she gaped
at something straight ahead. "My word!" she ejected in
shocked accents. "It is Mr. Harwood. What in the world is
he doing here?"

Julia followed her friend's gaze with her own, almost sag-

ging with relief when she saw Gideon Harwood standing
before a footman, presenting his invitation.

He had come after all. Thank God. As she thanked the
heavens above for granting her a second chance with the
man, she heard Caroline hiss, "Julia!"

Julia frowned at her friend's sharp tone. "Hmmm?" she
murmured, distractedly.

"You mustn't stare so at Mr. Harwood. People will talk."

Stare? Talk? Julia blinked, her relief-numbed mind slow
to process Caroline's words. When it finally did, she realized that she was indeed staring. Mortified, she tore her
gaze away, stammering, "I-I—It is just that I am stunned
to see him here."

"As am I," Caro said. She giggled, something utterly out
of character for her. "I must confess that I cannot blame you
for staring so. He is rather magnificent looking, is he not?"

It was on the tip of her tongue to say no, to deny that
she found him the least bit attractive; then Julia remembered the reason for her relief and she forced herself to
nod. Now seemed as good a time as any to initiate the
charade. "Yes. Magnificent," she concurred, stealing another glance at him through her lowered lashes. And he
truly did look magnificent, damn him, though it pained her
to no end to have to admit such a thing.

His perfectly tailored coat was dark blue, beneath which
he sported a white silk waistcoat that was cut deep in the
front to reveal the crisp linen frills of his shirt. As was
appropriate for the formality of the occasion, he wore
cream knee breeches, snug ones, she could not help noticing, a fit that emphasized the sleek athleticism of his build
in a manner that she found most admirable, in spite of her
reluctance to find anything about him to admire. He was,
after all, a blackmailing knave, which, by all rights of God
and man should make him repulsive to her in every way.
That he was not, made her seriously wonder at the state
of her own character.

Determining that it must be tragically flawed—how could
it not be, what with the unprincipled nature of her
thoughts?—Julia sighed and dropped her gaze lower.

Like most of the men present that evening, Mr. Harwood's annoyingly handsome legs were clad in white silk stockings. Unlike most of those other men, however, his stockings were spotlessly clean. As were his gleaming black pumps, which were fashionably tied rather than buckled. Now pretending to smooth her glove, she swept his entire length with her critical gaze.

Hmmm. All in all, he looked quite presentable—beyond presentable, to be fair—something that should have pleased her in view of the fact that she would be calling him husband in six short weeks. But she was not pleased—she would not be pleased. Never! Sternly commanding herself to be displeased by what she saw, and failing miserably, she ventured a glance at his face, hoping without any real expectation to find a flaw she could criticize there.

He was smiling at something one of the footmen said, revealing a flash of exceedingly white teeth. Straight ones, she noted with reluctant interest, and what appeared to be a full set of them. That meant that his breath would most probably be fresh, untainted by the putrid odor of rotten teeth. And that meant that it might not be so very dreadful to kiss him.

Kiss him? Julia's heart froze in shock at her insupportable thoughts. Good heavens! Her character must be in a far worse state than she had imagined to be having such thoughts about a man she knew to be beyond all contempt. More than a little alarmed she looked away, bowing her head to hide the blush she could feel stinging her cheeks.

Caroline laughed, a low, throaty sound that suggested that Julia's perusal of the disconcerting Mr. Harwood had been far more blatant than she had realized. "Perhaps you would like it to be *H* for Harwood after all, eh, Julia?"

"Of course—" Julia had been about to snap "of course not," but then she remembered her role in the charade and instead replied, "I cannot say, since I do not know the man." Was that really her voice, so shrill and unsteady?

Another laugh from Caro. "Considering the way he is looking at you, darling, I daresay that there is a very good chance indeed that you will be acquainted by the end of the evening."

Julia glanced up quickly at Caroline's words to find her-

self looking directly at Gideon Harwood. Having run the
gauntlet of footmen, he now stood a scant two yards away.
In the space of a heartbeat their gazes locked, and for several long seconds they stood staring at each other, the
world fading away as Julia struggled to regain her wits,
which had inexplicably fled her. As she stood helplessly
gazing into his starkly chiseled face, the hard set of his lips
softened and curved into a slow, arresting smile. Completely disarmed, she smiled back, somehow sensing that it
was the correct thing to do. Before she quite knew what
was happening, he nodded once and disappeared into the
ballroom.

"Well, well," Caro intoned, her soft voice laden with unmistakable meaning. "It would appear that you have made
a conquest this evening, and a most intriguing one, I
might add."

"Perhaps," Julia muttered, though how she managed to
speak for the—what? strain? chagrin? anxiety?—clogging her
throat, she did not know. Oh, devil take Gideon Harwood!
What was it about the blasted man that so unnerved her
every time he was in her presence? It was not as if he were
so very attractive. Or so she tried to tell herself.

"I must say that this dull evening has become rather
more entertaining for Mr. Harwood's presence," Caroline
remarked as they resumed walking. "To be sure, it should
prove most diverting to see how he fares in the *ton*."

Julia could not help wondering how she would fare as
well. Truth be known, as determined as she was to honor
her father's bargain, she was not so very sure how to go
about doing so. After all, she had to convince the *ton* that
she was in love with Gideon Harwood, and having never
actually been in that mysterious state before, what did she
really know about it? Oh, true. She knew about the intrica-
cies of courtship and the rules of the game to be played
within its boundaries. But courtship was courtship and love
was love, and even she knew that they were not at all the
same thing. She also understood that if she were to be
effective in her role of moonstruck ninny, she must extend
her performance beyond simply going through the motions
of courtship. Which left the question: How was she to act?

Perplexed, she contemplated her dilemma, smiling when she hit upon what she decided was the perfect solution. Perhaps she had never been in love, but her friends had at one time or another each fancied themselves to be so, and all had been most forthcoming when sharing their feelings. She'd also observed their besotted behavior firsthand, so the answer to her problem was quite simple: she would model her actions after theirs.

With that purpose in mind, she tried to recollect all that she had seen and heard. Hmmm. As she recalled, being in love meant cooking up schemes when with one's closest friends, bird-witted ploys calculated to thrust the lovelorn party into her desired sweetheart's path at every turn. Amy had a particular talent for waylaying would-be suitors, so she would be the one to emulate when acting out that detail. Yes, and then there was famous Helene's deft way of bringing every conversation around to whichever gentleman happened to be in her good graces at the moment. Hadn't Mr. Harwood suggested that she rattle on about him to all of her friends and acquaintances in order to appear appropriately smitten with him? Mmm, yes. He had. He had also said that they should exchange lingering looks.

As she mulled over his suggestions, Julia found herself wondering how he had come to propose them. Hmmm. Could it be that he had once been in love? Was there a woman somewhere for whom he had cared deeply, one who had quickened his pulse, and to whom he had freely given the tenderness that he could only pretend to give her? For some reason, one that she most definitely did not wish to explore, Julia found the notion of Gideon Harwood loving another woman rather—unsettling. Yes, and she did not like the sensation in the least, so she promptly thrust the thought from her mind and returned to the task of sorting out her role in the charade.

All right, then. Being as that it was her duty to please the vexing Mr. Harwood, she would act upon his suggestion of exchanging lingering looks, and yes, she would chatter incessantly about him while in company. She would also follow Amy's example and engage her circle in harebrained schemes to toss herself in his path. Since she had never before indulged in such silliness, doing so now should serve to convince her friends smartly enough of her infatuation with the man. In turn, they would gossip of her actions to their other friends and acquaintances. Brilliant! She had only to study and mirror Caroline's elegantly flirtatious manner, add a dash of Mina's blushing coyness, and it was certain to be whispered in every fashionable drawing room that Lady Julia Barham had a crush on Gideon Harwood. Why, he could not help but to be pleased by her performance.

And when they were alone? How was she to behave during those moments when they were out of their aristocratic audience's view? Julia frowned as she contemplated this new and decidedly delicate facet of her performance. Hmmm. There was the matter of the bargain she had just made with heaven to consider as well. If she had any intention whatsoever of honoring it, and she most certainly did, she must take great pains to avoid provoking, offending, or in any way insulting the exasperating man. In view of her less-than-charitable feelings toward him, her talents as an actress were sure to be sorely tested in the effort. Oh, what to do!

It took only a moment for Julia to decide upon the appropriate course of action: she would treat Mr. Harwood with courtesy, perfect, unfailing courtesy, nothing more or less. To be charming was out of the question, more than she could manage given her animosity toward him. But courtesy, well, surely she could grant him that? She had, after all, been schooled from the cradle to hide her feelings and to maintain a precise level of civility when in company. That she had mastered that art was something she had proved over and over again during her tiresome tenure in society, which only went to show that she had the ability to be agreeable to Gideon Harwood if she put her mind to doing so. Considering the circumstances, surely he did not expect any more than that?

Nodding to herself, she followed Caroline into the crowded retiring room. It was settled then. She would be polite, so very proper and decorous in her courtesy that Mr. Harwood would have no room for complaint.

CHAPTER 8

His presence had most certainly commanded the *ton*'s attention. Indeed, every pair of eyes in the ballroom appeared to be trained on him and were in danger of boring holes in his flesh for the intensity with which they watched him as he followed Lord Stanwell through the crush. Painted fans rose in their wake to hide their owners' faces, thus signaling the commencement of gossip. Gideon smiled. Excellent. Everything was going exactly as planned.

Now halting before his bride-to-be, who stood conversing with a stately brunette and a dumpy blonde with a curiously blanched-looking nose, Lord Stanwell exclaimed in a jovial voice, "Julia, my dearest girl, I have someone with me who very much desires an introduction."

"But of course, Father," she dutifully replied, smiling first at her father and then at him.

Thus cued, his lordship introduced, "Lady Julia Barham, allow me to present Mr. Gideon Harwood. Mr. Harwood has spent the better part of the past half hour expressing his admiration for you, my dear. Mr. Harwood, this is my daughter, Lady Julia Barham."

Gideon smiled and bowed, sweeping the woman before him with an assessing gaze as he inclined his head in formal salutation. She wore a gown of gold-shot bronze tonight, a color that made her skin glow like sun-warmed honey and deepened the amber of her eyes in a manner that he found unexpectedly striking. Even her hair seemed somewhat enhanced, richer in hue and more silken in texture, with each reddish gold strand gleaming as if lit by captured fire. As for her figure . . .

He discreetly eyed her womanly assets as he straightened back up. As with her skin, eyes, and hair, the gown showed her figure to its best advantage. True, she still looked overly slender, at least for his taste, but the low-cut neck of the bodice revealed a bosom that even he had to admit was surprisingly fine. As she murmured an appropriate response to their introduction, he appraised the overall picture she made.

While her looks had improved over the past two days, she still could not by any means be termed a beauty. Then again, he was hardly a judge of English beauty. Having spent the majority of his manhood in India, his tastes naturally ran toward earthier women: exotic, sable-haired beauties with mysterious sloe eyes, ample curves, and skin like tawny satin.

"Mr. Harwood, may I also have the pleasure of presenting two of my daughter's bosom bows? This is Lady Caroline Riddell"—he indicated the brunette, who nodded—"and Lady Wilhelmina Edicott." The plump blonde smiled the sweetest and most genuine smile Gideon had seen all evening, instantly winning his admiration.

"An honor," he murmured, bowing again.

That formality complete, Lord Stanwell turned back to his daughter, booming in a voice loud enough to be heard by all those around them, "Mr. Harwood has expressed a rather urgent desire to dance with you, my dear. It seems that he noticed you at Vauxhall Gardens on Sunday night last and was bewitched by your beauty." He clapped Gideon on the back as if they were the greatest of friends. "Though my daughter shall no doubt have my head for telling you this, Harwood, she spied you as well and has been unable to speak of anything else since."

All around them fans snapped open, the sibilant hiss of whispers arising from behind them as a dozen pairs of feminine eyes regarded them from beneath raised eyebrows.

"Oh, Papa! How could you?" Lady Julia exclaimed in a chagrined tone, playing the mortified maiden to perfection.

"Zounds, girl. You have hardly made a secret of your crush. Besides, since Harwood here"—another clap on Gideon's back—"has freely confessed his admiration for you, I see no harm in his knowing of your feelings."

Mindful of his audience, Gideon smiled and smoothly interjected, "Please do not be distressed, my dearest Lady Julia. As your humble and ardent admirer, I would sooner die the most agonizing of deaths than see you suffer so much as a moment of torment." Ha! And she thought him incapable of inane repartee.

She looked momentarily taken aback by his flowery speech, as if indeed stunned by the revelation of his unexpected talent. Then she smiled and murmured, "You are far too kind, sir."

"It is you who are kind to have granted me the precious gift of your favor, a gift that you may be certain I will cherish like the priceless treasure it is." Now in the spirit of his bantering game and rather enjoying the sport, he added in a theatrical voice, "Since you have been so very gracious in honoring me with your regard, may I be so bold as to call you an angel, my dear Lady Julia? For that is what you are. Indeed, how can you not be an angel when the sight of your face elevates my spirit with its beauty and the gentleness of your nature warms my heart with a rapture that can only be heaven-born?" He smiled as the gossiping hiss escalated to an electrified buzz. Perfect.

Her celestial ladyship again seemed at a loss, gazing at him in a queer manner that made him wonder at her thoughts. Before she could respond, a gentleman seeking a dance from Lady Caroline approached them. After introducing the amiable young man as Viscount Cleland, Lord Stanwell prompted, "Did you not wish to dance with my daughter, Harwood?"

"More than anything on heaven and earth," he gushed, casting the object of his feigned infatuation what he hoped was a moonstruck look.

She bit her lip, as if to stifle whatever retort had sprung to her tongue, and then smiled as if delighted by the prospect of dancing with him. "I should be honored, Mr. Harwood," she responded with a sincerity that rang true, even to his skeptical ears. It seemed that her ladyship possessed a talent for acting as well.

As Gideon offered his arm to escort her to the dance floor, he glanced at Lady Wilhelmina, who watched them with a rather wistful expression. His heart instantly went out to her. Poor chit. He would be willing to bet his entire fortune that she sat out the greater part of every ball. Hating the thought of the gentle creature suffering the humiliation that came from such neglect, he said, "Lady Wilhelmina, would you do me the honor of promising me your next dance?"

She blushed and graced him with another of her guileless smiles. "Yes. Of-f-f course, Mr. Harwood," she stammered, visibly delighted by his request. "It shall be a pleasure to do so."

"You are most gracious, dear lady," he countered with a smile that mirrored hers in its honesty. His next partner thus secured, Gideon led Lady Julia onto the dance floor.

"It was exceedingly kind of you to ask Mina to dance, Mr. Harwood," she murmured as they made their way through the crowd. "For all that she is the dearest girl in the world, her looks are considered to be rather, well, unfashionable, so she often lacks partners at balls."

Gideon shrugged one shoulder. "I asked her because I find her charming. If the gentlemen of the *ton* are too witless to see her fine qualities, then perhaps she is better off without them."

"I could not agree with you more," she returned, gazing at him in a way that again made him wish that he could read minds. If he were to hazard a guess at her thoughts, he would have to say that she was surprised to the point of being puzzled by his response. She seemed about to say more, her expression thoughtful as she opened her mouth, then she closed it again and turned her attention to the assembling dancers. When she saw their positions, she frowned and whispered, "Oh dear. A minuet. Do you think that you can manage a minuet, Mr. Harwood?"

Gideon snorted at the patronizing nature of her question. "Of course I can manage a minuet. In spite of what you might think, one need not have a title to master the steps."

She opened her mouth and then closed it again, as if censoring whatever she had been about to say. When she finally did speak, it was to apologize. "Please forgive me, Mr. Harwood. I did not mean to give offense. My intent was simply to spare you embarrassment should you not know the steps. Being as that we are strangers, I am unacquainted with the extent of your knowledge of dancing, so please do forgive me if my question seemed condescending. I most certainly did not mean to suggest a slur on your birth."

Aware that they were being scrutinized, Gideon forced himself to smile as he softly flung back, "Indeed? You had no such scruples about doing so when I called on Tuesday."

Following his lead, she returned his smile. "Yes. And I must apologize for that as well. I can only plead to being overwrought by my unexpected plight. Surely you understand?"

"Oh, I understand well enough," he snarled through the clenched teeth of his false smile. "You made your opinion of me abundantly clear. And do not tell me that you did not mean what you said. I have learned that people generally reveal their true feelings when they speak in haste, for they speak precisely what is on their mind without taking the time to choose their words and cloak their meaning in neat little lies."

She sighed as they stopped before their places on the dance floor. "Please, Mr. Harwood, I do not wish to quarrel with you. I am trying to make the best of our situation, as you, yourself, suggested I should do."

"Fine, then. Since we seem to quarrel every time we speak, perhaps it would be for the best if we do not attempt further conversation." With that, he moved into position for the first figure of the minuet. Now standing facing his haughty bride-to-be, who was displaying her formidable acting talent by beaming as if she were truly enjoying herself, he bowed as the music began, to which she sank into an answering curtsy. The honors thus completed, they moved into the first figure.

The minuet, which his mother had insisted he learn what seemed like a lifetime ago, had in his mind always been far too long and tedious to qualify as an amusement. And he had loathed every second he had spent learning it. Now, however, reflecting back on those days in the tiny curate's cottage and the hours he had spent with Bethany and Caleb going through the motions of the courtly dances his mother had insisted they study, he saw that they had in truth been some of the most magical moments of his life. Especially those occasions when his father joined them in their instruction, partnering their beautiful mother with an exuberance that had never failed to turn the lesson into a jolly romp. They had all been together then, happy, healthy, and full of love for each other and the simple life they led. What he wouldn't give to go back to those carefree days!

As Lady Julia passed in front of him, making a half turn on a *demi-coupé,* she smiled broadly and murmured, "We really must have some conversation if we are to convince the *ton* of our infatuation with each other."

She was right, of course, though what they should say, he could not even begin to imagine. Performing a *pas marché* with his right foot crossed behind his left one, he replied, "Fine. What do you suggest we talk about?"

By now they had completed the first loop of the S formation in which they danced and had come face-to-face in the center of the figure. She seemed to consider his question as they passed each other obliquely on the right and executed the necessary steps to complete the second loop of the S. It was not until they had again met in the center that she replied, "Pleasantries shall suffice, I should think."

"What sort of pleasantries?"

What sort of pleasantries indeed? In view of the fact that he bristled at just about every word she uttered, whatever could she say that would not cause him offense? Deciding that a compliment should be safe enough, she remarked, "I must say that you dance superbly, Mr. Harwood." And it was true. Not only were both his timing and steps precise, he moved with a grace that she would never have believed possible for a man his size, had she not seen it for herself. As she watched him perform a perfect *jeté échappé,* she found herself wondering how he had come to be such an excellent dancer. After all, such skill was utterly unexpected in a commoner.

Thus as he presented her with his white-gloved hand, which she could not help noting was as immaculately clean as his stockings, she quizzed, "May I inquire as to how you came by your expertise, sir?"

"The same way you came by yours, I daresay. It was a course in my daily lessons," he replied, joining the group of dancers forming a small circle in the center of the figure. Executing a series of intricate minuet steps, they moved around the circumference until they were in position to present their left hands. "My compliments to your teacher, then," she said, placing her hand lightly on top of his. "He succeeded admirably in teaching you."

"She," Gideon corrected her, moving his hand from hers to prepare to retrace the circle. "My mother taught me."

Julia digested that surprising tidbit of information as they performed the contretemps of the minuet, which consisted of hopping and advancing forward to again join left hands. That a parent would actually take the time to teach their child anything, much less dancing, which she knew from her own lessons to be an exceedingly time-consuming proposition, was an utterly foreign notion. She also found herself rather envying him the closeness he had clearly shared with his mother. What would it be like to have a mother who loved her enough to lavish her with such attention?

She did not have to think to know the answer to that question. It would be a joy beyond all other pleasures, of course, a delight that she would never experience since neither of her parents had ever cared for her beyond the brief displays of approval they granted her when she proved to be a credit to them.

Now presenting both hands to Gideon in commencement of the fifth figure of the dance, she said, "Your mother sounds wonderful. How very fortunate you were to have been raised by such a person." She could not keep a note of wistfulness from creeping into her voice.

He glanced at her quickly, a faint frown knitting his brow as if he found her comment very queer indeed, though why he would do so, she could not imagine. "She was. She was the best of women."

"Was?" Julia echoed. "Then she is—"

"Dead, yes," he interjected shortly. Hands joined, they made a single rotation.

"I-I am sorry," she stammered. And she was, genuinely so. His mother sounded like someone she would have liked to meet. So much so, that for a moment she had actually thought that marriage to the despicable Mr. Harwood might not be so very unbearable if it meant becoming part of a family led by a woman capable of such love. Disappointed, she cast about for a new subject, trying to remember what she had heard about him. She finally settled on saying, "I hear tell that you spent several years in India."

"Yes."

When he did not expand upon his response, she quizzed, "And how did you find it?" Their arms were rounded and raised at shoulder level to form a circle.

He released her hands to *demi-coupé* and then *pas glissé*. "Different." Again he refrained from elaboration.

Again she prompted him, "Different? In what ways?"

"A thousand ways, but none that would be of interest to you."

"You might be very surprised to learn what interests me."

"Perhaps, but I doubt it." By now they were nearing the end of the final figure.

For a moment Julia was tempted to challenge his remark, to tell him exactly what she thought of his high-handed dismissal of her ability to think beyond fashions and the frivolities of society. But, of course, she could not do so. So she curtsied in response to his bow, which concluded their dance, and satisfied her affront by injecting a note of hauteur into her voice as she replied, "We shall see, I suppose," though truth be told she doubted if he would ever care enough about her to learn of her interests.

Sighing, she took his arm and allowed him to escort her off the dance floor. Oh, well. What did it really matter? What did anything matter as long as her siblings were safe? And they would be safe as long as she maintained the facade of civility she had erected this evening.

Courtesy. Perfect courtesy. That was her concern, not convincing Gideon Harwood that she had worth beyond her position in society. She would take care to never forget her purpose in the future.

CHAPTER 9

Four routs. Four, no, five balls. Two picnics. A visit to Vauxhall Gardens. Two plays at Covent Garden. An opera at King's Theater. A balloon ascension in the park. One military review. A visit to the Royal Academy to view hackneyed paintings of insipid maidens, frolicking lambs, and exotic fruit. Seven drives through Hyde Park at the fashionable hour. And what was now his sixteenth call at her house bearing nosegays, bonbons, and whatever other frivolous token Gilchrist deemed appropriate for genteel courtship, and still, after three and a half weeks of keeping almost constant company with Lady Julia Barham, he had yet to see her display anything that resembled a genuine emotion. Why, if she were any more stiffly polite, even a trifle more rigidly correct, she would be in danger of shattering from brittleness.

Yes, and as if that were not quite tedious enough in itself, there was the matter of her conversation, or at least what she passed off as such. Bloody hell! Could it possibly be any more inane? Why, the very thought of being forced to endure yet another chirping review of the weather or monotonous tea-blend comparison was more than he could bear.

Gideon savagely tightened his grip on the nosegay he carried, unmindful that he crushed the intricately cut paper doily that formed a frill around the dainty bouquet of daffodils, roses, heartsease, periwinkle, and mignonette. The entire situation was intolerable—she was intolerable, damn it! Every second he spent in her company was a torment, an endurance test of just how much dullness a mortal man could bear without running mad from boredom.

Muttering a silent oath, he paused at the gate of the central Grosvenor Square Park through which he had just passed, waiting for a speeding gig and a more sedately paced traveling coach to go by before crossing the street. The fascination he had experienced when first observing Lady Julia's abrupt shift from a supercilious virago to a mealymouthed model of decorum had most definitely deserted him now. And he had to admit that he had indeed been fascinated by her dramatic change in behavior, his curiosity piqued to see how long she could maintain her pretense of civility before being overcome by her innate sense of superiority and breaking beneath the strain of being cordial to a man she had made clear she viewed as so much dirt beneath her dainty slippers.

But she had not broken, not even during those moments when they were alone and she was free to speak her mind without fear of being overheard by the *ton*. A pity, that. He far preferred the shrewish arrogance with which she had treated him during their initial interview to the banal courtesy she had bored him with since. She had at least been interesting in her scorn.

Snorting his frustration, Gideon more marched than walked around the corner of North Audley Street and started down Upper Brook Street. To be fair, their charade did require that she treat him with a measure of aristocratic cordiality, which was exactly what she was doing, he supposed. In view of that fact, he should probably give credit where it was due and say that she was doing an admirable job of playing her part.

Well, at least it was admirable if he were to judge it from the flurry of invitations he had received of late, many from London's leading hostesses. Impossible though it seemed to him, the *ton* appeared to have interpreted the remote, almost sterile courtesy with which Lady Julia Barham treated him as the formation of an attachment on her part. While he was wise enough to know that the invitations had been tendered out of a desire to watch the progress of their novel romance rather than from any real acceptance of his person, that same wisdom also made him see that he had been granted the rare opportunity to experience life in London's highest society and judge for himself if he truly wished his siblings to be a part of it.

And now that he had done so, did he still desire it?

At the moment, he was inclined to answer no. From what he had seen, life in the *ton* was miserable, an existence populated by artificial people living empty lives, who spent their days fraught with fear of unwittingly doing or saying something that might make them the target of the vicious gossip that was the heart of the *beau monde*. To be sure, one had only to look at Lady Julia to see the dreary sort of misses they spawned. Or her sisters, whom he had met at the picnic their mother had given Friday last. How many times during the dull affair had he heard them lauded as prime examples of breeding?

Gideon shuddered at the thought of the younger Barham daughters. Poor chits. Never in his life had he seen more exquisitely mannered children, nor had he encountered ones so tragically lacking in spirit. It had quite broken his heart to see them, tamed and drained of the enchanting exuberance that was a natural part of childhood. They could have been dolls for the way they had sat so stiff and still in their chairs beneath a tree, dolls carved of wood and clothed in a silken elegance that thrust upon them a maturity far beyond their tender years. Thinking back, he could not recall them uttering a single word outside of the rote courtesies with which they had responded when someone had deigned to speak to them. Never once had they smiled or laughed, nor had they engaged in the frolics one expected from children at picnics.

Lord Stanwell had said that Lady Julia was devoted to her sisters and spent much time in their nursery guiding and counseling them. If what he had seen was a result of her training, then he most certainly did not want her in charge of Bliss's education. He would not allow it! Better that Bliss remained a hell-bound hoyden than be tamed into a lifeless husk of decorum.

Gideon was now in view of the Palladian-style Barham mansion, an impressive, golden-brick structure boasting five center bays and an Ionic portico that formed a balcony crowned by a triangular pediment. As was usual for this time of day, there was a queue of stylish gigs and blooded mounts lining the street outside it, bearing testimony to the fact that Lady Julia had not been lying when she had claimed to have a bevy of suitors. Indeed, whenever he called there were at least half a dozen titled swains vying for her favor, all waged in a petty competition involving the exchange of genteel glares and cloaked insults as each struggled to outdo the others with the lavishness of the compliments he bestowed upon every aspect of her person.

Well, they were welcome to her and good riddance. For unless she suddenly displayed qualities that showed her capable of influencing Bliss in a desirable manner, which he rather doubted she would do at this late date, he saw no reason to continue their farce. After all, his sole purpose for agreeing to the bargain was to benefit his siblings. And since he had now determined that the disadvantages of the *ton* far outweighed the advantages it could offer them, what possible reason was there for him to marry Lady Julia?

He contemplated his decision for several moments, carefully considering everything he had heard and seen while in society, wanting to make certain that there was not some benefit he might have overlooked in his admittedly prejudiced view of the woman and her privileged world. After doing so, he slowly shook his head.

While he could think of a dozen compelling reasons why he should not wed her, he could not find a single one why he should. That being the case, he must end their charade. Today. He would linger until all of Lady Julia's suitors had taken their leave, and then beg a moment alone with her to inform her of his decision. No doubt she would be relieved, especially when he made clear that he was prepared to honor his end of the bargain and allow her father's shameful secret to remain just that, a secret. He would then be free to wash his hands of the duplicitous Barhams and be done with them once and for all.

Now feeling as if he had been granted a new lease on

life, which indeed he had, Gideon smiled and nodded as he passed Darby, Lord Stanwell's senior groom, who sometimes tended his gig on those occasions when he drove to the house, which was usually only when he was to escort Lady Julia somewhere. Having grown accustomed to hard exercise while in India, Gideon chafed at the sedentary life favored by prosperous Londoners and thus often elected to walk when conducting business about town, deeming most of the required distances not worth the trouble of ordering his horse saddled or carriage harnessed. Nodding again, this time at Noah, the youngest of the grooms, who grinned and greeted him gaily, he strode purposefully up the shallow front steps and rang the bell.

As always the door was guarded by Cuthbert, the Barhams' wizened majordomo, who smiled as if genuinely pleased to see him. Then again, perhaps he was, for Gideon had noticed that he was the only one of Lady Julia's callers who had bothered to learn the man's name and regularly ask after his health, something he did now.

"My word, Cuthbert! I must say that you look in prime twig today. I take it that the camphor liniment you have been using has helped your rheumatism?" he said, giving the servant a light but jovial clap on his stooped shoulder.

The majordomo's welcoming smile widened into a toothy grin. "Indeed it has, sir. Indeed it has. Why, I feel in such plump current that one would think I was sixty again." He cackled at his own witticism, a dry, airless rasp reminiscent of footfalls on parched autumn leaves.

Gideon, too, chuckled. "Excellent! I must say that that is quite the best news I have had all week."

"Yes? Well, I am sorry to say that I cannot improve upon that by telling you that Lady Julia is alone. She is presently entertaining five callers, among whom, I regret to report, is Lord Wolton." Cuthbert's age-rumpled face took on a decidedly pained expression as he conveyed that last bit of information.

Like Gideon, the majordomo harbored a less-than-charitable opinion of the foppish, ill-mannered Lord Wolton, whose general policy on servants was to treat them as rudely as possible and remind them of their inferiority at every turn. It was a policy he had attempted to extend to Gideon the first time he had called at the Barham residence, one he had abandoned quickly enough when treated to a sample of Gideon's own policy on dealing with bumptious nincompoops. Thus as Cuthbert announced him to the group gathered in the Peacock drawing room, a name that Gideon had concluded referred to its vivid blue-green walls since there were no peacocks or their feathers in evidence, Lord Wolton was forced to limit his demonstration of disapproving superiority to sniffing and looking away in a direct cut.

Ignoring him, Gideon bowed first to Lady Aurelia, who always served as chaperon during afternoon calls and whose charming manner he privately thought Lady Julia would do well to emulate, and then to Lady Julia herself.

Lady Aurelia smiled graciously, setting aside her ever-present needlework to offer him her hand. "Why, Mr. Harwood! How very kind of you to call," she said, her rich voice warm with sincerity and her beautiful face a study of cordiality. "It is always a pleasure to welcome you to our home."

"It is you who are kind in receiving me, my lady," he countered, briefly clasping her proffered hand in his. "And I can assure you that the pleasure is all mine."

Lady Julia favored him with her usual forced smile. "I must say that you have arrived at a most propitious time, Mr. Harwood. Lord Crompton is about to describe the new livery he has ordered for his footmen." She graced his lordship with one of her affected little smiles. "I, for one, cannot wait to hear the details."

It was all Gideon could do to restrain his urge to groan aloud at the dreary prospect. The last time he had called, his lordship had been engaged in selecting wallpaper for his dressing room, and had described what seemed like a thousand different paper patterns in tediously minute detail. After doing so he had arbitrarily decided that he preferred paint, at which point he began to list every available tint along with a thorough description of each. He no doubt would have bored them all into a coma from the dullness of his droning dissertation had Lady Aurelia not delicately hinted at the fact that he had long overstayed the prescribed time limit for calls, which according to the rules of etiquette should not exceed twenty minutes, thus forcing him to take his leave. He could only hope that her ladyship would be as vigilant today.

Hiding his chagrin behind a bland mask of politeness, Gideon dutifully presented Lady Julia with the offerings he carried, responding, "Since I do not wish to detain you from something to which you are so clearly looking forward, my lady, I shall seek a seat immediately and allow his lordship to proceed with what will no doubt prove to be a most stimulating discourse." Selecting a comfortable cane-backed armchair next to the distinguished, silver-haired Lord Dunsbee, whose wry wit he rather enjoyed, Gideon braced himself for the tedium that lay ahead.

"Please do carry on, Lord Crompton," Lady Julia prompted brightly.

Lord Crompton, a plump, priggish earl who seemed cursed by a perpetual cold, blew his nose with a violence that suggested more nasal mucus than a human head could possibly hold, and then did as requested. "As you know, my household livery is presently made up of a-a—"*A-choo! Sniffle! Sniffle!* Another fierce nose blow. "It is of a medium grayish blue superfine, which, to my way of thinking, is-is"—*A-choo!*—"exceedingly dull."

"I should imagine it is," Lord Dunsbee muttered just loud enough for Gideon to hear, referring, of course, to Crompton's penchant for wearing unusual colors, the combinations of which, more often than not, clashed. Today was one of his mismatched days, his attire consisting of a carrot-orange coat, plum waistcoat, and breeches in a peculiar shade of ash gray.

Sneezing twice and again blowing his nose, his lordship continued. "After visiting several of our city's finest drapers and viewing their wares, I have concluded that the new ones simply must be made up in mustard broadcloth. I found the most delightful shade at Dougherty's, which has been promised to me at a singularly excellent price." He clapped in glee at his bargain, an action that prompted yet another fit of sneezing.

"Mustawd, you say?" Lord Wolton quizzed, his eyebrows rising in a manner that clearly communicated his condemnation of the notion. "Oh, deah. I do hope that my eahs ahe playing twicks on me and that you did not say mustawd, my good fellow."

"And what is wrong with mustard, pray tell?" inquired Lord Tidwell, a tall, normally good-natured young viscount who just happened to be wearing mustard-colored breeches.

Lord Wolton shrugged. "I only meant to call to attention the fact that Cwompton's hewaldic colows call foh the use of awgent lace. A pity, weally, that. Oh is eveh so much mohe elegant." Argent, which was silver, and or, gold, were terms that referred to the heraldic metals featured on titled families' coats of arms, and usually determined the metal to be used in the buttons and braided lace that trimmed their footmen's livery.

"Our footmen's livery is trimmed in argent lace, and I have always thought them to look exceedingly fine," Lady Julia pointed out with admirable equanimity. "I am quite certain that Lord Crompton's servants shall look equally splendid."

A-choo! A-choo! Sniffle! Lord Crompton, of course.

Lord Wolton pursed his lips, visibly annoyed at being taken to task for his thoughtless slight to his hostess's family. "Awgent lace on woyal blue, such as youw footmen weah is indeed vewy pleasing, my deah, and is one of the few instances when awgent compahes favowably to oh. But awgent and mustawd?" A disdainful sniff. "I think not."

Lord Crompton blew his nose loudly.

"I rather think that it depends entirely on the shade of mustard. The contrast can be quite striking if done correctly," stated Lord Newmarch, a short but handsome viscount with a notorious fondness for tall phaetons and driving fast. Though he and Lord Crompton were famous for their public exchanges of wildly humorous insults, they were, in truth, the best of friends, and woe to anyone who dared to abuse one within the hearing of the other. Now lifting his quizzing glass to peruse Wolton's characteristically preposterous attire, his dark eyebrows rising at what he saw, he added, "In view of the fact that you selected a most unsuccessful combination of argent and mustard for the coat you wore to court a fortnight ago, I suppose that one can understand your aversion to the pairing. However, I am certain that Crompton learned from your failure, and shall do far better for himself."

"My coat was buttewcup silk shot with silveh, not mustawd, and I will have you know that it was counted a gweat success in the ciwcles that twuly matteh," Lord Wolton heatedly retorted, his color rising beneath his rouge in a manner that made his use of cosmetics all the more obvious.

"Indeed? And which circles are those?" inquired Lord Dunsbee, lifting his quizzing glass to join Lord Newmarch in his cool scrutiny of Lord Wolton. As if on cue, Lords Crompton and Tidwell followed suit.

"Yes. Do tell. We really want to know," baited Tidwell.

Lord Wolton's narrow chest puffed out in his affront and his thin lips all but disappeared as they crimped into an angry line. Glaring at the assembly of quizzing glasses and raised eyebrows, he bit out, "The highest ciwcles, I can assuwe you. Ones that do not suffeh the pwesence of nabobs in their midst."

That last, of course, was a jab at Gideon. Now rising, wobbling unsteadily as he struggled to find his balance on his high-heeled shoes, he snapped, "Since I am not inclined to suffeh one now, I shall bid you a good day!" He paused only long enough to bow to the ladies, almost losing his balance in the process, before exiting the drawing room as quickly as the mincing steps required by his shoes would allow him.

"But you still have not told which circles admired your coat," Dunsbee called out to his retreating back. "It is important that we know so that we do not unwittingly seek the opinion of one of their members should we meet him at our tailors' shops." When Lord Wolton did not deign to respond, he shrugged. "Pity. Now I shall have to wonder." A sigh. "Ah, well. I suppose that it is time that I take my leave as well, though it pains me to depart the company of two such charming ladies." With that, he rose. "Lady Aurelia, Lady Julia, a pleasure as always." He bowed. "Gentlemen." A nod. And then he, too, quit the room.

He had no sooner stepped over the threshold than Cuthbert appeared announcing Lord Farndell and the Duke of Dollimore, both of whom Gideon knew from the tone of their conversation to be friends of Lady Julia rather than suitors. That she should have male friends, especially ones like Farndell and Dollimore, who clearly possessed a superior wit, astonished him to no end. For while he understood that it was a nobleman's duty to take an aristocratic bride such as Lady Julia, he could see nothing in her person that might possibly entice a man to call strictly for the pleasure of her company. Then again, if she were the sort of chit he had known all his life perhaps he would see qualities in her that currently escaped him.

The next hour passed agreeably enough. Crompton and Newmarch entertained them with a droll duel of wits, after which they retired to their club to share a bottle. Tidwell followed on their heels, claiming an engagement with his mother, after which Farndell joked about the man's fawning devotion to his mimsey-mum, as Tidwell referred to his overbearing mother, and how he could never wed since no woman could ever measure up to dearest Mimsey-mum.

Three more callers came and went, during which time Lady Aurelia discreetly inquired if there was something in particular Gideon required, hinting at his breach of etiquette in remaining in their company for so long. He replied no, thanked her for her thoughtfulness, and then made a show of repositioning himself in his chair to assume a lounging pose that clearly conveyed his disinclination to move any time in the near future.

When, at last, Lord Thurkittle, Lady Julia's final caller departed, and Gideon still made no move to leave, Lady Julia smiled wanly and said, "I am sorry, Mr. Harwood, but I am afraid that I must excuse myself in order to prepare for the play I am to attend with Lady Amy this evening. Pray do pardon me?"

Thus signaled that the moment he had patiently awaited had at last arrived, Gideon replied, "I shall do so only after you grant me a word in private. There is a matter of some urgency that we must discuss. Perhaps we can take a turn about the garden?" He gestured to the formal garden that lay beyond the French doors at the far end of the room. Well aware that she would not deny his request, he rose without awaiting her response, saying to her aunt, "If you will excuse us, Lady Aurelia? I promise that I shall not detain your niece for more than a moment, and that we will stay well within your view."

Always a model of genteel courtesy, she smiled and nodded. "But of course, Mr. Harwood. I daresay that the air shall do our dearest Julia good. To my knowledge, she has not so much as poked her nose outside the entire day."

Gideon bowed, and then escorted Lady Julia outside. As was her custom during those times when they were alone, she did not deign to speak, waiting instead for him to do so, her patrician face arranged in its usual expression of vacant sociability.

The afternoon was a fine one, warm with just the slightest breeze that carried the fragrant sweetness of the honeysuckle that draped the garden walls in a tapestry of delicate cream and silvered green. The garden itself, though small, was laid out in a series of individual gardens divided by carefully raked sand paths, each containing a geometric topiary around which was planted a single genus of flower along with a host of its more exotic variations.

As they descended the graceful sweep of steps leading from the rear terrace to the garden below, Lady Julia prompted, "I do not wish to be rude, Mr. Harwood, but I truly have an engagement for which I must prepare. Please do be kind enough to state your business so that we might resolve it posthaste."

Gideon nodded. "As you wish. I have requested this moment alone to tell you that I have decided that I cannot marry you."

She came to an abrupt halt, gaping at him with eyes so wide that they looked in danger of bulging from their sockets. "W-w-what?" She more squeaked than spoke the utterance, her mouth working as if she wished to say more but could not manage the words in her shock.

"I no longer wish to wed you," he repeated, though, of course, it was obvious that she had heard him the first time.

She remained silent for several moments, visibly stunned, then said in a small voice, "I am afraid that I do not understand, sir."

Of course she didn't understand, Gideon thought sardonically; she could not possibly understand. In her conceit, it was no doubt beyond her to even imagine that there was a man in the world who did not wish to wed her and who would not gladly sell his soul for the privilege of doing so—something that he, himself, had come dangerously close to doing.

As always happened when he remembered his weakness in the face of temptation, Gideon was gut punched by self-loathing. Unreasonably blaming her for his failing, despising her for being the lure who had all-too-willingly baited her father's hook, he chuckled darkly and ground out, "No, I am sure you do not, my dear. And I doubt that you shall ever be able to do so, so I will not waste either of our time by trying to explain. Let it simply suffice to say that I have decided that I no longer wish to be a part of the *ton*. And since gaining entrée into that august circle was my sole objective in wedding you, I can see no reason in making us both miserable by continuing with our farce. Thus I am calling an end to it here and now."

She could not have looked more puzzled. "But why?" She shook her head, her delicately arched eyebrows drawing together in her bewilderment. "Everyone in the *ton* has received you quite graciously. Well, except for Lord Wolton, but no one cares a fig for his opinion, as you saw today. And my father said just yesterday that he is certain that he can secure you a membership at Brooks once we are wed." Another head shake. "All and all you are meeting with far greater success than either my father or I could have imagined. Why ever would you wish to quit the *ton* now when you are all but assured of entrée? We have only to announce our engagement next week as planned to—"

He cut her off with an impatient hand gesture. "As I said, you could never understand my reason. I am calling off the bargain, and that is that. Nothing you can say or do shall change my mind, so I suggest that you simply accept matters as they are."

He was about to add his promise to uphold his end of the bargain and keep silent on the matter of her family secret, when she retorted in a low voice that practically vibrated with restrained anger, "I will have you know, sir, that I am not some witless child to be patted on the head and dismissed without so much as a by-your-leave. Indeed, after all the effort I have gone to to satisfy your demands, you owe me at the very least an explanation of your sudden change in plans." To her credit, she managed to maintain her brittle smile and expression of vapid courtesy throughout her indignant little speech. Then again, perhaps it was not so much her doing as that they had simply become permanently affixed after being in place for so long.

Gideon shrugged. "Fine, then. You shall have one, though I do not expect that you will ever be able to truly fathom what I am about to say. The truth of the matter is that I do not like the *ton* or most of the people in it, nor have I found a single benefit to be gained from inclusion into it that could possibly outweigh the misery one must suffer in order to be a member."

"If what you say is indeed true, then it is you who lacks an ability for comprehension, for you cannot see the extraordinary value of what is being offered." Though her face remained complaisant and her delivery even, a note of the hauteur she had displayed during their first interview had crept into her voice.

"Then perhaps you would care to enlighten me on what I have failed to comprehend?" Not that he actually cared what she might have to say on the subject. It was just that he could not resist challenging her when she took that arrogant tone with him.

She favored him with a stiff nod. "Gladly. However, may I suggest that we walk while I do so? My aunt is watching and I do not wish her to suspect that something is amiss."

Gideon snorted at the absurdity of the reasoning behind her proposal. "No doubt she will catch on to that fact quickly enough when I suddenly cease calling."

"True. But if she believes that we are arguing or engaging in any other such unpleasantness now, she will come out and remove me from your presence. It is her duty as my chaperon to do so."

As tempting as he found the prospect of having her tedious ladyship snatched from his presence, Gideon did as requested and resumed their leisurely stroll through the garden. After all, he had had his say, so it was only fair that she should have hers as well. When they had walked for several moments, and she had yet to take advantage of the opportunity he had presented for her to do so, he prompted, "Well? I believe that you were about to emancipate me from my ignorance in regard to the *ton*."

She glanced up at him, her smile firmly in place. "Yes, of course, Mr. Harwood. But first, might I inquire after your initial desire to enter the *ton*? What was it that you wished to gain that you have since decided is impossible?" Again, she was all that was agreeable.

He shrugged. "Let me begin by saying that my wish to enter the *ton* had nothing whatsoever to do with any great desire to be a part of society. Though I shall no doubt shock you in saying so, I am perfectly content with my station in life."

She blinked twice, visibly confused by his response. "Then what—" She shook her head, her smile faltering as her brow knit into a frown. "Why—I mean—" Another head shake, this one accompanied by a look that begged him to answer the question she clearly sought to ask.

"Why did I agree to a bargain from which I would gain nothing I desire?" he supplied.

She nodded.

"Because while I have no use for the *ton*, I thought that being a part of it might provide advantages for my siblings, my youngest sister in particular. But now, after viewing the females in the *ton*, seeing what is expected of them and how they are required to behave, I have decided that she is far better off as she is."

Her ladyship's aristocratic nose promptly rose in the air. "And what is wrong with the way we females in the *ton* behave, pray tell?" There was more than a note of hauteur in her voice this time.

Gideon shrugged again. "Nothing, I suppose, if you like affected, overbred chits who are so well tamed that they cannot entertain an original thought or express an honest emotion."

She sniffed. "If that is truly your perception of us, then you are every bit as ignorant of society as I suspected." Her facade was definitely crumbling around the edges now. "While there are admittedly many females such as you describe, there are scores of others who are counted as clever and original, and are much admired for their naturalness. Why, you have only to observe one of the many women held out as paragons by the *ton* to see that what I say is true."

He could not help snorting at her claim. "Please believe me when I say that I have done exactly that. Indeed, I have spent almost every second of my time in your precious *ton* observing such a woman, one who is touted by all as being the paragon to end all paragons. It is from her that I formed my poor opinion. Well, her and her equally ideal sisters."

"I cannot even begin to imagine whom you mean, sir," she retorted, the precision of her accents clearly betraying her growing vexation.

"Can you not?"

"No."

"Come now, I should think it would be more than obvious."

She seemed to consider; then her eyes narrowed and she halted in her steps. "You cannot possibly be referring to—"

"You, yes," he interjected dryly.

Her eyes narrowed a fraction more, glittering in a way that made them seem in danger of shooting sparks. "You truly are an insufferable man," she hissed, two vermilion spots appearing on her cheeks in her anger. "How dare you presume to judge me?"

He chuckled, cynically amused by her question. "And why should I not judge you? By your words and actions you have certainly presumed to judge me, and yet you know far less about me than I know of you." That much was certainly true. Aside from the mechanical inquiries that came from the idle chitchat that made up the preponderance of her conversation, her high-and-mighty ladyship had never bothered to learn anything about him and his life.

That piece of logic earned him a withering look. "I know enough to recognize you for the blackguard you are. Anyone possessing so much as a shred of decency could see that only the worst kind of scoundrel would engage in the vile sort of bargain in which you entered with my father."

"Perhaps. Then again, if I am a scoundrel what does that make your father? It takes at least two to strike a bargain, you know." She opened her mouth, most probably to put him back in his lowly place, but he cut her off before she could speak, forcefully demanding, "And what of yourself, my dear Lady Julia? It seems to me that you agreed to play your part in all of this rather too easily. To my way of thinking, your ready acceptance of your role makes you every bit as morally corrupt as you seem to think me to be. Your actions most certainly are not those one would consider to be appropriate for a lady. Not a true one, at any rate."

Her mouth dropped open in her affront and she emitted an outraged squeak. Jerking her arm from his to brace her hands on her hips in a stance that was no doubt calculated to convey the magnitude of her indignity, she expelled, "And what, pray tell, do you know of ladies?"

"A great deal more than you, judging from your present behavior."

She ejected a scornful noise, halfway between a sniff and a snort. "I would wager that you never met a real lady before insinuating yourself into the *ton.*"

"Then it is a good thing that we are not wagering, for you would lose," he countered in a reasonable voice. "I have met a great many women in my time who I would readily term as such, most of whom will never set foot in your exalted *ton.*"

Her arms were folded across her chest now. "Indeed? Well, then. Since you style yourself as such an authority on the virtues that qualify a woman to be termed a lady, pray do share your vast knowledge."

"Gladly, but do you not think that it would be advisable

to resume our stroll while I do so? We most certainly would not want your aunt to spirit you away before you have received the full benefit of my instruction." He presented his arm with a flourish.

She stared at it as if it were the most contemptible thing in the world and that in merely touching it she would suffer some sort of repulsive contamination. Then she sighed and took it.

As they embarked on their second turn around the garden perimeter, Gideon lectured, "A true lady is many things. She is charitable, compassionate, humble, considerate, selfless, and, of course, gracious to a fault. She is also brave yet modest, capable, sensible, merciful, and devoted to the welfare of those around her." He was thinking of his mother as he uttered that last, and her unfailing benevolence toward all she met, whether they were deserving of her goodness or not.

Smiling briefly at his fond memory, he continued, "Above all, a true lady is genuinely gentle and kind. She does not judge a person as less deserving of her respect just because he possesses fewer worldly goods than she, is less educated, or is born into an unfortunate set of circumstances. She most certainly does not judge on looks, for she is wise enough to know that those with the fairest faces can harbor the ugliest hearts, while those who are ill favored can have souls blinding in their beauty. She also does not judge from the gossip she hears. A true lady reserves her judgment for when she can honestly claim to know a person, which is to say that she knows him heart, soul, and mind—that is, if she judges him at all. The finest ladies of all understand that it is not their place to judge, and they simply accept a person, flaws and all, in hopes that others will accept her in the same generous spirit."

"If the women you describe are as impossibly perfect as all that, I daresay that they need never fear that others will not accept them," Lady Julia pointed out with a sniff.

"Then you mistake what I say, for the truest ladies are far from perfect, and never try to deceive anyone into believing that they are. They—"

She cut him off with a derogatory noise. "Such stuff and

nonsense! A true lady takes pains to correct her faults, just as she always strives to present herself in the best possible light. A *true* lady has a cultivated understanding of what is expected of her at all times, and possesses a thorough knowledge of her society's mores, manners and ceremonies that enables her to behave in a manner that closely approximates its ideal of perfection."

"Ah, but the manners that make a true lady go beyond the empty gestures and rote pleasantries taught for the sake of appearances," he rebutted. "Her every word and gesture is a sincere expression of her inner goodness, goodness being at the core of every true lady."

"By which, I suppose, you mean to imply that I possess no goodness." She out-and-out snorted in her annoyance, which in Gideon's book was very unladylike indeed, though he had to admit that he far preferred her snorts to her sniffs. "I must say that you take a great deal upon yourself in thinking that you know me well enough to render such a judgment."

"I am not judging you, I am merely doing as you requested and sharing my views on what makes a lady," he smoothly returned. "If you find yourself wanting in comparison—"

"Indeed I do not, sir," she snapped. "What you have described thus far is a most undisciplined sort of female, one whose manners and bearing would make her a scandal in the *ton.*"

He nodded. "A terrible scandal, yes. Nonetheless, it is exactly the sort of lady into which I desire my sister to grow. In view of that fact, surely you can see why our bargain will never do."

"Yes, I can. I can also see that you are doing your sister a dreadful disservice by denying her the chance to learn to be the sort of lady possessed of the breeding to elevate her station in life. For despite what you may think, Mr. Harwood, as much as you may wish her to be accepted and admired for her naturalness and the goodness of her heart, the fact of the matter is that society has put forth a set slate of rules dictating how a lady must act. And unless she learns to observe them and behave in the prescribed manner, she will never be granted the opportunity to display her finer qualities. My sisters are—"

"Your sisters are exactly the sorts of chits I do not wish my sister to be."

Her face contorted in outrage, the fragments of her polite facade collapsing beneath the weight of her affront at his insult to her siblings. "I will have you know, sir, that my sisters are the dearest creatures in the entire world. And in declaring that you do not wish your sister to be like them, you are saying that you do not wish her to be loving, and obedient, and graceful, and beautiful, and everything else that is fine and good. Why, you could not find a more perfect pair of darlings than my sisters should you search all of England."

"They most certainly are perfect, I shall grant you that," he grated harshly. "Rather too perfect for my taste. They are like a pair of dolls, pretty and wooden, and wholly lacking in the natural merriment and energy of youth."

"And who is guilty of judging unjustly now? You have seen my sisters but once, sir, and under circumstances where displays of youthful energy would be viewed as highly improper." Her nose had risen in the air as far as it could go, and her chin had taken on a decidedly defiant set. "After all of your high-minded nattering against the sin of groundlessly judging others, you certainly seem eager to do exactly that." A sniff. "Then again, why should I be surprised that you would do so? As in the case you described of a woman being a lady, a part of what makes a man a gentleman is his wisdom to render a fair judgment. And since we have established that you shall never be a gentleman—" She raised her eyebrows, her silence pregnant with the insult of her unfinished sentence.

Gideon shrugged, refusing to be baited. "My remarks about your sisters were observations, not a judgment. If you will recall, I said that they are too perfect for my taste, thus allowing that their impeccable manners probably suit the tastes of others."

"I hardly see a difference."

"Then permit me to explain." Without awaiting her consent, he clarified, "An observation is simply a comment noting what one has seen and how they have interpreted it. As such, it allows that there are other equally valid views on the subject in question. A judgment, on the other hand, occurs when a person takes all opposing views on a subject into consideration, and renders a decision based on which one proves true in his mind."

Another sniff. "I suppose that you mean to tell me that your previous condemnation of all the females in the *ton* was not a judgment, but a mere observation?"

"No, it was a judgment. Then again, I have spent enough time in the *ton* that I feel qualified to rule on what I have seen and experienced. However, to set the record straight, I do not find all the females completely without merit."

"Indeed?" she sneered with an infuriating air of superiority. "Well, then. Perhaps you would be good enough to tell me which females have met with your approval so that I might learn from their stellar example?"

Again he refused to be baited. Nodding cordially at her request, he replied, "For all that she is viewed as exceedingly unfashionable, Lady Mina possesses a certain artlessness that is most refreshing. And I find your aunt, Lady Aurelia, exceedingly gracious and charming."

"Aunt Aurelia?" She drew back, frowning as if she could not quite believe her ears. "Surely you jest, sir?"

"I can assure you that I do not," he retorted acidly, his honor prompting him to rise to the defense of the woman who had always treated him with kindness. "I have found her ladyship's demeanor to be beyond reproach. Indeed, you would do well to learn from her example."

She emitted a singularly derogatory noise. "If you find her such a paragon, perhaps it is she whom you should wed. Please do, in fact. You would be doing us all an immense service in taking her off our hands." Her voice rose an octave with every word she spoke until she practically shouted the last line.

Gideon raised his eyebrows in amused wonder at her heated response. "My, my. Such passion. If I did not know better, I would say that you were behaving like a woman scorned, my dear." He paused to chuckle. "Do not tell me that you are jealous? That you have developed feelings for me and actually wish to wed me?"

"Of course not," she spat. "The only thing that I have developed for you is a deep and abiding distaste."

"In that instance, I should think you would be pleased by the news that you shall not have to wed me. Thrilled, in fact."

"Oh, I am thrilled—beyond thrilled! And if I never see you again, I shall count myself the most fortunate woman in the world."

He sketched his most elegant bow. "Your wish is my command, my dear. Let it never be said that I do not honor a lady's wishes."

CHAPTER 10

It was impossible. She could not do it. She simply did not have the courage.

Julia gripped the black iron railing outside of Gideon Harwood's Grosvenor Square residence, her knees growing weak as she gazed up at the modest yet substantial brown brick town house with its red dressings and keystone-crowned windows. But she must do it. She had no choice. Somehow, somewhere, she had to find the mettle to march up to that door and demand to see the master of the house.

The very thought of doing so made her tighten her hold on the railing, a grasp that clenched into a convulsive stranglehold of panic as she was assailed by another, even more daunting consideration: What would she do if he actually consented to see her? What could she possibly say to convince him to reconsider their bargain and compel him to wed her?

And wed him she must. For if she did not, she and her siblings would most certainly be tossed into the street, destitute and disgraced, while her parents faced the ghastly prospect of debtors' prison. At least that was the grim picture her father had painted the night before when he had called her into his study in response to a note he had received from Mr. Harwood, which he had read aloud. And a most hateful note it was, curtly phrased and devoid of the perfunctory yet placating courtesies that usually prefaced a missive bearing ill tidings.

Oh, true. She supposed that the tidings might not be considered so very bad if one could judge them by their words alone. After all, the beastly man had promised to uphold his end of the bargain, even as he released them from all obligations of theirs. But as her father had pointed out, and quite astutely she might add, a promise from a blackguard like Mr. Harwood could in no way be trusted, especially in view of the fact that he had not returned the debt voucher her father said her mother had signed. He had then gone on to explain how their family would remain poised on the brink of ruin for as long as the villain possessed that voucher, and how they would be completely at his mercy, slaves to his every wish and whim for fear that he would call the ruinous debt due.

To say that their situation was dire would be a vast understatement, and it was unlikely to improve any time soon, if ever, unless, of course, she could somehow change Mr. Harwood's mind about the bargain and persuade him to wed her. After all, even an unscrupulous character like Gideon Harwood would not stoop so very low as to ruin his wife's family. He would not dare. Not if he wished to continue his business dealings in town, the majority of which currently involved the purchase of various London properties from *ton* members.

At least that was the sort of business Amy said he was engaged in, and the slyboots should certainly know, thanks to her talent for wheedling from her father any information she desired. It was a talent she had been practicing quite rigorously of late, ever since Mr. Harwood had begun courting Julia, a talent that had unearthed numerous tidbits about the man, most of which astounded her. Why, had she not known better, his lordship's glowing accounts would have led her to believe Gideon Harwood to be a man of sterling character.

Indeed, according to Lord Shepley's reports, Mr. Harwood was regarded as exceedingly honest and trustworthy in London's most prestigious business circles. And while the *ton*'s social doors were closed to him—well, at least they had been before she had feigned an attachment to him—the men of the *beau monde* were more than eager to include him when it came to matters of finance and commerce. They were also said to respect him. If Lord Shepley could be believed—and why would he lie?—both Gideon Harwood's intellect and ethics were held in high regard. So high, in fact, that his opinion on matters of business was frequently solicited by those in lofty places. In short, he was much admired by Lord Shepley and his circle. And as everyone in London knew, Lord Shepley's circle was comprised of the most influential and discriminating men in the realm.

Wondering at Mr. Harwood's ability to deceive a group of such astute men, Julia pried her fingers from the railing and urged her suddenly leaden feet in the direction of his front steps. Then again, why should she be surprised? The man could be exceedingly charming and agreeable when he put his mind to being so, something she had observed first-hand during their brief courtship.

In point of fact, Caro considered him to be quite the gallant, while Mina seemed half in love with him. The Duke of Dollimore had dubbed him a capital fellow and had been seen riding on Rotten Row with him, a very high compliment indeed. And then there were the estimable Lords Mellanby, Crankshaw, and Pettiford, all of whom rallied around him at every gathering and were said to frequently call at his home. Why, even the perpetually disapproving Aurelia approved of him, having pronounced him a most pleasing gentleman. As did her mother, whose coquettish fawning over the vile beast was an embarrassment to behold.

Julia sighed. Truth be told, she could not really blame them for feeling as they did. If she were to be brutally honest, she would have to admit that she, too, would be taken with Gideon Harwood were she not aware of his true character. He was rather handsome, after all, in an aggressively masculine way. Yes, and his manners were remarkably elegant for a commoner. Then there was the matter of his meticulous grooming. Not only was his clothing always immaculately clean, his dark hair gleamed as if washed each day, and he smelled of soap rather than the heavy perfume that so many men used to conceal their

disdain for bathing. Oh, and one must not forget his excellent teeth. Or his intriguing air of mystery. Or the warm,
husky timbre of his laughter and the way the hard lines of
his face softened when he smiled. Or—

Or the fact that he is a blackmailing wretch, Julia harshly
reminded herself, discomfited by the odd sense of yearning
that threatened to overcome her as she pictured that fascinating smile. But enough of such featherbrained musings!
She had far more pressing concerns to occupy her mind
than how the blasted man looked and smelled, such as how
she was going to persuade him to marry her.

Now standing at the shallow flight of stone stairs leading
up to his door, Julia contemplated that very question. It
was the same one that had robbed her of her sleep the
night before, making her toss and turn and grow dizzy from
her whirling thoughts. As had happened then, she was no
closer to finding an answer now, at least none that offered
hope of success for her quest.

She sighed again. Well, for all her indecision there was
one thing for certain, and that was that she could not stand
in front of Mr. Harwood's house all day. Indeed, should
anyone of consequence see her loitering there, on foot and
unchaperoned, there was sure to be a scandal, the shame
from which her mother would never recover. Or so her
mother would claim.

Wincing at the thought of the lectures she would be
forced to endure from her parents should such a catastro-
phe come to pass, Julia shot a nervous glance about her,
making certain that she was unobserved. Save for several
tradesmen making deliveries to the houses, a crossing
sweeper clearing the foulness left by horses the night before, and an assortment of street hawkers crying their wares
to the servants who had stepped from the dwellings to purchase the daily household needs, there was no one to mark
her presence. Then again, it was scarcely past eight in the
morning, far too early for the occupants of the houses on
the fashionable square to venture forth, which was exactly
why she had selected this time of day for her clandestine
assignation. To be sure, not only was her potentially ruinous visit to a bachelor household unlikely to be observed,

the earliness of the hour all but ensured that Gideon Harwood would be at home.

True, but the hour is not getting any younger for your procrastination, she sternly reminded herself. Heaving another sigh, this one in resignation to her duty, Julia ascended the first of the five front steps, her mind again grappling for a plan to swing the pendulum of Mr. Harwood's favor back toward marriage to her.

She climbed to step number two as she mused. Hmmm. She supposed that she could appeal to his vanity. Yes, she could pretend to have become hopelessly enamored with his person and try to convince him that she wished to marry him out of a newly awakened sense of love.

Step number three. But was she actress enough to play such a scene convincingly? Another sigh. No, probably not. Besides, Mr. Harwood hardly seemed the sort of man to fall for such a transparent ploy.

Step number four. Well then, maybe she should try apologizing, though exactly what that would accomplish she did not know. Simply apologizing for losing her temper in the garden would neither address his reasons for withdrawing from the bargain, nor would it revise his intent to do so. On the other hand, she would probably do well to do so, so as to prevent him from thinking her to be impossibly ill-tempered.

Step five. Fine. She would apologize and then she would—she would what? Again she delved into her tangled thoughts, straightening an abstraction here, unknotting a concept there, until—aha! She hit upon a new idea: she would plead on behalf of her siblings and throw herself on his mercy. He did, after all, seem to harbor an inordinate fondness for his younger sister, at least judging from their conversation in the garden, so he was bound to be sympathetic toward the plight of her sisters and brother.

Then again, probably not. She stood on the stoop now. How could she possibly hope to gain his sympathy toward children he disliked as much as he did her sisters? And it was apparent from his comments that he regarded them with implacable displeasure.

Before she could further contemplate that disheartening

detail, the door swung open and a maidservant carrying a bucket and scrub brush stepped backward over the threshold, laughing raucously at something the man accompanying her said. As she turned in an abrupt twirl to face forward, the fitfulness of her movement due, no doubt, to her state of frenzied hilarity, the soapy contents of her bucket splattered far and wide, showering the front of Julia's fashionable golden brown silk pelisse. Her brand-new pelisse, to be exact.

Julia gasped her dismay at the sight of the widening splotches. Oh! And after all the effort she had put forth to look nice for Mr. Harwood.

"Gor, miss," the girl expelled in breathless horror, her blue eyes round and growing bright with tears as she gaped at the calamitous results of her recklessness. "If I'd known ye was 'ere, I'd 'ave—I'd 'ave nivver—" She broke off with a rending sob, her plain, freckled face crumpling as she began to weep in earnest. "0-0-0! Jist look at yer loverly coat, miss. Courter's gonna sack me fer sure this time."

"Now, now, Peg. We will have none of that," chided the man who had provoked the maid's ungoverned mirth, calmly surveying the mishap from the threshold. He was a roguish-looking fellow with a shock of unruly black hair and gypsy-dark eyes that presently regarded Julia with an interest that she found far too bold by half. "I am sure that our master will square matters right enough with Miss—" He raised one eyebrow in query, impertinently bidding Julia to present her name.

"Lady Julia Barham," she supplied in her most aristocratic tone, emphasizing the word "lady" in an attempt to put him in his place.

The maid emitted a short shriek, the contents of the bucket again sloshing over the brim in her agitation. "Lady? Oh, gor! I'm sacked fer certain, I is."

"You shall be sacked if you do not stop your screeching," the man retorted, his face registering what Julia found a satisfying degree of surprise at her identity. "Now to the kitchen with you, girl. You can scrub the stoop later."

The maid sniffled and bobbed a curtsy to Julia, her face as tragic as if she bore the knowledge that the world would end tomorrow. Then again, for her, perhaps it would if she lost her place. "I'm 'eartily sorry, my lady," she said in a jumbled rush. "I dinna mean to spoil yer coat. Truly, I dinna. I—"

"It was an accident, nothing more. So please do not give the matter a second thought," Julia interjected, the precariousness of her own situation giving her a new understanding, and sympathy, for the girl's fear of losing her place. Like she and her siblings, Peg, too, would no doubt find herself begging in the streets if Mr. Harwood chose to withhold his mercy. "As for the Courter person you fear will sack you, I see no reason whatsoever why they need ever hear of the incident. The same goes for your master. I take it that we can trust—" It was her turn to solicit the man's name, which she did by peering at him down her nose with an air of condescending expectation.

He bowed in an appropriately subservient manner. "Simon Rowles, Mr. Harwood's majordomo. At your service, my lady."

Majordomo? Though Julia had easily identified him by his speech and clothing as one of the upper servants, his youth had led her to assume him to be a footman on his way to enjoy a morning off, or perhaps Mr. Harwood's valet. Repressing the urge to frown in her surprise, she coolly inquired, "I take it that you can be trusted to hold your tongue in regard to this matter, Rowles?"

He nodded. "But of course, my lady. Whatever you wish."

She nodded back. "It is indeed my wish."

The girl graced her with a watery, but exceedingly grateful smile. "Oh, thank ye, my lady. Thank ye! Ye can be certain that Peg McCain ain't nivver gonna fergit yer kindness."

Rowles inclined his head in approval at the maid's speech. "Very nicely said, Peg. Now to the kitchen with you." He snapped his fingers three times, spurring her to obey.

She bobbed another curtsy to Julia, and then did as directed, but not before casting her benefactress another thankful smile.

When she had disappeared from sight, Rowles said, "That was most gracious of you, my lady. I daresay that this is only the second time in her unfortunate life that poor Peg has been granted such kindness from a stranger."

"The second?" Her sympathy for the girl now piqued, Julia found herself genuinely interested to hear the story at which the majordomo hinted.

"Yes. The first being when Mr. Harwood saved her."

"He saved her?" This time Julia could not refrain from frowning her surprise. "How?"

"He discovered her lying in our alley about a month ago, burning with fever. No doubt she would have perished had he not given her shelter and summoned the surgeon." He shook his head. "However, I need not tell you of my master's generous nature, my lady. I daresay that you know it well enough."

Julia could only stare at him, too stunned by his account to do anything more. That the villainous Gideon Harwood was capable of such compassion was almost beyond belief.

"But, of course, I am certain that you did not come here to discuss such things with me," Rowles added, skillfully guiding the conversation back to the business at hand. "No doubt you wish to see Mr. Harwood?"

She nodded. "Yes, please. It is imperative that I speak with him posthaste on a matter of great importance." Her heart sank in the next instant as the majordomo's face took on a look of genuine regret.

"I am sorry, my lady. But Mr. Harwood is not at home. There was a last bit of business that required his attention before he leaves for the country this afternoon."

Her sinking heart abruptly plunged to the pit of her stomach at the news of his impending departure. "Mr. Harwood is leaving?"

The majordomo frowned, visibly perplexed. "He has business at his estate in Lancashire. Surely he informed you of his plans?"

"No." She more squeaked than uttered the word in her distress. If he left London now, she might never get the chance to plead her case. Indeed, there was a distinct dan-

ger that he would call her mother's debt due before returning to town.

Rowles's frown deepened at her response. "Do pardon
me if I overstep my bounds, my lady. But I must confess
to being surprised."

"I do not know what you mean," she mumbled, her mind
barely registering his remark in her anxiety.

"It is just that there isn't a servant in Mayfair who has
not heard that our master is courting you, and that the *ton*
expects you to be engaged before the end of the Season.
That being the case, I should have thought that you would
be the first person he would inform of his plans."

Not about to report that his master had jilted her, she
replied, "Perhaps he knows how sorely I shall miss him,
and has thus decided to tell me the news today, before he
leaves, so as to save me from fretting over his departure."
She surprised even herself with the smoothness of her lie.

He accepted her fabrication with a nod and a smile. "Ah,
yes. I am certain that that is indeed the case. It is just like
Mr. Harwood to be so very considerate."

"Yes," Julia murmured, feeling suddenly ill as a new and
horrifying thought struck her. What if the business that
commanded Mr. Harwood's attention so early in the day
was the calling in of her mother's debt? It made perfect
sense that he should wish to do so now, after the dreadful
scene in the garden. The more she considered the possibility, the more likely it seemed. Indeed, what else could it
be?

"My lady, are you quite all right?" Rowles inquired, both
his face and voice reflecting alarm.

"I-I am fine," she somehow managed to squeeze past the
dread strangling her throat.

He shook his head, unconvinced. "You do not look fine.
You look ready to faint." He stepped back then, holding
the door wide to reveal an elegantly appointed foyer.
"Please. Do come in and rest, my lady. Mr. Harwood will
never forgive me if I do not take proper care of you. Your
abigail—" He halted abruptly, glancing up and down the
street, his dark eyebrows drawing together as if suddenly

noticing that she was alone. "By the bye, where is your maid?"

Julia thought quickly. "She is in the Grosvenor Square Park." Deciding that it was a viable lie, she added, "She begged so prettily to stroll through it while I conversed with your master that I simply did not have the heart to deny her petition." The truth, of course, was that she had not brought a maid at all since she did not wish anyone to know of her shocking mission.

To her relief, the majordomo readily accepted her explanation. "I can see that you are every bit as kind as our master," he said, gazing at her with such approval that Julia could not help feeling shamed by her lie. "Nonetheless, it was highly improper for her to leave you as she did. You must give me her name so that I can have her fetched while you rest. In the meantime, I will have Mrs. Courter, the housekeeper, see to your needs."

"No, no thank you, Rowles. That shall not be necessary. I truly am fine," she replied, her voice surprisingly confident for her growing panic at being caught in her lie. As she spoke, she slowly backed away from the door.

"At the very least, you must allow me to summon a footman to escort you in your search for your maid. I cannot in good conscience allow you to wander the square unattended. Or perhaps I should have Mr. Harwood's carriage take you home? I know that he would—"

"No, but thank you, Rowles." She injected a note of firmness into her voice, one that brooked no argument. "Now I shall bid you a good day." Without waiting for him to respond, Julia retreated from the door as quickly as she could without compromising her semblance of composure. Well aware that he watched her go, she crossed the street at a deceptively leisurely pace and entered the park, disappearing down one of the graveled paths to take refuge behind the cover of the lush shrubbery.

As soon as she was certain that she was out of sight, she collapsed on the nearest bench and surrendered to her despair. She had failed in her mission, miserably. That meant that she and her siblings would most probably be reduced to begging on the streets within a fortnight.

And it would all be her fault.

She hugged herself, tears trickling down her cheeks as she wallowed in her remorse. Oh, if only she had tried harder to charm Gideon Harwood. If only she had kept her temper in check when he had announced that he was calling off the bargain, and had instead worked to change his mind by showing through her example that he was wrong about the women in the *ton*. If only . . .

Oh, what did it matter? Julia sobbed her defeat. Their fates were sealed and there was nothing to be done for it now.

CHAPTER 11

Shweet! Tat! Tat! Tat!

"Vah mujhakō chirhātā hai,"—he teases me—Jagtar said, scowling up at Kesin, who dangled upside down by his feet from a tree branch. In spite of the pains the Sikh took to keep his pet restrained on those occasions when he accompanied Gideon about town on business, the cunning little beast had somehow learned to liberate himself from his tether, a trick he had demonstrated a quarter-hour earlier as they had passed this particularly tempting stand of lime trees edging Grosvenor Square Park.

Gideon, who never failed to be amused by the pair's madcap antics, laughed at the droll picture they made. It did indeed appear that Kesin taunted his master, having first led him on a wild chase around the perimeter of the park, weaving in and out between the narrow iron fence rails to elude capture every time Jagtar lunged near enough to seize him. And now hanging mere inches out of reach, chirping and whistling as if mocking the Sikh's failure to catch him.

Laughing again, Gideon glanced around the square, scanning the milling street hawkers and their wares in search of fruit with which to lure the animal from the tree. It took only a moment to spy what he sought, and a moment more to make his purchase. Thus armed, he returned to where Kesin hung, the beast now swaying as he twittered and scratched what was no doubt a flea on his belly. Temptingly waving his juicy offering, he called, "*Kesin! Mīthē angūr*"—sweet grapes—hoping to appeal to the creature's voracious greed for fruit.

The recalcitrant beast pulled itself up to crouch on the branch, emitting a series of sharp chirps as it stood peering down at the grapes with owl-eyed interest.

"*Mīthē angūr*," Gideon repeated, again waving the succulent purple bribe. For several seconds he was certain that the animal would accept his inducement, unable to resist the temptation of grapes. Then it grunted once and turned its back, making a show as it began to groom its woolly fur with its comblike lower teeth.

Jagtar sighed, his voice brisk with frustration as he pleaded in his native tongue, "Have pity on me. This habit of yours is very bad."

Kesin ignored him.

The Sikh sighed again and shook his turbaned head, saying to Gideon, "I feel he won't come. He is very careless."

As if loath to disappoint his master's low expectations, Kesin grunted once and whistled twice, then grasped the branch of the neighboring tree into which he quickly disappeared, thus proving that a slow loris was not always so very slow.

Expelling a foul oath in his native tongue, Jagtar raced around the railed perimeter of the park in pursuit and disappeared through the nearest entrance gate.

Gideon followed at a more dignified pace, chuckling and shaking his head. He had just passed through the gate when the air was rent by a piercing scream, a high-pitched female one, to be exact, coming from the direction in which Kesin and Jagtar had disappeared. Wondering which of his companions had provoked it, and there was no doubt whatsoever in his mind that the unexpected sight of one or the other had prompted it, Gideon lengthened his stride, heroically rushing to the woman's rescue.

Not, of course, that she would actually require rescuing if the source of her alarm was indeed the abrupt appearance of the Sikh or his queer pet. To be sure, for all his ferocious looks, Jagtar was gallant to the point of being chivalrous when it came to women. As for Kesin, well, he

was tame enough . . . unless he was hungry, in which instance he could be bold, especially if presented with the
opportunity to steal food, fruit in particular.

Suddenly recalling a recent incident in which the beast
had assaulted the housekeeper's bonnet as she had primped
for church before the foyer mirror, Gideon quickened his
jog to a run. The bonnet in question had been trimmed
with artificial cherries, and the loris being an animal was
naturally unable to distinguish at a glance real fruit from
the artificial fruit that was all the rage for trimming ladies
hats and coiffures.

As he rounded a particularly dense hedge, he heard another shriek and a panicked, "Help! Oh, please! Somebody
help me," followed by a plea in Jagtar's unmistakable voice
as he sought to calm the terrified woman. Since the soothing words were being uttered in his native tongue, a lapse
due, no doubt, to the Sikh's own panic in the face of the
woman's hysterics, they failed to have their desired effect.
A half-dozen more steps and Gideon burst upon the scene.

The woman, who was clearly highborn, judging from her
expensive brown silk pelisse and matching bonnet, the latter of which was trimmed with artificial apricots and
knocked askew to obscure her features, was poised in a
defensive crouch behind a park bench, using it as a barrier
to shield herself against Jagtar and Kesin, both of whom
looked every bit as terrified of her as she was of them.
Indeed, poor Kesin stood frozen directly in front of the
bench, where he had no doubt tumbled after what Gideon
suspected had been his foiled attempt at apricot larceny,
while Jagtar helplessly flailed his arms and gibbered in
Hindi, something that the woman seemed to interpret as
a threat.

As he watched, she popped up from behind her cover,
waving a handful of pebbles menacingly at the Sikh, shouting, "Go away! I shall stone you if you do not leave this
instant! I swear I shall!"

Gideon's eyes narrowed as her bonnet shifted with her
movement, granting him a glimpse of the ringlets peeking
from beneath the brim. They were a distinct color, a rather

familiar shade of pale golden red. Surely their owner was not—could not possibly be—

"Lady Julia?" he ejected in querying incredulity.

She froze, her arm now raised and poised to hurl the stones. In the next instant her head whipped around, her eyes widening and her jaw dropping at the sight of him. Staring, as if she could not quite believe her eyes, she choked out, "M-Mr. H-Harwood?"

"Lady Julia?" he responded in an equally stunned tone, wondering what in the world she was doing in Grosvenor Square at such an unfashionably early hour.

Her arm dropped and there was a *plink! plonk! plunk!* as the pebbles tumbled in a pelting shower from her hand, one of which scattered wide to box Kesin in the nose.

G-r-r-r! Roused from its terrified trance, the creature growled and scampered back to its master, who kneeled to allow it to climb to his shoulder.

"Mr. Harwood?" she repeated, this time more loudly.

Gideon frowned, suddenly noting the redness of her eyes and nose, and the dampness streaking her cheeks. It was apparent that she had been weeping, and for far longer than the brief moments during which she had been frightened by Jagtar and Kesin. His frown deepening in his concern, he urgently inquired, "What has happened, Lady Julia? Are you hurt?"

"Oh, Mr. Harwood!" She more wailed than uttered the words. Before Gideon quite knew what was happening, she had flung herself at him, her arms hurling around his waist to cling to him. Gripping him as if he were her only salvation, she sobbed, "I have never been so very happy to see anyone in my entire life!"

Gideon stiffened beneath her hugging assault, astounded that the impossibly restrained Lady Julia would behave in such a—well, an unrestrained manner. Then he felt her tremble in a series of shuddering sobs and realized that she had resumed weeping. Instinctively wrapping her in his comforting embrace, he held her close, alternately patting and stroking her heaving back as he soothingly crooned, "There, there now, my lady. You are safe. Nothing shall harm you." To his surprise, he found that he rather liked the feel of her in his arms. For all that she was overly slender for his taste, she felt remarkably soft and feminine molded as she was against his body.

"Safe?" She sniffled and tipped her head back to gaze up at him with damp-eyed gratitude, her crooked bonnet slipping off to dangle over one shoulder by its ribbon chin ties. Lady Julia most definitely was not the sort of woman who looked pretty when she wept. Indeed, not only were her eyes and nose red, her fair complexion was blotchy and she sniffled uncontrollably.

Gideon smiled faintly at the sight of her, deciding that he far preferred this blotchy, disheveled Lady Julia to the pale, perfect one. This one, at least, seemed human . . . and young . . . and vulnerable . . . and almost lost in her distress. Struck by a startling rush of protective tenderness, he smoothed a fiery tendril of hair that was stuck to her wet cheek, gently confirming, "Yes. Safe."

She sniffled several times, staring soberly at his face as she absorbed his reassurance. Then she drew in a deep, sobbing breath and expelled in a quivering rush, "It was dreadful! I have never been so frightened in my life. First the horrid beast attacked me and then I was accosted by that—that"—she hiccupped and nodded at Jagtar, who stood at a distance soothing his terrified pet—"that fiend!" Another sniffle, this one loud and watery. "I simply shudder to think what might have happened to me had you not come to my rescue."

"I can assure you that you were never in the least bit of danger," he replied, her latest sniffle cuing him to retrieve his handkerchief from his waistcoat pocket.

Two more sniffles. "How can you"—*sob!*—"be so very certain?"

"Because the fiend is my manservant and the horrid beast is his pet."

She grew very still in his arms as she digested that tidbit of news, then sniffled again and said in a small voice, "Oh. I-I see."

Though he was surprisingly reluctant to do so, Gideon forced himself to release her, saying in a light, almost teasing voice, "At the risk of being deemed ungentlemanly for confessing to such a thing, I cannot help observing that you have a rather dire need for this." He presented his handkerchief with a grand flourish.

She smiled, a quick, spontaneous smile touched by an unexpected hint of humor, a smile that by all rights of God and man should not have made her look beautiful for her splotchy face and red eyes, but nonetheless did. "In this particular instance, I daresay that we can make an exception to the rule." Nodding once in thanks, she turned away, as she had no doubt been taught to do when dictated by necessity to tend to bodily needs while in company, and proceeded to blow her nose several times. Her nasal passages thus cleared, she pivoted back to face him, her expression sheepish.

"Better?" he inquired with a smile. How could he not smile when she looked so charmingly abashed?

"Yes. Thank you." She began to hold out his now-sodden handkerchief, intent on returning it, then pulled it back again, blushing as she murmured, "Er—I shall have this laundered and returned to you tomorrow, if that is agreeable?"

He shrugged. "Anytime will be fine. As it so happens, I have more than one handkerchief to my name."

She stuffed the object in question into her reticule, her lips curving into a half smile at his response. "Yes. I daresay that you do, though a gentleman should know better than to boast of such wealth." By her tone it was apparent that she had just attempted a jest.

Gideon chuckled his appreciation of her effort. "A thousand pardons, my lady. I see that I must redouble my efforts to mend my ways if I am ever to be counted a gentleman."

"As must I, if I am to remain worthy of being called a lady." She sighed and shook her head, her smile fading. "I fear that I owe your manservant rather more than a thousand pardons." Another sigh and headshake. "Poor man. I had no call to shriek at him as I did. He did nothing to warrant such rudeness, not really. His wicked pet, on the other hand—" She broke off with a wry face.

Again Gideon chuckled. When she left off her airs, she was delightful. Was this the Lady Julia the *ton* saw and admired? Finding himself unexpectedly admiring her as well, he replied, "Would it, perhaps, ease your mind if I were to tell you that you are not the first person to find their appearances alarming?" At her nod, he nodded back. "Well, it is true. You might also find it comforting to hear that in spite of their frightening looks, they are usually quite tame."

She seemed to consider his claim for a moment before accepting it with a faint smile and a nod. "If they are indeed as tame as you say, then I must beg an introduction. A lady cannot speak to a gentleman unless she is properly introduced to him, you know; therefore I cannot apologize to your servant unless introductions are made. And since I wish to begin mending my ways immediately . . ." She finished with a meaningful lift of her delicate eyebrows.

He sketched an abbreviated bow and offered her his arm. "Your servant, as always, my lady."

After placing her bonnet back on her head and making the necessary adjustments to right it, she took his arm, countering, "Spoken like a true gentleman, Mr. Harwood."

"I am glad to hear that I am making such rapid improvement. At this rate, I may actually qualify as a gentleman in, oh, I would estimate about ten years time, given my woeful lack of socially acceptable manners," he bantered.

Rather than laugh and banter back, as he expected her to do, she remained silent, gazing at the ground as they walked several steps. When she finally looked up again, her face was serious. "I am afraid that I owe you an apology as well, sir."

His eyebrows rose in his surprise. "Indeed?"

Nodding, she came to a halt. "I-I was wrong to make you think that your manners are in any way lacking. On the whole, they are excellent. They quite put to shame those of many of the *ton*'s finest gentlemen. Though I know that it by no means excuses my disgraceful behavior, I can only plead distress over the bargain as justification of my actions. I do hope that you can find it in your heart to forgive me, for I truly am sorry."

It was Gideon's turn to be struck silent, taken aback not
only by her apology, but by the humility with which it was
uttered. At length, he replied, "I will forgive you only if
you pardon me in return. I fear that I have not been so
very gentlemanly in the way I have baited you during this
past month." And he was indeed guilty of doing so,
pricking and twitting her at every turn in an attempt to
fracture her cool facade.

She glanced at him quickly, visibly surprised by his
words. Then she laughed and saucily volleyed, "But of
course I forgive you, sir. How can I not forgive the man
who so gallantly dashed to my rescue?" Her pardon thus
granted, they walked the rest of the distance to where the
Sikh and his pet stood, Lady Julia smiling in a way that
stunned Gideon with the radiance it lent her face. How in
the world could he have ever thought her plain?

Now stopping before Jagtar and Kesin, Gideon promptly
put his manners to use in making the requested introductions, which her ladyship acknowledged with a charm that
clearly enchanted Jagtar. When she had tendered her apology, the graciousness of her words and the sincerity of her
voice further winning Gideon's heart, she turned her attention to Kesin. Tipping her head in wonder as she gazed at
the exotic little primate, she exclaimed, "Such an odd creature! What sort of beast is it?"

"It is called a *sharmindi-billi*, my lady," Jagtar replied in
a respectful voice, dipping his head in deference to her
station.

Her brow furrowed as she tested the words on her
tongue. "*Sharmindi-billi.*" She darted the Sikh a querying
look, mutely inquiring if she had pronounced the name correctly. When he smiled and nodded, she looked thrilled by
her success.

"The English name for the creatures is slow loris," Gideon supplied, thinking how engaging she was in her almost
childlike curiosity. "They are often used by snake charmers
in India to draw crowds in marketplaces, rather in the same
fashion the street conjurer we saw at the balloon ascension
used his monkey to lure an audience. In fact, that is how
Kesin earned his keep until Jagtar took a fancy to him

and purchased him from his owner." Gideon grinned just
remembering the fierceness of the bargaining battle. In the
end the Sikh had paid an exorbitant price for the animal,
far more than its market value, but worth twice the price
for the entertainment it provided them.

"Then its name is Kesin?" she inquired, laughing as the
animal mirrored her move by tipping its nubby-eared head
to solemnly return her gaze. "I must say that that is a very
fitting name indeed in that it is as queer as its owner."

Gideon, too, laughed, enjoying her delight in the beast.
"It means long-haired beggar in Jagtar's native tongue, and
you are correct in that it is most appropriate. Why, one
would think that Kesin is never fed from the way he constantly begs for treats."

She continued her examination of the loris in captivated
silence for several moments, tipping her head this way and
that as she did so, her movements comically imitated by
the object of her scrutiny. At length, she shyly asked, "Do
you suppose that he would allow me to pet him? My sisters,
Maria in particular, adore animals, and they will be ever
so disappointed if I do not touch him and report the texture
of his fur."

It was on the tip of Gideon's tongue to propose that
Jagtar introduce Kesin to the children, the pleasure of Julia's company making him momentarily forget that he had
abandoned their courtship. Remembering in the next instant, he swallowed the offer, suffering a sharp pang of
regret as he replied, "As I mentioned earlier, he is quite
tame. However, since he has had as much of a fright as
you this morning, he might be a bit uneasy with the notion
of being handled by a stranger. Perhaps—"

Struck by sudden inspiration, he glanced around the
ground, searching for the grapes he had dropped when she
had flung herself into his arms. Now spying them and seeing
that they were only slightly worse for their unceremonious
tumble, he retrieved them, amending, "He will no doubt
be more than happy to oblige you if you present him with
a peace offering." He held up the grapes, eliciting a whistle
from Kesin. "The little thief cannot resist fruit, which is
most probably why he attacked you." At her look of incom-

prehension, he explained, "The apricots on your bonnet
look very real, and Kesin has developed a special fondness
for apricots since coming to England. My guess is that he
spied them and sought to steal one."

"I daresay that he would have been most disappointed
had he succeeded in his crime," she said with a laugh, taking the grapes. Now dangling them temptingly before the
loris, she coaxed him in a soothing voice to accept them.
It took only a moment for him to snatch them and begin
greedily devouring them.

Again her head tipped in her wonder, her expression
spellbound as she watched the animal eat. "Just look at his
hands," she marveled in an awed tone. "Why, they look
almost human."

"I can assure you that the presumptuous beast quite fan-
cies himself to be human from the way the entire household
dotes on him," Gideon responded wryly.

His companions laughed at his joke, the Sikh with reser-
vation and Lady Julia with unbridled gaiety.

Gideon grinned at their amusement. "Now, I believe that
you wish to pet him?"

"Mmm, yes," she murmured, her fascinated gaze still
fixed on Kesin, who was emitting little grunts as he stuffed
yet another grape into his mouth. "Just let me remove my
gloves." She diverted her attention long enough to draw
off her tan kid gloves and tuck them into her reticule. Rais-
ing her now-bare hand to commence with petting, she said
in a loud whisper, "How . . . I mean, where should I . . . ?"
She glanced helplessly at Gideon, searching for instruction
on how to proceed.

"Like this." He laid his hand over hers, ushering it to
the top of the animal's head where he guided it to stroke
down its back. As he did so, he could not help noticing
how delicate her hand felt, or how neatly it fit beneath the
curve of his palm. When Kesin remained calm, placidly
feasting on his treat, he drew his hand from hers, nodding
for her to repeat the action on her own.

Without further encouragement, she did so, stroking the
creature almost gingerly at first, growing more confident
with each caress. By now the redness and blotchiness had

all but disappeared from her face, leaving in their place a
pair of sparkling eyes and silken cheeks flushed with becoming color. At length, she murmured, "Such thick, lovely
fur . . . and so soft. Oh! I cannot wait to tell Jemima and
Maria about Kesin. I simply must see if I can find a book
with a picture and a description of slow lorises. I just know
that they will be every bit as enchanted as I am by the
creatures."

"You seem to love your sisters a great deal," he observed, not missing the raw affection in her voice every
time she spoke of them.

"More than anything on this earth. There is nothing that
I would not do or sacrifice for them," she fiercely declared.
"And I love my brother just as much. Little Bertie is just
over a year old and is ever so precious."

Gideon stared at her in stunned silence, caught off guard
by the unfettered fervor of her response. Then again, after
the way she had flown to her sisters' defense at his criticism
of them during their exchange in the garden, it should
hardly come as a surprise to learn of the depth of her devotion to them. Now realizing how very callous his remarks
had been and wishing to in some way make amends for
wounding her feelings, he said, "Perhaps you would do me
the honor of allowing me to present your siblings with a
book on the subject of India's creatures? I have a particularly fine volume with numerous color plates and descrip-
tions, slow lorises numbering among them."

She could not have looked more amazed, or thrilled, by
his offer. "You would do that?" she inquired in a breathless rush.

He nodded. "It will be my pleasure. I shall send it around
tomorrow, if that is convenient?"

She looked away quickly, but not before he saw her
cheeks infuse with riotous color. "I-I was rather hoping that
you might bring it around yourself," she murmured, her
gaze firmly glued to Kesin as she resumed petting him.

Gideon narrowed his eyes, his suspicions aroused by her
unexpected invitation. Wondering at her new game, he replied, "I cannot help saying that I am surprised that you

would harbor such a hope. I daresay that I need not explain why."

She stroked the animal several more times, then sighed and dropped her hand to her side. "Mr. Harwood, has it not occurred to you to wonder what I am doing here at this hour of the day, unattended?"

"The thought has crossed my mind, yes," he said, though in truth he had not noticed that she was alone. Then again, he was hardly accustomed to dealing with aristocratic chits who were not allowed to set so much as a toe outside their front door without an escort, so it was hardly something he would think to note.

She nodded. "Perhaps you would allow me to explain? Once I have done so, you will no doubt better understand why I harbor the hope I do."

He nodded back, brusquely. "I am listening."

"In private, please."

The fact that she sought privacy further hoisted the already raised red flag in Gideon's mind. As he had learned from past experience, a request for privacy from a member of the Barham family generally signaled the introduction of a proposal, one usually based on lies and deception. Intrigued, in spite of his determination not to be, Gideon glanced at the Sikh and said, "You may return to the house now, Jagtar. Please have my gig harnessed and brought around front in a quarter of an hour so that I can escort her ladyship home."

Jagtar brought his palms together beneath his chin and inclined his head. *"Bahut acha, Sahib"*—very good. He repeated the action to her ladyship. "My lady." That formality complete, he did as directed.

"Well," Gideon prompted when the servant was out of sight.

She gestured to the bench she had used as a shield. "Shall we sit, Mr. Harwood?" Her voice had resumed its former brittleness.

He cringed at the sound of it, instantly regretting granting her request. Nonetheless, he nodded. "As you wish, my lady."

When they were seated side by side, he again prodded, "Well?"

She refrained from responding for several moments, her hands nervously twisting the ribbon drawstrings of her reticule. Then she sighed and said, "I suppose that I should simply blurt out what I wish to say and be done with it." The brittleness had vanished, replaced by very real-sounding anxiety.

"That would be preferable, yes," he concurred, not about to be disarmed by her maidenly show of nerves.

She nodded and dropped her gaze to her hands, which continued to fret her purse strings. Taking a deep breath, as if to brace herself, she began in a frayed voice, "All right, then. The truth of the matter is that I visited your town house earlier this morning with the express purpose of begging you to reconsider our bargain. When you were not at home, I retreated here to nurse my disappointment. I need not tell you why I could not bring my maid."

Of all the things he had expected to hear, a confession to a desire to honor her end of the bargain was the last on the list. Hell, it was not even on the list, so unforeseen was it. Beyond astonished and now somewhere in the realm of flabbergasted, but not about to show it, Gideon coolly retorted, "No, you do not, though I would be interested to hear why you wish to reinstate our bargain. By your own acknowledgment, you are no more eager to marry me than I am you."

She made a helpless little hand gesture. "For the sake of my siblings, of course. As I said, there is nothing that I would not do or sacrifice for them. And if the price of saving them from being thrown into the streets to live as beggars is a loveless marriage, then so be it."

Again, Gideon was taken aback, though this time he did not bother to disguise the fact. "I cannot even begin to imagine what you are going on about," he said, frowning his consternation. "What does our bargain have to do with your siblings being thrown into the streets?"

"If you call in my mother's debt, we will be ruined, and my siblings and I will lose everything, including our home." She shook her head over and over again, clutching at her reticule in a manner that betrayed the terrible depth of her despair. "The very thought of my siblings starving in the streets—I-I—" Her fragile voice broke then, her tear-glazed eyes haunted with fear and begging for mercy as she met his gaze in a mute plea.

"Debt?" he echoed, his frown deepening as he tried to make sense of her words. "I do not—"

"Oh, Mr. Harwood, please!" she sobbed, the tears that welled in her eyes now brimming over to spill down her cheeks. "I am begging you, please—please!—do not ruin us! I will do anything, be anything you wish, whatever it takes to please you." She had released her reticule and now clutched at his arm. "All you have to do is tell me the sort of woman you desire and I shall be her. I promise. Please! Just give me the chance." Her breath was being ripped from her chest in rough, ragged sobs, and she could not have looked more sincere or desperate as she stared up at him, awaiting his answer.

Gideon returned her gaze, too stunned by her impassioned outburst to speak. When his wits finally returned, he narrowed his eyes and inquired, "Who told you that I was threatening your family with ruin?" Not that he really needed to ask. There was only one person who could be responsible for concocting such a heinous lie.

Her sniffles had returned along with her tears. "My father, of course." *Sniffle!*

"Of course," Gideon echoed in a grim voice.

"He said that if I do not wed you, our family will always"—*sniffle! sniffle!*—"be in danger of you calling in my mother's gambling debt. And since it is so very large—" She sniffled twice more and shook her head. "Well, I need not tell you the power that such an obligation gives you over us."

Gideon's eyes narrowed further as understanding began to dawn. It appeared that Lord Stanwell was up to his vile, cowardly tricks again, and again at the expense of his poor daughter. His already fathomless loathing for the detestable man deepening, he said, "Perhaps if you tell me what your father said in regard to the affair, I shall be better able to address your fears."

She sniffled several times in quick succession. "Since we both know the circumstances of the debt, I see no need to explain."

"Nonetheless, I very much wish to hear your father's side of the tale," he interjected, though he knew that he was not going to like what he heard. When she looked about to protest, he reminded her, "You promised to do anything I wish in order to persuade me to reconsider our bargain, correct?"

"Yes." Her voice was hoarse, almost a rasp.

"Then prove it."

She sighed and averted her face, closing her eyes, as if in doing so she could somehow shut out the ugliness of what she was about to report. "He said that you lured my mother into gaming with you the night we met at Vauxhall Gardens, and that you deliberately drove her into debt, probably through cheating, in order to blackmail your way into the *ton*. He said"—*sniffle!*—"that you then threatened to ruin our family by calling in the debt, unless he agreed to sponsor you in society and I promised to marry you. He told me that if I did not wed you, you would have he and my mother thrown into debtors' prison, and my siblings and me turned out into the streets to starve. So"—*sniffle! sniffle!*—"of course I bowed to your wishes. How could I not?"

How indeed? Gideon thought darkly, wishing that the villain were there so he could thrash him within an inch of his life. That his lordship would use his daughter's love for her siblings to manipulate her in such a manner was evil beyond his comprehension.

"I truly did try to do as you asked and be the sort of woman I"—*sniffle!*—"thought you wished for a wife. I did!" Those last words were rent by a heartbroken sob. "But I failed." Another wrenching sob. "Oh! I have made such a stew of things! Since you have decided that you do not"—*sniffle!*—"like me and no longer wish to be a part of the *ton,* my father says that you will most certainly call in the debt." Now grasping his arm with a strength that was almost bruising in her desperation, she sniffled twice and pleaded, "Oh, Mr. Harwood! I would rather die than see my poor siblings suffer so. They do not deserve such misery. If you will but give me a chance, I promise to make matters right."

Damn Lord Stanwell. Damn him to hell! Gideon's hands clenched into fists in his fury. Not only had the bastard besmirched his character with his lies, he had utterly crushed his daughter by using him as a threat against the siblings she adored. No wonder she hated him so. Now armed with a new understanding of the predicament in which he found himself inextricably tangled, he pondered his next move.

He could, of course, repudiate her father's lies and tell her the truth. Yet doing so would be cruel, even devastating in that it would mark her mother a whore, and she and her siblings as bastards. And she deserved better than that. Besides, what good would it serve in the end? Delivering such a blow most certainly would not improve her lady-ship's opinion of him. That is, if she believed him at all. And why should she? Why would she believe a virtual stranger over her own father?

"Please, Mr. Harwood. Say that you will reconsider the bargain." Her face was again blotchy and her eyes red as she gazed up at him in tearful appeal. "You shall not regret doing so, I promise."

Though Gideon frankly doubted that last, sympathy for her plight made him weigh the former. Hmmm. Maybe he should reconsider the bargain. After all, the real Lady Julia was not so very bad. In fact, Bliss could do worse than to emulate the charm she had displayed earlier that morning. And while he was on the subject of siblings, surely her love for her own siblings boded well for a harmonious relation-ship between her and his sisters? Deciding that it indeed did, he glanced down at her, debating what to do.

She promptly smiled through her tears, clearly trying to appear as agreeable as possible. That she should be so eager to please, so desperate to barter herself for the sake of her siblings wrenched his heart.

Hmmm. Rather than wondering what she could do for him, perhaps he should consider the good he might do her in restoring their bargain. And now that he knew the extent to which her father was willing to go to achieve his despicable means, he saw that it was indeed in her best interest to reinstate it, that marrying her would be akin to a rescue. To be sure, if he did not wed her, her father would most likely sell her to another man, one who might use her cruelly and make her life more miserable than it obviously already was. At least with him, she would be assured of safety and kindness.

Now cast in the role of reluctant hero, Gideon met her damp-eyed gaze and quizzed, "Is that truly what you wish, my lady? To wed me?"

She graced him with another of her smiles, this one less forced for her expression of forlorn hope. "More that anything in the world." *Sniffle!*

That she should desire above all else to wed a man she did not even like spoke volumes about the depth of her desperation, as well as the pathetic state of her life. It also made up his mind. Nodding, he said, "Then you may consider your wish granted." She opened her mouth, no doubt to thank him, but he halted her speech with a curt hand motion. "I do, however, place three conditions on doing so."

"Anything," she exclaimed, her splotchy face transforming into a study of joyous relief. "I do not care what the conditions entail. I agree to them, and gladly. I—"

Again he halted her. "Please. Indulge me by hearing me out."

If a person could actually beam, Lady Julia Barham did so as she gazed up at him. "But of course. As I promised, I shall do and be"—*sniffle! sniffle!*—"anything you wish."

"What I wish is for you to be yourself. That is my first condition. I have glimpsed the real Lady Julia this morning and have decided that I like her very much. Therefore, you must promise that instead of wearing a polite mask and pretending that all is well when it is not, you will instead express your feelings and allow yourself to behave in a natural manner."

There was no doubt whatsoever that the smile she gave him in response complied with that first condition. "I must confess that it will be a relief"—*sniffle!*—"not to have to hide my feelings from you. However, I feel it only fair to warn you that I am cursed with a rather"—*sniffle! sniffle! sniffle!*—"quick temper."

He waved aside her confession. "Yes? Well, and I am told that I sometimes snore, loudly. The point is we all have our flaws, and as a married couple we should not feel burdened with the obligation to hide them."

"Agreed." *Sniffle!* "And your second condition?"

"That you blow your nose. This instant. Your sniffling is driving me mad."

She smiled at his request and retrieved her own handkerchief, a dainty, lace-trimmed affair, from her reticule. Modestly turning away, she complied. That bit of business thus completed, she turned back to him, saying, "Done, sir. What is your third condition?"

"I want you to promise to be a companion to my sister Bethany, with whom you are of an age, and to make an attempt to tame my youngest sister, Bliss. While the former task should prove easy enough, pleasurable even, given Bethany's sweet nature, the latter will no doubt be a trial. Bliss is, er, a bit difficult." Difficult, unfortunately, was a vast understatement for the brat's wild behavior. Then again, what could one expect from a child who had survived life in Westminster's meanest rookery?

"Difficult or no, they shall be my sisters, so I will naturally love them and give them every consideration I would grant my own sisters," she declared, and there was no doubt whatsoever as to the sincerity of her pronouncement for the stoutness with which it was uttered.

"I take it that you agree to my terms, then?"

"To all three, yes."

"In that instance, I shall inform your father of my decision to resume our bargain, and direct him to announce our engagement as planned," he replied, fully intending to appraise Lord Stanwell of a hell of a lot more than that. Indeed, by the time he finished, the bastard would not dare to utter anything but the most innocuous pleasantries to any of his daughters.

"How can I ever thank you, Mr. Harwood?" She now looked at him much as the princess gazed at St. George upon slaying the dragon in a Christmas pageant of *St. George and the Dragon*.

"You may start by calling me Gideon. If we are to announce our engagement next week, an easing of the formality between us seems in order," he replied, rather enjoying being her hero, though, of course, he was nothing of the sort. A true champion would have found a way to right matters in a fashion that would not require her to sell herself into marriage.

"Gideon." She smiled and inclined her head in agreement. "And you must call me Julia."

He nodded back. "Very well. Julia it is. Now Julia, since we are to be wed, what do you say to a friendship? I daresay that being friends will make our marriage a great deal more comfortable for the both of us."

"I would like that very much, Gideon."

"Friends, then?" He offered her his hand.

She took it, her palm molding to his as their fingers entwined. "Friends."

CHAPTER 12

"You will look like a queen, Julia," Mina declared, reverently touching the overskirt on Julia's wedding gown.

"A vision of elegance," added Amy, laying the Brussels lace bridal veil over her hand to test its transparency.

Caroline, who fingered the swansdown trim on the stylish white satin pelisse Julia would wear over her bridal gown on the drive to and from the church, nodded in agreement. "I do believe that you shall be the most beautiful bride of the Season. Your gown . . ." She shook her head, as if she still could not quite believe her eyes. "I have never seen anything so magnificent."

The gown in question was presently displayed on a wicker dressmaker's form that stood before the gilt-framed Cheval mirror in Julia's spacious green, gold, and coral bed-chamber, thus exhibiting it from all angles. And as Caroline had pointed out, it truly was magnificent. Indeed, it was everything that Julia had ever dreamed of in a wedding gown.

Designed in the current fashion with a high waist and classical silhouette, the gown itself was a rather plain white satin affair, trimmed at its long, straight sleeves, flaring hem, and low V-neckline with bands of simple gold lace. What made it so very spectacular was the overgown.

Though most aristocratic brides chose the traditional bridal colors of silver and white, silver, unfortunately, did the most dreadful things to Julia's complexion. Thus the overgown, with its elbow length, triple puffed sleeves and high standing collar, had been made of intricately embroidered gold and white lace. As the dressmaker had so astutely and rhapsodically pointed out, gold not only warmed and flattered Julia's delicate coloring to perfection, it reflected the light with every movement, glistening like a cascade of sunlight that would follow her down the aisle in a shimmering six-foot train. Adding to the glittering splendor of the exquisite creation was an edging of gold point-lace flowers, which also lined the face-framing inner brim of the bridal bonnet she would wear on the ride to the church in the morning. Once at the church she would don a crownlike diamond and gold aigrette, over which she would drape the whisper-thin Brussels lace veil.

Famous Helene, who had been uncharacteristically agreeable ever since Julia had invited her to be one of her six bridesmaids, smiled with a sweetness that would have prompted a dozen sonnets, had there been a dozen iambically inclined bachelors present to witness it. "It truly is a lovely gown, Julia. I daresay that it shall even outshine the one your mother wore at her wedding last week, and at the time I thought that nothing could be grander."

"Or more romantic," interjected Mina on an enraptured sigh, now lifting the bonnet to examine the silk flowers wreathing the crown. "I do believe that your mother is the most fortunate woman in the world, Julia, to have a husband who insisted on wedding her all over again, after more than two decades of marriage, simply to show the *ton* how much he still loves her."

"Considering the success of the affair, I shan't be a whit surprised if such weddings become all the rage. Indeed, I venture to guess that there is not a married woman in the *ton* who has not flung Lord Stanwell's romantic gesture at her own husband and demanded that he follow suit." This was from Caroline, who had moved from the gown to examine the aigrette and its matching necklace and earrings, which lay on a velvet cushion atop a small table that had been placed by the gown for the express purpose of displaying Julia's bridal accessories.

Amy giggled. "From what my papa says, you are indeed

correct, Caro. Why only last night he said that Julia's father is rather less popular with the other gentlemen of the *ton* for the dissatisfaction his example has bred in their wives' breasts." Another giggle. "Nonetheless, for all that his lordship's gesture was romantic to the extreme, I must confess that it is Julia whom I envy. After all, she is marrying the dashing Gideon Harwood on the morrow."

"Mr. Harwood is a fine man. Pleasing in both speech and manner," Caroline acknowledged with a decisive nod.

"And worth a plum," added Helene. "With his wealth, he will be able to give Julia everything she desires."

"He is also exceedingly gallant," contributed Mina. Her face grew wistful then. "Oh, Julia! I do envy you. What I would not give to have such a gallant man fall in love with me and whisk me off to the altar."

Julia, who sat on a small tapestry-upholstered settee watching her friends admire her finery, smiled at Mina's starry-eyed yearning for romance. Genuinely hoping that what she was about to say would prove true, she replied, "It will happen to you, dear. I am certain it shall. Someday you will meet a man who is everything you desire, and he will sweep you off your feet and love you the way you deserve to be loved."

"Just like you and Mr. Harwood," murmured Mina, her expression dreamy as she contemplated the rosy future her friend predicted. "What a wonderful life you shall have, Julia, marrying a man who adores you so. You must love each other to distraction to be wedding after such a short courtship."

"Yes," Julia said, though, of course, she lied. She did not love Gideon, nor he her. As for their future, well, since that day in the park, when they had agreed to be friends, she had discovered that he was rather more pleasant than she had first thought, and had thus begun to believe that they might rub along tolerably well together. Of course, rubbing along tolerably well was a far cry from the wedded bliss Mina envisioned for them. Nonetheless, it was a happier existence than she had dared to hope for when she had first entered into the bargain.

"Loving you as he does, he is bound to give you a generous allowance," the ever-mercenary Helene said, seating herself next to Julia on the settee.

Caroline sniffed. "Is that all you ever think about, Helene, money?"

Helene shrugged one shoulder. "What else is there? Though, of course, I shan't take a fortune unless there is a grand title attached to it."

"We shall all wed men of fortune, and most of them will no doubt be of noble birth. After all, it is our duty and right to marry well," Caroline declared, settling in one of the three pale gold damask chairs that had been arranged opposite the settee in anticipation of the women's visit. "However, should I have to choose between a wealthy commoner with intelligence and wit, and a titled dullard, I would take the commoner any day."

"I want a handsome husband, like Mr. Harwood," Amy said, inelegantly plopping herself into the chair on Caroline's left, "though I doubt I shall get my wish." She shook her head, sighing as if beset by the greatest of tragedies. "Papa seems to have an unreasonable prejudice against any suitor who is under the age of eighty and does not resemble a toad."

"Well, I wish for a kind man." This was from Mina, who now helped herself to a slice of trifle from the refreshment table a servant had placed in the room a half hour earlier. "Though a title, a handsome face, and wit are all fine things, they are worthless if the man possessing them is not kind."

"Mina is correct in that kindness is the most important quality of all in a husband, for without kindness there can be no love in a marriage," Caroline conceded, giving Mina's arm a fond squeeze as the girl took the vacant chair on her right. "Our dearest Julia is very fortunate in that Mr. Harwood possesses all the qualities we deem important in a husband."

"Save for a title, of course," Helene reminded them.

"Yes," Julia replied, stunned to discover that what Caroline said was true. Gideon Harwood was indeed wealthy, witty, intelligent, handsome . . . and kind. Above all, he was kind.

As the other women launched into a friendly debate over which gentlemen of the *ton* possessed the required qualities for a husband, Julia contemplated her betrothed's unexpectedly benevolent nature.

His was the type of kindness that warmed the soul, the simple, humble sort made up not of grand gestures, but of small, thoughtful acts performed solely for the pleasure they brought the recipient. To her surprise and gratitude, her sisters had of late become regular beneficiaries of his altruistic largesse.

Since learning of Maria and Jemima's interest in animals, Gideon now often brought Jagtar and Kesin with him when he called, each time asking that the younger Barham daughters be invited downstairs to play with the queer little creature. Maria and Jemima were, of course, thrilled, and not only by the slow loris. That their future brother-in-law should find them worthy company made them smile in a way that brought tears to Julia's eyes for the fierceness of the joy it gave her to see their gladness. As for Aurelia, since the request for their presence came from Gideon, she naturally could not deny it, though Julia knew that it must pain the awful woman to no end to see her charges so happy.

And that was not all Gideon had done for them. There was the time he had taken them all to see a particularly fine traveling menagerie, after which he had treated them to cake and ices. Then there were the books he brought, the first being the promised one on the beasts of India, followed by a series of others, each one a lavishly illustrated volume about a different place full of strange sights and populated by mysterious beasts.

To Maria and Jemima's delight, he presented each new volume to them, rather than her, along with a dainty nosegay for each. He would then sit them beside him to discuss the newest addition to their library, making them laugh as he drolly pointed out the more unusual aspects of the country the book explored.

How her sisters loved their moments with Gideon! How they adored him. She rather adored him as well during those times, her heart kindled by the pleasure he brought

into her siblings' drab lives. But those were not the only
instances during which she had found herself feeling somewhat more warmly toward him than she knew she should.
Oh, no. To her consternation, she had begun to view almost
all of his actions with favor.

Not for the first time since that day in Grosvenor Square
Park, Julia wondered at her feelings for Gideon Harwood.
She should despise him, of course. After the way he had
cheated her mother, threatened her family, and blackmailed
her and her father, she should view him as the most repre-
hensible villain in the world. Shouldn't she?

And yet, how could she? How could she hate a man who
had shown her such gallantry? A man who was kind not
only to her and her siblings, but to everyone around him,
be they pauper or lord? Above all, how could she detest
Gideon, knowing, as she now did, that the heart of his
crime was simply loving his siblings too much? That that
was indeed the case was something she had discerned when
he had informed her that his unscrupulous actions had been
performed for their benefit and theirs alone, though beyond
stating that fact he had been oddly taciturn on the subject
of his sisters and brother, offering little insight into their
lives when he did mention them and surrendering even less
when she asked. To be sure, all she really knew about them
was that his sisters lived on his estate in Lancashire and
that his brother had somehow disappeared.

For what must have been the two-hundredth time since
coming to her conclusion, Julia wondered at his odd reluctance to speak of the family he so obviously adored.

And as always happened when she did so, she realized
how little she knew about the man she was to wed.

She was marrying a stranger in the morning.

Desperate to avoid the sickening sense of panic that always assailed her when she allowed herself to dwell on that
disconcerting truth, Julia turned her mind back to his love
for his siblings. That thought, at least, was somewhat comforting. It also served to lift her spirits with hope for her
own siblings' futures. After all, a man who cared so deeply
for his own family was certain to understand her love for
hers. Which meant that perhaps—just perhaps—if she played

her cards right, she might be able to persuade him to allow Maria, Jemima, and little Bertie to pay an extended visit to their home once they were wed. Yes. And if she were especially clever, she might even contrive to have them take up residence with her.

The mere thought of having her sisters and brother near, where she could see that all of their needs were met, both in body and spirit, surrounded her heart in a warm glow. Exactly how she was going to persuade Gideon to allow such a thing, much less convince her parents to release them into her care, she did not know. Nonetheless, she had hope, which allowed her to dream of future happiness. What did it matter that her husband did not love her, if her siblings were safe and happy?

"Julia?"

Julia blinked several times, frowning as the sound of Caroline's voice penetrated her thoughts.

"Are you quite well, Julia?" intruded Mina's inquiry.

Julia smiled apologetically, dragged back to time and place by their voices. "Pray do forgive me. I fear that I was woolgathering," she replied, surprised to hear that her voice sounded as far away as her thoughts had been only seconds earlier.

Amy giggled. "I daresay that I would be woolgathering as well if I knew that I was to pass tomorrow night in Gideon Harwood's bed."

"Amy!" Caroline and Helene exclaimed in a scandalized duet, while Mina looked baffled by their censure.

Amy rolled her eyes. "Oh, pish! We all know that the slyboots was hinting at the wedding night when she asked Julia that last question. Do own up, Helene." She slanted Helene a suggestive look, her eyebrows raised in barbed query.

By the answering frown marring the famed one's celebrated brow, it was clear that she was about to spar a spat. In no mood to suffer one of Amy and Helene's petty squabbles, Julia laughed and said, "Since the inquiry was addressed to me, I shall be the judge of its nature." She smiled and nodded at Helene. "What was your question, dear?"

If looks could kill, or otherwise maim their recipient, Amy would have been in a very bad state indeed for the one Helene shot her. Nonetheless, Helene managed to return Julia's smile and reply in a polite voice, "I simply asked if you were going to miss your bedchamber. You know how I have always admired it, the bed in particular." She indicated the green-lacquered satinwood bed with its gilded neoclassical garlands, oval crown, and artfully puffed swags and drapery.

"I am quite certain that a man like Mr. Harwood has a very fine bed of his own," Amy saucily interjected, not about to be deterred from her naughtiness. "So fine, in fact, that it will quite make Julia forget this one altogether."

"Amy!" Caroline again chided, while Mina frowned and Helene ignored the remark altogether.

Amy sniffed. "Spare me your missish sensibilities, Caro. If you were the least bit inclined toward honesty, you would admit that you are every bit as fascinated by the bridal bed as I am."

There was a pause during which Mina's frown deepened and Helene sniffed. Then Caroline carefully conceded, "I will admit that I am curious, yes. Nonetheless, curiosity is neither an excuse nor a license to engage in unseemly discussion."

"Indeed?" Amy countered. "Well then. If one cannot discuss those matters about which they are curious, then how, pray tell, are they to ever learn what they wish to know?"

"In this instance I daresay that you will learn quickly enough once you are wed, though I, for one, am perfectly content to remain ignorant about such matters for as long as possible," Helene deigned to respond. "From what I have heard, the lessons to be learned between the sheets are far from pleasant."

Poor, innocent Mina could not have looked more confused. "Lessons between the sheets?" She shook her head, her forehead now a maze of creases in her puzzlement. "I cannot even begin to imagine what you mean, Helene."

"She is speaking of the marriage act, dear. What men

and women do between the sheets once they are wed," Amy informed her.

Caroline nodded. "Yes. She is referring to the act that makes babies."

"But babies are made by angels, who plant them in their mother's womb in answer to a woman's prayers," Mina said in a bewildered tone. "Are you saying that men and women pray for babies together while between the sheets?"

"Er—not exactly," Caroline replied, casting a desperate look first at Amy, then at Julia.

Julia, who had thus far taken pains to avoid thinking about the marriage bed, shook her head, not wishing to do so now. As Helene had pointed out, she would learn quickly enough once she was between the sheets with Gideon. So why add to her worries by fretting over the inevitable?

Amy, however, had no such reservations. "Surely you have heard of coupling, Mina?" she inquired, gazing at Mina expectantly. When her query was met by a stupefied stare, she tried, "Mating?"

"I always thought that mating was a word for marriage," Mina said, looking beyond troubled by her misconception.

Amy sighed and shook her head. "I see that you truly are an innocent. Perhaps . . ." Her voice trailed off as she seemed to consider what to do next. Nodding at whatever decision she had reached, she quizzed, "Tell me, dear. Do you know the differences between men and women? The bodily ones?"

Mina's face instantly brightened. "Of course I do. Men are tall and strong, and women are small and soft."

Helene, who had four brothers and was thus aware of the differences to which Amy referred, snorted. "Silly goose! She is referring to men's and women's private parts."

"Oh?" Mina's face again crumbled into a frown as she absorbed that tidbit of information. In the next instant her eyes flew open wide and she flushed a dull red. "Oh."

"I assume you understand now?" Helene asked with a superior air.

"Umm—y-yes," Mina mumbled, her color deepening. "I-I—uh—once saw a n-naked boy infant, so I know that men have a queer little—umm—thimble down there and a pair of wrinkly"—she balled her hands to indicate the shape—"things instead of—of—well, you know."

Amy giggled, a sharp, agitated twitter that warned that they were about to be treated to one of her more outrageous remarks. "That thimble grows to be quite large, as do the—" She imitated Mina's descriptive hand gesture. "I know, because I stumbled upon Lord Epsley relieving himself in a corner of Lady Fleming's garden during her picnic last spring. He was so deep in his cups that he did not think to cover himself, so I was able to catch more than a glimpse of his manly parts."

"And they were large?" Julia blurted out before she could think to stop herself. She had naturally assumed that those parts remained as relatively small on an adult male as they were on an infant.

Amy nodded, her eyes growing round as saucers, as they always did when on a subject that fascinated her. "His thimble was this big." She indicated a length between her palms that was very large indeed. "Of course, I suspect that Mr. Harwood will be larger, seeing as that he is much taller and far more masculine than Lord Epsley."

"Do you really think so?" Julia asked, trying hard to keep the fear from her voice.

"Of course he will be larger. Everyone knows that commoners are far larger down there than noblemen, and that they are much more brutal in their mating," Helene said. She shook her head, her expression pitying. "Poor, poor Julia. I daresay that it will hurt terribly when he enters you."

"He will enter her?" Mina squeaked. "With his—" She imitated Amy's gesture by indicating an enormous length between her hands.

Amy nodded. "He will thrust it in the place between her legs."

"Over and over again until she is quite sore and bleeding," Helene supplied with a shudder. "I hear tell that it is a most dreadful experience and that a woman must do everything in her power to avoid having to submit to it."

Mina could not have looked more horrified, an expression that painted a perfect portrait of Julia's own feelings at that moment. Though Julia knew that a man's male part had something to do with making babies, she had not realized that he would thrust it up into that tender place between her legs. She shuddered, the mere thought of Gideon doing such a thing to her sending a rush of panic spurting through her veins. Her throat suddenly bone dry, she somehow managed to croak, "However did you learn of such things?"

"From my mother, of course," Helene replied, as if such discussions between mother and daughter were the most natural thing in the world. "She told me in order to save me from a bird-witted crush I once had on a merchant's son. She caught me kissing him, you see. I was only thirteen at the time—" She broke off, shaking her head, as if she still could not believe her own youthful folly. "At any rate, once she told me about the marriage act and how it would be especially torturous with a commoner, I have naturally since confined my interest in men to the grander titles in the *ton*. As Mama always says: The better bred the man, the gentler he will be in the bridal bed."

"Well, I found several books on the subject hidden in Papa's desk. And according to both the pictures and the text, the act is supposed to be pleasurable," Amy challenged.

"For the man, yes," retorted Helene with a sniff, "which is why men want to do it all the time. My advice to you, Julia, and it is the same advice my mother gave me, is that you encourage your husband to take a mistress posthaste, if he does not already have one. That way he shan't bother you beyond the purpose of begetting an heir or two."

"Oh, my!" Mina whimpered, now looking on the verge of tears. "This marriage business sounds frightful to the extreme. I am glad that I do not have a serious suitor."

"There, there, now, dear. I am certain that it is not nearly as bad as Helene paints it to be," Caroline said soothingly, reaching over to give Mina's arm a comforting pat. "To be sure, my mother seems quite content in marriage, as does Julia's mother, and most of the other women in the *ton*. If they were being subjected to such torture between the sheets, I doubt they would look so very satisfied with their lot."

"Caro is right," Amy said with a nod. "Besides, if the act were as awful as Helene claims, I am certain that we would have been told something to that effect in order to prepare us."

"Ah. But if we were told, we might refuse to marry, so it stands to reason that we should be kept ignorant of the horror that awaits us," Helene reasoned.

Julia had to admit that what Helene said made sense. Besides, why would her mother lie? Considering the Duchess of Hunsderry's eagerness for her daughter to make a brilliant match, it would hardly serve her purpose to lie about the bridal bed in a manner that would discourage rather than encourage Helene toward marriage. That being the case, it must be true—it had to be true! Fear welled up inside her, making her feel sick with dread. And the experience was bound to be all the worse for her—brutal even—since her groom was a commoner.

Wrestling with her now almost overwhelming panic, Julia reminded herself that Gideon was a particularly well-bred commoner. And what was it that Helene's mother had said on the subject of the bridal bed and breeding? Oh, yes: The better bred a man, the gentler he was in the bridal bed. That being the case, a man's breeding could surely overcome his commonness and gentle him in the marriage act. Couldn't it? Clinging to that faint hope, she choked out through her fright, "Surely a commoner as well bred as Mr. Harwood will be as gentle as an aristocrat between the sheets?"

"I am afraid that he shall not be able to help himself," Helene replied, casting her a sympathetic look. "Blood will tell, you know, and even the most tame commoner will revert to a savage when faced with his most primitive urges."

"Well I, for one, refuse to believe it. Any of it," Amy stoutly declared. "I am certain that Mr. Harwood will make Julia rapturously happy, both in and out of the marriage bed."

"As am I," Caroline said with a decisive nod. "As much

as Mr. Harwood loves our dear Julia, he is bound to treat her with gentleness and respect."

Rather than comforting her, as her friend had so clearly intended to do, Caroline's words merely deepened Julia's sense of foreboding. Gideon did not love her, which meant that he would most probably do nothing to control the primitive urges of which Helene spoke.

"Yes. I am sure you are correct, Caro," Mina added, though unlike Amy and Caroline, she did not look at all convinced of what she said.

Helene shrugged. "We shall see."

For several moments thereafter the women remained silent, each lost in her thoughts on the subject. Then Mina tremulously inquired, "Is there nothing good that can be said about the bridal bed?"

"It is where babies are made, which is a very lovely thing indeed," Caroline replied, giving Mina's arm a squeeze.

"And where jewels can be earned," said Helene with a sly smile.

"Jewels?" the other women exclaimed in perplexed unison.

Helene nodded. "Or gowns, or a coach-and-six, or whatever else a woman desires."

"Meaning?" Amy quizzed with raised eyebrows.

"Meaning that if you must endure a man's lust, you might as well use it to your advantage." Helene nodded again. "Mama says that if a woman is cooperative and makes the act pleasurable for her husband, then he will give her anything she wishes. She told me that you have only to see which women in the *ton* are sporting the newest and richest jewels to know which ones are willing to pleasure their husbands between the sheets. Men, she says, are easily led by their lust, and a clever woman will use it to get her way."

Julia's breath caught in her throat as she considered the possibilities of what Helene had just imparted. If what the Duchess of Hunsderry said was true—and again, why should she doubt her?—then perhaps she could *pleasure* Gideon into taking her siblings into his home. What did it matter that she would have to suffer pain and indignity to accomplish her goal, just as long as it all worked out to her satisfaction in the end?

That left only the question of how one pleasured her husband in a manner that would allow him to be led. Though it shamed her to do so, Julia forced herself to ask, "Did your mother by chance, um, say how a woman should go about pleasuring her husband?"

Helene shook her head. "When I asked—"

"You actually asked your mother such a thing?" Amy ejected, eyeing Helene with new respect.

Helene shrugged. "As I said, I was thirteen. I was far too young to know that it was unseemly to ask about such things."

"And what did she say?" Julia prodded, trying not to sound too desperate.

Another shrug from Helene. "She said that a man liked to have his private parts fondled and that if a woman obliged him, he would finish the act quickly and thus spare her much of her trial. She also said that if a woman is especially talented at fondling, that she might satisfy her husband without having to endure him thrusting his male part into her female one at all, though she did not explain how it is done." She shook her head. "I am sorry, Julia, but the only other piece of advice she shared with me is that a woman should take a snifter or two of brandy before going to her husband in order to make the marriage act more tolerable."

"If you like, I can tell you what I read in Papa's books," Amy offered with one of her twittering giggles. "Many of the acts described involve intimately fondling a man."

Though Julia would have rather been flayed than admit her need to learn about performing such vulgar acts, she made herself smile and say, "Please do. And thank you." As Amy launched into an enthusiastic and graphic description of what she had read, making Mina gasp aloud in shock, and Julia blush and tremble in turn, Julia resolved that she would do everything in her power to give Gideon the greatest pleasure of his life, no matter how painful and mortifying it might be to her.

By the time she was finished with him, Gideon Harwood would be her lust-led slave.

Chapter 13

She must look tempting, smell enticing, move with alluring languor, and . . . and . . . what else had Amy said?
Julia frowned, her index finger drumming a tense tattoo
against the bottle in her hand as she searched her nerve-
tangled thoughts for the oddments of her friend's instruction. She must . . . must . . . ?

Hmmm. Her frown deepened, only to ease in the next
instant as her power of recollection returned. Oh. Right.
She must speak in a low, seductive voice, if she must speak
at all, which Amy had said was highly unadvisable since
one of her father's books alleged that men did not like
conversation with their pleasuring.

Satisfied by the accuracy of her restored memory, Julia
nodded. Yes, that was correct. Furthermore, she must remember to feign breathlessness when Gideon took her into
his arms, so as to make him think that she had been rendered breathless in anticipation of his manly attentions.
Nothing pleased a man more than a woman desirous of his
attentions, or so another of the books had said. Once in
his arms she must fondle him in the mortifying manner
Amy had described, after which she must lie pliant beneath
his husbandly assault, accepting whatever horrors he in-
flicted upon her with a smile and an enraptured sigh.

Her already wavering courage abandoned her completely
at the prospect of that last, driving her to lift the bottle she
held for the fifth—or was it the sixth time?—in the quarter-

hour since her maid had left her alone to await her groom. Though the etched-glass toilet bottle normally contained the strawberry water to which she attributed the much-envied clarity of her complexion, she had taken Helene's suggestion under advisement and had replaced the cosmetic with brandy she had filched from her father's library sideboard. Praying that the inebriant would indeed ease her coming ordeal, she brought the bottle to her lips, grimacing in preparation for the harsh flavor and the burning sensation that had chased the fiery liquid down her throat during her first few samplings.

To her surprise, it tasted less caustic than before, the burning now little more than a mellow rush of warmth that seemed to radiate through her veins, heating her blood and stalling her growing trepidation. Pleased by the effect, she took another, deeper drink. Then another. And another, vaguely noting as she raised the bottle yet again that she had consumed more than half its contents. Now feeling somewhat more in control of herself, she turned her thoughts back to Amy's instructions, arranging them in an order that would best suit her purpose. That done to her satisfaction, she nodded and took another tipple to reward her initiative.

All right, then. Time to prepare for her husband-pleasuring. Consulting the list in her head, she determined that the first order of business was to make certain that she looked as tempting as possible. Taking another drink as she went, Julia purposefully marched into the dressing room that adjoined the bedchamber to which Gideon's housekeeper, the briskly efficient Mrs. Courter, had shown her upon her arrival at the town house earlier that evening.

Like the rest of Gideon's residence, well, at least that of it she had thus far seen, both rooms were decorated with an easy elegance that was as cozy as it was pleasing to the eye. She particularly liked the landscape pattern on the wall covering in the bedchamber, with its lush garden scene and colorfully plumed birds. And yes, she had spent more than a passing moment admiring the gracefully carved tester bed, her eyes dazzled by its richly embroidered silk drapery and coverlet, though at the present she preferred not to dwell overly long on that particular piece of furnishing. Now coming to a stop before the long Cheval glass that stood in the far corner of the blue, gold, and white dressing room, she turned her attention to taking stock of her appearance, sipping from the bottle as she considered her reflection.

Though she had no idea how a bride being led to the marriage bed slaughter should look, Leonie, her French lady's maid, who had been overseeing Julia's appearance since she was sixteen, had seemed to have an idea of her own and had thus prepared her charge accordingly. Gazing at herself now, garbed but barely in an almost transparent night rail with a low, lace-trimmed neck and tiny puffed sleeves, made up in soft cream linen, she decided that the woman might indeed have known what she was about. To be sure, if what Amy's father's books said was correct, and men truly were titillated by the sight of a woman's unclothed form, then Gideon would most definitely find her attire tempting . . . provided, of course, that he found the figure so blatantly displayed beneath the wisp of fabric pleasing.

Wondering, for the first time in her life, if her unclothed figure could be considered attractive, Julia lifted her gown, gathering it above her breasts to scrutinize her nude form.

Hmmm. She was well enough, she supposed, though she knew from the brief glimpses she'd had of the demirep, as Amy referred to the beautiful creatures she claimed served as rich men's mistresses, that her figure lacked the lush ripeness those women possessed. Indeed, though her bosom could not by any means be termed meager, it was not nearly as imposing as the bosoms of those women, which always seemed in danger of spilling from their perilously low bodices. As for the rest of her body . . .

She dropped her gaze lower, critically studying the faint indentation of her waist and the almost nonexistent flare of her hips. Aurelia said that she was shaped more like a boy than a woman. Examining herself now, Julia had to agree. Certain that a worldly man like Gideon would never find her slight figure tempting, she pivoted to view herself from a profile, searching for an angle from which she might look more voluptuous.

Her body looked surprisingly better from the side, softer and more feminine with the rounded curves of her breasts and backside adding the much-needed contours to her boyish form. Struck by inspiration at the improvement, she arched her back, striking a pose that exaggerated the flattering effect.

Perhaps, just perhaps, if she took pains to arrange herself so that Gideon viewed her from this angle when he entered the room, he might not notice her shortcomings. Yes, and if she promptly rushed into his arms and began doing those—those—things!—to his body, he was certain to be far too preoccupied by his lust to notice her lack of shapeliness. Pleased by her plan, she raised the bottle in salute to her brilliance, letting her hem drop back to her ankles as she drained the remaining brandy in a single gulp. Setting the now-empty bottle on the floor beside the mirror, a soft belch escaping her as she straightened back up again, she turned her thoughts to her next piece of husband-pleasuring business: She must smell enticing.

Now feeling strangely carefree, she sniffed first one shoulder, then the other, trying to ascertain whether or not she met with that criterion. Esprit de Rose. She nodded and smiled. Excellent. Wanting to make sure that the rest of her smelled as sweet, she lifted the front of her gown to her nose, her gaze drawn to her wedding ring as she inhaled. The ring was unlike anything she had ever seen before, a distinctive design of interlocking twists and swirls, the significance of which Gideon had explained after the marriage ceremony as they had been driven to her parents' home where the wedding feast was held.

Her gaze traced the gold-wrought loops and angles. The design spelled Harwood, something she could see quite clearly now that Gideon had explained the arrangement of the letters. A pleasurable shiver ran up her spine just remembering the gentle tickling of his fingertips against the flesh of her hand as he outlined each letter in demonstration of his explanation. Repeating the caressing motion over and over again as he spoke, the sensation of which had made her feel strangely weak and boneless, he had then gone on to tell how a Harwood ancestor had designed the ring three centuries earlier as a tribute to the woman he loved.

The ancestor, he said, had been a fierce, bold knight, whose pride in winning the heart and hand of a beautiful baron's daughter had led him to bestow upon her a wedding ring bearing his name, thus marking her as his own for all to see. Both the ring and the tale had been passed down through the subsequent generations, becoming a wedding tradition that Julia found enchanting to the extreme.

Enchanted all over again just thinking about it, she decided that the ring was the most wonderful piece of jewelry she had ever owned. Though it was not the same one the knight had given his ladylove, the original having disappeared along with Gideon's brother, Caleb, the fact that Gideon had bothered to have a replica of it made just for her, so as to include her in his family tradition, made her feel wanted. Welcome. A part of a family to whom the word "family" meant everything. In her mind it had been the most gallant thing a man had ever done for her, a courtly act worthy of the knight from whose loins Gideon's family line had sprung. A—

Knight? And a baron's daughter? Her breath caught in her throat as she was struck by a startling new revelation: since Gideon's line had come from the union of a knight and a baron's daughter, then he was not completely common. Not in entirety. Of course, Gideon himself could not in any way be considered a nobleman, or even gentry, since a knight's title could not be passed down through the generations. But as Helene's mother had said, blood would tell. So perhaps enough of his ancestors' genteel blood remained in his veins that it would temper his common blood in the bridal bed and thus prevent him from abandoning himself to his primitive urges. Before she could fully contemplate or rationalize her new theory, there was a soft rapping at her bedchamber door.

Her head was now whirling in a way that made her surroundings look strangely tilted. Julia weaved her way to the dressing-room door, clutching the jamb to steady herself as she called out across the bedchamber, "Yes?"

"It is I, Julia. Gideon."

Gideon? Oh, heavens! She pressed her hand to her mouth in dismay. She was not ready. Not nearly so. She had yet to practice moving with alluring languor—and then there was the matter of her voice. No doubt she would be required to say something, and she had yet to test her voice to discover which tone sounded the most seductive.

"Julia?"

She sighed. Oh, well. There was no help for any of that now. She would just have to do as best she could. At least she would look tempting and smell enticing. Of course, in order to do the former, she must first strike her selected pose. Thus prompted to action, she charged into the bedchamber, stumbling twice in her unsteadiness. Stopping in the middle of the room, which seemed to list first this way and then that way beneath her gaze, she glanced frantically around her, searching for the perfect setting in which to display herself.

Aha! The bed. Naturally.

Another knock. "Julia? Is something amiss?"

"A moment, please," she called out, noting with chagrin that her voice sounded unnaturally shrill. Lowering it an octave and injecting a breathless quality, she repeated, "A moment." Better.

Now arranged at the foot of the bed, standing in profile with her back arched and her arm raised to brace herself against the bedpost, thus compensating for her queer lack of equilibrium, she dropped her voice yet lower and called out, "Please enter."

He promptly obliged, only to stop short on the threshold, stiffening as if caught off guard by her appearance.

She graced him with what she hoped was a provocative smile, tipping her head to fix him with a languid, sidelong gaze. "Yes?"

He cleared his throat and nodded in response. "I am sorry to disturb you, Julia. I see that I have interrupted your nightly ablutions."

"Do not apologize. You are welcome to interrupt me any time you wish," she replied in a caressing voice.

He frowned, eyeing her as if he did not quite know what to make of her performance. "You are most kind, my dear. However, I promise that I shall not detain you long, since you are no doubt weary from the day's festivities."

"I assure you that I am not the least bit tired. And I very much wish to be detained by you." She practically purred the words, adding a suggestive emphasis on the word "detained."

Gideon raised his eyebrows, taken aback by her double entendre. There was no mistaking her meaning. Not with the way she postured against the bedpost, wantonly displaying her body in a garment that left nothing to the imagination. Not with the blatant invitation in both her voice and smile.

She wanted him to exercise his husbandly rights, and she wanted him to do so now.

That she would desire such a thing was completely unanticipated, unprecedented by so much as a hint that she would ever wish their marriage to go beyond name alone. Perplexed by her contrary behavior, he lowered his raised brows into a frown.

Though they had been friends since that day in Grosvenor Square Park, laughing and teasing and enjoying each other's company immensely, she had never once given any indication that she might welcome his more intimate advances. Granted, she had seemed to respond to the kiss he had been required to give her at the announcement of their engagement, her mouth pliant beneath his as she had melted into his embrace. But aside from that solitary kiss their physical intimacy had never gone beyond holding hands and an occasional peck on the cheek, the latter of which served simply to demonstrate their affection for each other to the *ton*.

Then again, they were wed now. Naturally the ceremony had served to change their relationship. To be sure, he had expected it to do so, just not so quickly or dramatically.

Suddenly wondering if her father was behind the change,

if he had, perhaps, instructed her to play the whore, Gideon stepped into the room. It made sense, really. After all, the happier he was with Julia, the safer Lord Stanwell's sordid secret would be. His insides coiled in anger at the very thought. If what he suspected was indeed true, then the bastard had no doubt used some new threat against Julia's siblings to bend her to his will.

Well, to the devil with Lord Stanwell and his insidious machinations! He would be damned before he would allow either Julia or himself to be manipulated by him again. He most certainly would not let Julia hawk her virtue like a wharf-side doxy to serve the blackguard's purpose.

Hard put now to hide his fury, Gideon forced himself to smile at his wife, saying in as gentle a voice as he could manage, "You do not have to do this, Julia. Not tonight. I had thought to wait to claim my husbandly rights until after you had become comfortable with being my wife." That much was true. In fact, he would not have come to her chamber at all tonight had he not received an urgent missive from Lancashire that required him to do so. Summarily reminded of the purpose of his visit, he added, "I came only to tell you that we must leave for Lancashire at dawn. I have had a letter—"

"You do not desire me?" she interrupted, her face falling and her tone forlorn.

"It is not that—"

"Then you do desire me?" She could not have looked more sweetly hopeful.

"Of course, I do. You are very lovely," he gallantly replied. Of course he lied. He was simply being kind. He did not desire her. Not in the least.

Or did he?

His eyes narrowed, seeming to see her anew. She stood bathed in the warm candlelight, a molten creature of fire and ivory. As befitted a bride, her hair was unbound, rippling to her waist in waves of flame-kissed gold. The sight of it, so bright and silky, made him long to bury his hands in it, to twist and coil it around them until her head bent back, allowing his mouth to ravish those ripe lips that beckoned him with their smile. He wanted to tear that web-thin gown from her luscious body and stroke the pale flesh beneath, to fondle and caress her until he awakened her passion and made her cry out in need.

Did he desire her? The sudden lust gripping his loins answered for him. Oh, yes. It seemed that he had developed a taste for her wan English beauty.

She moved then, her gait sinuous as she advanced toward him. Before he quite knew what was happening, she twined her arms around his neck, drawing his face down to hers, purring, "I desire you as well, Gideon. And I quite like being your wife." Her lips were a scant inch from his now. "So you see? There is no need to wait for me to become accustomed to the idea of our marriage. Indeed, I shall be exceedingly disappointed if you make me wait." With that, she pressed her lips to his.

That she was unaccustomed to kissing was apparent from her closed mouth and chastely pursed lips. Oddly aroused by her inexperience, Gideon groaned and crushed her into his embrace, pulling her up onto her tiptoes to give her a thorough lesson in kissing. She gasped, as if startled, her lips pulling from his.

He smiled wickedly, his voice thick with desire as he whispered, "Let it never be said that I am a man to disappoint a lady." He had the presence of mind to kick the door closed before reclaiming her lips with his.

His mouth was hot, hungry as it covered hers, his hands rough in their eagerness as he twined his fingers through her hair, pulling her face yet nearer to his. Eager to fully possess her mouth, to taste the sweetness within, he slid his tongue between her lips, lightly licking and caressing them, seeking permission to enter.

Julia granted it with a stunned gasp, a delicious shudder heating her body as his tongue invaded her mouth, twining with hers in a way that made her go limp in his arms. Amy had said nothing about such kissing, nor had she uttered a single word about the rippling excitement she now felt beneath the onslaught of his passion. It was a sensation unlike any she had ever felt before . . . fierce, demanding, intoxicating. And she could not seem to get enough of it. Driven now by her powerful response to him, she returned his kiss in kind, her body moving and molding against his as she opened her mouth yet wider, her tongue stroking his, coaxing and inviting his ardor.

His hand found her breast then, first squeezing and flattening, now closing over it to cradle it, his thumb teasing her nipple through the thin fabric of her gown. She made a mewling noise deep in her throat, instinctively moving against his hand to urge him on, her insides seeming to throb and burn beneath the pleasurable sensations radiating through her body. In the next instant his mouth lifted from hers, lowering again on her throat to press nibbling kisses down its length.

Julia moaned, her arms tightening around his neck in shameless abandon, guiding his kisses even lower. He growled once, and swept her up into his arms. Covering the distance to the bed in several long strides, he laid her on the coverlet, his mouth once more on hers as he came down beside her.

As he kissed her, his lips again shaping to hers, his tongue boldly plundering, he lifted her gown, slipping it up to caress the flesh beneath. His touch gentle, almost tickling in its lightness, he stroked up the length of her legs, tracing a meandering line over her thighs that made her nether regions pulse and melt, flooding them with damp warmth. Now he was on her stomach, brushing and massaging, now on her breasts, again teasing her nipples until they throbbed and ached. Then, in a single deft motion he pulled her gown up and off, tossing it aside as he sat back on his heels to admire her naked form.

Dear God, but she was beautiful! Her breasts were full and round, tipped by the most luscious nipples he had ever seen. Her waist and hips, though not particularly defined, were sleek and supple, womanly without being overblown. Her legs, too, were slender, but shapely and long, bisected at their apex by a triangle of golden red curls.

Mesmerized by the sight of her lying before him, her pale skin glowing as if powdered by ground pearls, Gideon combed his fingers through those womanly curls, stroking and teasing them. She trembled, a soft noise escaping her throat. His own body now racked by savage need, he let his fingers glide lower, dropping between her legs to touch and stroke her there.

Julia froze at the resulting sensation, electrified by pleasure. Then she moaned, her thighs parting to welcome his intimate invasion. Over and over again he caressed her there, at first gently, then firmly. Then he dipped his head down to taste her. It was unlike anything she had ever felt before, a delight beyond all imagining, one that seemed to swell with every brush of his tongue, with every nibble and suckle.

"Gideon," she gasped, begging for more, though what she wanted, she did not know. And then it happened, an explosion of ecstasy inside her such as she could never have imagined. Crying her rapture, she surged against his lips, clasping his face against her as wave after powerful wave of pleasure rolled through her, making her tremble and sob. When at last the sensation ebbed, she fell back to the mattress, spent.

"Oh, Gideon. That was a miracle," she whispered, as he drew her into his arms to cradle her nude form against his still-clothed one.

He chuckled and kissed the top of her head. "I am glad you approve, for I would not be a gentleman if I did not pleasure my lady. And we both know how hard I am trying to be a gentleman."

Pleasure . . . me? Reality crashed back to Julia at his words, instantly pulling her from her satisfied stupor. Oh, heavens! It was she who was supposed to be pleasuring him. He was no doubt feeling quite dissatisfied with her about now. Thinking quickly and praying that it was not too late to make amends, she bantered back, "And I shall never qualify as a lady unless I pleasure my gentleman in return."

To her relief, he grinned, a very wicked and delighted grin. "Your servant, my lady," he responded with a chuckle.

Julia smiled back, her mind frantically dredging up Amy's lessons, which had become trapped somewhere between her brandy-induced haze and the remaining fog of her passion. Hmmm. If she remembered correctly, the first

order of business was to kiss him again and then remove
his clothes. Fortunately for her, he was in undress, which
meant that he wore only a dressing gown over his breeches
and shirt, saving her the complication of having to divest
him of his coat, waistcoat, and whatever else men wore.

Now feeling bashful in her nudity, yet mindful of Amy's
counsel about men being titillated by the view of women's
unclothed forms, Julia rolled over onto her belly and
pressed her lips to Gideon's. As she kissed him, imitating
the tongue thrusts and swirls that she had found so stimulating when he had used them on her, she tugged at the
sash holding his red-and-gold patterned dressing gown
closed, determined to remove it as smoothly as he had removed her gown. It was firmly knotted and refused to
loosen.

Bridling her urge to snort her frustration, she lifted her
lips from Gideon's, gracing him with what she hoped was
a seductive smile before turning her attention to the obsti-
nate knot. After several moments of plucking and pulling,
it came loose. Expelling a sigh of relief, she opened the
garment, only to have her breath strangle in her throat at
what it uncovered.

It appeared that Helene had been correct when she had
predicted that his male parts would be enormous. They had
to be to make such a massive bulge in his breeches. Feeling
the blood drain from her face in her horror, she tore her
gaze away, forcing herself to smile as she resumed the business of undressing him.

He had the overly large male parts of a commoner.
*Please, God. Please! Make him have enough gentle blood
in his veins to wield them with care.*

The remnants of her earlier passion dissolving in her
mounting dread, she finished removing his dressing gown,
an act he helped her accomplish. When it was duly tossed
aside, her hands went to his neckcloth. That, too, fell by
the wayside, followed in quick succession by his shirt. As
he lay back down again, having sat up to allow her to strip
him of his shirt, she caught her first full glimpse of his bare
upper body.

He was rather lovely. And strong. Aggressively so, with

his broad shoulders, powerful arms, and muscular chest. Impressed, in spite of her trepidation, she let her gaze trace the tapering line of his waist, experiencing an odd fluttering sensation deep inside her as she noticed the rippling strength of his taut belly. Lovely, yes. He was very well made indeed. Lost in admiration, she dropped her gaze yet lower. When it touched the swelling mound on his groin, she jerked it back up again.

Think of your siblings, she frantically ordered herself, reminding herself of her purpose. If she could show him the same sort of pleasure he had just shown her, he was certain to allow them to stay with her as long as she pleased. Her determination thus bolstered, she again concentrated on Amy's lessons.

Now that she had his chest bare, she must kiss and caress it. Worship his body with her mouth and tongue, the book had instructed. Remembering how wonderful his mouth had felt on her throat, she started with his neck, imitating his soft nips and teasing licks. Down his neck and over the smooth tautness of his collarbone she trailed, then lower to cover the hard, sculpted contours of his chest with kisses, pausing at his flat male nipples to suckle them as he had hers.

Gideon groaned, his breathing becoming harsh and ragged as she continued downward, now biting, now sucking, and now lightly licking. Then she reached his belly, where she lingered, her teeth playfully biting, her tongue teasing and probing his navel. His groin tightened brutally in response, the wrenching in his loins making him whimper and thrash.

Dear God, it was too much! He could not bear it. It had been far too long since he'd had a woman to be able to endure such inflammatory fondling without disgracing himself. To his relief, she paused at the waist of his breeches, seeming to consider what to do next. His succor, however, was short-lived, for in what seemed like the next instant, her hands were on his fall, unbuttoning it. His breath froze in his chest, bated by his agonized anticipation. Any second now, she would expose him.

For several moments she fumbled with the buttons,

seeming to have trouble releasing them from their moorings; then the flap fell away, revealing the straining line of his sex. Again she paused, this time to gape at him, her eyes wide and her mouth forming an exaggerated 0.

Had Gideon not been in such a heat, he no doubt would have found her reaction to what was undoubtedly her first encounter with an erect penis comical. As it was, he was in too much torment over awaiting her next move to find amusement in anything at that moment. Fortunately, or unfortunately, depending on how you wished to view the matter, he did not have to wait long before she resumed her ministrations.

Her hands now faintly trembling, she pushed his breeches opening wider, taking care not to touch the flesh that lay swollen and throbbing against his belly. Grasping either side of the opening, she eased the breeches over his hips and down his thighs. Though Gideon had kicked off his mules when he had climbed onto the bed beside her, he still wore his stockings, which she paused to remove.

Grateful for the respite from her stimulation, he lay still, sucking in deep gasps of breath in an attempt to cool his lust while she fidgeted with his garter buckles. When she had at last removed his garters and stockings, an action followed by a hasty divestment of his breeches, she lightly stroked up his legs, as he had done to her, drawing tickling squiggles across his thighs and around his hips.

Gideon moaned, the muscles in his buttocks bunching and tensing in his carnal torment as she teasingly sketched patterns in the thatch of hair at his groin, each time drawing nearer and nearer to the beleaguered source of his discomfort.

Then she touched him, suddenly and without warning, her hand wrapping around his shaft to stroke his length. His body arched, a strangled cry tearing from his throat at the exquisite shock of pleasure. Again she stroked him, and again he responded with shattering urgency.

"No! No. I cannot . . . You must not . . ." he gasped out in a garbled, broken rush, grasping her shoulders to pull her away. Were he to allow her to continue pleasuring him, he would lose himself for sure, and he wanted to last long enough to show her the bridal bliss she deserved. The mere thought of taking her, of plunging his needful flesh into the honeyed sweetness he had tasted earlier made him growl, a guttural, feral sound, and wrench her into his arms. Now consumed by his raging urgency, he grasped the back of her head, his mouth hard and demanding as it captured hers, smothering her with his kisses.

Julia gasped, horrified by the sudden forcefulness of his assault. His primitive urges! He was possessed by his primitive urges. And he seemed to be taking no pains to bridle them. Her panic mounted as he began to move against her, the unleashed power of his body terrifying her as she felt his muscles bunch and twitch as he crushed her yet tighter into his embrace. In the next instant his hand was between her legs, opening and spreading her, his finger slowly penetrating her, as if gauging her size.

She stiffened at his intimate invasion, her legs clamping closed as she sought to escape it. "Gideon, no," she cried, but her protest was stifled by his kisses.

Still clasping her against him, he rolled her onto her back, his leg lodging between her thighs to part them. Then she felt his sex, hot and hard and thrusting, gouging her where his finger had been only seconds before.

She squeaked in panic. As large as he was, he was certain to hurt her terribly down there if he entered her. Considering his length, he might even kill her by ripping through one of her vital organs. Now mindless to everything but her primal sense of self-preservation, Julia shrieked and hammered at his back.

He pulled back, staring at her in shock. "Julia, sweetheart, whatever is the matter?" he murmured hoarsely.

She tore herself free, scrambling to the opposite side of the bed where she huddled, protectively hugging her knees to her chest. "You cannot—you must not—I cannot—" she jabbered in breathless hysteria.

"Julia. Please. Just tell me what is wrong," he gently implored, smiling with a tenderness that under different circumstances would have won her complete trust.

She sobbed, tears now coursing down her cheeks. "Primitive . . . common . . ." she blurted out incoherently, then broke off, shaking her head.

Gideon's eyes narrowed in his sudden comprehension. It had been an act. All of it. Her acceptance of him in the park. Her easy camaraderie in the aftermath of that encounter. Her response to his kiss at the announcement of their engagement. And now this, her eagerness to bed him.

She viewed him as primitive and common. And though she had tried valiantly to do her duty, no doubt at her father's bidding, she simply could not bring herself to allow a mere commoner to take her.

Damn her to hell, and take her blasted father with her!

Furious, more enraged than he had ever been in his life, Gideon rose from the bed, too choked by anger to speak. Donning his dressing gown with deceptive calmness, he finally managed to hiss, "I see. Well, my dear. I must congratulate you on doing what no one else has ever managed to do."

She sniffled, looking for all the world like the wounded innocent she pretended to be. "I d-do not understand." She frowned and shook her head. "W-what have I done?"

"You have played me for a fool, damn you," he spat. "Well, be warned, Lady Julia." He flung her title at her like a stone. "Now that I know your game, I shall not be fooled again. You may have gotten what you wanted from our bargain, my dear, but you will never find peace in your gains."

CHAPTER 14

Julia awakened with a start, jolted from her fitful slumber as the coach lurched to a rattling stop. From outside the conveyance came masculine shouts of command, the outriders and coachman, she groggily identified, having heard those same voices countless times during the past two days, followed by the hoofbeats of approaching horsemen. The horsemen, she assumed, were Jagtar and Gideon, both of whom had ridden the entire distance from London on horseback.

So have we arrived at last? she wearily wondered, as she had done every time they had stopped during the past few hours. Too stiff and tired from the rigors of the journey to investigate, she remained curled in her seat, her feet tucked beneath her rucked up skirts and her head lolling limply against the diamond-pleated satin squab in a pose that could only be described as undignified.

Not that her pose mattered. Unless Gideon summoned her, an advent that was as likely to occur as goats were to sing an aria, there was little chance that anyone would disturb her until they arrived at their destination. That being the case, there was really no need to trouble herself with moving.

On the other hand, if they had indeed arrived at Gideon's country house, the servants might even now be assembling on the stoop to greet her, as was customary for a household receiving a new mistress. In that instance, it

would hardly be an auspicious beginning on her part to
have a footman fling open the coach door to reveal her
slouched in her seat with her shoes off, her bonnet askew,
and her skirts tossed above her knees like a slattern.

Shuddering at the mere thought of courting such disgrace, Julia forced herself to lift her heavy head and unfold
her sleep-contorted limbs, her cramped muscles screaming
in protest with every move she made. After flexing her
spine and stretching her arms and legs, she was again lim-
ber enough to lean forward and search the floor for her
discarded shoes.

Though it was a deep, moonless night and the coach curtains were drawn, light from the coach lamps spilled around
the edges of the heavy satin draperies, illuminating the inte-
rior enough to allow her to easily locate them. One flat,
olive-green Spanish leather slipper was half wedged beneath the opposite seat, having no doubt been tossed there
when the coach had hit one of the numerous ruts it had
encountered that evening. The other lay upside down near
the door. Hastily donning them, she yanked down her olive,
orange, and tan striped silk carriage dress, smoothing it as
best she could, though it was obvious that it was wrinkled
long past any redemption her pressing hands could offer.

Sighing her disheartenment at the sight of it—for she
really did want to make a good first impression—she turned
her attention to her chip hat. Aside from a bent ostrich
feather and a crushed ribbon loop, the former of which she
straightened and the latter she puffed, both with satisfactory results, the frivolous confection appeared to have survived the journey relatively unscathed. Thankful for that
small blessing, she secured it in place and then leaned forward to lift the nearest curtain, wishing to verify her location. Her hand had no sooner found the tasseled pull cord
than the door swung open.

It was Jagtar. Then again, who else would it be? Since
their disastrous wedding night, Gideon had spoken to her
as little as possible, conveying all messages through his
manservant. Always a model of respect, the Sikh now
smiled and bowed his turbaned head. "My lady? The *sahib*
asks if you wish refreshment, please?" If he found the duty

of go-between for his master and mistress odd, neither his face nor manner betrayed the fact. Indeed, judging from his casual air, you would have thought that such chilly estrangement between a newlywed couple was the most natural thing in the world. Then again, perhaps in his country it was.

Whatever the instance, Julia was grateful for his discretion, so the smile she returned was a genuine one. Leaving his question open to decide for when she knew where she was, she leaned further forward to peer over his shoulder at what lay outside.

There was a two-story, L-shaped stone building with a wooden railed gallery running the entire length of its second floor. Judging from the series of small doors and windows on the upper level, which on the longer wing were set above a row of neat stables, and the tavernlike appearance of the smaller annex, she easily surmised that they were in the courtyard of a coaching inn—the Dun Horse, or so the sign proclaimed.

Only marginally more enlightened than she had been before looking out, Julia quizzed, "Where are we, Jagtar?"

"The village of Tarlington, my lady." Before she could ask where Tarlington lay in respect to Gideon's country seat, he added, "*Sahib* bade me to tell you that this will be our last stop before reaching his home. If you wish refreshment or need to leave the coach, you must do so now, please."

Though Julia was rather hungry and the inn seemed respectable enough, she shook her head, in no mood to exchange the gay pleasantries that were generally expected from travelers by the proprietors of such establishments. "You may tell my husband that I will remain as I am." Better to go hungry than risk being judged as rude, especially since it appeared that Tarlington lay relatively near to Gideon's village of Low Brindle. People did gossip, after all, worst of all in small towns, or so she had always heard. And as mistress of Low Brindle it was her duty to set an example for their tenants by being a model of graciousness.

As Jagtar brought his palms together beneath his chin, a signal that he was about to take his leave, she hastily in-

quired, "Do you, by chance, know when we will arrive at
Critchley Manor?" Critchley Manor was the name of Gideon's country house, Critchley being the surname of the
family who had built the structure a century earlier. From
what she had been able to ascertain from her snatches of
conversation with Gideon during their courtship, the current Critchley heir had been forced to sell the estate after
bankrupting himself in renovating the manor. If that were
indeed true, then the dwelling was bound to be very grand
for all its recent improvements.

"Two hours, my lady. No more."

Julia nodded. "And are we to tarry here long?"

"Since you do not wish refreshment, we remain only long
enough to change horses."

That meant that they would be departing in a moment
or two, since the stableboys at coaching inns were famous
for their skill at removing a spent team and harnessing a
fresh one in the span of a minute or less. As Julia nodded
in response to Jagtar's reply, she could hear the jangle of
harnessing equipage and the *clip-clop* of hoofs against flagstone, followed by the slight lurch of the coach as the weary
team was liberated. Any second now, they would be ready
to resume their journey. "Thank you, Jagtar," she said.

"Please, my lady. Is there anything else I may do for
you?"

She smiled again and shook her head.

Again Jagtar brought his palms together beneath his
chin. This time Julia allowed him to incline his head and
take his leave. Now alone, again cloistered in the stifling
confines of the coach, she opened the nearest curtain and
slid down the window, wooing the fresh night air. The road
dust in this part of the country was such that she had been
forced to ride with the windows shut the entire day, a very
miserable experience indeed, considering the fact that the
day had been unseasonably warm. Now leaning her head
against the window frame to savor the cooling caress of
the breeze against her face, she gazed out at the scene
before her.

Six rushlight lanterns hung from brackets along the upper
gallery, their flames creating a flickering web of shadows

and light that alternately revealed and then obscured the men and beasts in the courtyard below. Judging from the number of people and horses milling about, and the candlelight that glowed through the drawn curtains at nearly every window along the gallery, it was apparent that the inn was a favorite with travelers. It also appeared that Gideon's servants were well known here.

To be sure, the coachman and footman seemed on particularly intimate terms with the serving maid who had brought them tankards of what Julia guessed to be ale, teasing and bantering with her, and patting her broad backside in a manner that caused her to erupt into hoots of bawdy laughter. Two of the four outriders stood near the stone water trough sharing a flask with the stable clerk, while a third guffawed and clapped a groom on the shoulder, as if sharing in a private joke. The absent fourth outrider had no doubt gone ahead to alert the household of their master's imminent arrival. As Julia watched, smiling at the servants' easy camaraderie, Jagtar strolled past chattering in his native tongue to Kesin, who sat on his shoulder ignoring his lecture as he devoured some sort of treat. Gideon, as usual, was nowhere to be seen.

Julia sighed, her smile fading at the thought of her husband.

He hated her, despised her with every fiber of his being, a fact that he had made painfully clear with the few curt words, cold glances, and abrupt gestures he had deigned to grant her since their wedding night. And she despaired at ever being able to mend matters between them. How could she when he loathed her too much to suffer her presence for more than a moment, and then only because he could not avoid doing so?

Feeling as if her whole world was falling apart, she sank back into her seat, hugging herself as dark hopelessness crept into her soul. Oh! It was impossible! A disaster. She had ruined everything: her burgeoning friendship with Gideon, her chance at an amiable marriage, her hope of helping her siblings, and worst of all, perhaps even the bargain itself.

Dread settled like a weight in her heart at the thought of that last. Perhaps even now Gideon was plotting to call in her mother's debt. He most certainly seemed angry enough to do so, and with good reason. After all, she had not only failed to live up to her promise to do as he wished and be the sort of wife he desired, she had deliberately invited and then rebuffed his husbandly advances in a manner that had insulted and humiliated him.

She had called him common and primitive, and had pushed him away as if he were the most loathsome beast in the world.

Julia cringed in shame at the memory. With all she had said and done that night, was it any wonder that he had accused her of playing him for a fool?

Wishing that she could somehow turn back time and change the course of her actions, Julia hugged herself yet tighter. He had been right, of course. She could see that now. After much thought she had discovered that she was indeed guilty of his charge, that in her reckless desperation to aid her siblings she had tried to manipulate him to her will without any consideration for his feelings, or for the cost should she fail. And naturally she had failed. How could she not when she had neither the skill nor the experience to play that particular game well? She had failed, and now she must suffer the consequences. She only prayed that her family would not be forced to do so as well.

Unbidden, visions of her family paying the price for her foolishness flickered through her mind, horrifying ones in which her parents were being hauled away to prison in chains, ruined and disgraced, and her siblings sat huddled in a damp, cold alley, hungry, frightened and abandoned, their emaciated bodies clothed in rags, their tender flesh ravaged by chilblains.

Her soul seemed to shrivel within her at the knowledge that her imaginings might very well become reality, and soon. Oh! If only she could talk to Gideon and explain the truth. Perhaps if he understood her reasons for doing what she had done, perhaps if—but no. Why would he listen to anything she said? Why should he? With everything that had happened, with all the lies and deceptions that lay between them, why in the world would he believe her even if, by some miracle, he agreed to listen?

Now mired in despair, a dark place she had wallowed since her wedding night, Julia wondered what would become of her, of her family. She was on the verge of tears, again imagining the worst, when the coach door swung open. To her astonishment, Gideon climbed in and took the opposite seat. As she gaped at him, too stunned by his unexpected presence to do more, he rapped on the ceiling, signaling the coachman to resume their journey.

There was a shout and the crack of a whip, the rattle of harnesses, and then a sharp jolt as the coach jerked into motion. *Clip-clop! Clip-clop!* The horses' hoofs clattered against the hard flagstone paving of the courtyard, a sound that softened to a repetitious thud as they turned onto the clay-and-pebble surfaced road. As had been the case all day long, their passage stirred up clouds of hazy dust that now billowed and swirled through the open window. Scowling, Gideon leaned forward and closed it, leaving the curtain open to allow the lamplight to shine in. Settling back into his seat again, he folded his arms across his chest, his posture tense and his expression grim as he studied her, as if sizing her up, though for what purpose she did not care to speculate.

Not quite certain what to do or where to look, and tempted almost beyond resistance to squirm beneath his discomfiting scrutiny, Julia busied herself by fumbling with her reticule, finally opening the drawstrings to remove her vial of lavender oil, a known cure for hysteria. Uncorking it with what she hoped was an air of nonchalance, she raised it to her nose, stealing a glance at Gideon from beneath her lashes as she inhaled the calming fumes.

He wore a chocolate-brown riding coat, beneath which he sported a fashionable double-breasted waistcoat made up in green-and-gold patterned silk. As was appropriate for riding on such a long journey, his lower body was clad in tan leather breeches, tight, supple-looking ones, she could not help noticing, the snug legs of which terminated into a very fine pair of knee-high top boots. Like every other garment she had ever seen him wear, his riding clothes were cut to perfection and tailored to emphasize the magnificence of his physique.

Though Julia had tried hard to ignore such thoughts in the days following her wedding night, finding them too disturbing by half, as she looked at Gideon now she could not help remembering the sight of him lying naked before her. His powerful body had been truly beautiful in its symmetry and proportion, a miracle of sculpted muscle and lean sinew that rippled beneath the flawless covering of his sleek, tan skin.

Something deep in her belly fluttered at the memory of that skin. It had felt like satin beneath her touch, soft and smooth and incredibly fine-textured. That a man who was the epitome of raw masculinity could have such skin was almost beyond belief. More amazing yet, she now found herself aching to touch him again, to feel the size and weight and warmth of him pressed against her, and to have him touch her in return.

The fluttering in her belly quickened as she remembered the pleasure of his intimate caresses. The way he had stroked her . . . She sighed, her thighs parting in response to her memory. And when he had used his mouth, his tongue . . .

"Julia?" *Snap! Snap!* Fingers snapped before her face. "Julia!"

Julia squeaked and dropped the lavender she still held to her nose, startled from her sensual reverie. It was Gideon, of course. And it was clear from the annoyance in his voice that this was not his first attempt to gain her attention. Mortified, certain that he had noted her perusal of his body and had somehow discerned her wanton thoughts, she blushed and bent over, hiding her flaming face in the shadows as she searched the floor for her scent vial.

Oh! Whatever was wrong with her? And something most definitely was wrong; it had to be for her to be longing to lie naked with Gideon and exchange intimate caresses. After all, to do such a thing was certain to stir his primitive urges, and that was the last thing on earth she wished to do. Why, the very thought of again suffering those forceful kisses, that savage embrace, and the stabbing menace of his sex as it sought to . . .

"It is behind your left foot," Gideon's harsh voice again

interrupted. "And I might add that it is soiling the carpet.
That means, of course, that I shall be forced to endure the
smell of lavender for the reminder of this journey and on
a good many journeys hereafter. And I detest lavender."

Julia snatched up the offending lavender, which was indeed behind her foot, bristling at his imperious tone. Flashing him a look of haughty disdain, she straightened back
up again, rebutting, "Had you not bellowed at me so, I
would not have dropped it."

"I had to do something. I thought you were suffering a
fit and felt obligated to verify your health," he returned in
an infuriatingly reasonable voice.

Now searching her seat for the cork, though corking the
vial at this juncture was like closing the stable door after
the horses had escaped since the oil had all spilled out, she
retorted, "I cannot imagine what could have made you
think such a thing."

Gideon leaned over and plucked the cork from a fold in
her skirts, presenting it to her on the flat of his gloved
hand. "What else was I to think with the way you were
staring and trembling? Generally when one stares without
blinking for several minutes, with their mouth agape and
their face flushed the color of port wine, they are suffering
from apoplexy or some other equally unpleasant sort of
attack."

Julia accepted the cork with a sniff. "It must have been
a trick of the light, for I most certainly was not staring.
And if I was trembling, it was due to exhaustion from our
journey. Even you must admit that our haste has been grueling in the extreme."

There was a long pause; then he sighed and said, "Yes,
it has been grueling, and for that I must apologize. It was
never my intention that you should suffer discomfort. Unfortunately, circumstances have arisen that dictate our swift
dispatch to Lancashire." His voice sounded suddenly thick,
oddly frayed.

Julia glanced up quickly from the vial she was corking,
taken aback by the abrupt change in his tone. He was no
longer staring at her, but out the window, his strong profile
moving in and out of shadow in the rippling lamplight. With

an odd pang she noted how haggard his features looked
and the way his shoulders slumped, his demeanor suddenly
weary and defeated, like a man bearing a burden too heavy
to be borne. Her anger instantly cooled at the sight of him.
The circumstances he spoke of must be very dire indeed
for him to look so. Suspecting that those circumstances in
some way involved his sisters, she responded in a gentle
voice, "Jagtar indicated that there is some sort of urgent
business at your estate that requires your attention. I do
hope that nothing untoward has befallen your family?"

He drew in a deep breath, closing his eyes as he released
it in a heavy gust. "It is Bethany," he murmured, rubbing
his temples as if they ached.

Bethany. By his dark tone, it was clear that something
very bad indeed had happened to his adored sister. Julia's
heart instantly went out to him, understanding his pain at
his sibling's suffering all too well. Overcome with sympathy,
she started to lean forward to take his hands in hers, to
offer him comfort. Then she remembered the bitterness
that lay between them and resisted the impulse. Letting her
voice convey her compassion instead, she said, "Though I
do not know the nature of your sister's trouble, you have
my promise that I shall do everything in my power to
help her."

"Thank you." He more grunted than uttered the words,
the hand massaging his temples moving down to press
against his still-closed eyes, as if they, too, pained him.

"What I do not understand is why you did not ride
ahead," she continued, mindful of the agony he must be
suffering in his anxiety to be by Bethany's side. "You could
have made much better time had you not accompanied the
coach, but I am sure that you know that."

"Yes." His hand was still pressed to his eyes.

"Then why did you not do so? I would have
understood."

"What? And have my mother rise up from her grave and
haunt me?" He dropped his hand then and opened his eyes,
smiling wryly.

Julia frowned her bewilderment at his queer response. "I
am afraid that I do not understand what you mean."

SCANDAL **201**

"My mother always considered gallantry toward women an important quality in a man, and she took great pains to instill it in Caleb and me. To leave you to make your own way to Lancashire would have been ungallant to the extreme."

"Your mother sounds most admirable," Julia remarked, adding to herself that the woman had done a commendable job of drumming that particular lesson into her son's head. Most men would have shirked the duty of escorting a wife they despised, especially under such circumstances.

"Yes," he said, his smile fading. "And I feel that were she here now, she would urge me to explain to you about Bethany. For better or worse, you are now a member of the Harwood family, so it is only right that you should know the truth, though I pray that you will treat the knowledge with discretion."

"You may be certain that I will keep private whatever confidence you choose to share with me," she vowed.

"Bethany lost the child she was carrying."

Julia recoiled, stunned by the news. "Your sister was with child?"

He nodded once, his face now impassive.

"But—" She shook her head, frowning her consternation. "But I did not even know that she was wed. You never mentioned her husband. And since she lives on your estate, I naturally assumed—"

"I did not mention a husband because she does not have one. She never did," he interjected, grinding the words out from between his teeth. "I must caution you, however, that both my household and village believe her to be a widow— the widow of an American sea captain named Nathan Matland, to be exact, so she is Mrs. Matland to them. It is a lie that I, myself, put about. After all that Bethany has been through, I would spare her the shame of being branded a harlot."

Uncertain what to say or how to react in the face of such a shocking confession, Julia merely nodded and murmured, "I see."

"No. You do not see. I can discern as much from the prim condemnation on your face." His voice was sharp and lashing, gentling to a silken sneer in the next instant as he added, "Then again, I expected as much. However, once you hear the tale of her downfall, I daresay that you shall understand well enough. Indeed, I believe that you will find her situation rather parallels your own in that she whored herself in an attempt to save her sibling, in this instance our youngest sister, Bliss."

Julia gasped, stung by his scathing assessment of her actions. "How dare you accuse me of whoredom?"

"After your performance on our wedding night, how dare you deny it?" he flung back. "For all that you possess wealth and a title, bartering yourself as you did makes you no better than the lowest harlot who sells herself in alleyways for a farthing."

She stiffened in her outrage. "I will have you know—"

"Enough!" he barked, imperiously silencing her. "I have neither the time nor the patience to listen to your indignant protestations, so I suggest that you save them to share with someone who is interested in what you have to say."

"Why you—"

"Enough, I said!" His command was accompanied by a brusque hand motion. "Though it shall no doubt come as a revelation to you to learn that the entire world does not revolve around you, this conversation is about Bethany. I instigated it for her benefit, and hers alone. I did so because I do not wish for her to suffer your shocked expressions and reproving looks should Bliss spill the truth about her to you by mistake. Bethany deserves understanding, not scorn, and I shall not allow her to be slighted by you or anyone else. Do you understand?" His voice had grown soft, dangerously mild.

Julia shot him a withering look, not about to be cowed. "Perfectly, though I might add that you have grievously misjudged me if you think that I would censure your sister out of hand. For all that I am not as worldly as you, I do understand that circumstances sometime force moral people to do things that might be perceived as wrong, and I try to afford them every benefit of the doubt."

"Like you have done with me?" he inquired with a sardonic quirk of his eyebrows.

She shrugged, refusing to take his bait. "As you have so disagreeably pointed out, this conversation is about Bethany. Now, I believe that you have a tale to share that will help me better understand her plight?" She raised her own eyebrows, viewing him with an air of condescending query. "Like yourself, I do not wish to extend this interview any longer than is necessary."

He sketched an abbreviated bow. "Your servant, my lady."

She responded with an aristocratic wave of the hand. If he wished to play the peasant, then she would gladly act the role of queen. "Then pray do proceed."

He nodded once, his face hard and expressionless, his voice cold and exact as he complied. "Her downfall—all of my family's downfall, really—began with my father's death. Being a mere curate whose living was earned by the grace of the village rector, we were turned out of the cottage that went with his post the instant he was in the ground, in order to make room for the new curate and his family."

"Was your village so very large then, that it required both a rector and a curate?" Julia inquired, genuinely wishing to understand Bethany's story. The woman was her sister now, so it was her duty to do so.

Gideon shook his head. "Quite the contrary. It was a tiny, rather poor place. However, like many rectors in England, ours had several other, richer livings at his disposal, which, understandably, he preferred to pursue. That being the case, he hired my father to tend to the spiritual care of his parishioners in his absence."

"But—" she began, trying to further improve her knowledge of rectors and curates.

"But we digress," he interjected. "To make a very long story short, we were left with little money and even fewer resources. Since my mother was six-months gone with Bliss at the time, she had no choice but to take us to London and throw us on the mercy of her only living relative, a brother who lived in Cheapside. As it turned out, he owned a small wig-making shop that at the time was enjoying modest success."

"How old were you?" Julia asked. Exactly why such a

thing mattered, she could not say, but it suddenly did. Very much so.

"Seventeen. Caleb was fourteen, Bethany nine, and Bliss was born three months after our arrival in London."

"And how old are you now?" she countered, stunned to realize that she did not even know her own husband's age.

"Twenty-nine," he replied with a frown, visibly impatient with her questions.

She ignored his annoyance, her curiosity whetted by the meager morsels of personal information he had tossed her. "And your birth date?"

"February twenty-sixth, but I really do not see how it matters. We are discussing Bethany, not me. Remember?"

"But I—"

"My uncle, of course, was hardly pleased to be saddled with five extra mouths to feed," he cut in, overriding her protest by continuing his story. "Not a day went by that he did not remind us of the fact that we were living on his charity, though I can assure you that we all earned our keep fairly enough by slaving in his shop. Even Bethany worked, as young as she was."

"What did you do?" Again, she simply could not resist asking.

"I waited on customers, collected payment, did whatever heavy labor was required around the shop, and delivered the finished wigs." Though Julia expected him to again point out her digression from their subject, he instead shrugged and said, "It was while on my way to make a delivery one evening that I was set upon by a press-gang and pressed into the navy."

Julia's hand flew to cover her mouth in her shock at his disclosure. She had read stories in the newspaper about men being pressed into the navy, and it was said to be a most brutal fate. Indeed, a great many men did not survive the experience.

He nodded, unperturbed by her horrified reaction. "It is how I ended up in India, though that part of the story is neither here nor there."

But it was very much here and there to Julia. So much so that she could not resist blurting out, "But how?" She made a helpless hand gesture, shaking her head. "I mean, surely seventeen was far too young to be pressed into the navy?"

He chuckled, a dark, brittle sound. "I was nineteen at the time, and I can vouch for the fact that I was not the youngest wretch they captured that night. As to the how of the matter, several sailors attacked me and beat me senseless. By the time I regained consciousness, I was at sea and there was no escaping." Another mirthless chuckle. "I soon discovered that even the most reluctant recruit becomes willing after several days of starvation and beatings."

"Oh, Gideon! How very awful," she exclaimed, shaking her head over and over again at the dreadfulness of what she was hearing. "I cannot even begin to imagine what you must have suffered."

"No, you cannot," he retorted shortly. "So I suggest that we return to the purpose of this discussion."

"But—" she protested, too fascinated by his role in the story to let the subject drop.

He cut her off, his tone brooking no argument. "Let it suffice to say that I deserted at the first opportunity, which happened to present itself in Calcutta."

"Calcutta?" Julia frowned. "Whatever was a British naval ship doing in such a place?"

"The one I was on had been consigned to the Bombay Marine, charged with the task of protecting East India Company merchant ships from pirate attacks." His mouth pulled into a sour grin. "Considering the fierce reputation of the pirates in that part of the world, it is little wonder why the navy could not assemble a willing crew for that particular duty. But"—he shrugged one shoulder—"that is a tale for another day."

"It is one that I would very much like to hear," Julia said. "Then again, I suspect that you have a great many other fascinating stories to tell as well."

"I do, most of which are unfit for feminine ears." He shook his head once, sharply. "But again, that is neither here nor there. To return to the business at hand, I soon discovered that there was a fortune to be made in India, and spent almost nine years doing exactly that. I wanted to be so damn rich that my family would never again have to depend on the charity of others. I was determined to buy them everything they could ever want or need."

"It seems to me that you more than succeeded in your goal," Julia commented, his dedication to his family forcing her unwilling admiration for him to rise another notch.

"Did I?" The utterance was harsh, edged with bitterness.

She frowned, taken aback by his tone. "Of course you have. With all your wealth—"

"All the wealth in the world cannot buy back Bethany's virtue and self-respect," he spat. "It cannot buy back the innocence Bliss lost living in a Westminster rookery, nor can it bring back our mother. It seems that it cannot even find Caleb, though from the most recent reports I have had from my Bow Street Runners, he may no longer be alive to find."

"No! Oh, Gideon, no," she exclaimed, genuinely stricken by the news. Even she knew how desperately he had been searching for his brother.

Gideon's sculpted lips twisted into a snarl. "Oh, yes. It is quite possible that his corpse lies rotting in an unmarked burial trench by the road to Oxford, along with two highwaymen whose company he is now thought to have kept, driven to a life of crime from my neglect."

"You can hardly be blamed for neglect when you were struggling to secure your family's future," Julia argued, her heart breaking at the torment in his voice.

"The truth of the matter is that I had amassed an impressive fortune after only five years in India, certainly enough to have kept us all in luxury for the rest of our lives. Had I returned to England then, my mother would most probably still be alive, and my siblings would not have been left in the straits that led to their ruin. But it was not enough. No matter how wealthy I became, it never seemed enough to buy the sort of security I sought. Hence, through my greed I became guilty of neglect."

Despite his detached tone and shuttered expression, Julia sensed the soul-crushing depth of his self-condemnation, his vulnerability. Aching for him, wanting nothing more than to draw him into her arms and soothe him, like she did her sisters when they were hurt, but certain that her gesture would be rejected, she sought to comfort him by coaxing him to unburden and share his festering anguish. "When did your mother die, Gideon?"

"Two years ago. Bethany says that she sickened while nursing our uncle, who was suffering from the same fever that took our mother. He died the day before she did. Caleb, too, was terribly ill for a time, but Bethany managed to pull him through." He spoke softly, his voice devoid of inflection, projecting an impenetrable calm that was devastating to hear.

"And you learned of the tragedy upon your return to England?"

"I learned of it through a letter from Bethany. I had been sending my mother money for several years by then, enough that she could have taken our family away from the wig shop and leased comfortable quarters elsewhere. But apparently she felt a sense of obligation toward our uncle and would not leave him, especially after the shop fell on hard times. As I understand matters, the powder tax Pitt enacted three years ago made men abandon their wigs, which, of course, put quite a strain on my uncle's business. Since my life in India was rather nomadic in nature, and the post was slow to arrive from England, my mother had been dead for well over a year by the time I received the news. I naturally returned to London on the first ship. But I arrived too late." He shook his head, desolation emanating from him in palpable waves. "It seems that I am always too late." That last was uttered softly, as if he whispered it to himself.

"Too late?" she murmured, wanting to understand his feelings.

"I arrived in London to find the wig shop turned into a lamp-makers shop and my siblings vanished. It took the Bow Street Runners two months to find my sisters. They were living in a Westminster rookery, under conditions that make me shudder to remember them. Bethany was with child and very ill from her pregnancy, and Bliss had taken up with a gang of young thieves, stealing whatever she could in order to keep a roof over their heads and a few scraps on their table. She had been lying to Bethany, explaining her ill-gotten gains by claiming to be employed by a feather worker, cleaning and sorting feathers."

"You—you said that Bethany sold herself to save Bliss?" Julia quizzed, her voice catching on her sorrow at what Gideon and his family had suffered.

He nodded. "Bethany is a very beautiful girl with a winning way. Once you have met her, you will see that it is not just my brotherly pride speaking when I say so."

"I believe you," she said. How could she not? As handsome as Gideon was, he could not possibly have a sister who was anything less than beautiful.

He nodded again. "Apparently my uncle noted her charms as well, for he made her his shop assistant when she was only fifteen, no doubt thinking that her pretty face would draw customers. And by all accounts his ploy worked. When the news of Bethany's beauty spread throughout London, it attracted a great many noblemen to the shop, several of whom coveted her for their mistress and offered her the post. Being a moral girl, she naturally turned them down, though the offers were exceedingly fine. Then our mother and uncle died. The shop, which had been failing since the enactment of the powder tax, was forced to close soon after. Though Bethany and Caleb managed to provide for themselves and Bliss, Bethany by working as a millinery seamstress and Caleb by laboring for a wheelwright, matters took another bad turn when Caleb suddenly disappeared, much as I had done years earlier."

"And you now believe that his disappearance had something to do with an association with highwaymen?"

"Unfortunately, yes. All the clues we have found thus far point to his having been shot, and most probably killed, during a robbery gone awry. My guess is that desperation to provide for his sisters drove him to crime."

"But you do not know that for certain?"

"No."

"Then surely there is some hope left that you might find him alive." After all that the Harwood family had suffered, fate owed them the small favor of hope.

"Since the bodies of the highwaymen were never identified, I suppose it is possible that he could be alive. As for hope"—he shrugged—"if Caleb were alive, it seems that the runners would have found some evidence pointing to that fact by now."

"True. Then again, if he is indeed guilty of highway robbery, perhaps he has simply hidden himself well out of fear for the law. He might even have left the country." She shook her head, scrambling to find a plausible explanation, wanting to restore the hope he had so clearly lost. "It is not unheard of for people to turn up after being presumed dead for many years, you know." But even to her ears, her words sounded hollow and devoid of faith.

Gideon smiled at her attempt, though it was apparent from the bleakness of his expression that her words had failed in their purpose. "So I have heard. But again, we have digressed."

"Yes," she agreed, at a loss for anything better to say. "Pray do continue with your story."

"As you might imagine, Caleb's disappearance left Bethany and Bliss in terrible straits. Not only was Bethany unable to earn enough to provide for her and her sister, but Bliss had developed a certain fascination with a pair of young thieves she had met on the street, and had begun to pick pockets. They were sharing a Westminster cellar with two other families at the time. Being fearful that her sister would be arrested, and desperate to give her a better life, Bethany sought out one of the noblemen who had offered her the post as his mistress when she was working at the wig shop, and sold herself to him."

"Then it is his child she was carrying?"

His features hardened to stone at her question. "Yes."

"But you said that she was living in Westminster when you returned to London. If she was a nobleman's mistress and carrying his child—"

"The bastard abandoned her when she discovered herself pregnant," he interrupted, "which forced her and Bliss to return to Westminster. It is where I found them, and not a moment too soon. Bethany most probably would have died, she was so weak with illness from her pregnancy. As for Bliss, I shudder at what would have become of her."

"The man is a scoundrel and should be shunned from polite society—he will be shunned!" Julia declared, incensed that a man, especially a nobleman, would treat a woman with such callousness. "If you tell me his name, I shall make certain that he is cut from the *ton.*"

"If I knew his identity, I can assure you that he would suffer much worse than mere banishment from society. Unfortunately, Bethany has refused to tell me who he is."

Julia frowned her bewilderment. "I cannot think why she would protect him after the beastly way he treated her."

"It is me she seeks to protect. She is afraid that I might end up in jail, or worse, for what I might do to the bastard should I ever get my hands on him." He fell silent then, again staring out the window. Though he seemed composed, almost indifferent to the tragedy of what he had just imparted, the angry flickering of his jaw muscles told a far different tale, betraying the emotion ravaging his soul.

Again Julia was tempted to reach out to him, and again she squelched the impulse. Needing to say something, to offer some sort of comfort, she murmured, "You were right. I did not understand about Bethany, but I do now. And I very much want to help her in any way I can. Bliss, too. All you have to do is tell me how."

"Just be kind to them. Hate me if you must, but please be kind to my sisters." He looked at her then, and she saw the terrible bleakness in his eyes. "It is all that I shall ever ask of you."

Julia nodded, her throat so tight with emotion that she could barely speak. "I promise that I shall love them like my own sisters. If we find Caleb alive, and I shall pray that we do, I will love him too." Impossible though it seemed, she was beginning to believe that she might someday find it in her heart to love Gideon as well.

CHAPTER 15

She had promised to love the Harwood sisters as much as she did her own. And it was a promise she had managed to honor thus far—well, at least in regard to Bethany, who was every bit as winning and wonderful as Gideon had claimed her to be. Bliss, on the other hand . . .

Julia snipped a length of pale gold embroidery silk from the skein she held, heaving an inward sigh as she stole a glance at Bliss. The girl sat stiffly erect in an armchair by the drawing-room window, working the sampler Julia insisted she stitch. Though she looked demure enough in her white muslin gown and blue silk sash, with a pert, lace-trimmed day cap atop her smooth dark hair, her sullen expression and the viciousness with which she stabbed her needle into the coarse linen betrayed the explosive belligerence that Julia knew seethed just beneath the surface of her serene facade.

As Gideon had warned, Bliss was difficult—beyond difficult—her rude behavior having quickly won her the dubious honor of being the most ungovernable brat Julia had ever met. To make matters worse, she seemed to have taken an inordinate dislike to Julia the instant she clapped eyes on her, and not a day had passed since that she had not acted upon her enmity, treating Julia with such hostility that one would have thought that she was an invading foe.

Then again, perhaps that is what she perceives me to be, Julia thought, turning her attention to threading her needle.

And who could blame her if she did? After the way Gideon
had introduced them, an introduction that had consisted
solely of his barked command that Bliss obey her, what
else was the chit to think? Why, from the harshness with
which he had thrust her and her authority into his sister's
life, one would have thought that Julia's addition to the
household was meant as a punishment, not the blessing the
presentation of a new bride should have been. Add that
infelicitous beginning to the way he had behaved since, and
was it really any wonder that the girl resented her so?

Julia sighed again, this time at the thought of Gideon.
He was like a thundercloud about to erupt, dark and angry
and brooding, treating her with icy detachment and the rest
of the household with a glowering impatience that made
them scurry skittishly out of his way whenever they spied him
heading in their direction. To say that the atmosphere at
Critchley Manor was tense would have been a sweeping
understatement. Adoring her brother as she so obviously
did, Bliss naturally blamed Julia for his ill humor and had
on more than one occasion accused her of ruining his life.

Now satin stitching the highlights in the lion's mane, the
lion being one of several exotic beasts in the design she
was embroidering on the needle case she was making for
Maria's birthday, Julia admitted that she could not blame
the chit for loathing her as she did. Had she been in Bliss's
place, she might have felt much the same way, though, of
course, she would have expressed her dislike in a more
genteel fashion. No matter how upset one might be, it was
never permissible to curse, or screech, or stamp one's feet
like a savage on the warpath. One most certainly did not
rip down the dining-room draperies in a fit of temper, as
Bliss had done the day before when Julia had tried to correct her beastly table manners, or toss a pot of ink on
another person's gown, which was Bliss's reaction to her
efforts at improving the scrawling scribble the brat passed
off as handwriting.

Beyond frustrated by the situation, Julia tugged her
thread too hard, ruining her stitch and bunching the fabric
beneath it. It was impossible—Bliss was impossible! How

was she to guide the horrid child when she refused to grant her so much as a civil word?

Now adjusting her wayward stitch, Julia searched her mind for an answer, seeking the means to strike a truce with Bliss. When she had come to her wit's end and was still no closer to finding a remedy, she reluctantly considered taking her problem to Gideon and soliciting his assistance.

Though Gideon had known Bliss a scant five months, having been pressed into the navy when she was little more than a baby, he appeared to possess at least a modicum of control over her. Well, he did if one were to judge from the way the brat metamorphosed into a lamb whenever she was in his presence. Then again, perhaps her good behavior stemmed less from control on Gideon's part and more from an eagerness on Bliss's part to please the man she no doubt viewed as her rescuing hero. Whatever the instance, a word from Gideon on her behalf was certain to go a long way in promoting peace. The question was: would he help her? Would he even listen to her appeal?

Probably not, on both counts, Julia grimly decided, resuming her needlework. Though she would have thought such a thing impossible, her relationship with Gideon seemed to have worsened during the three weeks they had been in Lancashire, with Gideon absenting himself from the manor every day from dawn until well after dark, supposedly overseeing the estate. Secretly, Julia suspected that it was not so much estate business as a desire to avoid her that kept him away, a tactic that she had to admit worked very well indeed. To be sure, sometimes several days would pass without her catching so much as a glimpse of him. Why—

"Bloody friggin' rag!" Bliss abruptly exclaimed.

Julia looked up in time to see the girl's sampler hurling across the room.

Thwack! Crash! It mowed down a delicate pair of Harlequin figurines, toppling them from the console table upon which they sat to shatter against the hard marble floor below.

"Bliss! How could you!" she cried, tossing aside her own needlework to rush to where the once-beautiful statuettes lay in a rainbow of jagged shards. Kneeling down to examine the ruin, she added in a severe tone, "These figurines were made by Meissen, and are—were quite valuable. I cannot even begin to imagine what your brother will say when he discovers what you have done."

The impossible chit, who now stood with her arms folded across her thin chest and her lower lip thrust out in an all-too-familiar pose of petulant defiance, shrugged one shoulder, visibly unrepentant. "He's hardly likely to notice since he's never here."

She was right, of course, but Julia would be damned before she would let the crime pass unpunished. Determined that for once the brat would get her just reward, she rose to her feet, assuming her sternest expression and most authoritative stance as she countered, "In that case, you will tell him yourself."

Bliss sniffed, a most scornful sound. "Oh? And whose gonna make me?" Another disdainful sniff. "You?"

Reminding herself that she was an adult and must thus refrain from taking the brat's childish bait, no matter how sorely it chafed her to do so, Julia calmly but firmly replied, "If need be, yes. Furthermore, I expect you to clean up the mess you have made, after which you will go to your room, where you will wait until your brother returns home. At that time I shall fetch you and see to it that you make your confession and tender an appropriate apology." To her relief, her voice rang with a satisfying degree of command.

Bliss stamped her foot, her gray eyes narrowing in a way that always signaled the onset of a tantrum. "I will not! I don't have to do nuttin' you say! You ain't the boss of me!"

"Actually, I am," Julia coolly returned. "If you will recall, your brother put you in my charge. He also bid you to obey me, so I am indeed the *boss* of you."

Bliss's eyes were little more than slits now. "Don't you dare talk to me about my brother," she flung back, her youthful voice growing shrill in her anger. "Everyone knows that he can't stand to be near you. It's the reason he ain't never here." *Stamp!* The soft sole of her kidskin slipper struck the floor with an emphatic thump. "He hates you"—*stamp! stamp!*—as much as I do." *Stamp!* "More, even! He'd be happy if you kicked the bucket—dancin' a bloody jig. We'd all be." *Stamp! Stamp!*

"What a wicked, ugly thing to say!" Julia gasped, her palm itching to spank the brat. Not that she would ever do such a thing, no matter how tempting the prospect might be.

"It's true!" *Stamp!* "It's true!" *Stamp! Stamp!* "True! True! True!" *Stamp! Stamp! Stamp!* In a frenetic blur of movement Bliss snatched up a nearby vase, flinging it against the wall as she flew toward the door.

Well schooled by now in the brat's tactics, Julia hurtled to the right, effectively blocking her escape.

With an infuriated screech, Bliss dodged first to the right, then to the left, and to the right again, trying to confuse Julia as to which direction she intended to race around her. In the next instant she seized a heavy marble bust from a nearby shelf and dashed it to the floor, striking so close to Julia's feet that she was forced to jump aside to save herself from being struck. Her move had what was no doubt the calculated effect, for it allowed Bliss to dart past her and out the door, which she closed behind her with a resounding slam.

Recovering quickly from the shock of almost having her feet crushed, Julia stormed after her. She would not let the brat get away with such appalling behavior. Oh no, not this time. She was through with countering her tantrums with kindness, done with trying to understand them. What the chit needed was a lesson in discipline, a firm one, and she was going to get it. Now. If need be, she would physically drag Bliss back to the drawing room and force her to clean up the mess she had made, after which she would lock her in her room. It was high time the brat learned that such abominable behavior would not be tolerated.

Julia's purposeful march down the newly plasterwork-ornamented hallway was accompanied by the chaotic din of hammering, a megrim-inducing racket that was punctuated now and again by shouted calls from the army of workmen who had by now become a fixture of the manor.

For all that Gideon had told her about the Critchley heir bankrupting himself with the extravagance of his renovations, he had neglected to inform her that the man had run out of funds before finishing them. Thus Julia had arrived to find the house overrun with craftsmen of every description, and the structure itself engulfed in scaffolding and tarpaulins. There were also a million and one decisions to be made in regard to the work that as mistress she was naturally expected to make.

Now coming to the noisy, workmen-deluged entry hall, through which Bliss would have passed in order to make her way to the garden, which was her preferred post-tantrum hiding place, Julia's progress was arrested by Mr. Stoppard, the London architect Gideon had hired to oversee the completion of the renovations.

"My lady?" he hailed, waving what looked like yet another set of his endless design plans. "A moment, please?"

Julia sighed, forcing herself to smile as the man approached. "Mr. Stoppard?" she replied, hoping that he would not detain her long. Once Bliss had hidden herself in the garden, she was all but impossible to find.

The architect smiled and sketched a brief bow. He was a fine figure of a man, tall and elegantly slender, with a handsome face and a fine sense of fashion. "As you can see, my lady, things are progressing quite splendidly," he said, almost shouting in order to be heard over the sawing and hammering. "I must confess to being particularly pleased with the way the staircase came out. I do hope that you are equally delighted?" It was apparent from both his words and expression that he expected her to approve his work.

Though Julia was tempted to approve it without a glance in her eagerness to bring Bliss to justice, she knew that it was her responsibility as mistress of the house to make certain that the completed work was indeed satisfactory. And since she had been schooled from the cradle to always honor such duties, she forced herself to turn her attention to the staircase, reluctantly resigning herself to the fact that she would have little chance of catching Bliss for the time lost in her pursuit. As she examined the architect's creation, she had to admit that he had every reason to be proud.

Made of gold-veined white marble and railed with a gilt scroll-patterned ironwork balustrade, the wide, stately staircase rose from a vestibule of rich gold siena marble, branching off right and left halfway up to curve into the gallery above. It was a design that repeated itself for three more stories, forming a quartet of galleries that overlooked the magnificent entry hall below. Rows of bronze-crowned black marble columns adorned and supported each gallery, with the uppermost ones providing a buttress for a majestic glass-and-ironwork dome.

"It is splendid, Mr. Stoppard. I cannot recall having ever seen a grander staircase, not even in London," she said sincerely. "I am quite certain that my husband will agree." Not that she actually expected Gideon to comment upon it, at least not to her. Truth be told, she was not sure that he even noticed the renovations, since she had never seen him spare any of them so much as a passing glance.

The architect graced her with another smile, clearly gratified by her praise. "Excellent! I am glad you approve. Now about the ballroom floor . . ."

A half hour later Julia finally stepped out onto the back terrace that overlooked the Critchley gardens. Laid out in the Picturesque style, a style that prescribed to an informal arrangement of lush landscapes and meandering, serpentine avenues, viewing the gardens from here was rather like gazing upon a panorama of Old Master paintings. Scenes of untamed woodland dissolved into idyllic, sun-dappled glades; dreamlike wildernesses with romantic grottos gave way to glens where rustic bridges spanned tranquil lakes, and rainbows danced in the mists of sparkling cascades. Everywhere one looked were fanciful eye-catchers. There were arches and obelisks, rustic cottages and Grecian temples—there was even a mock ruin of a castle that sat in a fairy-tale forest near the edge of a flower-strewn meadow.

Though Julia knew that she would never find Bliss in this seemingly endless wonderland, she felt obligated to at least try. Who knew? For once, luck might actually favor her.

She had just descended the terrace steps and was about to take the path to her left, which cut through a mazelike planting of hedges and trees, when someone called out to her from her right. Shading her eyes from the glaring midday sun, she peered in the direction from which the voice had come, cranking her neck to look through the arched stone gateway that led into the private family garden.

It was Bethany, reclining on what Julia instantly recognized as the French chaise longue from the East drawing room. By her side sat a man she could not recall having ever seen before.

"Julia!" Bethany called again, merrily waving her hand. "Do come! There is someone I would very much like for you to meet."

Smiling, Julia did as requested, pleased to see Bethany up and about. To her knowledge, this was the first time she had left her bedchamber since losing her baby.

At her approach the man rose, revealing himself to be almost as tall as Gideon and every bit as splendidly built. Bethany waited until she had stopped by her side before making introductions. "Julia, this is Mr. English. No doubt Gideon has told you all about him since he is practically a member of our family."

Having been shielded from all unpleasantness while confined to her sickbed, Bethany was unaware of the trouble in her brother's marriage. Therefore she labored under the impression that he loved his new bride and that he thus confided everything to her. Not about to reveal the truth herself by admitting to a lack of communication with Gideon, Julia smiled, as if verifying the assumption, and nodded at their guest. "A pleasure, Mr. English."

"And this, Mr. English, is Lady Julia, Gideon's bride, but of course you have already guessed as much," Bethany continued.

Mr. English smiled and bowed. "The pleasure is all mine, Lady Julia. Please allow me to congratulate you on your marriage, and to wish you much joy in your union." He was a handsome man, almost sinfully so, with his sculpted features and thickly lashed dark eyes. Even his hair was extraordinary, black as ebony and falling almost to his shoulders in a glorious mane of silky waves and fat, gleaming curls. From the glances Bethany kept darting him, it was obvious that his remarkable looks were not lost on her.

"You are most kind, Mr. English, but please, I am simply Julia to my friends and family. Since you are said to be a bit of both, it is only right that we should put aside the formality of titles," she replied, not missing the admiring gazes he shot Bethany in return. And why should he not admire her? With her glossy, chocolate-brown ringlets, stunning sapphire eyes, and angelic face, she more than matched him in beauty.

His smile broadened at her cordial speech, revealing teeth every bit as excellent as Gideon's. "In that instance, you must call me Christian."

"Christian," Julia acknowledged, smiling back.

"Christian has just returned from Liverpool," Bethany explained, smiling as well as she glanced back and forth between her companions. "As Gideon probably told you, his Bow Street Runners found several witnesses who claim to have seen a man fitting Caleb's description at an inn there around the time of his disappearance."

"And Christian went to further investigate the claims," Julia easily surmised.

Bethany nodded. "Since the innkeeper harbors some sort of prejudice against runners and would not speak with them, it was decided that someone from our family must interview him. Of course Gideon could not go. He had just arrived from London with you when we received word, and could not leave his new bride. So Christian was kind enough to offer to go in his stead. He—" She broke off with a short, lilting laugh. "But how silly of me to ramble on so. Surely my brother told you all of this?"

For a moment Julia considered responding with a noncommittal murmur, her pride urging her to foster her sister-in-law's belief that all was well with her marriage. Then her curiosity about the outcome of the interview got the better of her, and she shook her head. "No. I am afraid not." Feeling obligated to supply an explanation for why her husband had neglected to mention such an important matter, she weakly added, "You must understand that Gideon has been terribly preoccupied with estate business of late."

"He has been having a rather bad time with his tenants, poor man," Bethany concurred, readily accepting her excuse. She sighed and shook her head. "Who would have guessed that a disagreement over weaving could cause such a hullabaloo?"

"Yes," Julia agreed. Though she knew nothing about the controversy to which Bethany alluded, she was aware that the majority of their cottagers were weavers by trade. She had managed to learn at least that much about the estate during her frequent visits to Bethany's sickbed.

Bethany sighed again. "Ah, well. Perhaps matters will improve after tonight."

"What is happening tonight?" This was from Christian, who Julia silently blessed for saving her from having to make the inquiry herself.

Bethany flashed him an apologetic smile. "I am sorry, Christian. I am so accustomed to you knowing everything about village affairs, that I quite forgot that you have not heard Gideon's plan." He smiled back in pardon, and she explained, "Gideon has arranged a meeting with the weavers tonight to discuss their differences. He hopes that doing so will smooth whatever lies between them, and stop their constant bickering. After that terrible fight on the village green—" She broke off, shaking her head. "Well, if anyone can right matters, it is Gideon. I daresay that he will want you there, Christian, just in case there is trouble. The meeting is at seven o'clock, in the tithe barn." She finished by favoring him with another smile, this one so radiant that it lit her entire face.

His answering one was equally dazzling. "You may be certain that I will be there."

Though Julia knew that she should be interested in the villagers' woes—after all, as mistress, it was her duty to be concerned about her tenants—she was far more intrigued to hear what Christian had found out about Caleb. Aware that the conversation had strayed too far from the subject to return on its own, she urged it back by saying, "I am sure that my husband will appreciate your presence there tonight, Christian, and that he will be just as eager as I am to hear what you discovered in Liverpool. I do hope that your mission met with success?"

Christian's gaze was still on Bethany, his handsome face a poignant study of tenderness and yearning. Politely tearing it away to look at Julia while he answered her question, he replied, "A bit of success, yes. It seems that the innkeeper rented a room to a man who not only fit Caleb's description, but was wounded as well, which Caleb was said to have been, if it was indeed he who was shot during that robbery a year and a half ago."

"If he was able to travel as far as Liverpool, then he could not have been too gravely injured," Julia commented, choosing to view the news with optimism.

Christian shook his head, his expression grim. "I only wish that that were the case. According to the innkeeper the man was in a very bad way, so bad that he most certainly would not have made it there without the aid of his companions. He also said that the man refused to summon a surgeon, in spite of the fact that he was in terrible pain. The reason the innkeeper remembered him so well was because he half expected him to die while under his roof."

"Do you suppose that his companions were highwaymen?" asked Bethany, her eyes troubled as she stared up at Christian.

"Perhaps, though they did not sound much like highwaymen to me. They were described as being a genteel woman of middle years and a male servant. The innkeeper said that the woman was quite lovely and obviously wealthy." He seemed about to continue in that same vein, then shook his head, as if changing his mind. "In any case, they spent only one night there, so he suspects that they sailed on one of the ships that left the following day. After two weeks of inquiry, I managed to ascertain that there were three ships to sail that day: one to Jamaica, another to Portugal, and the last to Brazil."

"Is there any way of knowing if Caleb was aboard one of them?" Julia inquired.

"There are passenger lists and such. However, since it is

doubtful that he would have used his real name, I searched for groups of travelers with two men and one woman. I found four. Two of the groups sailed for Jamaica, one to Brazil, and the other to Portugal. Since all the ships are currently out to sea on other voyages, I shall be unable to interview the captains and crews until they return. I left several liberal bribes at the wharf to ensure that we are notified the instant they dock."

There was a pause of silence, as each contemplated the news. At length, Bethany sighed and said, "I suppose that we should view all this as encouraging, but I must confess to being worried. Ocean voyages are perilous enough for a person in health. I can only imagine the danger to a wounded man."

"From what I have heard, Caleb is very strong. He is also young, which makes him resilient to illness and wounds," Julia pointed out, determined that the Harwood family should foster this new hope. After all they had suffered, they deserved the luxury of hope.

Christian nodded. "Add those facts to the ones that he had two companions to nurse him, and a ship's surgeon at his disposal, and I would say that there is a very good chance indeed that he is alive and well."

Bethany seemed to consider their encouraging words for a moment, then smiled faintly. "I suppose you are right, both of you."

"Of course we are right," Julia declared, reaching down to give her shoulder a reassuring squeeze. Looking back up at Christian, she asked, "By chance, was anyone able to say when the ships might return?"

"The ones that sailed to Portugal and Brazil are expected in a few weeks. It will be a bit longer for the other, but—" He broke off abruptly, frowning. "Pray do forgive me, Julia. How very rude of me to keep you standing all this time. Please sit." He indicated the chair he had vacated.

Julia shook her head. "As much as I am enjoying our conversation, I really must find Bliss. She—" She paused, hesitant to mention the brat's bad behavior in front of Christian.

"She had a tantrum and has run out here to hide," Bethany finished for her.

"Yes," Julia admitted, slanting Christian an abashed look.

Bethany laughed. "It is quite all right. Christian knows all about Bliss's wicked ways."

Christian made a droll face. "As you will soon discover, Julia, the Harwood women view me as a pet, and thus feel no need to guard their tongues when in my presence."

"We have made you our pet because we find you so very pleasing and enjoy spoiling you," Bethany countered, laughing again. Judging from the smitten look she gave him as she delivered her remark, Julia ventured to guess that he might exchange the station of pet for that of husband in the very near future.

Christian grinned, displaying his even white teeth in all their stunning glory. "If you like, Julia, I will find Bliss and bring her to you. As her pet, I am privy to her hiding places."

"I really do not wish to trouble you with such a thing," Julia demurred, loath to take him from Bethany's company.

He shrugged. "It is no bother. I had intended to find her anyway, and let her know that I have returned."

"Well . . ." She glanced with uncertainty at Bethany, who nodded her approval. Looking back at Christian, she smiled and finished, "In that instance, please do, and thank you."

"Then I am off." Stealing one last, worshipful look at Bethany, he disappeared down the path at the opposite end of the flowering knot garden.

"What a delightful man," Julia commented, claiming his abandoned chair. "And kind. Not many men would take an interest in a child Bliss's age."

Bethany smiled, a sweet, pensive smile. "They are very alike, Bliss and he, kindred souls."

"Bliss and Christian? Alike?" Julia frowned, taken aback by the concept. For the life of her, she could not even begin to see any similarities between the two.

"They are alike in that they both feel lost, which creates a bond of sorts between them," Bethany said. "That bond makes them understand each other in ways that other people cannot. Sometimes when I watch them together, I have the feeling that they find comfort in each other's company."

Julia's frown deepened. "Why ever would they feel lost?"

"Christian feels lost because he has no identity, and Bliss because—"

"How can Christian not have an identity?" Julia interrupted.

"Because he has no memory of his past."

"What!"

"He does not know who he is, or even how he came to be captured. You see, Christian was a slave when Gideon found him, the captive of a great Mogul leader. He—"

"A captive!" Julia gasped in shock. "How very awful for him! I once read an account written by a man who was captured by Moguls, and he suffered a most hideous ordeal."

Bethany nodded, her beautiful face growing grave. "I suspect that it was exceedingly terrible for Christian as well. However, since neither he nor Gideon have shared the details with me, I know little about his captivity. All I really know for certain is that his captors always addressed him as either Christian or English, which is why he has chosen to be called Christian English now. He is accustomed to answering to the names."

"Poor man. Are there no clues at all to his identity?" Julia inquired softly, moved by Christian's plight.

"Judging from his skill with a sword, Gideon at first suspected him to be a soldier, captured during some sort of battle. For a short while he even thought that he might be the younger son of a nobleman, given his cultured speech and manner. However, since we have thus far been unable to find military records to confirm the former, and no noble family in England has reported missing a son matching Christian's age and description, both theories now seem highly unlikely."

"How sad," Julia murmured. "It appears that he truly is lost."

"His past is lost, yes. Fortunately he was found by Gideon and given a new place in life." Bethany smiled then, as if struck by a sudden, pleasurable thought. "I must say that Gideon is equally fortunate in that he has gained a steadfast friend in Christian, as have we all. Something that you will learn soon enough for yourself, Julia, is that if a family member is missing from the manor, they are most probably at the dowager's cottage near the edge of the property, visiting Christian."

"Then that is where he lives?" Julia asked, forgetting that she was supposed to know such things.

Bethany eyed her queerly, but replied without commenting upon her ignorance. "Yes. For all that Christian can afford to purchase his own estate, he prefers to live in the cottage and help Gideon oversee his."

"Christian is wealthy?" Julia stared at her in surprise, incredulous that a man without either an identity or a past could possess the funds to purchase something as dreadfully expensive as an estate.

"Not as wealthy as Gideon, but yes." Bethany nodded. "Christian can most certainly be counted as plump in the pockets."

"But how? I mean, if he was a slave . . ." Julia let her voice trail off, finishing the sentence with a helpless hand gesture and a puzzled frown.

"It was Gideon's doing," Bethany replied, her pride in her brother evident in her voice. "Though he is far too modest to tell you of his kindness himself, Gideon helped Christian make a fortune of his own after he freed him. With all the poor man had suffered, he felt that the least he could do was make certain that Christian had the funds to search for his identity, or build a new one, if he so preferred."

"From what I have seen and heard, Christian seems more disposed toward the latter," Julia observed with a smile.

"He does, which I must confess to finding exceedingly odd," Bethany said, her expression growing troubled. "You would think that he would be eager to find out who he is, to discover his past. Yet, he has made no effort whatsoever to do so since returning to England." She sighed. "I sometimes wonder if he refrains from searching out of fear of what he will find."

"Or maybe there is something holding him here . . . perhaps the promise of a wonderful future that he wishes to explore," Julia countered meaningfully, hinting at Christian and Bethany's obvious affection for each other.

Bethany frowned and shook her head. "But that makes no sense. No matter where he goes, how long he is absent, or who he proves to be, he will always have a future with us and be welcomed as part of our family. He knows that."

"It could be that he does not wish to postpone his future here while he searches for his past. After all, there are some moments that must be seized and nurtured the instant they arrive, if they are to grow into something enduring," Julia tried hinting again.

Bethany merely looked at her, her frown deepening, as if she truly did not understand the intimation.

"I am speaking of love, dear," Julia clarified when it became apparent that Bethany was not going to grasp her meaning. "I have seen the way you and Christian look at each other. It is clear that you care for each other a great deal, and not just as friends."

Rather than blushing and looking pleased, as most women did at the mention of a burgeoning romance, Bethany recoiled, as if taken aback. Then she laughed, a tense, forced-sounding trill. "Christian and I? In love?" she exclaimed, as if such a thing were the silliest notion in the world. "Nonsense! We are just friends—like brother and sister. I have never thought of him as anything more, nor he me."

"Are you so certain that that is all he feels for you?" Julia persisted, far too familiar with the signs of infatuation to miss them when they were worn with such transparency.

"Very certain, yes."

"But—"

"We are friends. Nothing more," Bethany interrupted, her firm voice ringing with finality. "It is all we will ever be to each other. Even if Christian did have stronger feelings for me, which he most assuredly does not, I would not marry him. I could not."

"But why?" Julia demanded to know, perplexed that Bethany would turn away from the man she so obviously desired.

"How can you even ask such a question when you know what I have done, what I have been?" Bethany flung back, her face contorting into an expression of wounded reproach. "Surely you can see that I am unfit to be a wife? Especially to a man as fine as Christian."

"Bethany—" Julia began, wanting to make her see reason.

"No, Julia! Enough!" Bethany shook her head once, violently. "I do not wish to discuss the matter any further." By the glint in her eyes and the firm set of her delicate jaw, it was evident that she would brook no argument.

As much as Julia would have liked to pursue the subject, she refrained from doing so, not wishing to cause Bethany further distress. Also not wishing to leave matters as they were, she said, "Please forgive me, Bethany. I did not mean to upset you. It is just that I care about you and wish to see you happy." She was about to add the promise that she would not broach the subject again, but stopped herself from doing so, aware that it was a vow she might not be able to keep.

"Of course I forgive you, Julia. I know that you meant well." For all that Bethany's smile was wan, her words sounded genuine enough.

Now searching for a new topic of conversation to fill the leaden silence that had fallen between them, Julia murmured, "I do hope that Christian is not having any difficulty with Bliss."

"Oh, you have nothing to fear on that account," Bethany replied, her frail smile gaining strength. "She is never any trouble for him. As I said, they are very special friends."

"You also said that they are both lost, though you have yet to tell me why Bliss should feel so." It seemed a harmless enough topic to pursue.

Apparently it was, for Bethany promptly replied, "She does not feel safe."

Julia frowned, taken aback by her response. "But why? Surely she knows that she can trust Gideon to take care of her? Can she not see how devoted he is to her—to your entire family?"

"It is not Gideon she does not trust, but life. The poor dear has suffered so many changes, so much terrible tragedy in her short life. It has made her wary of happiness and of feeling secure, for experience has taught her that all good things can vanish in the blink of an eye."

"Yes, I can see how she might feel that way," Julia said, and she did. From what Gideon had told her, everyone Bliss had ever trusted to care for her had failed her in one way or another. Her anger with the child now diluted by sympathy, she murmured, "I wish there were something I could do to help her."

"You could discuss the problem with Gideon, and persuade him to spend more time with her," Bethany suggested.

It was all Julia could do to refrain from sniffing at the notion of Gideon allowing her to persuade him to do anything, much less listening to anything she had to say. Though she considered it highly unlikely that he would ever do either, she dutifully inquired, "Do you really think that that would help?"

Bethany nodded. "I am sure it would. You see, Julia, it is my belief that much of Bliss's fear stems from the fact that Gideon is never here. I do not know if you are aware of the fact, but these past three weeks is the longest period of time he has spent with us since returning to England. Before this we were fortunate to see him for a day or two once every fortnight, and then he was off to tend business elsewhere, or traveling the country in search of Caleb."

"He does have a great many responsibilities," Julia pointed out, though why she should feel compelled to come to Gideon's defense, she could not even begin to imagine.

"Oh, I was not criticizing him," Bethany countered with a smile. "How could I when so much of what he does is to benefit Bliss and me? I was simply trying to explain matters."

Julia smiled back. "And you are doing a splendid job of it." That said, she returned to the business at hand. "So you truly believe that Gideon's frequent absences make Bliss feel vulnerable?"

Bethany nodded. "After all the people she has lost, she cannot bear to have those she loves out of her sight for any length of time. It is almost as if she believes that nothing bad can befall her, or them, if they are near." She paused, as if to consider the matter, then shook her head and continued. "My guess is that her naughty behavior is a bid for Gideon's attention. After all, if she drives off her governesses, throws tantrums, and is utterly impossible, he must come home and deal with the problems she has created. Once he is near, she is all that is good and agreeable. Though you may find it hard to believe, Bliss is by nature a very agreeable child. Indeed, I cannot recall her having a single tantrum before Gideon's return from India."

"Well, she has certainly been having plenty lately, violent ones, and having Gideon home seems to have done nothing to curb them," Julia commented, heaving a frustrated sigh.

"My guess is that she is terrified."

"Terrified? Of what?"

"You, of course."

"Of me?" Julia pointed to herself, completely caught off guard. "Why ever would she be terrified of me?"

"Because you are Gideon's wife. And as his wife, you have it in your power to take him away from her, if you so choose. She also understands that a wife commands far more of a man's attention than his sister. I would say that she is afraid that he will abandon her for you."

"But—but that is absurd," Julia sputtered. And it was. As Bliss, herself, had pointed out, Gideon hated her and could not bear to be near her. It was the reason he was never at home.

Never at home? Understanding dawned then. While Bliss might have hated her for the reason Bethany suspected, had she indeed been the adored wife, the child most probably despised her for driving Gideon away. After all, when he fled from her, he fled from them all.

"Of course it is absurd," Bethany said, her voice penetrating Julia's thoughts. "Unfortunately, Bliss cannot see that, nor is she likely to do so unless Gideon shows her that her fears are unfounded."

"Have you told your brother any of this?" Julia asked. If she had not, she must convince her to do so. After all, Gideon loved Bethany, which meant that she would have a far better chance of persuading him to the plan than she could hope to have.

"Yes. I talked to him shortly after your arrival, but"— she sighed and shook her head—"it seems to have done no good. He is still almost always gone from the manor."

And of course it was all Julia's fault. Indeed, there was not a doubt in her mind that he would have heeded his sister's plea if he could have been assured of avoiding Julia's company while doing so. As it was, he seemed to think that what Julia had to offer Bliss was more important to her well-being than the measure of security his presence would give her, and had thus chosen to absent himself from both their lives. What he did not realize was that Bliss would not accept what Julia was trying to give her until he gave his sister what she needed from him.

"Since you are his wife, I thought that he might be more inclined to listen to you," Bethany was saying.

"I am not sure that my efforts would meet with any better success than yours," Julia said, her stomach knotting at the mere thought of trying to talk to Gideon. Not only would he not listen, but her attempt could easily result in an ugly scene. And she hated scenes of any kind.

"All I ask is that you try," Bethany persisted. "Do say you will try, Julia." She pressed her palms together in a gesture of desperate pleading, her face eager and her eyes beseeching.

"Well," Julia murmured, her mind spinning as she tried to decide what to do. She would like to help Bliss, very much, but could she? Was it even possible to make Gideon listen to her? She had tried so many times to talk to him, to explain what had happened on their wedding night and make him understand her side of the episode. But it had been to no avail. He had refused to hear her out.

"Please?" Bethany entreated.

Julia sighed. Something she had not tried yet was an

apology. She considered the idea for a moment, then decided that it had merit. Perhaps if she apologized and confessed the truth, rather than trying to rationalize and excuse her actions, she might disarm him enough that he would listen. Once she had his ear, she could address the problem with Bliss. Surely he would not refuse to hear what she had to say on behalf of his sister? Who knew? If she were able to break through the icy wall between them, they might be able to someday come to terms and find a measure of peace together.

"Say yes, Julia," Bethany urged.

Julia sighed again. It was worth a try. "Yes," she finally conceded. "I will try, but I cannot promise that doing so will achieve anything."

"Of course it will—I am certain of it!" Bethany exclaimed, her cheeks flushing a glorious shade of pink in her happiness.

Julia smiled back. She had promised to love the Harwood sisters as much as she did her own. Now was her chance to prove that she did.

CHAPTER 16

"Well done, Gideon!" Christian commended, guiding his bay gelding left at the fork in the road they traveled on their ride home from the village meeting. "Judging from the outcome of the assembly tonight, it seems that you were correct in that your tenants needed only to discuss their differences to see how silly their bickering has been."

Gideon smiled and nodded, well pleased with his evening's work. "Yes, once I showed them that they have been working at cross-purposes, matters progressed far better than I could have hoped. So much so, that I feel safe in predicting that from hereafter life in Low Brindle will be decidedly more peaceful than it has been in many a year."

"If the rampant goodwill displayed tonight is any indictor of the village's future climate, I would venture to say that we run the risk of becoming dreadfully dull in our harmony," Christian returned with a chuckle.

Gideon made a wry face. "I, for one, will take harmonious dullness over the stimulation of strife any day of the week. Indeed, at this point in time, I can think of nothing more gratifying than to have a market day pass without being called into the village to marshal a dispute."

"Well, I daresay that you will get your wish, now that you have acquainted your tenants with the benefits to be had in working together." Christian shook his head, again chuckling. "There is nothing like the lure of prosperity to make men put aside their petty squabbles and pull together."

The squabbles to which Christian referred were the product of a fierce price competition that had cropped up among Gideon's tenants, in which each of the weavers attempted to monopolize the traveling cloth merchants' business by underselling his neighbors, more often than not at a sacrifice to himself. Exactly who had started the nefarious practice and why were fodder for frequent and violent debate. Whatever the truth, the resulting enmity was regularly played out in the marketplace, with insults and accusations of inferior goods invariably sparking bouts of fisticuffs that sometimes escalated into a village brawl.

Needless to say, the feud succeeded only in driving away any merchant who ventured to the village in search of goods. For in spite of the fact that Low Brindle cloth was of good quality and could be had at a ludicrously low price, few men wished to risk life and limb to obtain it. Of course, each weaver blamed the others for their dwindling trade, which merely exacerbated matters. Thus, what had once been a thriving textile community had soon degenerated into a financially embarrassed battleground. And by the time Gideon had purchased the estate, the cottagers were struggling to meet their rents and the village had ceased to flourish.

Gideon, who had discerned the potential lying dormant beneath Low Brindle's pall of conflict, had spent several weeks analyzing the situation before finally devising a plan calculated to tempt the weavers into a truce and revitalize the stagnating village. Tonight had merely been the first step in that direction. By the time his plan reached fruition, Low Brindle would be a reckoning force in the cloth industry.

"So, what do you intend to do with all the goodwill you created tonight?" Christian inquired conversationally, shattering the companionable silence into which they had lapsed.

Gideon waited until a rapidly approaching dray wagon rattled past before responding, "My immediate goal is to form a village cloth guild, which all the weavers will be welcome to join. From what I have observed, guilds promote a strong sense of common purpose among their members."

"And that sense cannot help but further foster the unity you created tonight," Christian deduced with a nod.

Gideon nodded back. "Yes. And I intend to continue fostering it by showing them the power to be had in their combined number."

"Indeed?" Christian's voice reflected genuine interest.

Gideon nodded again, more than willing to introduce his brainchild. "My first order of business will be to suggest that the members pool their funds and purchase cotton in bulk. Not only will doing so allow them to buy it at a cheaper price, but it will also enable them to procure a much better grade than is currently available to them."

"Are you saying that as individuals, your weavers are restricted to buying certain grades of cotton?"

"It would seem so. After sending inquiries to several cotton brokers in Liverpool, I have discovered that the finest grades are available for sale only to those willing to buy in sizeable lots."

"But how will the per-bale cost of those finer cottons compare to that the weavers are presently using? Will it not be much more expensive?" Christian asked.

Gideon shook his head. "If we purchase several lots at once and are clever in our negotiations, the cost per weaver will be less than what they are now paying for an inferior grade. Furthermore, the finer cotton will allow for the production of the delicate muslins and calicos that are all the rage in London. And there is a much greater profit to be made from fancy goods than from the plain fustian most of my tenants are now producing."

Christian seemed to consider the idea for a moment, then said, "I believe that the weavers are currently selling their goods unfinished. Do you plan to advise the guild to continue the practice, or are you of a mind to employ finishers so as to keep the entire production confined to the village?" Finished as opposed to unfinished goods was cloth that had been bleached, dyed, printed, and/or whatever other treatment was required to make the newly woven fabric suitable for its designated purpose. It was a process that was commonly undertaken by cloth merchants, thus allowing them to create the colors and print patterns that best suited their particular markets.

Gideon grinned at Christian's response. It appeared that he was not the only one who had been studying the textile trade of late. Pleased to have someone with whom he could discuss the subject, he replied, "I would like to finish the cloth here, so as to allow us to sell directly to London shops and exporters. That, of course, will require an army of finishers and a properly outfitted factory."

"Hmmm. I daresay it will," Christian said. "Have you selected a location for a factory?"

"I had thought to convert the old mill. Not only is its size and floor plan suitable for the purpose, but the old waterwheels will provide power for the printing machine I intend to acquire."

"Yes, and the ready access to the stream will also prove invaluable should you or your weavers someday decide to invest in a steam-engine-powered loom," Christian pointed out thoughtfully.

"That too," Gideon replied.

"I daresay that you will eventually be required to purchase a London warehouse and showroom—and you will need salesmen who are familiar with the fancy trade." It was clear from the unbridled enthusiasm in Christian's voice that he was now fully warmed to their subject.

"I already own several London properties that would be appropriate for both purposes. As for salesmen"—Gideon shrugged one shoulder—"I am certain that Lord Shepley can direct me to an agency that will give me recommendations."

"Speaking of lords and such, will you not need someone in London to observe the *ton*? Your weavers cannot hope to supply society's cloth demands unless they are informed of each new rage the instant it takes hold. They must—" Christian broke off, chuckling. "But how mutton-headed of me! As a *ton* member, your wife can most certainly help you there."

It was all Gideon could do to refrain from snorting at that notion. Julia, help him? A mere commoner? Ha! His light mood darkening at the mere mention of his haughty, treacherous wife, he tersely replied, "I do not think that we can count on help from that quarter. Julia is far too preoccupied with her own affairs to take an interest in mine."

Though Christian's expression was lost in the shadow of his broad hat brim, it was clear from his abrupt head motion that he shot Gideon a sharp glance, as if startled by his response. At length, he murmured, "How very odd. She struck me as most interested in all of your affairs when I made her acquaintance this afternoon. Indeed, I cannot recall meeting a wife so involved with her husband and his family; nor have I ever had the pleasure of being presented to a more gracious lady. I must confess that I quite like your lovely Julia."

Bristling at his friend's blind admiration of the woman he judged worthy only of contempt, Gideon almost pointed out that Christian could not recall much of anything at all and was thus unqualified to judge any woman's merit. Squelching the ugly impulse in the next instant, he instead responded, "Yes? Well, I suppose that that should come as no surprise. Julia is a master in the art of appearances."

Again, Christian cast him a quick look. This time, however, his head tipped to an angle, allowing the light from the full moon to wash over his face in a way that clearly illuminated his features. He was frowning, as if deeply troubled. "I say, Gideon. A master of appearances is hardly the glowing picture one expects a happy groom to paint of his new bride. I do hope that you and Julia have not quarreled so very soon after your wedding?"

Gideon uttered a silent profanity, cursing himself for allowing his animosity toward Julia to show. For all that she deserved his scorn, she was still his wife and it was his duty to see to it that the rest of the world viewed her with respect. Thus reminded of his obligation, he carefully clarified, "My remark was not meant as a slur, but as a simple statement of fact. Julia is indeed well schooled in the art of appearances, as she is in every art the *ton* dictates a woman must master in order to be worthy of the title 'lady.' Since her expertise in such matters is one of the reasons I wed her, I daresay that my remark can be viewed as a recommendation to her credit."

They had reached the crossroad at the edge of the manor grounds now, where they usually parted company since Christian was required to go left to the dowager cottage, and Gideon to continue straight ahead to the manor. Both reined their mounts to a halt. Christian's docile gelding came to an immediate standstill while Abhaya restlessly danced and snorted beneath Gideon's restraint, his nostrils flaring at the scent of something he detected on the soft night breeze.

"While your recommendation of your wife's accomplishments speaks of a certain admiration for her person, I notice that you have yet to mention love," Christian observed, leaning forward in his saddle to reward his horse's obedience with a pat on the neck. "As you no doubt know, Bethany is of the opinion that you and Julia fell in love at first sight, and that you wed in haste because your passion for each other was such that it would not allow you to wait. But I—"

"But you do not believe it," Gideon interjected softly.

Christian shook his head. "No. It is hardly in your nature to be so impetuous about anything, much less something that is bound to have such a profound effect on the rest of your life."

"Well, you know what they say about love," Gideon replied flippantly, trying to decide whether or not to confide in Christian. For all that they were friends, the best of friends, in truth, he was hesitant to divulge to anyone the extent of the trouble in his marriage.

"A great many people say a great many things about love, most of them quite foolish," Christian retorted. "But are we really talking about love in this instance? You can tell me that it is none of my affair if you wish—hell, you can tell me to go to the devil and I shan't blame you a whit if you do, but I feel I must ask: do you love Julia?"

For a moment Gideon was tempted to take Christian at his word and tell him that it was indeed none of his affair.

Then he remembered all that they had been through together in India, and all the private, painful confidences that
Christian had shared with him about his enslavement. Sighing, he admitted, "No. I do not love her." He owed his
friend at least that much of the truth.

Christian merely looked at him for several seconds, his
face solemn in the moonlight. Then he shook his head and
said, "If you do not love her, why did you wed her? Of all
the men I have ever met"—he expelled a snorting laugh—
"well, at least of those I can recall meeting, I have always
considered you to be the most uncompromising in your
principles. And you have always made it quite clear that
you would either find the sort of love your parents had, or
forgo marriage altogether. Indeed, you were most adamant
on that point the few times we discussed the subject."

It was Gideon's turn to remain silent as he sought a
response that would answer the question honestly, without
revealing the heart of the truth. At length, he replied, "I
married her on a different principle, because it was the
right thing to do."

"The right thing?" Christian echoed, frowning his consternation. Then his jaw slackened and he ejected, "Good
heavens! Do not tell me that you compromised her?"

Gideon laughed, a rasping grate that sounded harsh, even
to his own ears. "Of course not. Julia is hardly the sort of
woman to be compromised. Let it suffice to simply say that
the marriage served both of our purposes, and leave it at
that." Now gripped in the black mood that always seized
him when he thought of his marriage, and wishing to be
alone with it, he crimped his lips into a semblance of a
smile and added, "But enough. It is late and I am weary.
Please do not think me rude if I take my leave now."

Christian shook his head. "I shan't. It has been a long
day."

"Then I will bid you a good night." As Gideon wheeled
Abhaya around to make his escape, Christian abruptly
called out, "Tell me that you at least desire her."

Gideon reined the stallion to a halt, caught off guard by
his friend's request. "Pardon?"

"Tell me that you at least desire your wife," Christian

repeated. "For all that you admit that your marriage is a loveless one, I would hate to go away from here thinking that you are shackled to a wife you do not, at least, desire."

Gideon did not have to rationalize, perjure himself, or even think twice in order to tender an acceptable answer to that one. He had only to open his mouth and utter the bitter truth. "Oh yes, I desire her."

Christian smiled. "I am glad, for where there is desire, there is a chance for love. Or so people say."

"So they say," Gideon acknowledged with a shrug, though in this instance he doubted if his desire would ever lead to love. Unwelcome erections, yes. Self-loathing, most definitely. But love? Ha!

They both fell silent then, perhaps because there was nothing left to say. Finally Christian said, "Well, good night, Gideon. I will see you tomorrow." With that, he was off.

Gideon made a soft clicking sound between his teeth, signaling Abhaya to walk. The animal tossed his head once and snorted, then complied, his gait smooth and his pace leisurely as he carried his master homeward down the shadowy, tree-lined lane.

Tell me that you at least desire her. Christian's words kept ringing through his mind.

Scowling, Gideon ordered himself to ignore them. Ever since his wedding night he had done everything in his power to avoid Julia, shunning her both in person and thought in an effort to evade the conflicting emotions that besieged him every time he remembered that night. And in most instances the ploy had proved successful. But tonight . . .

Tell me that you at least desire her.

But tonight he could not keep her at bay, could not keep from torturing himself with the terrible, treacherous emotions that arose in the wake of the memories those words evoked.

Tell me that you at least desire her. A grim smile twisted his lips. The awful truth of the matter was that he did not just desire Julia; he lusted for her . . . urgently . . . ruthlessly . . .

Shamefully.

And since their wedding night, when she had lain naked and pliant in his arms, he had been plagued by carnal thoughts of her that so beguiled him that he barely had the strength to resist them. Robbed of the fortitude to do so now, he had no choice but to grit his teeth and surrender to his memories.

She had been so sweet that night, so very alluring and titillating in her virginal attempts at seduction. The way she had touched him . . . a tentative stroke here, a shy caress there . . . He expelled a hissing breath, his groin contracting violently at the mere thought of those heated moments. Never in his life had he been so aroused, nor had he felt such delicious anticipation in wondering where a woman would touch him next and how. Never had he ached so to experience a lover as he had Julia.

Unbidden, the picture of her naked and lying before him flashed through his mind. His groin gave another savage wrench. God, but she was beautiful! A vision of wanton innocence, sprawled as she was in the autumnal splendor of her hair, with her pale flesh blushed and glowing in her passion. And there was no mistaking that he had awakened her passion. Not with the way she had quivered and moaned beneath his hands, not with how she had undulated against him and responded to his kisses.

Gideon smiled faintly at the remembrance of those kisses. They had tasted like brandy. Whether the flavor had come from his own lips, a memento of the brandy he had imbibed earlier that evening, or the betrayal of a snifter she had sipped to ease a fit of maidenly nerves, he could not say. All he knew for certain was that he would never again be able to drink that spirit without being reminded of her lips. . . .

Which is why you swore off brandy on your wedding night, you fool. He again gritted his teeth, this time in disgust at his fatuous musings. Damn it to hell! What was it about the blasted woman that bewitched him so? By all rights of God and man, he should feel nothing for her but loathing. Yes, and scorn, and contempt, and every other harsh thing a man should rightfully feel for a woman who had used and deceived him. He most certainly should not want her, not even in the basest sense.

But he did want her. Badly. He hungered for her—for the taste of her, for the feel and smell of her. He ached to take her as a man took a woman, to pleasure and possess her, and to fully awaken the passion that he had merely stirred in her on their wedding night.

She haunted him.

Expelling a string of vile curses in his frustration, Gideon forcibly dragged his thoughts from Julia, determined to exorcise her from his mind, if only for the moment. Desperate for something—anything at all—to keep it diverted, he turned his attention to the shadow land through which he rode, commanding himself to examine and study it.

It was one of those perfect, early-summer nights, soft and fragrant and full of mystery. The heavens above formed a deep purple dome, punctured by pinpoints of pure white light that swirled and stretched into infinity, like footprints left by the moon on its myriad journeys from twilight to dawn. Though the moon itself was now obscured by the lush canopy of tree branches overhead, its light seeped through the foliage to pierce the darkness below and dapple the road with silver. All around the night was alive with the sounds of burgeoning nature.

Now came the purring call of the nightjar as it swooped across the sky, preying upon the ghostly white moths that danced in shafts of moonlight. Now echoed the woodcock's croaking love song, accompanied by the owl's harsh screech as it made its nocturnal kill. And now sounded the short, gruff bark of a male fox, answered by a vixen's shriek in a courtship ritual as old as the woods that hid the lovers from prying human eyes.

But it was to no avail. Try though Gideon might to become entranced by nature's midnight magic, he simply could not keep his mind from straying back to Julia and that other, far more spellbinding night. Thus, by the time he reached the manor his mood had gone from dark to foul.

Now wanting nothing more than to deaden his mind with a bottle of port, he grunted once in response to his major-domo's greeting, more tossing than handing the servant his

greatcoat and hat in his impatience to be alone. Pausing in
the foyer only long enough to seize the branch of candles
from a nearby footman, whose duty it was to light the family to their chambers at night, he stalked up the stairs and
down the second-floor hallway, eager for the sanctuary of
his study.

It was well past midnight and the household had long ago
sought their beds, leaving the manor still and dark, a peaceful
haven where a haunted man could find respite from his
ghosts. The lateness also served to free Gideon from the danger of inadvertently stumbling into Julia. And at that particular moment, he would rather face the devil incarnate than his
enticing, nettlesome wife. He had just reached his study door
when someone called out from behind him.

"Gideon, wait. Please."

Gideon froze, his body stiffening as he instantly recognized the elegant, perfectly modulated voice.

Julia.

Damnation! What was she doing up and about at this
hour? And what the hell could she possibly want with him?
Seeing no choice but to find out, he donned the mien of
cool indifference he had taken to assuming in her presence,
then slowly turned, responding in a clipped syllable, "Yes?"

She advanced toward him, her slight form haloed in the
glow of the single candle she carried. As she drew near, Gideon could not help noticing how lustrous her skin looked in
the warm golden light, or how her unbound hair seemed to
capture and reflect the burnished splendor of the flickering
flame. Though she was simply dressed in a plain, coral muslin
gown, with her shoulders and arms draped in a delicately
embroidered green silk shawl, she could not have looked
more beautiful . . . or tempting. It was all Gideon could do
not to groan aloud at the sight of her.

She waited until she had stopped a scant yard from
where he stood, before replying, "I am sorry to disturb you,
Gideon, truly I am, but I must speak with you. I have been
waiting all evening to do so, so please do not turn me away
now." She finished her plea with a timorous smile, one that
he found immensely appealing, in spite of his determination
to ignore her disquieting charms.

Disgusted with himself for falling such easy prey to her wiles, Gideon jerked his head once to the negative, unwilling to suffer her presence any longer than necessary. "No. Not tonight, Julia. It is late, and I am in no mood to indulge you in one of your tiresome arguments."

Her smile began to slip at his rebuff, only to be caught and renewed in the next instance as she countered, "Then you mistake my purpose. I am not here to argue, but to offer you an apology."

"An apology?" His eyes narrowed in immediate suspicion, warning bells going off in his mind. When a Barham did the unexpected, one stood well advised to suspect that spurious intent lay at the core of their unorthodox action.

She nodded, her smile broadening a fraction. "I would like to apologize for my behavior on our wedding night."

Of all the topics she could have chosen for discourse . . . Gideon's jaw muscles tensed with a click of clenching teeth. Not about to be roped into that particular conversation, especially at that moment, he snarled through his gritted teeth, "Don't bother. I do not care to hear it, or anything else you might have to say on the subject. Now go to bed, and leave me in peace." Certain that that would terminate their interview, Gideon turned away, imperiously dismissing her.

He had just flung open his study door when she abruptly demanded, "Why?"

Expelling an inaudible curse beneath his breath, he forced himself to pivot back around and confront her challenge. Fixing her with a fulminating glare, one that had yet to fail in cowing an opponent, he tersely countered, "Perhaps I should ask you the same question, Wife."

Every bit the master of appearances he had claimed her to be, Julia's smile did not falter in the face of his ire. "Why what?" She shook her head, meeting his gaze with eyes as ingeniously guileless as her practiced smile. "I am afraid that I do not know what you are asking."

He made a rude sound. "For all my poor opinion of you, Julia, I never counted you as slow-witted. However, judging from your present performance, it appears that I must now add that regrettable trait to your extensive list of character flaws."

She drew in a sharp breath, and for a moment he thought that her mastery would fail her. Then she bowed her head and quietly replied, "I am sorry, Gideon. I apologize for my shortcomings, but I truly do not know what you mean."

Rather than disarm him, as her skillful show of humility was no doubt calculated to do, it merely deepened his skepticism. Emitting another disdainful noise, this one in incredulity that she would mistake him for a big enough fool to buy her act, he brusquely retorted, "Fine, then. Why do you suddenly feel the need to apologize now, after all this time? And why the hell are you so bloody insistent on doing so at this hour of the night?"

"I did not apologize before because I did not know how. And I wish to do so now because I have just found the courage to say what needs to be said, and I fear that it will not last until morning." Her voice was soft but firm, its candor unmarred by the telltale tautness or hesitation that often marked a lie.

Gideon frowned, caught off guard by her artless response. He had expected her to respond in the usual Barham manner by offering a glib but convoluted explanation. Or perhaps fall back on her customary litany of self-serving excuses and rationalizations. But this? His frown deepened in his consternation. Could it be that she was actually sincere in her desire to mend the rift between them?

For a moment he was tempted to believe that it was true, perhaps because he wanted there to be hope for their marriage. Then he came to his senses and dismissed the notion as drivel. After all that had passed between them, he should know better than to think that she would humble herself to him, a primitive commoner, unless, of course, doing so would in some way benefit her or her contemptible father.

His foul mood worsening at the realization of how close he had come to again letting her play him for a fool, he growled, "Save your vapid show of contrition for someone blind enough to believe it, *Lady* Julia." He more sneered than uttered her title. "I am familiar enough with your treacherous machinations to know that you would not bother to instigate a truce unless you had something to gain from doing so. And since I have no intention of providing the means to the end of whatever chicanery you have a mind to embroil me in, I will bid you a good night." Again he began to turn away, once more signaling an end to their meeting.

But again she would not be put off. "You are wrong about my motives, Gideon," she persisted. "The only end I seek to gain is peace, to simply live in harmony with you, nothing more."

"Just peace and harmony?" He raised his eyebrows in an exaggerated expression of sardonic disbelief. "And why would you so stubbornly pursue something that will reap so small a gain?"

"Because I am tired," she flung back, her mastery slipping a notch. "I am tired of living in dread of our every encounter and of feeling constantly crushed by the weight of your wrath. Most of all, I am sick to death of having to tiptoe around you for fear that the rage inside you will explode." She was staring at him intently, her brow furrowed and her voice taut with frustration. "Surely you are as tired of the tension between us as I am?"

He shrugged one shoulder. "I cannot say that it has affected me one way or another." It was a lie, of course. He, too, was weary of the strain that governed their marriage. Nonetheless, he could not bring himself to bend to her pleas for an armistice. He would not. His wounded pride forbade him to do so.

Julia's mastery of artifice abandoned her completely now, and she expelled an exasperated snort. "Then you are the only one to remain unscathed. In case it has escaped your notice, our hostility has put the entire household on pins and needles and has made Critchley Manor a most uncomfortable place to live. Even Bliss has remarked upon the uneasy atmosphere and has voiced her misery. As for Bethany, now that she has left her sickbed, she cannot help but see the true state of our marriage. Loving you as she does, she is bound to be pained at seeing you so unhappily wed. She is—"

"Enough! Do not think to use my sisters to promote your own selfish cause," Gideon interrupted harshly, though in his heart he knew that she spoke the truth. He *was* letting his animosity toward Julia poison all their lives.

"I was not trying to use your sisters, Gideon; I was merely stating a fact," Julia replied, her reasonable tone heralding the return of her mastery. "In spite of what you may think of me, I care about your sisters and their feelings. I also care about your household. So if you will not consider a truce for my sake or yours, I am begging you to do it for everyone else at Critchley."

As much as it went against the grain to do so, Gideon did consider it. How could he not when his sisters' happiness was in jeopardy? And it truly was at risk, especially in regard to Bliss. Indeed, despite his reluctance to admit the fact, even to himself, he had noticed that the enmity in his marriage was affecting the child, and badly.

Though Gideon would have preferred to be flayed alive than to concede victory to Julia, he saw no choice but to do so. For Bliss's sake. And Bethany's. As Julia had pointed out, Bethany would discern the trouble between them soon enough, now that she was up and about. If he could save her the pain of having her happy illusions about his marriage shattered by granting Julia her truce, then so be it. After all his sisters had suffered, they deserved to have a happy home, a peaceful one. What did it matter if he had to sacrifice his pride to give it to them?

That decision made, he sighed and said, "All right. I will agree to a truce, for my sisters' sakes, though I must confess to harboring some reservations about whether we will ever be able to completely put aside our ill feelings for each other. After all that has been said and done . . ." He shook his head, again sighing, this time at the enormity of the task before him. "I can only promise to try."

"That is all I ask," Julia replied with a nod and a smile. "Now please, allow me to take the first step toward burying our differences by letting me say how sorry I am, for everything. Truly, I never intended to hurt or offend you. Regardless of the impression I gave you, I admire and respect you, and I very much wish to be your friend."

Despite his best intentions to honor his vow, Gideon could not help scoffing at her ludicrous apology. "Accusing a person of being common and primitive, and cringing from their touch as if they were a leper is hardly the way a person acts toward someone they admire and respect. It most certainly does not demonstrate a wish for friendship, so please do not insult me further by trying to convince me that you harbor anything but scorn for me, because we both know how you truly feel."

"Gideon—" she began.

He cut her off. "No, Julia. I have heard quite enough for one evening. Now go to bed. We are finished." When she merely looked at him, he waved his hands in a shooing motion. "You have won. I have agreed to a truce, so go."

"No. Not until you listen to what I have to say."

One look at the stubborn set of her jaw and Gideon knew that he had no choice but to hear her out. Resigning himself to the fact that he would find no peace that night until she had had her say, he growled, "Then say what you must, and be done with it."

"About what happened on our wedding night, when I said—"

"I believe that our wedding night is a subject best discussed in the privacy of my study," he cut in, unwilling to think about, much less discuss, that disastrous night without a glass of port to fortify him.

She nodded. "Of course. Whatever you wish, Gideon."

What he wished was for her to go away and leave him alone. Since that clearly was not going to happen, he motioned her toward his study door, indicating that she was to enter.

Nodding again, she did as directed. Gideon followed at her heels, closing the door behind them. When she paused in the center of the cozy, book-lined room, awaiting his further instruction, he took her arm and guided her to one of the two simple rosewood armchairs that stood before his imposing desk.

Relieving her of the candle she carried, he commanded, "Sit," then wasted no time in lighting the mirrored wall sconces. That done, he stalked over to the sideboard and poured himself his much-needed snifter of port. He was about to return to the business at hand when his gaze fell upon the cut-glass brandy decanter. After a moment's consideration, he poured a snifter of it as well.

Now carrying a glass in each hand, he covered the short distance to Julia in several long strides. "Here. I thought you might need this," he said, extending the brandy to her.

She glanced first at the glass, then at him, her expression questioning.

"Brandy," he replied to her unspoken query. "Is it not your drink of choice when faced with the task of dealing with me?"

"You—you knew I had been drinking on our wedding night?" she sputtered, her cheeks infusing with color.

"Of course I knew. I could taste it on your lips," he said, his suspicion about her brandy-flavored kisses now confirmed. "As I recall, it was rather fine brandy."

Her blush deepened to a most becoming shade of dusky pink. "I—I suppose that I should explain about that too."

"Oh, I think I understand well enough," he replied, lifting her hand from her lap to place the glass in it. "I daresay that you felt the need to numb your senses from the degradation of being bedded by a primitive commoner."

She bit her lower lip and shifted her gaze to her glass. "I admit that I needed something to numb my senses. However, I can assure you that the need had nothing whatsoever to do with feelings of degradation at the thought of sharing the bridal bed with you." She jerked her head once in what was no doubt intended to be a head shake. "I needed it to alleviate my fear of what happens there. Helene told me that her mother said that the marriage act is not so very dreadful if one drinks brandy beforehand."

"Helene?" Gideon quizzed, seating himself behind his desk.

"Lady Helene Dunville. Her father is the Duke of Hunsderry." She paused to sip from her glass, grimacing at the taste. Her voice now husky from the liquor, she added, "You met them on several occasions. Surely you remember?" She peered at him in query.

He nodded and took a drink from his own glass, a deep one. "Yes, I remember them." How could he forget? They were everything he loathed about the *ton*: superior, self-involved, boring, and perpetually discontented with everyone and everything around them.

She nodded back. "Yes, well, after Helene told me of the horrors her mother said awaited a woman in the marriage bed, I thought it best to heed her advice and filch a bit of brandy from Papa's sideboard."

Gideon's eyes narrowed at her words, sudden suspicion flickering through his mind. "And what exactly did Her Grace say about the marriage bed to fill you with such dread?"

She averted her gaze to again stare into her glass. "I-I-er—surely I need not explain such things to a worldly man like you?"

"Yes, you do, since I know nothing of the bridal-bed horrors against which Her Grace warned her daughter."

Her face was a dull red now. "She says that men thrust their—their—well, you know"—she made a helpless hand gesture—"their male p-parts into the place between a woman's legs."

Gideon waited for her to continue, certain that there had to be more. When she remained silent, he drew back slightly, frowning his incredulity. "That is the horror then, being entered by a man?"

Julia nodded, her gaze still glued to her glass. "Her Grace says that a man thrusts his p-part inside a woman over and over again until she is torn and bleeding, and that a woman must do everything in her power to avoid the barbaric act."

"I see," Gideon murmured, taking another drink. And he did. If what Julia said was true, and he was certain that it was since he doubted if she had either the imagination or sophistication to make up such a tale, then Her Grace apparently felt a perverse need to poison her daughter against the pleasures of the flesh. Either that, or she was one of those pathetic women who truly did not enjoy the sexual act.

"Her Grace also says that the act is worse with a commoner," Julia continued in a stammering rush. "She says that commoners' m-male parts grow to be much larger than those of noblemen, and that they wield them with far more brutality. It is their common blood, you see; it makes them unable to bridle their primitive urges, so they revert to being savages between the sheets."

Primitive . . . common, she had cried out as she had shrunk from his amorous advances on their wedding night. Gideon's lips compressed into a taut line, his insides coiling in anger at the Duchess of Hunsderry for setting about such vicious and damaging lies. What had happened that night made sense now, all of it. Julia had not been shrinking from him, but from his passion. It had terrified her out of her wits.

Now wishing to get to the bottom of the matter so he could fully understand her fears, he gently probed, "Is that all you have heard about the marriage act, Julia?"

"Amy says"—she glanced up quickly to clarify—"Amy found books on the subject hidden in her father's drawer, you see." At his nod, she continued. "Well, they say that the marriage act brings pleasure to both the man and the woman. Helene, however, says that since the books were written by men, and that men want to do the act all the time since it feels good to them, that what the books say cannot be believed."

"Anything else?" he prodded, growing more appalled by the second. Good heavens! What sort of women was the *ton* breeding to believe such rot?

"Only that men can be led by their lust. According to Helene's mother, a woman can persuade a man to do anything she wishes by being cooperative during the marriage act and doing everything in her power to ensure that it is pleasurable for him. She also says that since a woman cannot always escape submitting to her husband, that she might as well use his lust to her advantage." She looked up then, her face a study of remorse. "That is what I tried to do to you on our wedding night, Gideon. I asked Amy to tell me what her father's books said on the subject of pleasuring men, so I could do those things to you and pleasure you into doing my will. But—but—" Her splintering voice broke then, leaving her to gaze helplessly at him, mutely pleading for his understanding.

"But you lost your courage," Gideon gently supplied.

She nodded several times, then regained her voice enough to hoarsely reply, "Yes, and I am sorry. Not about losing my courage, but for trying to use you in such a wicked way. In my desperation to win you over, I could not see how very wrong it was. But I can see it now, and I shall not blame you if you choose to hate me."

"I do not hate you, Julia," he reassured her with a smile, and it was true. Now that he understood what had driven her to reject his advances on their wedding night, his anger had all but dissipated. As for her trying to lead him with his lust . . .

"Then you forgive me?" she asked, her woeful tone spiked by hope.

"Only if you tell me what you wished to gain by pleasuring me to your will. Whatever it is, you must want it very badly indeed to perform an act that terrifies you so in an attempt to win it."

She returned his querying gaze in silence for several moments, then dropped it to stare into her glass, which she did as if suddenly fascinated by its amber contents. At length she sighed and confessed, "I had hoped to persuade you to permit my siblings to come stay with us."

Gideon frowned, taken aback by her response. "That is all? You wished your siblings to come to Critchley?"

She nodded without looking up.

"Why did you not just ask me to allow them to visit?" he said, not certain whether to be furious with her for not trusting him enough to simply ask, or with himself for making her feel that she could not. "Surely you cannot think me such an ogre as to deny you your siblings' company?"

"But you mistake my meaning. I was not trying to persuade you to let them merely visit; I wanted you to consent to allow them to take up residence with us. I sought to remove my sisters from Aurelia's control." She looked up, shaking her head over and over again. "Oh, I know that you admire Aurelia, and I do not expect you to believe me when I say that she makes my sisters' lives a misery, but it is true. She is awful to them, a terror, constantly criticizing and reproving them, and denying them even the smallest measure of kindness and affection. You once commented that my sisters are like wooden dolls. Well, that is Aurelia's doing. The poor darlings are afraid to do or say anything for fear of suffering her scorn and disapproval." By her fierce expression and impassioned tone, it was clear that she spoke the truth.

Again Gideon was caught off guard. "But what of your parents? Your mother?" he quickly amended, for he knew for a fact that Lord Stanwell did not give a fig about his daughters. "If matters in the nursery are so very dreadful how can she not see it and do something to remedy the situation?"

"Because she does not care to see it." Julia sighed, a sad, defeated sound, and again shook her head. "The truth of the matter is that neither she nor my father bothers to notice my sisters at all, unless it suits their purposes to do so. They do not care how my aunt treats them, just as long as they behave properly on those occasions when they are required to be presented to society. Bertie, being the heir merits more of their attention, but it is still far less than a child requires to feel truly loved, and I fear that he, too will grow up starving for affection. If they lived here, I could see that they were raised with the love and joy they are denied at home."

"And what of yourself, Julia? Was it the same when you were a child?" Gideon gently quizzed, shocked by what he was hearing. He had naturally assumed that the Barham children, being of the aristocracy, led a privileged life, filled with indulgence and pleasure. But he now saw that matters were much different, that his own childhood had been far richer than theirs, in spite of his parents' relative poverty.

"Aurelia did not come to live with us until I was almost out of the schoolroom, so I was raised by an entourage of nursery maids and governesses. While I cannot claim that they loved me, they were at least kind. Then again, nursery work was their chosen profession, where Aurelia"—yet another sigh, again paired with a head shake—"my father thrust the post upon her as a punishment."

Gideon choked on the port he had just swallowed stunned by her revelation. "What?" he managed to splutter. "Why?"

"For being stubborn and headstrong and eloping with a
scoundrel her parents had forbidden her to wed," Julia replied. "She was very young at the time, of course, just eigh-
teen, and exceedingly lovely. Being both beautiful and the
daughter of a marquess, she was naturally expected to
make a brilliant match. Well, to make a long story short,
her family's reservations about the man's character proved
correct, and she eventually ended up on my father's door-
step, destitute and widowed."

"And he took it upon himself to punish her folly by
forcing her to take a post she detests," Gideon concluded,
his opinion of her father dropping yet lower, if such a thing
were possible at that point. Not only had the bastard deliberately demeaned his wounded and disgraced sister, he had
injured his daughters by forcing them to be the recipients
of the woman's resulting bitterness. No wonder Julia was
so desperate to remove her siblings from her parents'
household. It was a most harrowing place to live.

"So do you forgive me yet?" she murmured, slanting him
a hopeful look.

Wondering how a bastard like Lord Stanwell could have
sired such a brave and caring daughter, he smiled and truthfully replied, "With all my heart."

"And you understand that I was not calling you common
and primitive on our wedding night? That I was—"

"Merely referring to my sexual urges, yes," Gideon dryly
interposed. For a moment he was tempted to reopen the
subject, to address and attempt to dispel her misconcep-
tions about the marriage act. Then he decided against it.
There would be time enough to do so later, now that they
had struck a truce.

"I spoke the truth when I said that I admire and respect
you, Gideon," she continued with a nod. "And I truly do
wish to be friends again, if you will have me for yours."

He broadened his smile and nodded back. "I would be
honored."

They were friends again, which renewed his hope for
their marriage. For like desire, friendship, too, could lead
to love.

CHAPTER 17

Julia gasped, too stunned to do anything else as she watched the standing needlework frame she had received from London just that morning sink slowly into the shallow Critchley Park lake. She had ordered the ornately carved rosewood frame specifically for Bliss, hoping that it would not only aid the girl in improving her stitchery, but that it would also provide a frame for her sampler that would prove too cumbersome to throw, should she decide to use it as a projectile during one of her frequent fits of bad temper.

But it appeared that she had greatly underestimated the delicate-looking child's strength. Now in the midst of a tantrum, this one over Julia's gentle attempt to correct the tangled mess the brat was trying to pass off as bullion stitches, Bliss had heaved the frame into the lake as effortlessly as if it were her usual embroidery hoop.

Her mind still too boggled to fully comprehend what had happened, Julia continued to gape at the partially submerged frame, her mouth flapping open and closed in speechless shock. Finally she managed to squawk, "Bliss! How could you do such a wicked thing?"

But Bliss had already darted off across the spacious lawn, having used Julia's momentary lapse in wits to make her escape. Torn between her wish to rescue the expensive frame and her desire to bring Bliss to justice, Julia glanced indecisively between Bliss's retreating back and the frame's curving cabriole legs, which poked out of the water at drunken angle, weighing her priorities. Then her simmering outrage abruptly exploded through the lingering haze of her shock, snapping her to a decision.

Unruly brat! If anyone was going to wade into the water and rescue the frame, it was going to be Bliss. Yes, and she would also wash and iron the sampler it held, after which she would be sent to bed without her supper to contemplate her abominable deed.

Her priorities now firmly in place, Julia dashed after Bliss. Holding her yellow-and-gold striped muslin skirts high above her knees as she ran, she shouted at the top of her lungs, "You come back here this very instant, Bliss!" Not, of course, that she actually expected the wretched child to heed her command. Oh, no. She called out simply to vent her mounting anger, which at that moment made her hands itch to throttle the brat.

Though Bliss was inordinately fleet-footed, a boon that when coupled with her head start gave her a distinct advantage over Julia, Julia was fueled by determination, which made her fly over the grass with unprecedented speed. Ignoring the startled glances she drew from the gardeners, who worked at raking up the waste left by the park's small flock of grazing sheep, Julia kept her eyes resolutely focused on Bliss's blue-muslin-clad back, willing herself to sprint yet faster.

The Critchley Park, while nowhere near as expansive as the gardens, was a pleasant place, lushly landscaped with ornamental shrubbery, shade trees, and a lake, the latter of which Bliss had begged to sit by this afternoon, complaining that the drawing room heat was far too oppressive to suffer. Dividing the park from the gardens was the stately manor house.

Renovated to reflect the popular neoclassical style, the dun-colored brick mansion boasted an impressive facade with Roman triumphal arches, garland swag friezes, medallions depicting classical scenes, and six Corinthian columns, each of which was topped by a statue carved to resemble a mythical deity. Twin flights of curving steps, both railed in elaborate black ironwork, swept up and then together, to meet in a crescent-shaped veranda, a graceful contour that was echoed by the lines of the iron and glass dome that rose from behind the pedimented portico above.

By now Bliss neared the wide drive, and Julia knew that she had only to cross it and slip through the bushes flanking the house in order to escape into the garden beyond.

And then that would be that. Bliss would have again won.

Though Julia was winded and her leg muscles screamed from the unaccustomed exercise, the very thought of the brat again evading justice gave her the strength to accelerate yet faster. She was almost close enough to grab the girl, who was now at the edge of the drive, when her single-minded concentration was shattered by the thundering sound of hoofbeats—rapidly approaching ones.

She glanced up to see Gideon and Christian tearing up the circular drive on horseback, clearly engaged in a race. Judging from their speed, they would never be able to stop in time to keep from running down Bliss, should she try to escape by crossing in front of them.

But, of course, Bliss would never be so very foolish as to do such a thing. To be sure, for all that she was head-strong and undisciplined, she was far too sharp-witted to risk life and limb, simply to win a contest of wills. Or so Julia told herself. But again she was wrong, as she so often was in her estimation of the chit. Bliss did not so much as pause at the edge of the drive.

"Bliss, no! Stop!" Julia screamed, throwing herself forward to tackle the child, to save her from mindlessly running in front of the horses. But she was not quick enough; Bliss had already darted beyond her reach.

Splat! Oomph! Julia landed on the graveled edge of the drive with bone-jarring force, brutally knocking the wind from her lungs. Too incapacitated to do anything more, she could only stare in mute horror as Bliss recklessly plunged forward—right into the path of the oncoming horses. In the next instant she disappeared in a blur of flailing legs and pounding hoofs, and the air was rent with a single shrill cry from Bliss, followed by a chaotic din of masculine shouts and horses' screams.

Unable to watch a second longer, Julia buried her face in her hands, feeling as though she would shatter to pieces. Bliss was dead and it was all her fault.

There was a sudden roaring in her ears, and for a moment she thought she might faint from the grief and horror of what she had witnessed. Then someone grasped her shoulder, reviving her senses. "Julia? Are you hurt?" an urgent voice inquired.

Julia looked up to find Christian kneeling beside her, his face as drawn and ashen as she knew her own to be. Her head now shaking over and over again in her anguish, she somehow managed to wail, "I am fine, but—oh, Christian! Bliss . . . she . . . I tried—" Then her voice failed her, rupturing into a fractured sob.

"Bliss is fine," Gideon's voice lashed out over the agitated snorts and whinnying of the horses.

Startled, Julia glanced to where Bliss should have been lying in a bloodied, mangled heap. She was not there, though her torn and crushed chip bonnet was, giving chilling testimony as to what would have happened to Bliss had she not somehow miraculously escaped the horses' hoofs. Her distress now surmounted by bewilderment, she looked up at Gideon to ask after the child, only to have the inquiry die on her lips unspoken when she saw Bliss lying on her belly, draped over Gideon's lap.

Apparently he had snatched her up and tossed her on his horse, rather like in the trick Julia had seen performed at Astley's Amphitheater. Unlike the Astley's rider, Gideon looked furious.

His condemning glare now flashing between her and Bliss, who had recovered enough from her scare to begin squirming in protest of her uncomfortable position, he demanded, "What the hell is going on here?" Julia opened her mouth to explain, certain that he blamed her for the near tragedy—and why should he not, since she was responsible for Bliss's welfare?—when he frowned down at his sister and growled, "What have you done this time, Bliss?"

"Me! Why'd you think I'm to blame?" the brat squealed,

her squirming now escalating as she struggled to slip off the horse.

Gideon flattened his hand against the small of her back, foiling her escape. "And why would I not think it?" he rasped.

Bliss lifted her head to shoot him a sullen look. "I dunno why you're taking her part." Her lower lip thrust out to create a particularly petulant pout. "You don't even like her. Everyone knows it's true."

By now the gardeners and grooms had all rushed forward and stood gaping, having witnessed the near-fatal accident from afar. Fitzroy, the elegant Critchley majordomo, along with Mrs. Jobbins, the grandmotherly housekeeper, had dashed out onto the veranda upon hearing the commotion, and they too stood transfixed by the spectacle before them. Only Roger, the youngest stableboy, had retained the sense to take charge of Christian's abandoned horse.

Gideon slanted Julia a sharp glance, as if thrown off guard by his sister's allegation; then he looked back down at Bliss, shaking his head. "You are wrong, Bliss. I like her very much."

"Ha!" Bliss scoffed. "If you liked her, you wouldn't always be running away from her."

"Again, you are mistaken. However, I must admit that I have allowed estate business to take me away from her far more than is proper, a neglect that I fully intend to remedy now that I have settled matters with my tenants." Though the anger in his voice had cooled a degree, he still spoke loud enough for their audience to hear his every word. "Indeed, it is that purpose that brought me home early today. I had thought to spend the afternoon in my wife's charming company." He shifted his attention from his scowling sister to smile at Julia, who Christian was assisting in rising.

She smiled back, pleased that he would take such a step in furthering their reconciliation. Feeling the need to say something to acknowledge her appreciation of his effort, she nodded and replied, "I cannot think of a more pleasant way to pass an afternoon than in your company, Husband.

Now that you have settled your business, we have much to catch up on."

"Yes, we do, and I must thank you for your understanding, my dear. No new bride should be forced to suffer the neglect you have endured in my preoccupation with my estate. I do hope that you will forgive me and allow me to make amends." His steel-gray eyes locked into hers, the unflinching candor of his gaze bearing testimony to the sincerity of his penitent speech.

"Of course I forgive you, Gideon. I understand that estate matters must take precedence over coddling me, and that your worry over your tenants has made you gruff of late," Julia replied, touched that he would not only apologize to her, but would also take measures to explain his actions in front of the servants, thus silencing the gossip about their marital discord.

By now Bliss was struggling so hard that Gideon had to pull her up into a sitting position and clamp her against his chest to keep her from slithering over the side of the horse. Ignoring the brat's yelp of protest, he countered, "You are most gracious. However, you can be certain that I shall—"

"Let me go, Gideon! I can't breathe," Bliss squawked, tugging at his arm in an attempt to pry it from around her waist.

"Not until I learn what possessed you to dive in front of my horse," Gideon growled, both his face and voice losing all traces of their former softness as he again directed his attention to his wayward sister.

"It was all her fault." Bliss tossed Julia a resentful look. "She was chasing me."

"And why exactly was she chasing you?" Gideon quizzed, looking from Bliss to Julia in search of an answer.

Bliss opened her mouth to respond, but Julia cut her off before she could speak, not about to engage in an argument with the chit in front of the servants. "Perhaps it would be best if we discussed the matter inside, Gideon. The sun is getting rather hot, and I daresay that Bliss could do with a nap after the fright she has suffered." Turning to the gardeners, who still stood gawking from the edge of the drive, she instructed, "Bliss's needlework stand met with an, um, unfortunate accident by the lake." She slanted a glance at Gideon, who grimaced, easily divining the truth. "Might I impose upon you to rescue it from the water?"

"Yes, and do be kind enough to have it brought to my study," Gideon added, swinging from his horse with Bliss still in tow.

Doffing their billycocks, the men hurried off to do as bidden, while the grooms sprang forward to lead Gideon's horse away.

Christian, who had been observing the proceedings with an odd half smile, turned to Julia and said, "I have brought Bethany a book she expressed a wish to read. If she is receiving, I would very much like to present it to her."

Julia nodded. "She said something about finishing the watercolor she has been painting of the castle ruins. I am certain she will welcome your company."

Gideon, who now grasped a glowering Bliss by her upper arm and was practically hauling her along, nodded his approval for Christian to seek his sister. His gaze, however, was on Julia, and he was frowning as if he did not at all care for what he saw. His lips compressing into a taut, angry line, he barked, "Fitzroy, Mrs. Jobbins, please come here this instant."

Julia stared at him in confusion, mutely seeking an explanation for his sudden displeasure. But he was no longer looking at her. He had transferred his attention to the servants, who rushed down the steps to do his bidding.

He barely allowed them time to come to a stop before dictating in curt, clipped accents, "Mrs. Jobbins, we will be requiring soap, water, towels, bandages, and whatever else you think might be needed to treat a deep cut. Please see that they are delivered to my study posthaste."

A fresh wave of distress swept through Julia as the meaning behind his words, and the reason for his anger, instantly hit home. "Oh, Bliss. I did not realize that you are hurt," she cried, making a move to go to the child.

Gideon halted her. "I said that Bliss is fine, and she is," he bit out, thrusting his struggling sister at the majordomo, who promptly latched on to both her arms, thus shattering any illusions she might hold about escaping him. "Fitzroy, please escort my sister to her chamber, and see that she stays there until I summon her," he commanded. Without sparing either the servant or his sister so much as a second glance, he turned back to Julia. His hard face and sharp tone now softening, he said, "It is not Bliss who is injured, my dear. It is you."

When she merely looked at him, frowning her incomprehension, he gently lifted her left arm to display an ugly gash and several long abrasions, mementos, no doubt, from her fall at the edge of the drive. A quick glance down at her skirts revealed them to be smeared with blood.

Though Julia had been too preoccupied to notice the wounds before, now that Gideon pointed them out, they hurt like the devil. Biting her lip to contain her sob at the pain, she mechanically followed Gideon's lead as he escorted her to his study, where he seated her at a table set near an elegant tripartite window. After opening all three window sections, something that did much to relieve the room's heat, he divested himself of his coat, hat, and gloves, and her of her bonnet, then sat in the chair next to hers to again take her wounded arm, this time to examine it.

As he bent his head over it, angling her arm toward the window in order to view it in the best possible light, Julia focused her attention on his hair, trying to divert her mind in a desperate attempt to keep from bursting into tears.

He truly did have lovely hair . . . so thick and lustrous. It was lighter than it had been during his tenure in society, the chestnut and russet highlights streaking its sable darkness now more pronounced from the hours he had spent riding in the sun these past weeks. He had also allowed it to grow longer, and it now spilled over his collar in a tousle of glossy waves. She was remembering how silky it felt to the touch, when he looked up.

His face serious, he murmured, "I am afraid that the gash is deeper than I first thought. However, there does not appear to be any gravel in it, for which I am grateful."

Julia, who had always been able to tend to her sisters' scrapes and bruises without flinching but could never look at her own wounds without feeling ill, just stared at him,

suddenly feeling too weak and nauseated to do more. He
seemed about to say something more when there was a
scratching at the door.

"Enter," he called out, carefully pressing his clean handkerchief to the gash to staunch the bleeding.

It was Mrs. Jobbins with a basket containing the requested supplies, followed by her assistant, a tall, rather
nondescript woman named Sarah, who bore a large bowl
and a pitcher of water.

"On the table, please," Gideon directed, rising to allow
the servants access to the table.

Signaling for Sarah to follow, the housekeeper bustled
across the room. "I brought everything you asked for, sir,
as well as a wormwood infusion, just in case her ladyship
has bruises in need of treatment." Mrs. Jobbins indicated
the earthenware pot she had just pulled from the basket. "I
also thought that a needle and thread might be in order."

"Needle and thread?" Julia squeaked in alarm. The omi-
nous roaring returned to her ears with a vengeance at the
thought of what the need for such implements would bode.

"Just in case your arm requires stitching, my lady," she
replied in what Julia thought to be an inappropriately
cheerful voice, considering the situation. Then again, the
plump, rosy-cheeked housekeeper was known for her unfailing good humor, so perhaps she simply could not help
sounding so.

"Oh my," Julia whispered, the roaring in hers ears now
accompanied by a roiling sensation in the pit of her
stomach.

Gideon, who stood behind her chair with one hand still
applying pressure to her wound and the other resting on
her shoulder, gave her shoulder a reassuring squeeze. "Everything will be fine, sweetheart," he murmured. "I shall
take excellent care of you. I promise."

"You, sir?" Mrs. Jobbins paused in arranging the supplies to frown at him in surprise.

"Yes, me." His hand continued to squeeze Julia's shoulder, lightly kneading and massaging it, soothing and comforting her.

"But sir, do you not think that you should entrust her

ladyship's care to someone such as myself, who is experienced in dealing with wounds?" the housekeeper protested, her brow furrows deepening beneath her face-framing froth of gray curls.

"Oh, I can assure you that I have had more than my share of experience in tending wounds, Mrs. Jobbins, many of which were quite wicked in nature."

"But stitching, sir?" the housekeeper exclaimed on a rising note of disbelief.

Julia, too, wondered at his experience. However, being as that she was his wife, the servants naturally expected her to already know about such details, so she filed away her questions to ask for when she was alone with him.

"I have stitched more people than I can count, myself included, and I am pleased to report that we all survived without any ill effects," Gideon replied. "Besides, I have yet to ascertain whether or not my wife requires stitching, something that needs to be done without further delay."

The housekeeper eyed him dubiously. "Perhaps Dr. Horrock—"

"I passed Dr. Horrock on the road earlier. He was on his way to the Popplewell cottage to assist the midwife in delivering Mrs. Popplewell's baby," Gideon cut in. "It is a breech, which will no doubt keep him there for the remainder of the day."

Mrs. Jobbins's faded blue eyes widened at the news. "A breech?" She clucked in sympathy. "The poor, poor dear, and this being her first baby and all."

"Yes, I daresay the woman is in for a rough time," Gideon said. "I thought you might prepare a basket of whatever you think the family will need, and have a footman take it around. Tell him to remain at their service until the baby is born and to contact me promptly should they require anything we can provide."

"Well . . ." The housekeeper hesitated, casting Julia an uncertain look. "If you are sure you can manage matters here."

"Quite sure," Gideon confirmed.

"My lady?" she deferred to Julia.

Though Julia was not nearly as sure of Gideon's medical

expertise as he was, she forced herself to smile and nod. After all, it would never do for the servants to think that she placed less than perfect trust in her husband.

"Then I will prepare the basket straightaway. I must say that it is most kind of you to remember the Popplewells in such a fashion, sir," the housekeeper said, her formerly disapproving face now beaming with approval at her master's charity. Signaling to her assistant, who stood at the opposite side of the table having completed her task of pouring the water and arranging the towels, she crisply directed, "Come along, Sarah. I will need your help in the stillroom." Both women bobbed a curtsy, then hurried off on their mission of mercy.

Gideon resumed his seat by Julia's side. Drawing the water bowl and towels nearer, he again lifted Julia's injured arm. "I am going to cleanse your wound now. I will be as gentle as I can, but I am afraid that it still might hurt a bit."

Julia nodded mutely, unable to speak for the dread constricting her throat. Almost as afraid of disgracing herself as she was of the pain she knew awaited her, she braced herself as best she could, focusing on the clear azure sky beyond the window as she frantically prayed, *Please, God, please do not let me shame myself by crying or fainting.*

But Gideon proved to be as good as his word, working quickly yet with a touch so gentle that Julia's fear was soon surpassed by wonder at his skill. Why, aside from the sting of the soap he used to clean the gash, she suffered next to no pain at all. Thus, by the time he had finished bathing her arm, she felt strong enough to steal a peek at his face. When she saw his expression, she promptly regretted her impetuous courage.

He looked grim, clearly displeased by what his cleansing had revealed. Before she could avert her eyes again and hide the fear she knew was reflected in their depths, he glanced up and caught her looking at him. The instant their gazes touched, his face softened and his lips curved into a faint but reassuring smile. "I am sorry, Julia, but the cut is deep and needs to be stitched. Fortunately it is not very long, so it should not take more than five or six stitches to close it."

Five or six stitches? Julia bit her lip and looked away, feeling herself blanch in horror at the prospect. Though she had never been stitched herself, she had once witnessed a scullery maid who had cut herself while cleaning the knives being stitched. Judging from the way the girl had screamed and cried, it had been an exceedingly torturous ordeal.

An ordeal that she, herself, was now about to suffer.

The roaring rushed back into her ears, this time with a deafening volume. Now almost wishing that she would faint, Julia forced herself to again look at Gideon, to face her fate bravely, as befitted her station as a lady.

His lips were moving and he was gazing at her in query, as if asking a question. She shook her head once to clear the roaring. "Pardon?"

His expression softened another degree, as if he understood exactly what she was going through and sympathized with her plight. "I asked if you would like some brandy before I begin."

She shook her head. Though she could have done with the calming effects of brandy, she doubted if her stomach would tolerate it at the moment. And for all that she might end up weeping, she did not want to add to her humiliation by vomiting.

"As you wish," he replied, laying her arm on the table to reach for the dreaded needle and thread.

Julia watched in fascinated horror as he first cut a length of thread, then lifted the curved needle. Had the needle been that large only moments ago? And so wickedly sharp? Shuddering at the realization that the gruesome implement would soon be stabbing her flesh, she tore away her gaze.

"Julia?" Gideon's voice pierced the black sheen of her panic.

Julia looked at him, swallowing hard to clear the metallic taste of fear from her mouth.

Apparently she looked as miserable as she felt, because he grew very still at the sight of her and an odd expression passed over his face. After a moment or two he smiled, a slow, gentle smile that made the breath catch in her throat for the tenderness it betrayed. Taking her face in his hand to cradle her cheek in his palm, he murmured, "I know you are afraid, sweetheart, and it is quite natural to be so. I thought that I would faint from fright the first time I was faced with being stitched."

"And—and d-did you?" she whispered hoarsely, her breath again catching, this time at the warmth in his eyes as they captured hers. If he had fainted, then he would not think any less of her if she did so as well.

He chuckled. "No, but I did scream, and quite loudly at that." Another chuckle, this one accompanied by a head shake. "I stopped the instant it was pointed out that the surgeon had yet to begin his work."

Julia could not help smiling at his droll confession. "How old were you at the time?"

"Six or seven. I cut my leg falling off the churchyard wall. I was playing at being a crusader storming a citadel full of bloodthirsty infidels."

"Why, you were little more than a baby," she exclaimed, her heart going out to him for having suffered so at such a tender age. "How very dreadful for you."

"Not at all. The doctor gave me some sugared almonds, which was a very rare treat indeed. I was so intent on devouring them that I barely felt it when he finally stitched me." He tipped his head, grinning broadly. "Say now, there is an idea. Would you care for some sugared almonds to divert your mind?"

It was obvious what he was doing, of course. He was trying to ease her fear with his teasing. And to a small measure it was working. Touched that he would make the effort, she smiled back and said, "That is a fine offer, Gideon, and I thank you, but I am afraid that my stomach is rather too knotted to eat them."

His grin faded at her response, and his handsome face again grew solemn. "This shan't be so very bad, Julia, I promise. I do not wish to brag, for as you, yourself, pointed out, a gentleman never brags"—he flashed a brief smile at his own jest—"but I truly have become quite deft with a needle over the years. So much so, that I feel confident enough of my skill to promise that the stitching will be over before you know it has begun."

His voice was so soothing, his manner so very kind and

reassuring, that she could not help but to have confidence in him as well. "All right then, Gideon. I will take you at your word. Do what you must."

Gracing her with another smile, this one disarming enough to make her smile back, albeit wanly, he dropped his hand from her cheek and picked up the threaded needle. "Ready?"

She nodded once, screwing her eyes closed in anticipation of the first shock of pain. Again he dabbed at the wound with the cleansing cloth, and again he did so with such care that she was spared all pain. He was angling her arm in preparation to begin, when he surprised her by asking, "Would you like to hear how I came by my stitching skill?"

"Yes, please," she replied in a strangled whisper, grateful to have something besides her impending pain to contemplate.

"I learned from a French surgeon who befriended me in India. When I expressed an interest in his profession, he taught me a bit about medicine. Enough that I was later able to aid the native soldiers under my command when they were wounded in battle."

Julia winced as he took the initial stitch. "Are you saying that you joined the army after deserting from the navy?" she asked, forcing herself to ignore her discomfort. This was the first time he had volunteered information about his life in India, and she was far too intrigued to hear what promised to be a fascinating tale to allow her pain to spoil the telling. Besides, as he had promised, this stitching business did not hurt so badly.

"No. I became a mercenary."

"A what!" Her eyes flew open to gape at him in astonishment. He was, of course, concentrating on her arm, so she ended up staring at his strong profile.

"A mercenary," he repeated, as if it were the most ordinary profession in the world.

She frowned, not quite certain what to make of his startling revelation. From what she had read, mercenaries were ruthless, greedy scoundrels who would do anything, kill anyone for a price. Then again, everyone knew that much of what was written about such subjects these days was nothing more than wild exaggerations of the often dull truth. Needing to separate the facts from the fiction, but almost afraid of doing so for fear of discovering that the more sinister aspects of what she had read were true, she stammered, "What, er, what exactly did you d-do as a mercenary?"

He smiled, as if he discerned her thoughts and found them amusing. "Nothing as nefarious as the title mercenary would imply. I trained the troops of Indian chieftains and princes."

Julia barely felt the next stitch in her impatience to learn more. "But how—I mean why—" She broke off, shaking her head, trying to decide which of the thousand questions circling her brain to ask first.

"How did I become a mercenary?" he supplied, looking up from his ministrations long enough to flash her a wry smile.

"Yes, that is, if you do not mind telling me." He had once said that his Indian adventures were a tale for another day. Julia held her breath, hoping that today would be that day.

He finished the stitch he was making, his free hand tightening on her arm to steady it as she flinched, then replied, "I do not mind."

"Truly?" she exclaimed, thrilled that he would take her into his confidence. He was such a private man. The fact that he would offer to share a part of himself that she knew he seldom shared with anyone proved that he was genuinely committed to honoring their truce.

"Truly," he confirmed. "Where would you like me to begin?"

"At the beginning, of course." Now that they were friends again, she wanted to know everything about him.

He seemed to consider, then nodded. "As you know, I was pressed into the navy in London, and deserted in Calcutta. What I did not tell you is that the navy trained me in gunnery, something for which I proved to have a remarkable talent. Again I do not wish to brag, but I am also an expert with a sword."

"Indeed?" She frowned and shook her head. "However did you come by such a skill?" The teaching of swordsmanship was generally confined to boys of gentle birth, or those whose prospects included a military career, neither of which described Gideon.

"From an old fencing master who lived in our village when I was a boy. It was rumored that he had once taught at court, and that he had retired to our village to escape some sort of scandal." He shrugged one shoulder, as if dismissing the account as nonsense. "Whatever the instance, my mother held the opinion that all cultured men must have a knowledge of swordsmanship, so she bargained to do the man's baking in exchange for lessons for Caleb and me. My mother, you see, baked the best meat pies and puddings in Yorkshire. Everyone said so." He smiled then, as if in pleasure of the memory.

Julia allowed him to savor his remembrance, waiting for his smile to fade before pointing out, "That explains how you came by the skills to engage in your, er, unusual profession, but not how or why you adopted it."

Another one-shoulder shrug. "I did so because I had no other choice. I was alone and without money in a foreign land, where I could not even begin to speak the language or understand the customs. Since I also did not dare to return to the ship for fear of the punishment I would suffer for running away, I was willing to do almost anything to survive. So when a small band of mercenaries came to my rescue in a marketplace shortly after my arrival, I was more than happy to join their ranks."

"How did they rescue you?" she interjected, captivated by his story.

"I was caught stealing bread and they created a diversion that allowed me to escape. I found out later that they did so because I was young and an Englishman. When they discovered that I was also skilled in weaponry, they invited me to join their band of merry men."

Julia smiled faintly at his offhand Robin Hood reference. "Then they were Englishmen as well?"

"They were French and German adventurers, but they deemed England near enough to Europe for me to be considered as one of their own people." Another shrug. "On the whole they were a rough lot with no education and only modest ambition. Save for the doctor, they were little more than swords for hire. Then again, so was I, at least in the beginning."

"A sword for hire," she repeated softly, liking the exotic sound of the title.

He nodded without looking up. "At first I was content to simply fight for whoever would hire us. The pay was fair, and the actual battles were few and far between. Since I aspired only to earn enough to bring me home to England, I found the arrangement satisfactory. But then I saw the fortunes being made by the men training the troops with whom we fought, and I grew ambitious. You see, Julia, the Indian rulers are always feuding among themselves or fending off foreign invaders, and they have learned from experience that the European method of fighting is far superior to their own. Thus, they are willing to shower riches on anyone who can teach their troops European battle tactics. Being an Englishman with military training, brief though it was, and experience in fighting with native troops, I was considered to be more than qualified for the job."

"What of the men you met in Calcutta?" Julia asked, awed and more than a little envious of his adventure.

"They served under me for a time, and then went their own ways. Except for the doctor, who eventually returned to Calcutta and made a tidy sum tending to the Europeans living there, I never saw them again."

"And Christian? Bethany said that you rescued him in India." The moment the question slipped out, she hastened to amend, "Not that I wish to pry into Christian's affairs."

There was a pause, during which she heard what sounded like scissors snipping thread, then he looked up to meet her gaze. "You are correct in that Christian's story is his own to tell. However, I can tell you that I found him wounded on a battlefield after a skirmish with the Mogul prince to whom he was enslaved. Like me, Christian is skilled in weaponry and so he had been forced to fight for his master." He shook his head. "At any rate, when I discovered that he was a captive, I had him carried to my camp and nursed him back to health. We have been friends ever since."

They fell silent then, with Gideon returning his attention to Julia's arm, while Julia contemplated all that she had heard. At length she sighed. "Oh, my! What a wonderful, exciting life you have led, Gideon. I must admit that I am quite envious."

"It was neither exciting nor wonderful. It was hard and exhausting, and my bones still ache from sleeping on the ground," he growled, but he did so with a touch of humor. "I also do not want you to think that I fought without scruples. I might have been a mercenary, but I still had my principles. I would not train any troop that bore any hostility toward England and might someday use the skills I taught them against my own countrymen. Nor would I be of service to any man with a reputation for brutality or unfairness, no matter what he offered me."

"That was very honorable of you," Julia commented. Not that she was surprised that he would adhere to such high principles. Aside from the matter of his blackmail, an offense that she was finding increasingly bewildering in the light of his otherwise sterling character, he had proved to possess an extraordinary sense of honor.

"The devil's honor, some would say," he countered with a dark chuckle. Now looking up, he added, "I have only to bandage your arm, and we shall be finished."

"You are done stitching?" Julia glanced down in surprise to see her wound neatly sutured. He had not lied when he had claimed to be skilled with a needle and thread. Relieved to have escaped what she knew could have been a grueling ordeal under less skillful hands, she shot him a grateful look, saying, "You are indeed a master of stitching, Gideon."

He smiled, a slow, lazy smile that did the strangest things to her heart. "And you, my dear, are very brave."

She smiled back, feeling suddenly shy as her awareness of his charms came crashing back with a tongue-tying vengeance. Struggling to unknot it, she somehow managed to reply, "It is easy to be brave when one has such a superb doctor at their service."

"Ah, but I am not just referring to your courage during my stitching, as commendable as it was," he returned, now wrapping her arm in a clean white bandage. "I saw how you tried to stop Bliss from running in front of my horse. The way you hurled yourself at her without any thought for the injury you might cause yourself was very brave indeed."

"It-it was?" Julia stammered, a warm glow spreading through her at his praise.

He nodded. "Very. Now promise me that you will never do anything so very foolhardy again."

"Pardon?" She frowned, taken aback by his unexpected reproof.

"I want you to promise that you will never again behave in such a foolhardy manner," he repeated. "While I am pleased that you care enough for my sister to take such a risk for her, I would prefer not to have to stitch you again."

The warm glow seeped away. "Oh, I see." And she did. For all his patience and kindness, he viewed having to stitch her as a nuisance. Feeling as if she should apologize for inconveniencing him, she murmured, "I am sorry for being such trouble. I promise that I shall not bother you if I require stitching in the future."

He looked up quickly, shaking his head. "You misunderstand me, Julia. The reason I do not wish to stitch you again is because I do not like seeing you hurt. However, should the need to do so again arise, please know that I do not find stitching you the least bit of trouble. Indeed, I want you to promise that you will come directly to me and let me do it for you."

The warm glow was back, enveloping and embracing her. "I will, Gideon. I promise," she vowed with a smile and a nod.

He nodded back. "Good. I also want you to feel free to bring your troubles to me and to know that I will help you with them in any way I can." He had finished bandaging her arm and now took her hands in his, lacing his fingers through hers in a firm clasp. "I know that we had a rather bad start to our marriage, but now that we have sorted matters out, I would very much like to try to make a go of it."

"You would?" she said, her heart flip-flopping crazily in

her chest as he again smiled that slow, lazy smile, this time displaying those splendid teeth.

Another nod. "Mmm, yes. You see, my dear, I have decided that I rather like having you for my wife." His voice was little more than a whisper now, taking on a warm, caressing intimacy that sent a queer tingle down Julia's spine.

With the tingle now ending in a funny little quiver in the pit of her stomach, she faintly replied, "And I like having you for my husband, Gideon." How could she not at moments like this?

His smile broadened into a grin that was nothing short of devastating to her senses. "I am glad, for it is my fondest hope that you will someday be my wife in all aspects of the word. That you will one day trust me enough to allow me to show you that the marriage act is not the horror the Duchess of Hunsderry claims it to be, but a miracle that brings great pleasure to both the man and the woman."

Julia's brow knit at the mention of the marriage act, but she was far too caught up in the intimacy of the moment to feel fear at it. Wanting to believe him, to believe that she could again experience the bliss she had enjoyed on their wedding night without fear of what would follow it, she desperately searched his eyes for the truth, seeking proof of his claim. "Truly?"

He returned her gaze steadily, his compelling gray eyes gentle and filled with such tenderness that her heart cried out to believe him. "Have I ever broken a promise to you?"

She thought for a moment, then shook her head. "No."

"Then please believe me when I tell you that I will never do anything to hurt you. While it is true that the marriage act can be painful for a woman the first time, the pain quickly passes and she experiences pleasure. Do you remember how it felt when I pleasured you on our wedding night?"

Julia blushed. How could she forget? It had been wonderful—better than wonderful. Why, just thinking about it sent an electrifying charge of excitement rushing through her veins.

Apparently her blush gave him his answer, because he

smiled. "The marriage act will bring you the same sort of pleasure, only better. You will find that—"

Scratch! Scratch! Whatever he was about to say was interrupted by scratching at the door. Tearing his gaze from hers to glare at the door, he barked, "Yes?"

It swung open to reveal Fitzroy, accompanied by a green-and-gold liveried footman, who carried Bliss's needlework frame. "You asked that this be brought to you, sir," Fitzroy intoned in his clipped, precise accents, signaling for the footman to present the stand. "We cleaned and dried it as best we could, but I fear that the sampler is quite ruined."

Gideon gave Julia's hands, which he still held, a quick squeeze, then rose to take it from the servant. "Thank you. That will be all."

When the men had departed, closing the door behind them, Gideon studied the sodden sampler. After a moment of doing so, he murmured, "Would you care to tell me what happened? I daresay that the tossing of the frame into the lake had something to do with Bliss dashing in front of my horse."

Though Julia had truly meant to speak with him about Bliss the night before, as she had promised Bethany she would do, the hour had grown too late for her to do so by the time she and Gideon had finally struck their truce. Presented with the opportunity to do so now, she explained her troubles with Bliss, as well as her and Bethany's views on why the child behaved as she did, to which Gideon listened with a thoughtful expression.

When she at last fell silent, he frowned. "So you and Bethany think that I have been neglecting Bliss, do you?"

"No! Not neglect," Julia rushed to reassure him, terrified of destroying the newly laid foundation of their friendship by again offending him. "No one could be a better brother than you, or do more for their siblings. It is just that Bliss needs to feel as if she is a part of your life . . . an important enough one that she can feel safe in the knowledge that you care too much for her to ever abandon her. But how is she to feel that way if you never pay her special notice? As I said, Bethany believes that her tantrums and abominable behavior are nothing more than bids for your attention."

"And you truly think that a bit of special notice from me will help cure all that?"

Julia nodded. "It might also help cure the resentment she feels toward me. After all, she can no longer blame me for driving you away from her if you are here and lavishing attention on her."

He seemed to consider what she had said, then nodded back. "All right then. I will do it and with pleasure. However, please be advised that I intend to take equal pains in lavishing attention on you as well. As with Bliss, I have been derelict in my notice of you for far too long." The warmth had crept back into his voice.

"And I shall enjoy the attention every bit as much as Bliss will," she retorted with a smile. And she would.

He smiled back, visibly pleased by her response. "Now that that is settled, I suppose that we should decide what to do about this business with the needlework frame."

"We must start by punishing Bliss," Julia replied decisively. "It is high time she learns that there are consequences to her wicked actions. She must also be made to finish her sampler. Otherwise we will have given in to her tantrum, and I refuse to reward her bad behavior."

"I agree, and I promise to mete out an appropriate punishment. However, I do not think that it will be possible for her to finish this particular sampler." He carried the frame over to Julia so she could see the cloth it held. "Between the dunking it took in the lake and the servants' efforts to clean it, I fear that it is indeed quite ruined."

Julia had to agree. It was ruined. She sighed. "I suppose that I will just have to draw her a new one."

Gideon contemplated the spoiled sampler for several moments, smoothing the sodden fabric with his palm as if trying to discern its design. At length he replied, "With your permission, I would like to help with the drawing."

"You would?" she ejected in surprise, thrilled by the prospect of his continued company.

He looked up, a playful smile lurking at the corners of his lips. "Yes. I have an idea that just might solve all of our problems with Bliss."

CHAPTER 18

"Shiva cut off his head? Truly?" Bliss gaped up at Gideon, her gray eyes wide and her mouth forming an exaggerated O at the gory turn the story he was telling had just taken.

"In one stroke, whiz—splat." He drew the edge of his hand across her throat, illustrating the murderous action.

She chortled her delight. "O-o-o! I bet Parvati was mad enough to spit when she found out what Shiva had done!"

"Perhaps a bit," he replied, visibly amused by her bloodthirsty glee, "but I daresay that she was more sad. After all she was Ganesa's mother, and it is the saddest thing in the world for a mother to lose her child."

"His mother?" She drew back, tipping her head to fix him with an incredulous stare. "Why'd you call her his mother?"

"Well, did she not make him from the scurf of her body and give him life by sprinkling him with water from the Ganges River?"

Bliss nodded.

Gideon nodded back. "And is that not what mothers do when they give birth, create children from their body and give them life?"

Bliss grew very still, her eyes narrowing and her frown deepening as she contemplated his theory. At length she slowly conceded. "Hmmm. Perhaps she was his mother after all." She granted him a conciliatory smile and nod.

"So what did she do when she found him with his head chopped off?"

"As I said, she was very sad. So sad, that she could not be comforted. When Shiva saw how much his action had grieved his beautiful wife, he sent his messengers to find Ganesa a new head. The first beast they found was an elephant sleeping by the Ganges River, so they lopped off its head, whiz—splat"—another decapitating motion—"and brought it back to Parvati. She planted it on her son's shoulders, which promptly restored his life. And that is why Ganesa has an elephant's head."

Bliss stared at him in saucer-eyed silence for several moments, as if visualizing the scene in her mind, which no doubt she was, given her vivid imagination. Then she glanced back down at the sampler before them and demanded to know, "But why does he have four arms and only one tusk?"

Julia, who had paused on her way to Bethany's chamber to observe the pair through the open library door, smiled at the picture they made. They sat on a comfortable, fan-shaped Italian sofa, Bliss with her feet tucked beneath her and her slight form snuggled against Gideon, while Gideon lounged with his long legs stretched out before him and his arm resting casually on her shoulders. Bliss could not have looked happier, nor Gideon more relaxed. Both were so caught up in the story that neither noticed her standing there.

The tale Gideon recounted was the Indian myth about Ganesa, the Hindu god of prudence and wisdom, a deity traditionally portrayed as short and pot-bellied with yellow skin, four arms, and an elephant's head with one tusk. The odd being was only one of the many equally strange creatures that Gideon had chosen to incorporate into the sampler design he had created for Bliss. And oh, what a wonderful design it was!

Unlike most samplers, which were comprised of an alphabet, a proverb, or a verse, and a pastoral scene that often included the family members of the child stitching it, Gideon's sampler was a whimsically illustrated map of India, bordered by scenes portraying fantastical beings from

Indian mythology. To Julia's delight, he had narrated each scene as he sketched it, enchanting her not only with his exotic tales, but with his wry wit and easy charm. He had also outlined his idea for resolving their troubles with Bliss.

His plan was a simple one. He would deliver the new sampler to his sister with the expected command that she stitch it, coupled with an unexpected promise to tell her the stories the scenes depicted as each was embroidered to his and Julia's satisfaction. Since Indian deities had a penchant for rainbow-hued flesh, and were often depicted as a bewildering hodgepodge of human and animal parts, Bliss would be required to consult with him on a daily basis so that he could determine the proper colors of silk to be used for each figure. Doing all of this, he had explained, would not only ensure that Bliss learned her needlework, but it would also allow him to pay her special notice without arousing her suspicion at his sudden interest.

Though neither of them had voiced the fact, they both knew that the stories and floss selection would serve another, more important purpose: It would foster conversation between him and Bliss, giving them something to talk about until such a time that they became well enough acquainted to chatter easily about everything and anything, or nothing at all, as was the way with close siblings.

And so Gideon had presented the sampler to Bliss the following day. As he had hoped, she had been intrigued enough by his promise of stories that she had consented to stitch it—an agreement that Julia had to admit the girl had more than honored thus far. Indeed, she had taken to stitching with such care and diligence that not a day passed that Gideon had not praised her progress, a prize that seemed to please her even more than her story rewards.

Oh, that was not to say that Bliss did not genuinely enjoy Gideon's tales. It was clear from her enthusiastic questions and interjections during their telling that she indeed did. However, Julia doubted if she would have found them nearly so thrilling or expressed half as much interest in them had they been told by anyone other than the brother she so obviously adored.

A month had now passed since the inauguration of the

sampler experiment, and Julia had to acknowledge that it was a resounding success. Not only did Bliss seem happier and more at peace, but her tantrums had dwindled to an occasional foot stamp and pout, and she had started to treat Julia with a tentative yet sincere cordiality that promised to someday blossom into friendship. Much of that last could, of course, be directly attributed to Gideon's change in demeanor toward their marriage.

Smiling at the thought of that change, Julia shifted her gaze from Bliss to her husband, her heart fluttering in her breast at how handsome he looked as he threw back his head and laughed at something his sister said. True to his word, he had begun to lavish attention on her as well, and not a day had passed since he made the promise that she had not discovered something new and wonderful about him while in his company.

An invisible warmth embraced Julia at the thought of those times, and she was suddenly moved by a deep, almost irresistible longing to draw nearer to where he sat. Checking the impulse out of courtesy to Bliss, who she knew cherished her moments with Gideon as much as she did, she forced herself to remain where she was and be satisfied with simply contemplating him from afar.

He was such an exciting man, so strong and vital, and almost intimidating in his intelligence. Everything about him spoke of absolute confidence . . . the directness of his gaze, his regal yet relaxed posture, the sovereignty in his voice. He wore it with the ease of a man who had set out to conquer the world and had won, projecting a quiet sense of power and authority that instantly commanded other men's respect.

Oh, how he thrilled her!

He also charmed and delighted her as no man had ever done, especially during those moments when he spoke of his childhood in Yorkshire. Never in her life had she laughed so hard as when he recounted his youthful pranks, never had she been so very moved as when he spoke of his love for his parents, his voice growing reverent and his eyes glittering with the intensity of his emotions. Unlike most people of her acquaintance, who drifted through life

in search of love, never quite certain how to give it or
whether they had truly found it, Gideon had experienced
love from the cradle, which enabled him to recognize and
understand it. Secretly Julia suspected that it was that
ability that made him the man he was today: A man of
unfailing kindness and generosity; a caring, loyal, and
compassionate man. A man so utterly magnificent that she
could not help feeling as if she were somehow a better
person simply by being allowed to be his friend.

And they truly were friends now, good ones, and growing
closer every day. Of late he had even begun to confide in
her and seek her counsel, soliciting her advice on matters
that ranged from the kinds of wine they should purchase
to stock their cellar, to how his newly formed cloth guild
could best cater to the *ton*'s textile needs. In doing so he
made her feel important. Necessary. A much wanted and
appreciated part of his life. And for the first time ever, she
felt pride in herself. True pride. The kind that had nothing
to do with her noble blood or place in society, and everything to do with the fact that someone as admirable and
highly regarded as Gideon found her worthy of his respect.

Gideon Harwood respected her. Her! Not who she was
or what she stood for, as most people did, but for what
was inside her, what she thought and felt. Gideon viewed
her as capable and intelligent, sensible and strong.

And she loved him for it.

She loved him? Julia rocked back on her heels, pressing
her hand to her throat in her astonishment. Good heavens!
Could it be true? Had she fallen in love with her husband?
Thunderstruck by the very notion, she refocused her eyes
on the man before her, who at the moment was laughing
at his sister's attempts to tickle him, searching her heart
for the answer.

Did she love him?

She let her gaze sweep him from head to toe, unable to
resist lingering here and there. That she found him attractive was undeniable, just as she could not deny that she
liked and respected him. She also could not deny that of
late she had begun to feel other things as well: strange,

unfamiliar sensations that overwhelmed her every time he was near.

There was the way her heart turned over whenever his gray eyes touched hers, and how the warm sound of his laughter sent shivers rippling up her spine. And then there were his smiles, those beautiful, arresting smiles. The way his firm lips curved over his even white teeth, slowly and with an almost sinful languor . . . They seemed to beckon to her, promising a pleasure that made her long for the courage to abandon her fear of his passion and sample the sweetness he offered. As for his voice . . .

She closed her eyes to listen as he bantered with Bliss, letting the deep, rich tones of his voice roll over her, to caress and embrace her senses. Something deep inside her seemed to melt at the sound, its fevered heat seeping through her veins like liquid fire, making her feel hot and flushed and weak all over. Everything about him was so compelling, so magnetic and deliciously disturbing . . .

Oh, what he did to her! She thought about him constantly, craving him when they were apart and hungering for him when they were together. She was utterly and completely undone by him.

So, did that mean she loved him?

Slowly she opened her eyes to again consider him, her fingers twitching at the sight of him, aching to touch him.

Did she love him?

Her heart gave a hard, painful lurch in reply.

She did. She, Lady Julia, loved Gideon Harwood.

She must have gasped aloud in her shock, because both Gideon and Bliss looked up. Gideon's lips promptly curved into one of his irresistible smiles, while Bliss regarded her with an expression of polite query.

Compelled to say something to explain being caught lurking in the doorway, she smiled, albeit a bit unsteadily, and somehow managed to babble, "I wanted to tell you that I will be in Bethany's chamber, should either of you need me." Without awaiting their response, she turned on her heel and fled.

Though Julia wanted nothing more at that moment than

to be alone, to ponder her startling discovery in peace,
Bethany had begged her help in putting away the garments
she had made for her lost baby, and Julia did not have the
heart to leave the woman alone in her sad task. And so
she made her way up to Bethany's chamber, her confusion
and dismay at her feelings for her husband growing with
every step she took.

She loved Gideon, sweetly and profoundly, and to such
blissful distraction that it now seemed impossible that she
had not recognized her feelings for him right away. Then
again, how could she be expected to do so when it should
have been impossible for her to feel them for him at all?
After the way he'd threatened her family with ruin and
blackmailed her into marriage . . .

But she no longer cared about any of that. And no matter how hard she tried to do so, no matter how many times
she told herself that it was foolish to entrust her heart to
a man capable of such villainy, she simply could not force
herself to believe that loving him was wrong. How could
she when he treated her with such kindness, with such
honor and gallantry? Truth be told, she was finding it increasingly difficult to reconcile the admirable gentleman
Gideon had proved to be with the blackguard her father
claimed him to be. So much so, that had his accuser been
anyone but her father, she would never have believed the
charges.

But, of course, she had no choice except to believe them.
For not only was it her duty to believe her sire, but Gideon
had not denied his charges when she had voiced them that
day in the park. And surely a man free of guilt would have
protested his innocence?

But again, she could not bring herself to care. Besides,
she had already decided that his crimes were forgivable,
since they had been committed out of love for his siblings.
Yes, and then there was the fact that his actions had caused
no real harm to her or anyone else. So . . . So . . .

So why torture herself over things that no longer mattered, and would never again matter, at least to her? Julia
turned down the corridor where Bethany's chamber lay,
nodding her satisfaction at the logic of her reasoning. She

could twist the facts any way she pleased and examine them from every angle, but the only thing that would matter in the end was that she loved Gideon Harwood. And truly, where was the wrong in that? He was her husband. She had wed him for better or worse, so why not choose better? Why not follow her heart and love him, as was her right and duty as his wife? Of course, in order to truly love him as a wife loved a husband, she must submit to the marriage act.

A whisper of fear wound through her at the mere thought of doing so. For all that Gideon had promised that she would find the act pleasurable, she could not quite bring herself to believe that it was true.

Oh, it was not that she suspected him of deliberately trying to mislead her. She was quite certain that he believed what he said, that he genuinely thought that he had brought pleasure to the women he bedded. But those women had no doubt been mistresses and other wanton creatures, whose business it was to please a man. And Helene's mother had said that such women only pretended to enjoy the act in order to gratify the men paying for their services. Besides that, Julia could not imagine how any woman could enjoy having a man stick his male part in that tender place between her legs, especially when she had found it so very uncomfortable when he had stuck his finger in there on their wedding night.

Then again, Amy had read . . .

Oh! If only she knew a woman experienced in such things with whom she could discuss the matter, one who would speak frankly to her about the marriage act, and whom she could trust to tell her the truth. At least then she would know what to expect and could prepare herself accordingly.

By now she had reached Bethany's door. Forcibly shoving her thoughts aside to mull over later, she knocked, entering the room in the next instant at Bethany's bidding. As with everything else in regard to his sisters, Gideon had spared no expense in furnishing the chamber.

The walls were covered with a magnificent flowers and fruit wall paper in muted shades of rose, white, and crimson, and the room was elegant yet cozy, the formality of its furnishings made homely by their casual arrangement.

Against one wall stood a dainty, pink-satin-festooned bed with a gilded canopy and domed cupola, flanked on one side by a comfortable gold and white damask bergère, in which Julia had spent countless hours sitting during her visits to Bethany's sickbed. Situated on the facing wall was a gold-veined white marble fireplace, before which sat a pair of armchairs, a needlework stand, and a small table scattered with books. The wall to the right featured a matching pair of tapestry settees and a row of crimson-velvet-draped casement windows; the one on the left boasted an exquisite floral marquetry secretary, at which Bethany currently sat writing.

She rose at the sight of Julia, smiling in welcome as she rushed forward to greet her. Though Bethany was always lovely, she looked particularly so today, dressed as she was in a frilled blue and white dotted gown with her hair arranged in an artless cascade of curls. Taking both Julia's hands in hers to give them an affectionate squeeze, she said, "You are such a dear to help me this afternoon. I cannot thank you enough."

Julia gave her hands a squeeze in return. "There is no need to thank me, dear. We are sisters now, and sisters help each other. Is that not so?"

Bethany's smile broadened, her soft pink lips parting to display her pearly teeth. Like all the Harwoods, she was blessed with excellent teeth. "Yes, we truly are sisters." She dropped Julia's hands to give her a quick hug. "Oh, I am so happy that you are here, Julia. I cannot tell you how many times I have longed for a sister my own age with whom I could talk and share confidences. And now my wish has come true."

"As has mine, for I, too, have wished for such a sister," Julia admitted honestly.

Bethany pulled back from their hug, smiling with a radiance that would have made Julia envious of her beauty had she not been so kindly disposed toward her. Looping her arm through Julia's to lead her toward the bed, she said,

"Then let us be the best and dearest of sisters, and vow to come to one another when we find ourselves troubled or in need of advice."

Julia smiled back, nodding her agreement. By now they had drawn near enough to the bed for her to see that there were stacks of tiny garments laid out on the pink coverlet. On the floor nearby sat an open trunk, waiting to receive them.

"I know that I should have put these away weeks ago, but I simply could not bring myself to do it," Bethany murmured, stopping at the edge of the bed. Her face was tender, her eyes shadowed as she gazed down at the only thing left of the child she had never known, and would never have the chance to know.

Julia wrapped her arm around Bethany's shoulder to draw her close, giving what small solace she could offer. "There is no wrong in keeping them near, not if they give you comfort."

"They do," Bethany whispered, reaching down to pick up one of the garments. It was a beautifully stitched pelisse of striped linen, trimmed with frothy muslin frills. "For all that my baby never drew a breath in this world, I still loved it." She smiled gently, wistfully, at the dainty wrap in her hands, her expression growing dreamy and faraway. "Oh, what hopes I had for it, what wonderful plans. I used to imagine all the marvelous things we would do together . . . the games we would play, the stories I would tell, how I would sing it to sleep at night and wake it with kisses in the morning." She looked at Julia then, her beautiful sapphire eyes clouded with tears. "Did you know that it was a girl? A beautiful daughter."

Julia shook her head, her own vision blurring in sadness at the other woman's grief. This was the first time Bethany had expressed pain at losing her baby, and while Julia had guessed that she felt some sorrow at the loss, she also could not help wondering if, perhaps, she was not a bit relieved as well. After all, the child would have been a bastard, a constant reminder of her shame.

Now feeling shame at herself for having imagined sweet

Bethany capable of such selfishness, Julia hugged her closer and crooned, "Of course she was beautiful. How could she not be with you as her mother?"

Bethany smiled tremulously, visibly fighting her tears. "She could have grown up to resemble her father, and she still would have been beautiful. He was an inordinately handsome man."

"Indeed?" Julia murmured, for a lack of something better to say. Truth be told, she was at a loss as to how to comfort Bethany. What did one say to a woman mourning the death of a child? For all that her own mother had lost three babies, she had never been called upon to confront whatever grief she might have felt at the event.

Bethany nodded. "He was also kind and charming."

"Kind?" Julia drew back, frowning her consternation at her sister-in-law's glowing description of the man who had wronged her. "How can you say that he was kind when he abandoned you in such a heartless manner?"

Bethany shrugged one shoulder, a gesture reminiscent of her siblings. "Because it is the truth. He was never anything but kind and considerate when we were together. As for his abandoning me and our baby"—another one-shoulder shrug—"that is simply the way of the world. Noblemen have no use for their bastards or the women bearing them, and more often than not they cast them off without a second thought. I understood those terms when I accepted my nobleman's offer, so I have only myself to blame for not taking better precautions against being caught."

Julia sniffed. "You take far too much upon yourself in shouldering so much of the blame."

"Perhaps," Bethany replied, gazing again at the garment in her hands. "However, it hardly matters now. What is done is done, and there is no point in dwelling on it."

But Julia could not help dwelling on it a bit longer. "The man behaved like a scoundrel and does not merit such forgiveness from you. I should think that you would despise him for what he did to you." Had she been Bethany, she would have loathed the man to her dying day.

"You mistake my meaning, Julia. I do despise him, and I most certainly do not forgive him for the thoughtlessness with which he cast me off. However, I must be fair and accept my share of the responsibility in the matter. As I said, I knew the risks in what I did. I gambled and I lost."

"Well, I think that you are exceedingly brave and noble," Julia declared, not wishing her new sister to think that she in any way condemned her actions. "It was beyond courageous of you to sacrifice yourself for Bliss the way you did. I can only imagine how dreadful it must have been for you to do so."

Bethany looked away, but not before Julia saw a blush creeping into her cheeks. "It was frightening at first. After all, I had never been with a man and did not know what to expect. But then, well"—she shot Julia a sidelong glance from beneath her inky eyelashes—"since you are wed and we have agreed to be sisters, I suppose that you will not mind if I speak frankly?"

Julia nodded. "Please do."

"Perhaps it brands me as a harlot to confess to such a thing, but I enjoyed being intimate with him. He was so gentle and patient with me; he always made certain that I found my pleasure."

"You . . . liked it?" Julia choked out, stunned by her admission.

Bethany nodded.

Julia stared at her averted face, wanting to pursue the subject and ask the questions weighing on her mind, but not quite certain how to do so without revealing her innocence. After all, she had been wed to Gideon for two months, and Bethany naturally expected that she was experienced between the sheets. Settling on evasiveness, she murmured, "Do you suppose that the marriage act is so very pleasurable for all women?"

Bethany tipped her head to meet her gaze, her lips curving into a faint, knowing smile. "If they have a caring, considerate lover, yes. A woman cannot help but to find pleasure in the act if a man takes pains to see that she is satisfied."

Julia considered her words, watching as she began to carefully fold the pelisse she held. She did not doubt that Gideon would be a caring and considerate lover. Well, at least he would be until he was overcome by his primitive urges. Nonetheless, the mere fact that Bethany had not found having a man stick his male part in her womanly place unpleasant gave her hope that it might not be as torturous as Helene's mother had said. Then again, Bethany's lover had been a nobleman, which meant that his male part was smaller and more refined than Gideon's common one. And that meant—

"Oh, but how silly of me not to have thought of such a thing before," Bethany exclaimed. "I shall give these garments to you and Gideon for when you have your first child."

Julia felt her jaw drop, caught off guard by the notion of bearing Gideon's child. For all the contemplation she had given to what happened in the marriage bed, she had spared little thought as to the consequences of those actions. She must have looked as flabbergasted as she felt, because Bethany glanced away quickly, saying, "Oh. How thoughtless of me. Of course you do not want them. You will naturally wish to stitch your own."

"It is not that, dear. I would very much like to have them," Julia rushed to explain, her heart aching at the forlorn note in Bethany's voice. "Indeed, I could not hope to make anything nearly so lovely on my own. It is just that I thought that you might wish to save them for your own children. After all, it is hardly unreasonable to expect that you might someday wed and have more children."

Bethany refrained from response for several moments, busying herself with wrapping the pelisse in tissue paper. At length she sighed and said, "I shall never have another child, Julia."

"How can you say such a thing with certainty?" Julia argued, not about to allow Bethany to deny herself the hope of future happiness, just because of something she had done in the past. "It is entirely possible that you might marry and—"

"I shall not have more children, because I cannot," Bethany interjected quietly. "There were complications with the birthing, and the doctor said that I shall most probably never be able to conceive another child."

"Oh, Bethany, no!" Julia cried, stricken by the thought that a woman as loving and gentle as Bethany would never have children. "Perhaps the doctor was wrong—"

Bethany silenced her with a head shake. "No, Julia. All the doctors Gideon brought from London said the same thing."

It was Julia's turn to shake her head, which she did over and over again, not wanting to believe what she was hearing. "Bethany . . . I . . . I am so sorry," she finally managed to say, though the words hardly seemed adequate in such a situation.

Bethany smiled gently. "You are a dear to care so about me, Julia. But the fact remains that I shall never have another child to wear these, so it would please me immensely to someday see my niece or nephew clad in them."

"Then you shall," Julia declared. "And I shall be proud to see them so finely clothed."

"I will also be glad to help you make some new ones, if you wish. Since my baby came early, there are several pieces I did not have a chance to finish. I was making—"

Whatever she was about to say was lost as the door burst open and Bliss came bounding into the room. "Do come quickly, Julia!" she cried, hopping from foot to foot in her agitation.

"Why, whatever has happened, Bliss!" Julia exclaimed, rising in alarm. "Do not tell me that there has been an accident?"

Bliss made an exasperated noise. "Do I look as if someone has had an accident?"

Julia had to admit that the girl was smiling rather too broadly for something bad to have happened. Shaking her head at her own silliness for not having noted the detail herself, she asked, "What is it, then?"

"A surprise," Bliss countered cryptically, skipping across the room to seize her arm. Giving it an impatient tug, she urged, "Come and see! Hurry! Hurry! Hurry!"

Julia cast an apologetic look at Bethany, who laughed and said, "Well, you heard the child. Go and see your surprise."

Without further prompting, Julia allowed Bliss to lead

her downstairs, almost having to run to keep up with her.
"In here," Bliss said, stopping before a closed door, behind
which lay the freshly renovated Blue drawing room. When
Julia merely looked at her in query, she snorted and said,
"The door won't open by itself, you know. Open it!"

Unable to form even a vague notion of what she might
find in the room, she did as directed. In the next instant
she was greeted with a chorus of, "Julia! Julia!" and her
sisters came flying at her. Behind them stood little Bertie
and his nurse, the former promptly breaking free from the
latter's restraining hold to toddle after his sisters.

"Maria! Jemima! Bertie!" Julia cried, opening her arms
to receive them. The next few moments passed in a joyous
blur as the siblings engaged in a boisterous reunion. When
they had all hugged and kissed and exclaimed over each
other to their mutual satisfaction, Julia swept Bertie up into
her arms, saying, "How very lovely! I had absolutely no
idea you were coming!"

"That is because it was supposed to be a surprise, silly,"
Maria chortled, visibly pleased by the success of their ploy.

Jemima grinned and nodded. "It was all Gideon's idea.
He sent a note to Aunt Aurelia instructing her to bring
us here."

Julia's elation deflated a fraction at the mention of Aurelia.
"Oh," she murmured, looking around the room in expectation of seeing the horrid woman frowning at their unruly
conduct. When she did not see her there, she glanced back
at her sisters and inquired, "Where is Aurelia?"

"Gideon asked to speak with her in his study." This was
from Maria, who was straightening her deep-crowned straw
hat, which had been knocked askew in their loving fray.

"I daresay that your sisters and brother are tired and
hungry from their journey," interjected Bethany's voice.
Julia glanced in the direction from which it had come to
see her sister-in-law standing on the threshold, grinning at
the scene before her. "When Gideon informed me of their
visit last week, I had the room next to yours prepared for
your sisters, and the one across from it for your brother
and his nurse. If you would like to take them up and get
them settled, I will have Cook send up a light repast."

"I shall do that, and thank you. But please do come in and meet my siblings first," she replied, looking around for Bliss so that she could introduce her as well. When she found her absent, she asked, "Where is Bliss?"

"Here," Bethany said, pulling Bliss from where she was skulking just outside the door. The child scowled as her sister urged her into the room, her jaw tensing as her gray eyes darted between their elegant visitors. For all that she was trying so desperately to look brave, she could not have looked more daunted and uncertain.

Julia's heart instantly went out to the child. Beckoning for her to draw nearer, she smiled and said, "Bliss, do come meet my sisters, Maria and Jemima, and my brother, Bertie. Like you, dear, Maria and Jemima adore animals, so I was hoping that I might persuade you to introduce them to our country creatures while they are here." Shifting her gaze to her siblings, she explained, "Bliss knows all the animals that live in our gardens and park, and has tamed many of them to eat from her hand."

Bliss came forward as directed, but her scowl did not ease and she merely jerked her head in response to the introduction.

Maria, however, was unperturbed by Bliss's less-than-gracious welcome, a fact she demonstrated by grinning and exclaiming, "Please do introduce us to your animals, Bliss!"

"If you wish," Bliss muttered, now staring at the floor.

"Perhaps we can take the book Julia sent us on country creatures with us, and read all about the animals as we meet them," Jemima chimed in, her pretty face lighting up at the prospect of their outing.

"If you wish," Bliss repeated in a bored monotone. Though she still stared at the floor and her face remained fixed in a scowl, Julia could see the beginnings of a smile twitching at the corners of her mouth.

After introducing Bethany, who tendered a warm welcome, Julia handed Bertie back to his nurse and took each of her sisters by the hand. "Well then, I suppose that I should show you to your quarters now."

They had just trooped over the threshold on their expedition upstairs, when Julia glanced back to see Bliss standing alone in the drawing room, watching them go. Though she still scowled, Julia could see the longing in her eyes, her hunger to be included. Feigning a frown, as if displeased by the girl's loitering, she called out, "Well? Are you coming, Bliss?"

Bliss's scowl slipped in her surprise. "You want me to come?"

"But of course. I cannot get my sisters settled without you. I am counting on your help in acquainting them with the manor."

She did not have to ask twice. Bliss hurried to join them, visibly struggling to resume her scowl, but dismally failing.

CHAPTER 19

It was a half hour later when Julia returned downstairs, having overseen the maids in unpacking her siblings' trunks and settling them down to eat the meal Cook had sent up. Her smile, which had become a permanent feature since her sisters' and brother's arrival, broadened at the thought of the scene she had just left. Bliss, who had completely overcome her initial shyness and suspicion of their visitors, had been outlining a schedule for viewing the garden creatures with a precision that would have done a general proud, while Maria and Jemima listened with unconcealed awe of their new friend. By all appearances, the girls were well on their way to becoming bosom bows.

Though Julia knew that she should have stayed with her siblings a bit longer and made certain that they finished their meals, she was much too anxious to seek out Gideon and thank him for bringing them to her to do so. That he would do something so very thoughtful merely strengthened her conviction in the right of loving him. Now happier than she had ever been in her life, she more skipped than walked down the stairs, coming to an abrupt halt as she passed the open front door.

Gideon's coach had been brought around and Aurelia stood next to it, supervising the footmen as they lashed several trunks to the roof. Mystified as to what her aunt could be doing, she went outside to investigate.

"Aurelia?" she hailed, interrupting the woman's explanation of why the trunks must be strapped just so.

Aurelia turned at the sound of her voice.

Julia gasped, recoiling in shock at the expression on her aunt's face. She was smiling broadly and with such uncharacteristic pleasure that Julia could only gape at her, too stunned to do more.

"Julia, my dearest girl!" Aurelia cooed, sweeping her into what from anyone else could have been interpreted as a fond embrace. "How splendid you look. Marriage must agree with you."

At that moment, Julia would have been far less stunned had her aunt sprouted horns than she was at being hugged by her. Struggling to find her tongue, which had abandoned her in her surprise, she somehow managed to sputter, "What has happened?"

"The most marvelous thing in the world. Your husband has offered me a splendid new post in London." She more gushed than uttered the words in her enthusiasm.

Julia blinked her astonishment. "He did?"

Aurelia nodded. "I am to be a spy of sorts for his cloth guild. It shall be my duty to go about in the *ton* and report upon the latest rages in fashion, so as to enable the guild members to properly cater to society's cloth needs. Your husband has offered me a handsome salary, fine quarters, and all the trappings necessary for me to enter the *ton*."

It took several moments for her aunt's words to penetrate Julia's surprise, but when they did, she could not contain her elation. "Then you will no longer be in charge of my sisters?"

"As much as it pains me to leave the darlings, no," Aurelia replied, though, of course, she looked and sounded anything but pained by the prospect. "But never you fear about them. Your husband said that he would write your parents and request that the dears take up residence here. As he pointed out, country air is much more healthful for children." She gave Julia's shoulder a pat, gazing at her with something strangely akin to approval. "I must say that your Mr. Harwood has turned out to be a stellar husband. Not that I am surprised, mind you. I always thought him to be far and away your most promising suitor."

Had Julia not already been hopelessly in love with Gideon, he would have won her heart in that instant. Not only had he brought her siblings to Critchley Manor, but he had also rid them of Aurelia in a manner that ensured that she would not be reclaiming her old post anytime soon. Feeling as if she would burst with gladness, she bid Aurelia a hasty farewell, then rushed off to find Gideon, eager to express her gratitude.

She found him in his study standing before a bookcase with his back to the door, running his index finger along the leather-bound spines of the volumes it held as he searched for a particular title. Apparently she made a sound as she entered the room, because he turned, his lips curving into one of his fascinating smiles when he saw her.

Smiling back, she stopped several feet from where he stood, struggling to find words that would adequately express her appreciation for what he had done. When she could find none, she followed her heart and ran to him. Flinging her arms around him to seize him in a fierce hug, she exclaimed in a babbling rush, "You wonderful . . . marvelous man! Thank you! Oh, thank you for bringing my siblings here and ridding us of Aurelia . . . not that a mere thank you is enough for what you have done. Words alone can never express my gratitude. I-I—" She broke off then, rising up on her tiptoes to press her lips to his, letting them say everything she felt inside.

There was no shyness in her kiss, no hesitation or virginal reserve as she claimed his mouth with hers. There was nothing but a joyous abandonment of her fears, a rush to show him how much she loved him. And her love was all that truly mattered now. It strengthened and empowered her, giving her the courage to trust his passion. Indeed, how could she not trust it? For all that Gideon was of common birth, he had proved to be the very embodiment of nobility. And somehow she just knew that he would be the caring, considerate sort of lover Bethany had described, the kind of man who would temper his primitive urges and do everything in his power to make certain that the marriage act was as pleasurable as possible for her.

Emboldened by that belief, she began to move her mouth

hungrily over his, brushing and melding and showering them with kisses, now and again running the tip of her tongue teasingly along the parting of his lips, coaxing them to open for her.

He froze beneath her sudden amorous assault, as if stunned and uncertain what to do. Then he emitted a soft, strangled growl and crushed her into his embrace. Encouraged by his response, she molded her body to his, undulating against him in her mounting desire as she caught his lower lip between her teeth, now nibbling, now softly sucking and licking it. He groaned into her mouth and grasped her buttocks, dragging her yet further up onto her tiptoes to deepen their kiss.

His lips were hard and urgent as they ground against hers, his tongue hot and ruthless as it plundered and probed her mouth. Something deep in her belly began to stir and twist, coiling into a pulsing knot that made the secret place between her legs grow damp and tingly.

Unbidden, her hands began to move over him, clutching at his broad shoulders, caressing his strong back and arms, and finally grasping his firm buttocks. They bunched and tensed in her hands, a hoarse cry tearing from his throat as he arched back and then slammed forward, driving his manhood against her. She could feel the violence of his arousal, the heat and size of him. By now the place between her legs had begun to throb and ache. Wanting him to touch her there as he had on their wedding night, to pleasure and relieve her, she rubbed against his hardness, mutely begging for his intimate caress.

Gideon sucked in a hissing breath, the feel of her luscious body squirming against his stimulating him with an intensity that brutally gripped and tightened his groin. The way she jerked and surged against his inflamed sex—dear God! It was almost more than he could bear. And yet he could not pull away, though he knew that he should do so before he completely lost control and again terrified her with his passion. How could he leave her arms when he wanted to go on kissing her forever? Heaven help him, but he could not seem to get enough of her, of the sweet taste of her mouth, the womanly smell of her skin, the feminine softness of her body, or the titillating sound of her muffled moans.

Wanting yet more of her, he clasped her tighter against him, his breathing growing harsh when he felt her breasts swell and spread against his chest, her hard nipples seeming to burn his flesh through the thin fabric of her gown and his shirt. In that instant it took every ounce of his willpower not to ease her back onto the floor, to resist his urge to spread and mount and take her. The way she was thrusting her sinuous hips against him, fast and frenzied—he groaned and trapped them in his hold, clutching them tight in an attempt to tame her wildness.

Her hands began to move over him now, kneading and caressing him, recklessly slipping here and sliding there, feeding his carnal madness. Then one of them squeezed between their bodies to grasp his sex, giving it a soft tweak. The raw shock of the resulting sensation served to drag him back to his senses, and he violently ripped himself from her embrace, knowing that to tarry there could only lead to disaster and disgrace. Trembling all over from the intensity of his need, he quickly put distance between them, forcibly resisting his urge to fall to his knees and nurse his painful erection.

"W-what is wrong, Gideon? D-did I do something wrong?" Julia asked in a bewildered whisper. She was staring at him with stricken eyes, tiny furrows forming between her elegant brows.

"That depends entirely on what your intentions were," he gritted out, wishing that she would go away so he could shift his sex to a more comfortable position in his fashionably tight breeches, if such a position were indeed possible to achieve, considering the degree of his arousal.

She looked away, but not before he saw the beginnings of a blush stain her cheeks. "I-I was just trying to show you how grateful I am for what you did for my siblings," she stammered.

Gideon's eyes narrowed at her response, understanding dawning in his mind. It appeared that she sought to tender what she viewed as payment in arrears from their wedding night, apparently believing it due since he had given her what she had sought to gain in her misguided attempt to seduce him. Incensed that she would think him base enough to expect such a payment, that she could believe him so utterly lacking in character as to use such a ploy to force her between his sheets, he growled, "I did not do what I did to manipulate you into bedding me out of gratitude. I—"

"You did it because you are the kindest, dearest, most thoughtful and generous man in the world, and you knew that it would make me happy," she interjected softly. She moved forward then to cup his cheek in her palm, tipping his face down to force him to meet her gaze. "Gideon, please believe me when I say that I never once suspected your lovely deed of being anything other than an example of your fine nature. How could I when I consider you the most honorable man I have ever known?" She tilted her head to one side, her lips forming a faint smile. "Are you truly so very blind that you cannot see how I feel about you?"

Gideon returned her gaze in silence for several beats, searching her beautiful amber eyes for signs of those feelings. When he found what he sought, his breath stilled in his chest. There was tenderness, admiration, respect . . . and desire.

Desire? He exhaled sharply. Oh, yes. Her eyes were sparked by the unmistakable gleam of desire. She was looking at him with the smoldering eyes of a woman who very much wanted the man who stood before her. Barely able to believe what he was seeing and wanting to be sure of her feelings, he hoarsely whispered, "Are you saying that you have learned to care for me a little?"

She laughed, a warm, throaty ripple. "More than just a little, Gideon. I care for you very much, enough that I must confess to having fallen in love with you."

His mouth quirked into a stunned smile. "Indeed?"

"Indeed. And I am ready to be your wife in all ways, if you want me." She was tracing the line of his jaw with her thumb now, her touch almost excruciating in its erotic gentleness.

If he wanted her? Gideon groaned and pulled her back into his arms. "How can you even ask if I want you, sweetheart? A man would have to be mad not to want you." His erection, which had started to subside during their conversation, returned with a groin-wrenching vengeance as she nestled against him. His hips gave an involuntary jerk in needful response, jabbing her with his hardness.

She drew back with a laugh, fixing the culprit with a wicked look. "My, my. I see that you were not lying when you said that you want me."

Gideon glanced down at himself as well, making a wry face. "As I said, a man would have to be mad not to want you. However, this particular man does not intend to be intimate with you until he is satisfied that you are indeed ready to accept his husbandly advances. In view of your fear of the marriage act, it might be best if we discussed the matter first, so that I can explain—"

"Could you not just show me instead?" she interjected, snuggling against him in a manner that brought him precariously close to spilling himself.

"Julia," he groaned, determined to make her see sense.

But again she interrupted him, this time stunning him by guiding his hand between her legs, compelling him to touch her through her gown. "I want you to pleasure me like you did on our wedding night, and I want to learn to pleasure you in return. While you are correct in that I fear having you stick your male part into my female place, I am willing to trust you to make the experience as wonderful as you said it could be." Now rising up on her tiptoes to kiss him, she seductively pleaded, "Please?"

Emitting a feral growl in reply, Gideon swept her up into arms, his stride long and purposeful as he carried her to the door. Flinging it open with a force that sent it crashing into the abutting wall, he stepped over the threshold and marched down the hall.

"Whatever are you doing, Gideon?" she exclaimed on a musical laugh, clinging to his neck.

"Taking you to my bed. It would hardly be seemly for me to pleasure you on my study floor in the middle of the day, though I must confess that the thought did cross my mind."

"But what will the servants think when they see you carrying me off to your bed like this?"

"They will think that we are finally behaving like a newlywed couple." With that, he started up the white marble stairs, his long legs taking them two steps at a time.

They fell silent then, remaining so for the rest of their trek, though Gideon could not resist stealing a kiss or two as they went, promises of passion that Julia eagerly accepted. They were approaching their destination when they encountered Roger, the fourth footman, who was going about his duty of trimming the wall-sconce wicks. He stopped abruptly at the sight of them, casting them a startled look, his mouth flapping open as if to make an inquiry. In the next instant it snapped closed again to form a knowing grin, and he rushed ahead to open Gideon's bedchamber door.

Gideon spared him a nod. "Thank you, Roger. Now go away, and tell the other servants to keep away as well." Their privacy thus secured, he entered the room, kicking the door shut behind him.

This was the first time Julia had been in Gideon's chamber, and she could not help gaping in awe at its foreign splendor. It was a spacious room, decorated in an array of jewel-bright colors and accented with gilding that appeared to be pure gold, filled with the most wonderful things she had ever seen.

There were fabulous Indian tapestries on the walls, some portraying fantastical myths, while others depicted strange cities, all revealing the rich heritage of the land from which they had hailed. On the floor lay several beautifully loomed carpets, each different yet harmonious in pattern. And scattered about on display stands and tables were ancient-looking artifacts and sculptural figures, the history of which Julia hoped Gideon would someday share. As for the furniture . . .

Oh my! She had never seen anything so very lovely in her life. It was like lace carved out of teakwood, every table, every chair and chest a masterpiece of flowing arabesque foliage, inlaid with enameled floral designs. The bed, too, was almost beyond imagination. Both the headboard and footboard had been carved to resemble pairs of elephants, which stood back to back, their trunks raised to support a tentlike canopy of gold-embroidered and -fringed red silk.

It was to that whimsical bed that Gideon took her, depositing her on the gold-and-red patterned damask coverlet. He then stepped back and began to methodically strip off his clothes. When Julia started to rise, thinking that she should follow suit, he commanded, "Sit, Julia. I shall not allow you to undress until I explain about my male parts and you see that they are not as fearsome as the Duchess of Hunsderry has led you to believe. If you remain clothed while I do so, you will be free to leave the chamber should you decide that you are not truly ready to experience the marriage act."

Though Julia felt more than ready at that moment, she remained perched on the edge of his bed, watching him with undisguised interest as his body was revealed. He was every bit as magnificently made as she remembered, all sleek sculpted muscle and smooth tawny skin, more perfect in form than any man had a right to be.

Captivated by the sight of him, she let her gaze roam over the torso he had just unveiled, admiring the dramatic contours of his powerful chest, the massive breadth of his shoulders, and the sinewy definition of his strong arms. If ever a man was the picture of masculinity it was Gideon . . . her Gideon . . . her husband.

A quivering thrill ran through her at the thought that this splendid man was all hers: hers to keep and hold, hers to love to her heart's desire. Now moving her gaze lower, she traced the tapering line of his waist, her pulse quickening as it traveled inward to scrutinize the rippling grid of his taut belly. As she stared, his hands moved to the buttons at his waist, clearly intent on removing his breeches. Not quite ready to be confronted with the reality of what she was about to do, she dropped her gaze to stare at the carpet beneath her feet.

After a moment or two of studying its pattern, during which she struggled to fight her sudden rush of panic, Julia forced herself to look up again and murmur, "Come here, Gideon," telling herself that she must meet her fear straight on if she were ever to master it.

He kicked aside his discarded clothes and did as she directed, moving forward to present himself to her in all his naked glory. As he came to a stop before her, she tipped her head back to smile up at his face, saying, "Do you know how beautiful you are, both inside and out?"

He grinned, a slow, rather wolfish grin that sent her pulse racing yet faster. "I am glad I meet your approval, my lady."

"I cannot imagine you not meeting with any lady's approval," she returned, wistfully wondering how many other women had had the privilege of seeing him like this, women who had no doubt known what to do with his lovely body.

As if discerning her thoughts, he cupped her face in his hands, his grin sobering to a tender half smile as he said, "Ah, but you are the only lady whose approval matters to me. And if you are pleased, then I am happy."

She turned her head to kiss his palm. "Oh, I am pleased, my love. Everything about you pleases me."

"Then I hope that I shall continue to do so in everything I do." He moved his hands from her face then, reaching down to take her hands in his. "Now, sweetheart, I want you to look at my male member so I can explain how it works."

Hiding her reluctance to obey, Julia did as requested, heaving a silent sigh of relief at the sight of him. His sex was flaccid now. And while it still looked too large to fit inside her, it was not nearly as intimidating as when it was hard. She slanted him a querying look, wondering what to do next.

"Touch me," he instructed, guiding her hands to him.

She hesitated for a moment, then cupped him in her palms, her fingers trembling slightly as she wrapped them around him. As she held him, he began to harden and grow. Not certain if she should continue to hold him, she started to let go.

He grasped her wrists, stopping her. "It is an erection, Julia, and it is nothing to be alarmed about. An erection is a sign that a man is exceedingly attracted to the woman he is with. He must harden like this in order to be rigid enough to enter her."

Julia continued to hold him, watching him grow in fascinated silence. At length, she frowned and inquired, "How does it feel when you get an erection?"

"Tight and tingly and a bit achy. Probably the same way your woman's place feels when it needs to be pleasured."

The exact way her woman's place felt now as she stared down at him. He had become fully erect and had risen from the cradle of her palms to jut aggressively from the inky V of hair at his groin. Though Julia knew that she should be terrified at the sight of him, she instead felt oddly excited, titillated by her feminine power to prompt such a response from him.

"I want you to give me a firm squeeze now." When she shot him a surprised look, he commanded, "Do it." When she did, albeit gingerly, he quizzed, "What do I feel like to you?"

She thought for a moment, then replied, "Hard, but you yield a bit when I squeeze you."

"Exactly." He crouched down before her to meet her gaze, reaching down as he did so to circle her hands around him. "No matter how hard a man's erection might get, it will never be too hard not to yield and mold to a woman's softness when he enters her. It most certainly is not the punishing battering ram the Duchess of Hunsderry claims it to be."

"I-I suppose not," Julia conceded, glancing back down at where their hands remained wrapped around him. He released his hold then, telling her to open hers as well to expose him. When she did, he guided her fingers to his sheath, showing her how it slipped back and forth, thus demonstrating the manner in which he would further yield to her. After urging her to test his entire length for pliancy, which to her growing relief she discovered was pliant indeed, he sat back on his heels, concluding, "So you see, sweetheart? I am not so fearsome down there after all."

"No," she agreed, now beginning to believe that he might fit inside her after all. She stared between his splayed legs, thoughtfully contemplating everything she had learned. Still a bit confused about several details regarding the matter, she quizzed, "The Duchess of Hunsderry claims that men of common birth have much larger male parts than noblemen. Is that true?''

To her surprise, Gideon threw back his head and laughed. "I daresay that most noblemen would take exception to that theory, since a large penis is generally thought to denote superior virility." He grinned broadly. "Do remind me to thank the duchess for her compliment the next time I see her."

Julia could not have been more bewildered. "Then it is considered to be a good thing for a man to be large down there?"

"A very good thing. And aside from Her Grace, most women seem to agree. However, it is not true that a man's bloodline determines his size, at least not in the manner Her Grace claims. I can honestly tell you from having bathed in Indian palace bathhouses with both noblemen and commoners, that there is no correlation between social station and genital size."

"And what about Her Grace's views on commoners' primitive urges?" she inquired, readily accepting his explanation on the matter. How could she doubt him when he spoke with such candor?

"Like his size, a man's behavior between the sheets has nothing whatsoever to do with whether he is a commoner or a nobleman. It is entirely dependent upon his character. If a man is gentle and courteous by nature, then he will be so during lovemaking."

And if anyone was gentle and courteous by nature, it was Gideon. Her wonderful Gideon. Julia smiled, feeling an enormous weight lift from her mind. With Gideon as her lover, she truly did have nothing to fear from the bridal bed. Now wanting nothing more than to experience it and to learn whatever other sensual lessons he could teach her, Julia leaned forward and dropped a kiss on his mouth, saying, "You are an excellent teacher, my love, for I find that I am no longer afraid." Kissing him again, this time lingering over his lips to nibble his lower one, she added, "In fact, I find that I am anxious to proceed to our next lesson in lovemaking."

With a grin he pulled her into his embrace, dragging her

off the bed to cradle her between his legs, clasping her clothed form against his nude one. "Your servant, my lady," he whispered into her ear, pausing between each word to tease and nibble her lobe.

Julia moaned her pleasure, tipping her head to urge him on. He promptly obliged, pressing soft, sucking kisses to the place, his hot breath tickling her flesh in a way that she found almost unbearably erotic. Melting bonelessly against him in her bliss, she sighed, "How I love you, Gideon!"

On down her neck he kissed, each thrilling brush of his lips sending sparks of primal heat shooting through her veins, making her body feel warm and heavy, and her pulse skitter alarmingly out of control. He was kissing around her jaw now, moving over her chin and steadily upward until he at last found her mouth. Letting his lips hover over hers, he whispered, "For the record, I love you, too, sweetheart." Then his mouth swooped down over hers, claiming and possessing it.

Julia's instinctive response to him was so powerful that her body instantly quickened, and her mouth eagerly answered the sensual demand of his lips, greedily drinking in the fire and fierceness of his desire. Over and over again he kissed her, his lips ravishing and worshiping hers, delighting and stirring her. She arched and squirmed against him in fevered response, clinging tightly to his neck as his tongue began to tease and stroke and twine with hers, feeling as if she might die from the rapture of his kisses. Then his lips abruptly left hers and he pulled away, holding her at arm's length.

For a long moment he simply looked at her, his breath tearing from his chest in harsh, labored gusts, his eyes hot and openly lustful as they roamed over her face and form. Then he growled, a low, primitive sound, and buried his face against her throat. Resuming his kissing there, he groaned, "Dear God, Julia! How I want you!"

How she wanted him too! Unable to voice her desire for the sobbing moans swelling in her throat, she tangled her fingers in his thick hair and urged him on. And on he went, the sleek silk of his mouth inching lower and lower, brushing the curve of her arched throat, his tongue circling and caressing her pulse point, kissing over her collarbone and then down until he reached the swell of her breasts. Again he paused, this time lifting his head to gaze almost reverently at the sloping softness of her cleavage, his hand lifting to gently trace the contours with his fingertips.

The shock of his tickling touch against her sensitized skin was electrifying, sending currents of raw fire surging through her breasts, making them throb and ache to be fondled. She moaned her need and undulated against him, pressing and rubbing her now-burning nipples against him, begging him to touch them. "Gideon, please," she gasped, though how she managed to speak for her breathlessness, she could not say.

To her sensual bereavement, he instead pulled away, grasping her chin to force her to meet his gaze. Staring deeply into her eyes, he whispered, "Are you quite certain that this is what you wish, my love?" His voice was breaking with huskiness, betraying the urgency of his own need.

"Yes. Oh, yes!" she gasped, nodding several times in her eagerness to proceed.

He searched her eyes for a moment or two, as if seeking signs of fear or hesitation. When he found none, he pulled her back into his embrace and reclaimed her mouth with his. Her lips instantly parted and he plunged inside, his hands moving to the hooks at the back of her gown, deftly unlatching and opening them. A short while later Julia felt her bodice sag and the neckline began to slip over her shoulders. Again he pulled from their kiss, this time to ease the garment off her.

Eager to be rid of it, she helped strip it from her passion-fevered body, and then made short work of discarding her underclothes. Now clad only in her white silk stockings, she stood wantonly before him, a thrill of feminine power racing through her at his expression of enraptured awe as he drank in the sight of her nudity. Languorously striking what she hoped was a seductive pose, she whispered, "Make me your wife, my love." The words no sooner left her mouth than he scooped her up in his arms, engaging her lips in a another kiss as he placed her on the bed.

Rather than join her there, Gideon remained standing by

the bedside, admiring and savoring her beauty. She was exquisite with her flawless ivory skin and autumn-bright hair . . . sheer perfection, every slender line, every graceful curve and lush contour of her body a miracle of feminine beauty. She stirred and aroused him as no woman had ever done before, especially lying as she was before him with her skin flushed by passion and her lips swollen from his kisses. She was gazing up at him with such trust, such unbridled longing that any remaining doubt in his mind as to whether she truly wanted him was instantly erased.

A ragged sob escaped him, the mere sight of her making him ache in ways that he had never before imagined possible. She was so seductive, so willing and inviting, that simply looking at her was making his sex throb with a fierceness that boded ill for his control. Aware that he might not be able to last much longer in his current state, he lowered himself onto the bed beside her, intent on preparing her to receive him.

Never in his life had Gideon felt such urgency, such raw and rampant need. Yet he forced himself to love Julia slowly, thoroughly, wanting her to savor and enjoy the experience, to make certain that she never again felt fear at the prospect of receiving his husbandly attentions. Thus he kissed and caressed every luscious inch of her, coaxing and wooing her passion with his hands and mouth.

Following her writhing body's uninhibited directive, he paused on her breasts, lifting and cupping their sweet bounty in his hands to knead, fondle, and suckle them. When she began to thrash and arch in mindless urgency, her thighs opening in brazen demand, he let his hands meander downward, massaging in a soft, circular motion as he lingered over her slender waist and flat belly. She wiggled and squirmed in inflamed response, urging him lower, her sobbing moans giving voice to her sensual torment.

Tormented by need himself and feeling as if he might explode from it at any moment, Gideon abruptly dipped lower to comb through her feminine curls. She shuddered and jerked, opening her legs yet wider, splaying them to reveal her glistening womanhood, begging him to touch it. Struggling to govern his now-overwhelming urgency, Gideon gently parted her slick flesh, opening it until he exposed the hardened bud of her desire.

"Gideon, please," she whimpered, jerking her hips at him, begging him to touch her there.

Still exposing her, Gideon lightly caressed her thighs, stroking up the inner contour and around the edges of her woman's place, taking care not to touch her most sensitive spot as he traced down her other leg.

She gasped, thrashing in frenzied need. "Gideon, I need—"

"This?" He touched her bud with one finger.

She surged against him, her legs straining yet further apart. "Yes. Oh, Gideon, please."

Again he did not immediately comply, teasing her by merely holding his finger against her. Maddened by her need, she began to rub against him, imploring him to stroke and fondle her.

Gideon chuckled, though what he really wanted to do was straddle her and bury his beleaguered sex into the tempting place she was thrusting so tantalizingly at him. Knowing that he could not do so until she was properly prepared, he began to stroke her, now softly, now deeply, now dipping down to taste her, further parting her as he did so, trying to gauge her readiness for him to begin spreading her feminine opening.

Julia drew in a shuddering breath as hot, tingling threads of pleasure spread throughout her, feeling as if she would die if he did not take her to that blissful place he had taken her on their wedding night. Yet every time she came close to the edge of it and was about to take the plunge, he stopped her, pulling her back.

"Gideon," she mewed in protest as he did so a third time.

"Not yet, love," he murmured, beginning his torment all over again.

She could barely breathe as he traced the damp edges of her womanhood, slowly circling inward, now and again grazing the place that ached most. Over her most secret recesses he glided, his finger pushing inside her just the slightest bit and then withdrawing, traveling upward to fondle her throbbing bud.

Over and over again he repeated the motion, each time pushing deeper inside her. Julia became so swept away by the thrilling sensations washing over her, that she did not object when he finally pushed all the way in. Remaining inside her for a moment or so, he withdrew, reentering her in the next instant. She froze, a squeak escaping her when she felt two fingers inside her, gently opening her.

"Am I hurting you?" Gideon murmured, his other hand moving back to her most needful place to calm and soothe her.

She instantly relaxed as liquid warmth shot through her nether regions. When he touched her there, it was not so bad having his fingers inside her. Besides, having him inside her did not precisely hurt; it just felt strange and unfamiliar. Aware that she must tolerate being entered by something much larger than his fingers if she were ever to be his wife, and wanting that more than anything else on earth, she forced herself to smile and whisper, "No, love. You are not hurting me."

"Good." He pulled out, reentering with three fingers. This time she felt uncomfortably stretched, and she instinctively closed her legs to protect herself.

He stopped her, coaxing them wide again. "I know, sweetheart, I know," he crooned, lowering his head to suckle her bud as he lightly began pumping her with his fingers.

After several moments, during which she lay tense and acutely aware of his fingers moving inside her, she again began to relax and drift toward her climax.

And again he stopped her before she could get there, pulling his mouth away as he withdrew his fingers. Instead of reentering her, as she expected him to do, he further opened her legs, bending her knees to push them up to her belly. Bringing her to the brink again with his mouth, he left her hovering there, letting his fingers replace his lips as he rose to his knees to position himself between her thighs. Gathering her into his embrace with one arm, he reached down and again entered her with his fingers. After preparing her a bit more, he pulled out, slowly reentering her with something that filled her opening completely.

Julia looked down to see his tip inside her, gaping at where they were joined in wide-eyed shock.

"Does it hurt, love?" he inquired, anxiously searching her face for signs of pain.

She considered for a moment. Now that he had been in for a moment, he seemed to have molded to her shape, exactly as he had promised, so it really did not hurt. Pleased by their success, she shook her head and kissed him.

"Promise me that you will tell me if I do hurt you, and you wish me to stop," he instructed, kissing her back. His hand moved back down between her legs to stimulate her again.

"Mmm." She nodded once. As always happened when he touched her there, she instantly relaxed. When she had again melted back against the mattress in her pleasure, he carefully moved deeper. She gasped, but she did not tell him to stop.

Now barely able to contain himself at the feel of her tight virgin's flesh embracing him, Gideon moved yet deeper, continuing to stroke her slick bud as he did so.

Degree by slow degree he entered her, stopping only when he felt the fragile barrier of her maidenhead. Knowing that it would cause her pain to break it, he gathered her tighter into his embrace, whispering, "Sweetheart, I am going to fully enter you now. I am afraid it will hurt at first, but I promise that it will get better. However, if you wish me to stop now and withdraw, I shall do so." Heaven help him! He would probably die from the intensity of his need if she told him to do so, but he would stop anyway. He loved her far too much to do anything that might spoil their future happiness together.

She opened her eyes to meet his, gazing into them as if uncertain how to respond. Then she bit her lower lip and said, "Do it. If you say that it will get better, then I believe you."

Gideon smiled tenderly at her display of bravery. He could tell that she was indeed very frightened of what he was about to do, and yet she loved him enough that she was willing to place her trust in him. Capturing her mouth in a passionate kiss, his hand still fondling her between her legs, he thrust hard, taking her maidenhood.

She cried out into his mouth, her whole body stiffening at the shock of her pain. Though Gideon wanted nothing more in that instant than to plunge into her taut warmth again and again, and relieve his now-unbearable arousal, he forced his hips to remain still, letting her adjust to him.

Rather than push him away and demand that he pull out, as Gideon half feared she might do, Julia stayed as she was, her only movement to pull her mouth from his and bury her face against his chest. For several long moments he simply held her, soothingly stroking and patting her back. Now and again he felt a deep shudder run through her and heard a muffled sob.

By and by she looked up, and brokenly whispered, "What do we do next?" Her face was red and damp with tears, and her lower lip was impressed with tooth marks where she had bitten it.

Gideon's fiery urgency instantly cooled at the sight of her distress. "Nothing if you are in pain." Caressing her hair, he cradled her against him, his voice tender yet husky with remorse as he added, "I am sorry this is hurting you so much, love. Perhaps it would be best if I stopped now and we tried again some other time. Now that I have taken your maidenhood and stretched you a bit, it should not hurt the next time."

She shook her head, her endearingly blotchy face growing adamant. "No. I do not want to stop until you have found your pleasure." When he began to protest, afraid of causing her further pain, she silenced him with a kiss. "Gideon, I love you and I want to be your wife in all ways. Besides, now that you have been inside me for a while, it does not hurt so very badly." She moved her hips a fraction, as if testing the motion, nodding at her findings. "You were right when you said that it would get better." Another cautious thrust of her hips, another nod. "Yes, I do believe that I shall be fine now."

Gideon stared down at her with narrowed eyes, unconvinced. "Nonetheless, it might be best if—" He broke off with a strangled groan, his body jerking in heated response as her hand snaked between his legs and grasped his manly sac, her thumb lightly caressing the sensitive ridge behind it. "Where the hell did you learn that?" he gritted out, his urgency returning with a groin-flaming fury.

She smiled sweetly. "From Amy, of course. Her father's books suggested all sorts of interesting ways to help a man find his pleasure. Like this." She tickled the underside of his sac again, this time trailing up between his buttocks.

Gideon yelped, almost losing himself at the resulting sensations. "Julia . . . please . . ." he moaned, desperately fighting off his approaching climax. Damn it! He would not lose himself now, not like this.

"Then let me give you pleasure as a wife should," she replied, twining her arm around his neck to pull his head down to kiss him. As she captured his lips with hers, she arched up, grasping his tense buttocks to thrust him deeper inside her.

It was too much. The last of his control snapped and with a hoarse cry, he thrust back. She tilted her hips to take him deeper, her legs wrapping around his hips to urge him on. That was all the encouragement he needed, and he plunged in again. And again and again, his body heaving and convulsing in his passion, while hers writhed against him in electrified response. Gradually she found his rhythm and they began to move as one, thrashing and arching in frenzied pleasure, Gideon's every forceful stroke driving them closer and closer to what they both sought. When they began to swirl into rapture, they did so together, crying out in unison as their senses exploded. They climaxed in perfect harmony.

"Oh, Gideon! You were right. It is wonderful," Julia sighed, when she could at last speak.

Gideon chuckled and kissed her. "I am glad that I did not disappoint you, sweetheart."

She giggled and kissed him back. "The only way I shall ever be disappointed is if you do not do to me again what you just did, and soon."

CHAPTER 20

"My turn! My turn!" Bliss exclaimed, hopping up and down in her glee at their game.

Gideon smiled. "I should think that you both would have had more than enough turns by now," he said, lowering the giggling Jemima from his horse into the arms of a waiting footman, who in turn eased her to the ground.

The instant her feet touched the drive, she, too, began jumping up and down, joining Bliss's chorusing demands with her own cries of, "Again, Gideon! Again! Again!"

The prim, sober child Jemima had once been had all but disappeared in the weeks she had been at Critchley Manor, replaced by a sweet hoyden with a contagious giggle and a mop of golden curls that could never stay combed, no matter how much Julia fussed over them. At the moment she looked more like a ragamuffin than the lady she was bred to be, with her blue satin sash crushed and half untied, and her white muslin gown smeared with grass stains from the boisterous game of Prisoner's Base the entire family had played an hour earlier.

The family. His family. Gideon's smile broadened at the thought of the unorthodox brood he jokingly referred to as his tribe, his joy bubbling over as he shifted his gaze from the two girls' bright, eager faces to where several other tribe members took their leisure in the Critchley Park.

A red, blue, and yellow Oriental carpet had been spread beneath a cluster of shady oak trees, upon which sat Bethany, Maria, and Kesin. Bethany, who was engaged in sketching Maria and Kesin, had set aside her sketchbook and pencil to help Maria with the bonnet she was making for Kesin. Maria and the droll little primate had become fast friends over the past weeks, due in part, no doubt, to Maria's constant feeding of the beast, and the girl had decided just last Monday to adopt him as her baby. That, of course, required that she make him a frilly infant's bonnet to wear. Oblivious to the indignity that awaited him, Kesin sat beside his new mother as if he were a miniature person, which he most probably thought he was, doing what he did best: devouring fruit.

As Gideon admired the charming picture they made, chuckling at the notion of Kesin in a bonnet, there was a nearby eruption of childish shrieks and chortles. Glancing in the direction from which they had come, he saw Jagtar swinging a delighted Bertie high in the air, dipping down as he did so to plop the boy on his shoulders. Bertie's pretty French nurse, Jolie, looked on with a smile, exchanging glances with Jagtar that spoke of an interest that went beyond their mutual adoration for the young lordling upon whom they presently doted.

Gideon watched the trio's jolly antics for several moments, and then took in the entire scene, wishing, not for the first time in the past weeks, that he had a talent for painting so he could capture the precious moment on canvas. Of course, the picture would not be truly complete without Christian, who was in Liverpool interviewing the captain whose ship might have carried Caleb to Jamaica, and Julia, who had been summoned inside to settle a laundry dispute. After all, they were an integral part of the core around which the entire family was formed, with Christian being the peacekeeper, and Julia the nurturer, under whose gentle care they all thrived and bloomed.

As always happened when he thought of Julia, Gideon's heart soared with happiness. For all his dreams of having a quiet, satisfying life, he had never once dared to hope that he would someday find the euphoric bliss and profound peace he had found in loving Julia. She was everything he could have ever wished for in a wife: kind, caring,

capable, intelligent, beautiful, and sensual to the point of
voluptuous naughtiness.

He out-and-out grinned at that last. Oh, but she was a
lusty little baggage, as hungry for him as he was for her,
and never shy about provoking his passion. Not that it took
much for her to do so, not when her slightest touch inflamed and seduced him.

Unbidden, the memory of her latest provocation sprang
forth and sizzled through his mind, its smoldering heat
threatening to sear his loins to cinders.

He had been awakened by his arousal at dawn to find
Julia beneath the covers fondling him. When she had discovered him awake, she had mounted and taken him at her
wanton leisure, controlling and teasing his desire until he
had at last wrestled her to the mattress and driven them
both to paradise. Simply remembering the way she had
moved beneath him, how she had wrapped her beautiful
legs around his hips to urge him faster and deeper, made
him long to march into the house and carry her off for an
afternoon of carnal games, something he knew she would
enjoy as much as he.

A powerful sense of contentment swept through him at
the knowledge that he had found his perfect mate. And
Julia truly was perfect in every way. Not only was she the
perfect wife, exemplifying the word in all the expected
ways, but she was also the perfect lover, one of those rare
women blessed with innate sensuality. Why he had only to
caress her for her to—

"Gideon!" *Whap!* Someone slapped his leg, unceremoniously demanding his notice. That someone was, of course,
Bliss, who now stood with her hands braced on her hips,
scowling at his inattentiveness. "It is my turn, Gideon," she
insisted in an exasperated tone.

"Again. Oh, I want to go again!" Jemima chimed in. Her
sash had been further loosened from her jumping up and
down, and had slid down almost to her hips. To Gideon's
way of thinking, she looked exactly as a child should.

A silken laugh drifted from the opposite side of his horse.
"Well, you heard the child, Gideon. Again."

Gideon glanced to his right to see Julia standing beside

his horse, her eyes sparkling with amusement and her ripe
lips curved into a teasing smile. Though she was demurely
dressed in a pink-and-white sprigged muslin gown, her V
neckline offered him an unobstructed view of her soft white
cleavage from his current vantage point. Letting his gaze
roam freely over the delectable contours, the same path his
kisses had taken that morning, he drawled, "Again, you
say?"

"Again," she confirmed, a response echoed by Bliss and
Jemima from the left of his horse. She laughed again, a
rich, throaty ripple, tipping her head to slant him a saucy
look. "You would not wish it to be said that you disappointed a lady, would you?"

Gideon tossed her a grin as lascivious as his thoughts.
"Never, my lady." Locking his gaze into hers for a brief,
heated glance, he wheeled Abhaya around, urging the animal to a quick trot as he guided it down the long, curving
drive. When he was a goodly distance from where Bliss and
Jemima stood, he turned around again and took his
position.

The game they played was not a game at all, but an
exhibition of a feat in horsemanship he had learned while
in India and had often used on the battlefield. It was the
same trick he had employed to snatch Bliss out of harm's
way the day she had dashed in front of his and Christian's
horses. When Bliss had related the incident during their
earlier round of Prisoner's Base, well, at least her version
of it, which completely eliminated her culpability in the
near tragedy, Jemima and Maria had clamored for a demonstration. And what had begun as a simple display of
horsemanship had quickly been adopted as a game by the
children, all of whom clamored for a turn at having Gideon
gallop up to them and snatch them up into the saddle
with him.

It was something they had been playing at for a half hour
now, and while Gideon genuinely enjoyed frolicking with
his youngest tribe members, he was of a mind to play a
more interesting game now that Julia had made her
appearance.

Shifting his narrowed gaze from the girls at the edge of

the drive to where Julia sauntered across the lawn toward Bethany, her enticing hips swaying temptingly beneath her flimsy skirts, he urged Abhaya to a gallop, leaning low over the animal's neck as they picked up speed. He was almost to where Bliss waited when he abruptly steered the horse around her, racing across the lawn to snatch up Julia. She shrieked in surprise as he swung her up onto his lap. Recovering her senses in the next instant, she laughed, snuggling against him in a way that hardened both his sex and his resolve to have his way with her. From behind them he heard Bethany, Jagtar, and Jolie's shouts of laughter, punctuated by Bliss and Jemima's disappointed protests.

Ignoring them all, Gideon urged Abhaya toward a distant, wooded grove, his hand roaming from Julia's waist to cup her breast. As always happened when he fondled her, she moaned and melted against him.

"Wicked man! Whatever possessed you to carry me off like that?" she teased in a husky whisper, her hand wandering downward to squeeze his manhood through his breeches.

And as always happened when she fondled him, he hardened completely and surged against her. "I was merely following your directive, my sweet," he murmured, his fingers now slipping down her neckline to stroke her nipples. Like his manhood beneath her hand, they instantly hardened to his touch. "You did say 'again,' did you not?"

"But the children," she demurred between her soft moans of pleasure. "What if they should follow us?"

Now concealed by the trees, Gideon drew Abhaya to a halt. "They shall not follow us. Bethany is certain to know what we are about and keep them away." That said, he dipped down and claimed her luscious mouth with his. No matter how often he kissed her, no matter how thoroughly, their fevered hunger for each other made every time feel as if it were the first one, stirring uncharted sensations that drove their passion to exhilarating new heights.

True to her naughty nature, Julia began moving her hands all over him, her body squirming and jerking in a way that finally forced him to pull back to see what she was doing. She was working to position herself so that she

sat facing him, straddling his lap. Liking the idea and the
possibilities it presented, Gideon aided her in her endeavor,
effortlessly lifting her so she could shift her legs. Now in
the desired pose, she curled her legs around his hips, drawing his pelvis between them.

The sight of her thus, with her skirts rumpled up around
her waist to expose the white-silk-encased length of her
legs and her woman's place pressed tantalizingly against his
hardness made Gideon sob aloud in need.

She smiled, clearly enjoying his sensual torment. Slanting
him a sultry glance, she slipped her hand down his
breeches. Grasping his engorged sex, her fingers lightly
working his most sensitive place, she murmured, "My, my.
What have we here?"

Gideon groaned in inflamed response, his own hands
moving beneath her skirts to caress her womanhood. When
he found it damp, he knew that he had to have her, then
and there.

Apparently they were of like mind, because her hands
were now on his falls, unbuttoning them. A moment later
he sprang forth, straining and pulsing, and ready to take
her. Emitting a rough growl, he grasped her buttocks, lifting
her up to sheath himself in her honeyed warmth. Commanding Abhaya to stay, he thrust deeply inside her, plunging in again and again until they collapsed against each
other, quivering in ecstasy.

For several blissful moments they remained like that, sag-
ging in each other's embrace in boneless rapture, with Gideon still inside Julia. At length Julia straightened up, a
frown creasing her brow. "Do you hear that?"

"What?" Gideon murmured, kissing her furrowed
forehead.

"That noise. It sounds like a coach or a wagon coming
up the drive."

Gideon forced his thoughts away from the fact that he
was again hardening inside her to concentrate on listening.
He, too, heard the rumbling, which indeed sounded like a
rapidly approaching vehicle. Promptly losing interest in the
noise in favor of nibbling Julia's ear, he confirmed between

nips, "I do believe you are correct. I daresay it is the kitchen staff returning from market."

"Market day is Wednesday. Today is Friday," she pointed out.

"Mmm," he responded, working his way down her neck.

"Gideon! Do pay attention," she chided, pulling away.

"I am paying attention. You have my full attention." He thrust his hips, driving his again-erect sex deeper inside her to demonstrate the fact.

"And I love that sort of attention," she replied, giving him a playful thrust back. "However, do you not think that we should go and see who it is? It could be Christian returning with news of Caleb, you know."

Gideon considered her logic for a moment, moving inside her as he did so, enjoying the feel of her. Then he sighed and reluctantly withdrew. "I suppose you are right. Besides if it is Christian with news, he will send someone to fetch us, and it would be highly unseemly for the servants to catch their mistress with her skirts tossed up like a doxy."

"Indeed? And would it not reflect equally poorly on you for them to catch their master tossing up their mistress's skirts on the back of his horse in the middle of the day?" she inquired with a laugh, tugging her bodice back into position.

He chuckled. "Ah, but it is different for a man. I daresay that such roguishness would serve only to add luster to my manly reputation."

She gave his cheek a playful cuff for his impudence, to which he responded with a kiss. Then they got down to the business of straightening their appearances, well, at least as best they could. Several minutes later they emerged from the trees to see a coach stopped at their door and bustling activity all around it. Not recognizing the vehicle, Gideon glanced at Julia in query.

Apparently she did not recognize it either, for she murmured, "Who do you suppose it could be?"

Gideon, who had drawn Abhaya to a halt in order to study the scene, shrugged. "I cannot say. However, there looks to be a crest painted on the side."

Julia squinted at the crest, as if trying to make out the details. Unable to do so for the distance, she shook her head, musing, "Perhaps it is someone who is lost and is seeking directions. Or a traveler in need of aid."

"Or it could be a spy sent by the *ton* to report upon our marital progress," Gideon contributed with a chuckle. "The only way to know for certain is to go and see." With that purpose in mind, he spurred Abhaya forward, cutting across the park lawn to where three footmen had begun to unlash the trunks atop the fashionable blue and gold vehicle, while two grooms moved forward to take charge of the six gray horses. They were halfway there when Gideon heard Julia groan.

"It is the Duke of Hunsderry's crest," she muttered. Gideon looked down in time to see her make a face. "I wonder what the Dunvilles could be doing here? They are hardly the sort of people to drop by a person's country house simply for the pleasure of their company."

Though Gideon, too, was less than thrilled by the prospect of having to suffer the insufferable Dunvilles, he gave Julia a reassuring hug, saying, "Again, the only way to know for certain is to find out." They had now drawn near enough for him to see that their sisters had rushed over to the coach and now greeted their callers. As he watched, Bethany curtsied to the duchess, an imposing harridan decked out in purple and black, who Maria appeared to be introducing, while a footman helped Lady Helene from the coach. A moment later, Lady Wilhelmina Edicott emerged.

"Why, it's Mina," Julia exclaimed, her glum expression brightening at the sight of her friend. "Her Grace must be on a matchmaking mission."

Gideon frowned. "Matchmaking? Here?"

"Well, not here. My guess is that the group is either going to or returning home from a country house party hosted or attended by a gentleman Her Grace wishes to secure for Helene."

"And how did you come to that conclusion, pray tell?"

"Because Mina is with them. Her Grace always invites one of Helene's plainer acquaintances to accompany them to gatherings where there will be likely gentlemen present, so as to make Helene appear all the more beautiful in contrast."

"I rather prefer Lady Mina's looks, myself," Gideon commented truthfully. "At least a man knows what he is getting with her."

"That is because you are a man of rare good taste," she retorted, tipping her head back to invite his kiss.

He obliged, but quickly, since they were almost to the coach now. He had just lifted his lips from hers when Jemima rushed to the edge of the road, calling, "Do come, Julia! We have company."

Julia made another face, only to promptly rearrange it into an expression of bland cordiality as two grooms rushed over to help her dismount.

"You must pardon me if I greet our guests from horseback," Gideon whispered into her ear, as one man joined his hands to make a step, while the other hovered by his side in preparation to steady Julia as she stepped down. "My breeches are soiled from our romp, which will show if I dismount. Since it would never do for Her Grace to think that I am completely consumed by my primitive urges . . ." He finished his sentence with a meaningful lift of his brows.

She snorted. "I truly do not care what Her Grace thinks. I love you, and that is all that matters."

Gideon grinned, pleased that she valued their love above the *ton*'s opinion. Dipping down to kiss her cheek, he murmured, "Have I told you today how much I adore you?"

"Only a dozen or so times. You are rather behind in the number today. I shall expect you to work very hard to correct your oversight." Tossing him a saucy look, she dismounted. After pausing to smooth her gown, she took Jemima's hand, allowing the child to pull her around the coach to where the assembly had congregated. Gideon followed them on horseback.

"Julia, oh Julia!" Mina cried, rushing forward to hug her friend. "How I have missed you!"

Julia hugged her back. "I have missed you too, dear."

Helene came forward then to give Julia a dutiful hug, while Mina turned to Gideon. Flushing a blotchy pink that perfectly matched the three spots on her chin, she stammered, "It is wonderful to see you again, too, Mr. Harwood."

Gideon smiled and inclined his head. "The pleasure is all mine, Lady Mina. But do call me Gideon. Julia speaks of you so often and with such fondness that I have begun to view you as a member of our family."

Mina's blush deepened. "Gideon, yes, and you must call me Mina." She could not have looked more flattered.

"Mr. Harwood." This was from Lady Helene, who rudely pushed Mina aside and now stood in front of her, gracing him with a simpering smile.

"Lady Helene," he responded in like insincere coin.

She continued to gaze at him expectantly, clearly waiting for him to lavish her with the same sort of pretty welcome he had given Mina, no doubt believing it to be her God-given due as the toast of the *ton*. When he merely turned his attention to her mother, who Julia was formally welcoming to their home, the disagreeable chit sniffed and turned away.

As he watched the Duchess of Hunsderry, he could not help wondering at the titled bucks who so eagerly thronged around Helene at every gathering. One glance at her mother would have been more than enough to put him off the chit forever. As it was, he could barely keep from grimacing his distaste at the sight of the hideous creature. With her obviously dyed black hair, thickly pasted pock-marked skin, and overly rouged cheeks and lips, Her Grace truly was a horror to behold.

Well, at least to his eyes. The *ton*, however, seemed to find her quite elegant. Then again, they considered anyone with plump pockets and a title to be the height of elegance. Nonetheless, there was one opinion he held that he doubted anyone in the *ton* would dispute. And that was that Her Grace had an overly sharp tongue, which she wielded as a weapon to bring about the downfall of anyone who did not meet with her exacting, if rather arbitrary, standards. At the moment she was using that tongue to take Julia to task for allowing Jemima to run about like a hoyden.

"Really, Julia! I cannot even begin to imagine what could be going through your mind to allow the girl such liberties. You know what they say: an ungoverned child will grow into an unprincipled adult. My dearest Helene was allowed only an hour of play each day, and then only under the strictest supervision to ensure that she did not engage in unseemly activity, such as running and making unnecessary noise. And just see how splendidly she turned out. Lord Shepley, on the other hand, allowed Amy to run willy-nilly and to go her own way in matters that the chit had no business whatsoever in deciding for herself, and just see—"

"What an enchanting creature she has turned out to be," Gideon smoothly inserted, not about to allow the odious woman to insult someone Julia counted as a bosom bow. "You are correct in that Lady Amy is a stellar example of womanhood, Your Grace. Indeed, aside from my wife and Lady Mina, I count her as quite the most charming girl in the *ton*."

Helene sniffed at being omitted from his compliment, an annoying sound that was echoed by Her Grace as she lifted her spectacles from where they dangled against her bony chest on a gold chain. Fixing him with a condescending stare through the thick lenses, she sneered, "Yes, well, I daresay that you would find her so, Mr. Harwood."

Gideon nodded and smiled, deliberately misunderstanding her slur. "Thank you, Your Grace. You do not know how much it means to me to be acknowledged as a fine judge of character by a paragon such as yourself." He could not have sounded more fawning.

Julia and Bethany, who now stood behind the awful woman, clapped their hands over their mouths to stifle their guffaws, while Bliss emitted a loud snort. Poor Mina merely looked confused.

The duchess opened her mouth, no doubt to have another go at taking him down a few pegs, but he cut her off before she could speak by quizzing, "By the by, Your Grace, to what do we owe the pleasure of your company?"

For a moment it looked as if she might ignore his inquiry and proceed with her setdown, then she seemed to think better of it and dropped her spectacles back into place.

"The cream of the *ton* was invited to Lord Waddington's lodge in Westmorland for a hunting party, but the place turned out to be so barbaric that Helene and I simply could not stay." She sniffed her disdain. "How his lordship could expect ladies of quality to suffer such abominably crude accommodations, I do not know." Another sniff, this one more contemptuous than the last. "At any rate, His Grace elected to stay and kill things with the rest of the gentlemen, so Helene and I were forced to return home alone."

"And our dearest Mina," Gideon interjected, infuriated at the woman's insistence on dismissing the girl as if she did not exist.

When Her Grace sniffed again, he was tempted to offer her his handkerchief, as he had once done with Julia. "Yes, even Mina could not be expected to endure such wretched conditions." She heaved a much-put-upon sigh and shook her head. "Since we are three helpless women traveling alone, we have decided that it would be best to spend our nights at acquaintances' country houses whenever possible. After all, a beauty such as Helene is bound to excite interest at inns, which puts her at risk to suffer advances from the common ruffians that frequent such places. Your house happens to be on our route, so . . ." she finished the sentence with a shrug.

Gideon smiled and inclined his head in what would normally denote a gracious acceptance of her explanation. "But of course you are welcome here, Your Grace." He paused to slant Julia a sardonic look. "Heaven knows we would not want your darling Helene to become the target of some dreadful commoner's primitive urges."

"Yes, and a pinch of cinnamon would do wonders in improving your cook's recipe for bread pudding," the Duchess of Hunsderry said, scraping her plate with her fork to scoop up the last of the dessert she had spent the past fifteen minutes maligning. "My cooks have always benefited immensely from my advice, or so my friends tell me, so you would be wise to heed it as well, Julia, dear, and pass it on to your cook."

Gideon, who had spent the past two hours listening to

the harridan criticize everything about her dinner, from the weight of the silver to the rise on the bread, feigned a pleasant smile and inquired, "Have you had a great many cooks to advise, Your Grace?"

She sniffed. "Seven in the past two years, ungrateful wretches! They stay only long enough to benefit from my culinary wisdom and then leave."

Gideon suspected that they left out of annoyance at Her Grace's caviling, but he kept his opinion to himself out of respect for Julia. For all that she claimed not to care for Her Grace's opinion, she had been born and bred to be a part of the *ton*. They were her circle. Her friends. And to be cast from their company could not help but to cause her anguish, and he would rather be damned than see her hurt. Thus he contented himself with wryly commenting, "Such gross ingratitude makes one wonder at the state of the world, does it not?"

"Indeed it does," the duchess agreed, her words punctuated by a soft belch. Having now all but scraped the delicate Oriental pattern off the china plate before her, she set down her spoon, adding, "I noticed that you have a reasonably fine pianoforte in one of your drawing rooms. Perhaps Mina and Bethany can amuse themselves with music while the four of us play cards." She lifted her spectacles to eye Bethany with a look of condescending query. "I assume that you have had some instruction in music, Bethany?"

Bethany, who was chatting companionably with Mina, while Helene sat pouting on her other side over the lack of fawning being directed toward her, looked up to respond. Before she could speak, Gideon answered for her. "My sister has a talent for both singing and the pianoforte, and is quite proficient on the harp as well. Since I have had the honor of hearing Mina play the pianoforte on several occasions, which she does quite charmingly"—he smiled at Mina, who in truth possessed only modest musical talent—"perhaps she and Bethany will honor us with a harp and pianoforte duet?"

Mina flushed, visibly thrilled by his praise. "B-but of course, sir. It would be a p-pleasure," she stammered, while Bethany smiled and nodded in agreement.

The duchess shrugged. "I daresay that their efforts would be vastly improved by the addition of my dear Helene's singing, but alas, we cannot spare her if we are to play cards."

"I shall be perfectly amenable to forgoing our card game if Helene would prefer to sing. Indeed, Helene possesses such a lovely voice that it would be a treat to hear her," Julia said. She smiled at Helene, who instantly brightened at the compliment.

Gideon smiled as well. The sly minx! It was obvious to him that she sought not musical entertainment, but an excuse to escape yet more of Her Grace's tedious conversation.

"Pshaw, Julia!" Her Grace scoffed. "Do not tell me that you harbor the same prejudice against cards as your mother?"

Julia drew back, frowning. "Pardon?"

Gideon cringed inside as he waited for the other shoe to drop. Bloody hell! What had Lord Stanwell been thinking to invent a lie that could be so easily uncovered through casual conversation? But, of course, the answer was obvious: In his desperation to squirm out of his predicament, the bastard had not bothered to fully consider his story.

"Why surely you know of your mother's low opinion of cards and gambling?" Her Grace replied, lifting her spectacles again, this time to peer at Julia with an air of quizzical superiority.

"No," Julia admitted. She could not have looked more nonplussed.

The duchess sniffed and lowered her spectacles. "How very odd that you should not know such a thing about your own mother, especially when you have been in the *ton* for so long. Then again, you have never had the close sort of relationship with your mother that Helene and I share, so I suppose that your ignorance should come as no surprise." She shrugged, another belch escaping her as she did so. "At any rate, I must say that I have always considered your mother's steadfast refusal to engage in wagering to be rather poor form. Bad *ton*, frankly. And were she not such a spendthrift in other regards, I would be forced to suspect her of cheeseparing."

Julia was staring at him now, her eyes full of the questions he knew must be running through her mind. Damn it to hell! Why did this have to come about now, when their love was so new? Why could it not have happened several years down the road, when they were settled in their life together and secure in their marriage? Feigning interest in his dessert to avoid meeting Julia's gaze, Gideon wondered what he could possibly say to her to explain the matter. The truth was out of the question, of course. He would not wound her in such a manner.

"Are you saying that you have never known my mother to gamble?" Julia inquired. Her eyes were now boring holes in him.

Another sniff from Her Grace. "Never. Even your father is rather less inclined to gamble than most men. Indeed, I cannot recall him ever wagering more than a few pounds."

"How very interesting," Julia murmured, her soft voice pregnant with a meaning that only Gideon could understand.

Uttering a silent oath, the foulest one he knew, Gideon forced himself to glance up at Julia, knowing that to further evade her gaze would serve only to mark his guilt. Her head was tipped to one side and she was staring at him with a look of bewildered suspicion. The instant their gazes touched, her eyebrows lifted in mute query.

He grimaced and shrugged one shoulder, hoping that she would take the gesture as a plea of ignorance. Determined to cut the damning conversation short, he glanced at their guests, smoothly suggesting, "Shall we retire to the drawing room, ladies? I can assure you, Your Grace, that I have no prejudice whatsoever against gambling and will gladly engage you in a friendly wager." Praying that in branding himself a gambler he might put Julia off, he rose.

As the rest of the party followed suit, Julia said, "Bethany, do be a dear and show our guests to the Blue drawing room. Gideon and I will join you shortly." She shifted her gaze to him, her expression conveying that she would brook no argument from him.

Gideon nodded, his gut giving a sickening wrench at what awaited him. Good God, what was he going to tell her?

The door had no sooner closed than Julia rounded on him demanding, "The truth, Gideon. I will know the real reason why my father insisted that I wed you."

"What makes you so certain that what your father told you is not the truth?" he countered, nimbly dodging her question.

"Because Her Grace has neither the wit nor the imagination to make up such a thing about my mother. Besides, now that I consider the matter, I truly cannot recall my mother ever retiring to the card table at any gathering." She shook her head, her expression mulish. "No, Gideon. It is clear that my father lied about his reason for forcing me to wed you, and I will have the truth now."

"Has it never occurred to you that your mother might not like the Dunvilles any more than we do, and that she has sought to escape Her Grace's company by refusing to game with her? As for whether or not she indulges in cards at gatherings, how can you honestly claim to know that she abstains? From what I have observed, you are far too occupied with dancing and being fawned over by your admirers to possibly mark anyone else's actions."

Another head shake. "Perhaps I could accept those explanations if the rest of my father's story made sense, but it does not. It has not for a long while now, not since I have discovered what a fine man you are. You, Gideon Harwood, are far too noble to ever be guilty of cheating and blackmail. Please do not insult me by trying to convince me that he told the truth." She was inching toward him now. "So tell me: why did my father force me to wed you?"

Gideon frantically searched his mind for a response, one that would satisfy her. The best he could find was, "Has it never occurred to you that this might be a private matter between your father and me? One that you have no business in knowing?"

"It became my business when I was forced to wed you, Gideon. Can you not see that?" Now stopping before him, she grasped his arms to stare beseechingly up into his face.

"I love you, Gideon. More than I ever dreamed I could love anyone, and not a day goes by that I do not thank heaven for the good fortune to be your wife. And yet, what kind of a marriage do we truly have if you will not confide in me? How am I to believe anything you might say in the future if we have this lie between us?" Her hands tightened on his arms. "Gideon, if you cannot trust me enough to tell me the truth in this, then I shall be forced to conclude that our love is a lie. And I cannot live in a marriage built of lies."

Gideon stared down at her, stunned by her words. "Are you saying that you will leave me if I do not tell you?" Was that really his voice, so hoarse and frayed?

She nodded once, then let go of his arms and stepped away. "I shall have no choice but to leave Critchley Manor. I do not know where I will go or what I shall do, but anything will be better than staying with you." When she met his gaze again, he saw that her eyes were bright with gathering tears. "You see, Gideon, if I stay I shall never have the strength to keep myself from you, for I love you too much to do so. And then I will be forced to despise myself. So it is better that I leave and starve, than stay and be stripped of all self-respect."

Gideon felt the blood drain from his face, devastated by the thought of losing her. And yet, how could he tell her the truth when it would surely destroy her?

How could he not tell her, given the choice?

True, he could create a new lie, a clever one that would explain everything quite neatly and spare her all pain. But would that not simply widen the web of deception between them, one in which he might someday find himself caught? And if he were caught in a lie a second time, she would leave him for certain and never return. Besides, she was right. What kind of a marriage could they possibly have if it were built on lies?

Suddenly tired, more world-weary than he had ever been in his life, Gideon admitted that they could have no marriage, not without a foundation of truth to build it on.

"Gideon, please. I love you so much," she pleaded. Rising up on her tiptoes to take his face in her hands, she gazed deeply into his eyes, whispering, "Gideon, if you have done something that shames you and you are afraid to tell me for fear that I will despise you, please know that there is little on this earth that could shake my love for you. Whatever it is, we shall work it out. I promise." She rose higher and pressed a kiss to his lips.

That kiss, coupled with the sweetness of her plea, undid him. For all that he hated the thought of hurting her, he had no choice. Besides, it was possible that she might someday learn the truth for herself if she dug deeply enough for it, which knowing his Julia's tenacity, she very well might do. At least if he told her himself, he would be on hand to help her come to terms with the fact that she and her siblings were bastards, and would remain so under the current laws of England, in spite of the fact that her father was now legally wed to her mother.

Resigning himself to his terrible duty, Gideon sighed. "All right, Julia. You want the truth, so you shall have it. I know that this is going to be difficult for you to hear, but—"

At that moment two footmen entered the room to clear the table. Nodding cordially at them, Gideon grasped Julia's arm and pulled her from the room. Nodding again, this time at the majordomo and housekeeper, who conversed at the end of the hall, he escorted her into the small antechamber next door.

Now alone again, he said, "I suggest you sit, Julia."

There must have been something in his face that told her that what he had to say was very bad indeed, because she did as he advised without question. When she had settled into one of the dainty straight-back chairs set against the wall, he kneeled before her, taking both her hands in his. Holding them tightly, prepared to pull her into his arms and comfort her, he told her the truth. By the time he had finished, her face had blanched to the color of ash and silent tears coursed down her cheeks.

"Julia, sweetheart," he whispered, when she simply sat there staring at him with wet, haunted eyes. "It will be all right. I swear it."

A great, rending sob ripped from her chest. "No, Gideon. Nothing shall ever be right again. I am a bastard and so are my siblings. Should anyone ever learn the truth—" She broke completely then, weeping as if her heart would break.

Gideon stood, scooping her up to cradle her in his lap as he took her seat. She struggled weakly against him, but he crushed her to him, stilling her. Kissing the top of her head, his hand moving soothingly on her back, stroking and massaging it, he crooned, "Hush, love. No one will ever learn the truth."

"But if they do—"

"If they do, there is bound to be a scandal, true, but I doubt if it will have a lasting effect on your family," he interjected. "Your father wields far too much power in society to suffer the repercussions a lesser man would be forced to endure in a like situation. Furthermore, everyone knows that there are a great many noble bastards in the *ton*, and as long as no one talks about the fact, no one really cares."

She sniffled. "But this is different. Most of those bastards are products of their mothers' indiscretion, born within a legal marriage. Since their mother is married to a man who chooses to claim them as his own, there is no real scandal. Besides, no one can truly prove that they are not their father's children. But my father was married to someone other than our mother when we were born, so there can be no question as to our legitimacy." *Sniffle!*

Gideon felt in his waistcoat pocket for his handkerchief. "At least you can take comfort in the fact that your father is now legally wed to your mother. That might help matters, should the secret ever come to light." He pulled out his handkerchief and presented it to Julia.

She blew her nose. "And I have you to thank for that. It appears that I have a great deal to thank you for." Fresh tears welled up in her reddened eyes. "Oh, Gideon! You truly are the best man on earth, a perfect gentleman. While I-I—" She shook her head, a sob fracturing her voice. "All those weeks in London that I spent looking down on you, all those times I belittled your common blood and lorded

my nobility over you . . . it was I who was not worthy of
you. And I never shall be. I-I—'' Her voice ruptured into
another sob, and she resumed weeping in earnest.

The wrenching sound of her anguish ripped through Gideon's heart, making it bleed at her pain. Gathering her in
his arms to hold her close, he murmured against her hair,
''But of course you are worthy, sweetheart. You are the
perfect lady and you are perfect for me. We are perfect for
each other. Nothing can ever change that fact, just as nothing will ever change my love for you. You promised me
that we could work out whatever troubles arose from me
telling you the truth, and I expect you to honor that
promise.''

''But Gideon—'' She began to protest, tipping her head
back to meet his gaze.

He silenced her with a kiss. After lingering over her lips,
rejoicing at her passionate response, he lifted his mouth
from hers to stare down at her blotchy face. Smiling tenderly at the sight of her red nose, he said, ''We have laid
the foundation for truth in our marriage now, so I see no
reason why we should not build on it. Unless, of course,
you do not forgive me for allowing myself to become entan-
gled in your father's lie.''

She sniffled. ''Of course I forgive you. How could I not
when your intentions were good? For all that you are too
humble to take credit for your gallantry, I see that you wed
me for my own protection.''

''And I will continue to protect you for as long as we
both might live, if you will allow me to do so.''

She smiled then, albeit wanly, but it was a smile nonetheless. ''There is nothing on this earth that I would love more,
except you, of course.'' With that, she twined her arms
around his neck and kissed him.

Gideon had just deepened their kiss and he was considering snubbing their company in favor of carrying her upstairs, when there was the sound of footsteps running down
the hall. A moment later there was a pounding at the door,
and a voice he identified as belonging to his normally reserved majordomo, shouted, ''Mr. Harwood! Mr. Harwood!
You have an urgent message from Liverpool.''

Julia and Gideon pulled from their kiss in unison to stare at each other. "It has to be news of Caleb," Julia exclaimed, her formerly forlorn face transfusing with excitement. Slipping from his lap, she tugged him up onto his feet, urging, "Well? Do go see."

Without further prompting, Gideon went to the door, returning with a sealed message and a bottle of port. When he had read the letter, pausing once to study the bottle, he could not contain his whoop of joy.

"Well?" Julia eagerly quizzed.

"We have found Caleb." He more laughed than uttered his response in his happiness.

"Where? How?" she cried, snatching the letter from his hand.

"He is in Portugal. The ship that sailed for Portugal the day Caleb is thought to have left England arrived in Liverpool two days ago, and Christian had the opportunity to interview the captain. The wounded man the captain described as sailing with him on that voyage not only matches the description of Caleb I gave Christian, but the captain showed him this." He held up the bottle.

When she glanced first at the bottle, then up at him, frowning her incomprehension, he lifted her left hand, placing her wedding ring next to the emblem etched into the bottle. Her eyes widened and she gasped. "It matches perfectly."

"Do you not remember me telling you that the original Harwood wedding ring disappeared with Caleb?"

"Yes, but"—she made a helpless hand gesture—"but how? And why is a copy of the ring etched into the bottle?"

Gideon shook his head. "I cannot explain the etching. However, Christian was able to learn that Caleb has assumed the name Jonathan Iverson, and that he is now a winemaker in the Douro Valley. It seems that he married the widow of a port winemaker with a vineyard there. According to the captain's account, the woman assisted in nursing Caleb on his voyage to Portugal and they fell in love then."

Gideon's already wide grin broadened at the thought of

his headstrong brother falling in love and settling down. "At any rate, the captain encountered Caleb on his last voyage while at"—he paused to peer at the letter in Julia's hands; when he found what he sought, he nodded—"it was at a lodge in Villa Nova. I assume from the letter that the Portuguese call their shipping warehouses lodges. Whatever the instance, the captain thought highly enough of the port Caleb was selling there to purchase a large quantity to import to England, and has contracted to buy more. He is scheduled to return to Portugal in a fortnight, and Christian has secured passage for us on his ship."

"Oh, but this is wonderful news!" Julia exclaimed, throwing her arms around him in an enthusiastic hug. "Of course we must go."

Gideon grinned and hugged her back. The news was more than wonderful. It made his life complete.

EPILOGUE

Portugal

"So the woman the innkeeper reported seeing in your company that night was Lady Silvia, and the man was her footman," Gideon clarified.

Caleb nodded. "I did not know who else to turn to when I found myself wounded and pursued by the law. Lady Silvia had always been kind to me, so I took the chance and went to her."

"And of course she helped you," Gideon interjected.

Another nod from Caleb. "Yes. It was she who removed the bullet and arranged for my passage to Portugal. Without her aid and that of her manservant, I most certainly would have died . . . if not from the lead in my belly, then at the end of a rope." He paused then, a shadow passing over his face. "I am grieved to hear of her death. She truly was a great lady."

"Indeed she was," Gideon murmured.

"As is my darling Hannah," Caleb added, kissing the dainty blond woman who sat by his side. "I owe my life to her as well. I doubt I would have survived my wound without her care."

Hannah smiled, a sweet, loving smile that instantly transformed her ordinary face into one of breathtaking beauty. "And I doubt if I would have survived this past year without you by my side, dearest."

"I believe that you two met on the ship to Portugal?" Gideon quizzed.

"That is correct," Hannah said. "I was returning home to Portugal after burying my husband in England. Like me, he was English, and I thought it only proper that he should be buried in his homeland."

"How did he come to own a vineyard here?" Julia asked. The woman was her newest sister, so of course she wished to know all about her. Julia could not help smiling her pleasure at the addition. One could never have too many sisters to love . . . or brothers, she added, glancing at Caleb.

That he and Gideon were brothers was obvious from their remarkable height, strong physiques, and boldly sculpted faces. Yet unlike Gideon, whose features were unrelieved by the slightest softness, Caleb's were tempered by the same beauty that Bethany had inherited, something that made him appear almost pretty in contrast to Gideon's starkly masculine looks. Like Bethany, Caleb's eyes were a deep sapphire blue, and his thick, wavy hair was the same chocolate brown as hers, though his was liberally streaked with honey and gold from long hours spent toiling beneath the hot Portugal sun. And when he smiled, Julia could not help noting that he possessed the excellent Harwood teeth. All and all Caleb Harwood was an exceedingly handsome man.

It was a fact that was clearly appreciated by Hannah, who gazed at him as if he had hung the moon and stars as she answered Julia's question. "My first husband determined that there was a fortune to be made in producing port wine, so he purchased this vineyard. He was a London wine merchant, you see, so he understood the wine business. What he did not know was how grueling it would be to tend the vines." She sighed and shook her head. "In the end it proved to be too difficult, and I was left a widow with only this house and vineyard to my name. Fortunately, the purchase of the vineyard included pipes of aged port that proved ready to bottle, and with Caleb's help I was able to bottle and sell it at a fine profit." It was her turn to kiss her husband. "Our darling Caleb has turned out to be an excellent businessman. I daresay that my first husband would have been pleased by the success he is making of the vineyard."

"I must say that it is some of the finest port I have had the pleasure to taste," Gideon commented.

Julia nodded. "Gideon sent a case of it to our good friend Lord Shepley. He is certain to recommend it to the *ton,* which will make it all the rage in London."

Gideon chuckled. "I do hope that you are prepared to keep up with the demand."

Caleb and Hannah exchanged pleased grins. "Most assuredly, brother," Caleb replied. "After all, I have a wife and family to support now." The family to which he referred was Hannah's two young sons from her first marriage.

"I must say that Caleb was most fortunate to meet you as he did, Hannah," said Bethany, who had been listening to the conversation in silence. "It is just too bad that it had to be under such sad circumstances. Please do accept my condolences on the death of your first husband."

Hannah inclined her head in acknowledgment of the other woman's sympathy. "It was indeed a very sad time for me, but caring for Caleb helped to ease my grief somewhat."

"Was that when you began to fall in love?" Bethany shyly inquired.

"Not exactly," Hannah countered with a soft laugh. "We started out as friends. Being as that I am some years older than Caleb, I naturally never expected a romance to blossom from our friendship. All I knew was that he needed a place to stay, and I needed a strong back to help run the vineyard. So I proposed a bargain that we help each other. He accepted and, well, I suppose that you can guess the rest."

Caleb coiled his arm around his wife's shoulders to draw her near. Kissing her cheek, he said, "I must admit that I loved Hannah the moment I saw her leaning over my cot. However, it was only right that I allowed her a suitable period for mourning before declaring my feelings."

"What a lovely tale," Bethany exclaimed on a sigh.

Caleb grinned. "It is also an amazing one in that she

accepted my proposal. After all, I was a highwayman running from the law with only a golden ring to my name."

"Ah, but you truly were not a highwayman, darling," Hannah retorted. "You never actually robbed anyone."

Caleb made a droll face. "That is because I was shot before I could do so."

"Nonetheless—" Hannah began.

But Caleb interrupted her, interjecting, "Nonetheless, I rode with the intention of committing robbery, and in the eyes of the law I was guilty. Had I remained in England I would have lived in fear of being discovered and hung."

"There is no proof that you were there that night, Caleb. Even my flock of Bow Street Runners was unable to find any real evidence pointing to that fact. So if you and Hannah desire to return to England to live, you are perfectly free to do so," Gideon said.

Caleb and Hannah exchanged a quick glance; then Caleb replied, "Our life is here now, so we will remain in Portugal. However, I promise that we will return to England soon for a visit."

Gideon nodded. "I suspected that you might feel that way, and I must say that I am thrilled that you have found such happiness here."

"It appears that we have both found great happiness," Caleb returned, nodding at Julia.

Gideon flashed Julia a smile that quite took her breath away. "Indeed it does."

"What I want to know is whose idea it was to etch the Harwood family emblem into your port bottles." This was from Bethany, who was gazing at the happy couples with a rather wistful expression.

"It was Hannah's," Caleb said, gazing at his wife with obvious pride.

Hannah nodded. "When all of our letters to you and Bliss were returned, and your neighbors either did not respond to our queries or could not tell us your fate, I began to wonder if perhaps Gideon might have returned from India and taken you away. From what Caleb told me, Gideon had acquired the wealth to live as a gentleman, and all proper English gentlemen drink port. It was my hope that he might someday see a bottle of our port and recognize the emblem, which would in turn lead him to us here."

"And it worked splendidly," Julia exclaimed. "How very clever of you, Hannah."

Hannah smiled, visibly pleased by her praise. "I daresay that I should give the Harwood family ring to you, Julia. After all, it rightfully belongs to the bride of the eldest Harwood male."

"I have a ring of which I am exceedingly fond, so if it is all the same to Gideon, I would prefer that you keep it. It is the ring Caleb placed on your finger when he wed you, so it should stay there." She glanced at Gideon, who gave his permission with a smile and nod. Returning her attention to the couple before her, she added, "Besides, if you intend to use the ring emblem as your brand, then it belongs here."

"Since there appears to be little danger of my name being recognized as that of a wanted highwayman, perhaps I will resume its use. With your permission, my dear"—he kissed the top of Hannah's head—"I would like to call our port Harwood's."

"I was going to suggest that myself, since it is only right that the name should match the brand. I—" She broke off with a laugh as her stomach gave a loud rumble. "But where are my manners? It is long past time for dinner, and you all must be starved. As you can tell, I most certainly am. If you will excuse me, I shall go see to the matter now."

When she had bustled off to tend to her duties as hostess, Caleb, too, rose. "I should go see what sort of trouble my boys are getting your girls into."

Of course they had brought Bliss, Jemima, and Maria with them. Being as that it was London's Little Season, Julia's parents had raised no objections to Julia's proposal that she bring her sisters on the journey.

"I believe that I will retire to my chamber and write to Christian until dinnertime," Bethany murmured. "I have so much to tell him."

Now alone, Julia said to Gideon, "She really does love Christian, you know."

Gideon nodded. "Yes, and Christian loves her, though neither will admit to the fact."

"Would you mind if they wed?"

"No, of course not. Christian is a fine man and I would be honored to have him for a brother. However, it is impossible for them to do so until he discovers his past. He could have a wife somewhere."

"Perhaps that is what keeps him from searching for his identity," Julia mused. "Perhaps he would rather live with the hope that he might someday wed Bethany, rather than risk discovering that it can never be."

"Perhaps," Gideon replied.

They both fell silent then, losing themselves in their thoughts. Over the past weeks, Julia had come to terms with her father's devastating secret, and had decided that Gideon was correct. Everything was indeed all right, and it would remain so as long as she had Gideon in her life. Oh, that was not to say that she no longer worried that the *ton* would learn the truth about her parents' marriage. She did. It was just that she had gained the confidence to believe that she could weather anything the future might bring, so long as Gideon was beside her.

Filled with the peace of knowing that Gideon would always be by her side to strengthen and comfort her, no matter what happened, Julia gazed down at the freshly harvested vineyards that spread out below the arbor-covered veranda where they presently sat.

The vineyards had been planted on a series of steep terraces carved into the harsh Douro River Valley wall, below which flowed the Douro River, the color of which perfectly matched the clear azure sky above. They had traveled down that river from their arrival port of Oporto, since it was the quickest route to Caleb's sprawling white *quinta*, as the vineyard estates where called. And if Julia lived to be a hundred, she would never forget the sun-drenched majesty of the Douro Valley, with its violet-shadowed gorges, quaint villages, and picture-perfect landscapes. She would also never forget the passion with which Gideon had made love to her as they had drifted on the current. Wishing that he would whisk her upstairs and repeat his magnificent performance, Julia shot him a longing glance.

Apparently passion was not among whatever was on his

mind, for he was gazing off into the distance, his eyes unfo-
cused and his expression rather grim. Taken aback that he
would look so at a time that should be filled with nothing
but happiness, she murmured, "A penny for your
thoughts, love."

Gideon blinked twice before turning his attention to her.
Smiling rather sheepishly, he said, "I was just contemplating the fact that Caleb will be remaining in Portugal. I
know that it is exceedingly selfish of me to feel so, but I
must confess to being disappointed that he will not be returning to England with us."

"I would have loved that as well," Julia replied. "However, he has promised to visit us, and there is nothing to
keep us from visiting him here as well. So we must try to
content ourselves with that comfort." She studied him from
beneath her lashes for a moment, wondering if this might
be a good time to tell him her news. She had thought to
wait until after his reunion with his brother, so as not to
detract from the occasion. But in light of his glumness, it
seemed that this might be the perfect moment to do so
after all. Glancing away again, she slyly added, "Of course,
it will be a while before I shall be able to make this trip
again. At least nine months, I should guess."

Gideon frowned, only to look stunned in the next instant
as the meaning of her words sank in. "Are you saying
that—that—"

When his mouth opened and closed several times without
issuing forth any more words, Julia laughed and supplied,
"Yes, Gideon. You are going to be a father come spring."

"A-are you certain?" he sputtered.

This was the first time Julia had ever seen her impeccably
poised husband at a loss. Laughing again, she tossed back,
"Very. I cannot imagine why you would look so surprised.
It was bound to happen as often as we make love."

He continued to gape at her for a moment longer; then
he expelled a loud whoop. Jumping to his feet, he pulled
her from her chair and crushed her in a fierce but careful
hug. "A baby! Oh, Julia, my love, this is the most marvelous news in the world! I thought that my life was complete
when we found Caleb. But now it truly is."

"As is mine," Julia said with a smile, rising up on her tiptoes to twine her arms around his neck. Drawing his face down to hers, she murmured, "Now love me, Gideon."

With a grin, Gideon captured her lips with his. When he had kissed her into breathlessness, he scooped her into his arms and carried her upstairs, where true to the gentleman he was, he did not disappoint his lady.

New York Times **Bestselling Author**

Jo Beverley